COPS AND ROBBERS

POLICE SCOTLAND
BOOK 6

ED JAMES

PROLOGUE

ALLY PUSHED THE BODY OF HIS GUITAR AGAINST THE AMPLIFIER, sending squalls of feedback through the room. He reached down with his free hand and adjusted the controls, making the noise swell like a siren.

Roddy was still pounding away at the drum kit, eyes closed, lips twitching as he silently counted time.

Ally unstrapped the guitar and propped it against the amp, letting it squeal even louder, the noise filling his head. He got down on his hands and knees and started adjusting the fifteen Boss and Fender units on his pedal board. When the delay kicked in, he nudged the reverb up until his amp started shaking in sync with his teeth. Then he sat back on his haunches, listening to the blissful racket echoing around the drums and bass. He waited for a beat, then slammed his right hand on the overdrive pedal. A beautiful hiss burst out of the speaker. He listened to it for two bars, then hit a distortion. The sound curved in on itself, shriller and harsher. He pumped the wah-wah pedal with his left hand, creating a wave of sound, squeezing the feedback, warping it.

Somewhere in that wall of noise, he picked out Roddy's clattering drum pattern. The signal. He looked over at the rugged drummer, now counting the beats open-mouthed. Four bars left, three, two.

Gary noodled away on his bass, head down, hiding behind his

dark fringe, holding the frenzied guitar riffs and drum patterns together with a measured heartbeat. Then a flash of hair and Gary locked eyes with Ally, grinning.

Ally nodded back, then at Roddy.

The drummer swept into a snare roll, shouting the count but nobody could hear it over the din.

Ally snatched up his guitar and stomped pedal after pedal. Then crashed in with a chord on the final beat. He let his guitar ring, let it compete with Roddy's dying cymbals, the drone of Gary's bass throbbing.

Gary was the first to come out of their shared trance, flicking his cabinet's power button off and resting his bass against it. 'If there was anyone here, they'd be going mental right now.'

'Too true.' Ally sat back on his amp and reached down to switch it to standby. He looked around their practice room. White-washed walls, bare wooden ceiling, concrete floor, the equipment of two bands rammed into the small space. And as damp as a fortnight in the Highlands, even with the dehumidifier wedged in the corner filtering their sweat out of the air.

The glamour.

A sign of things to come? Low budgets and tiny venues?

Ally tried dismissing the thought with a sigh. 'Won't be long before we have a proper crowd. More than just our uni mates, anyway.'

Roddy snorted. 'You almost missed the last chord there, you amateur. You're overdoing it with the pedals.'

'I was tempted to put another one on.' Ally shrugged. 'Reckon that'll do it for tonight, bro?'

'Four times through that bloody set is enough for anyone.' Roddy rummaged around behind his drum kit and tossed a can of beer in Ally's direction.

He caught it one-handed. 'Cheers.' One of those cheap supermarket lagers that tried to look expensive. All fur coat and no knickers. He tugged the ring-pull and a gush of foam burst out. *Man...* He held the can out to avoid getting it all over his clothes, shoes, guitar or — God forbid — his pedals. It slopped on the concrete floor, yet another sticky patch.

Gary took a slug of vodka, neat from the bottle, and swept his dark hair back with his free hand. He held the bottle up and toasted the others. 'That was good.'

Roddy opened another, frowning. 'The practice or the booze?'

'Both. Now you've almost stopped making mistakes.'

'Enough.' Ally stifled a yawn. 'Anyone fancy a pint?'

'No, mate.' Gary's mouth twisted into a mischievous grin. 'Tonight's the night.'

'You still on about that?'

'Aye, and I won't stop until you finally do it.' Gary walked over and placed both hands on Ally's shoulders, breathing harsh vodka fumes. 'The deal was, I arrange the gig and you go for a wee wander. I've arranged the gig, so...'

'You're such a bloody child.' Ally brushed Gary's hands off. 'Alright. Fine.' He reached over for his guitar bag and stuffed his Telecaster inside. 'What do you expect to find down there?'

'That's the thing.' Gary rested his bass on the stand. 'I was reading an interview with Expect Delays.' He took another swig of vodka. 'Neeraj, the guitarist, said they used this very practice room we're in. Or one of the neighbouring ones, anyway. Said that one night they found a weird door. Course they opened it and guess where it led?' He looked at his bandmates, wide-eyed. 'He said there's this old street that went right under the Old Town. Can walk for miles under here.'

Roddy stowed away his sticks. 'And you think it's that door downstairs, don't you?'

'Got to be. And I reckon if we follow their lead, we'll get signed, too. It's *fate*.'

Ally started sweating despite the cold.

That door... looked ancient, like it had been there for centuries. Like a portal to Edinburgh's hidden history of grave robbers and body snatchers.

He cleared his throat. 'Gary, I don't think the music industry works like Harry Potter. Secret portals, magic spells, fate and fame and—'

'A deal's a deal.'

Ally looked around at Roddy, but the drummer was packing away his cymbals. He glanced back at Gary. 'It's dark down there. Don't think my phone would cut it.'

A beaming grin spread over Gary's face as he whipped a torch out of his hoodie pocket. Heavy duty, like it could light up the castle during the Tattoo. He moved closer, prodding Ally in the chest with it. 'A. Deal. Is. A. Deal.' Each word was punctuated with another poke.

Ally looked over at Roddy.

'Don't look at me.' The drummer downed the rest of his can, the silence as uncomfortable as the squalid room. 'This is between you pair.'

Ally closed his eyes, searching for an excuse that didn't make him seem like a wee boy — a scared wee boy. Came up with nothing. He opened his eyes and checked his watch. Shit. Still another fifty minutes till they had to lock up and clear off. No chance he could stall until closing time. He folded his arms and tutted at Gary.

The bassist just stood there, staring, grinning, waiting. And holding that torch out.

Ally snatched it out of his hands. 'Right, fine.' He marched out of the room, head down.

The corridor led to a staircase, the stone steps worn in the middle. Up to Edinburgh and safety, down to the other three rooms. And to that bloody door. Looked like it had been shut for a reason and kept shut ever since.

He waited, fresh sweat trickling down the sides of his ribs. His ears were still buzzing from their racket. The muffled sound of another band bled through a door way back down the corridor, a woman singing, "The dress seems to fit, but you won't wear it."

Sound good. Better than us, maybe.

Then Roddy dropped the keys, same as he did every single time. He picked them up and locked the door.

Gary grabbed Ally from behind. 'Come on!'

One last sigh, then Ally headed down the stone stairs, faster than he should have on the scuffed steps. He stumbled, almost slipped, but caught himself on the clammy wall, the lack of white-wash the only difference to their rehearsal space. The torch shone into the gloom, lighting the heavy door at the bottom. *Sod it.* He raced down, the beam bouncing, then stopped, getting his breathing back under control as the other two's footsteps slapped towards him. 'You are coming with me, aye?'

Gary rubbed his hands. 'Of course.'

Roddy toasted him with a fresh can in his mighty fist. 'Wouldn't miss this for the world.'

Ally nodded like it was no big deal, then opened the door. He waved his torch around and his fears disappeared like startled ghosts.

An old street, a paraffin lantern hanging from the stone wall. Reminded him of Mary King's Close, the tourist attraction he'd visited on a school trip. The guide said the Old Town was built on top of the older buildings, an entire city under the city, a cavernous maze of tunnels, eventually closed off and left to crumble. This was real, not the little section made safe for tourists and schoolkids.

He breathed in the damp air, the hairs on his arms standing up. The smell was the same as in their rehearsal room, but you could taste it down here.

A hand gripped his shoulder and vodka breath whispered in his ear: 'Time's a marching...'

Ally took a shallow breath through his nose and set off, his trainers padding over countless years of stone dust, his torch picking out bricked-up doorways and windows. The low ceiling stretched away into darkness like a long mine shaft.

God knows what's above, maybe the Royal Mile?

His light hit a brick wall. End of the road.

Ally waved the torch about for the others to see. 'This far enough?' He turned around and lit up another brick wall to his left. Behind, Gary covered his eyes. Then Ally shone it over to the right.

No wall. Just a dark tunnel. A crossroads where two of the roads had been bricked up, leaving only one option for progress.

Ally shone the torch into the tunnel, the beam dying deep in the gloom. Goosebumps tickled his arms. 'Right, lads, do you want to head back or—'

'Keep going.'

Ally kept the torch pointed down the dark shaft and marched on.

Another hundred steps ought to do it. And if Gary didn't see it that way, he can get to—

'What was that?' Roddy stopped dead, his shoes skidding in the loose grit.

Ally spun around, his torch flaring over the walls in a wild zigzag. 'What?'

'Swear I heard something.'

Ally shone the light all around. Up. Down. Nothing. Then on Roddy's wide smile.

Bastard's trying to scare me.

Ally gritted his teeth and strode deeper into the dark, the torch cutting over ancient flagstones and dilapidated stone walls. This far in, they were wet, stale water slicking the rough stone, not quite puddling, but not far off.

The light flashed across a sign. Ally whipped the torch back to take a second look. A butcher's shop, the doorway bricked up like all the others.

Another fifty paces and the path angled to the left. He reached the crook of the bend and stopped. 'This is it. I'm done.'

Roddy's breath was loud in the darkness.

Ally turned around and shone the torch in their faces.

Gary glared at him as he took another sip of vodka. 'This is nowhere near far enough, mate. Keep going.'

The torch caught a twinkle in Roddy's eyes.

Ally wanted to smash it on the floor. *Sick of this.* 'Come on, man, I–'

'*I* say when it's over, not you.' Gary stabbed his chest with a sharp finger. 'Or I can just cancel that gig?'

Ally stared at him, knowing he couldn't argue. *Wanker.* He turned and stomped off, quicker than before. *The sooner this is over...*

Something glinted in the pale light.

What the hell?

Ally stopped dead and flashed the torch around, dropping his voice to a whisper. 'Hold on, I swear I saw something.'

'Quit it.' Gary huffed. 'That didn't work when Roddy tried it and it won't—' Something metallic sparkled on the floor. Gary's voice shot up an octave. 'Look! What the hell is that?'

Ally flicked the torch back again, trying to locate the mysterious metal object.

Roddy stepped up closer with a laugh. 'Arrr, maybe it's gold! Maybe it's trrreasure!'

Ally bent down, training the torch across every inch of ground.

Another glint. He stopped, his heart in his throat, pounding so hard he could barely breathe. *Get a grip, man!* He took a deep breath and held it. In the high-pitched silence, he felt like he was deep underwater, every instinct screaming at him to get back to the surface.

Then he knelt down to get a closer look at the glinting object. Long and thin. A screwdriver, covered in something brown.

What the hell?

He twisted the front of the torch to widen the beam and light up the surrounding area. And then he gasped like a little child.

A body was propped against the wall.

DAY 1

Friday

1

THE ALARM WENT OFF, A GUITAR RIFF THE SIZE OF A STADIUM rattling out of the clock radio.

Dire bloody Straits.

Cullen slapped the snooze button, hoping it was just a bad dream and he still had hours of sleep left. Nope. The green lights showed 06:00.

Dire Straits blasted out again and Cullen jerked awake. He hit the button hard. Then forced himself to sit up, his head throbbing like his brain was going to squidge out of his ear. Almost as bad as a hangover. He turned on his bedside light and looked for Sharon.

Her side of the bed was empty. Almost. A pair of yellow eyes peered up at him from the bottom of the bed, surrounded by a mass of ginger fur.

'Are you man-marking me, boy?'

For once, the cat didn't answer.

Cullen swung his legs off the side of the bed and pushed himself up. He took a deep breath, centred himself, then dropped to the floor and did a press-up. 'One.'

His belly hung a little lower than he would have wished.

'Two.'

Used to be a midriff. A washboard stomach.

'Three.'

Ten years of strong lager and takeaway pizza, some return on that investment.

'Four.'

Should get back into running.

'Five.'

Or hit the gym again with Craig Hunter.

'Six.'

If he ever answered my texts.

~

CULLEN WANDERED INTO THE KITCHEN, THE RADIO PLAYING AT LOW volume. Dire Straits had given way to Eric bloody Clapton. *Bad to worse.* His chest and arms ached. Sweat soaked his T-shirt shoulders, which hurt but not as bad as the rest of him.

Sharon perched on a stool at the breakfast bar, stirring a mug of tea. DS Sharon McNeill, on duty even on her day off. Dark hair in a tight ponytail, blouse and trousers.

Cullen leaned in and kissed her on the cheek. 'Morning.'

'Morning.' Sharon took a sip, staring at her laptop. 'How's my favourite Acting Detective Sergeant?'

'It's just temporary.'

Eyes still on the screen. 'First step on the career ladder, darling.'

'We'll see.' Cullen sat down opposite her. 'By the way, Mum's cancelled. We're not going there tonight.'

'That's good.'

Cullen grinned. 'You're not listening, are you?'

She looked up at him, her eyes puffy and bloodshot. 'What?'

'Jesus, Sharon.' Cullen reached across and caressed her cheek, stopping her from turning back to the screen before he could get a better look at her eyes. 'Are you okay?'

She sniffed. 'It's only a cold.' She rubbed her nose, then gently but firmly pushed his hand away. 'I'm a big girl. Had to get it on my day off. And we're supposed to be driving to your parents' tonight, right? Or did she really cancel?'

'No, I was winding you up. Do you want me to cancel?'

'Nah, I'll be fine.' Sharon took a sip from the cup. 'I'll pick you up from work. To tell you the truth, I'm looking forward to having a weekend off together, even if it is up at your parents' house.'

Cullen gave her a stern frown. 'Come on, they're not that bad.'

'They're not. You're really lucky having parents like them.'

Yeah, just wait till we get there and Mum starts interrogating me on whether I've finally got in touch with my sister.

Cullen yawned, feeling like it split his face in two.

She shook her head, trying and failing to suppress a yawn herself. 'You need to grow up, mister. Looks like you were in late again last night, am I right?'

'Domestic that turned violent. Rumbled on and on. Got a confession, PF's happy. Not that I get to speak to her.'

She pinched his cheek. 'Oh, Scott, you're the golden boy just now.'

'Shut up...' Cullen brushed her hand away, warmth spreading over his cheek. He busied himself with the toaster, sticking two slices on and fiddling with the setting to avoid the usual disaster. That thing was like a Scottish tan — bread white to burnt in seconds. He checked his watch, then felt the kettle, tepid. Coffee at the station. He sat on the stool next to Sharon, keeping an eye on the toast and the tell-tale smoke. 'You never told me how your interview went?'

She didn't reply.

'You didn't even text me. Was it that bad?'

'What?' Still distracted. 'No, it was good.' She shut the laptop and dropped her hand to stroke Fluffy. The cat was standing between them, guarding Sharon against Cullen. 'I've been looking at houses.'

Cullen gestured at the laptop. 'I take it that means the interview went well?'

'Not counting my chickens, but I've found a couple of nice ones. A new build in Ravencraig and an old cottage in Garleton.'

'I'm *not* moving to Ravencraig.'

'Four bedrooms for one eighty.'

'And there's a reason for that. It's in Ravencraig. Besides, we don't need four bedrooms, unless...'

'Unless I'm planning on starting a family? No need to worry.' She patted his stomach. 'Fat chance of that while you're this out of shape.'

The toast popped up, shrouded in smoke.

Cullen jumped up and got a plate out of the dishwasher, checking it was clean before he shovelled crunchy peanut butter on the toast. He took a bite and chewed slowly. *Delicious.*

Sharon turned up her nose. 'I hate that stuff.'

'This guy I worked with, Craig Hunter, total fitness freak, he swears by it. Says it's good for you if you want to get back into shape. Lots of protein.'

'And fat. It *can't* be good for you in the quantity you eat it, whatever that gym monkey tells you.'

'Craig's a good guy.'

'Sorry.' Sharon took another sip of tea. 'I'm stressed about this job, Scott.'

'You'll get it. And if you don't, you'll be fine anyway.'

Sharon stared at the counter.

Cullen took his plate and sat next to her. 'Hey. This isn't the Sharon I know and love.'

She snuggled in close. 'I don't feel like her.'

Cullen kissed the top of her head. 'You'll be fine.'

'What if I'm not?' His chest muffled her voice.

'Look, there are plenty of other things going on just now. Task forces, specialist units. Might be good to get some other experience. You've been in CID for ages. Maybe you need a change?'

She sat upright, her eyes focused on her mug. 'You're right. I'll be fine.' She drained the mug.

On the radio, the DJ piped up to announce the next track in a mid-Atlantic drawl: 'Coming up, the new single by Edinburgh band Expect Delays, and what an awesome title they've chosen for this one — *Cops and Robbers.*' Which he pronounced *Cobz 'n' Robbuz.*

'All I need.' Cullen bit into the toast. Almost into his tongue too.

The song kicked in, half-spoken lyrics riffing on innocent childhood memories of playing cops and robbers, then segueing into an up-tempo rant about the game playing out in the adult world where foreign governments will rob the country while the cops sit around drinking cups of tea, cups of tea, cups of tea...

Cullen glanced at Sharon, nodding her head to the synthetic

beat. She caught his look and pushed her empty cup away and Cullen burst out laughing. 'Jesus, how can you listen to this?'

'Better than the shite you do, Scott.'

Cullen grabbed his chest as though he had been stabbed in the heart. He spread the next slice of toast, heaping even more peanut butter on.

Sharon picked up a copy of *The List* and pointed at the moody shot of Expect Delays on the cover. 'Good interview in there.'

Cullen took it and pointed to the singer. 'Is his hair combed forward?'

'You're obsessed.' She inspected it with a shrug. 'Are you jealous?'

'Seriously, is it?' Cullen took a closer look. No doubt about it. Mike Robertson had grown his hair out on top and styled it into one of those emo fringes, sweeping it over his forehead like a curtain to cover his creeping baldness.

'Be thankful you've got a full head of hair yourself.' Sharon caressed the back of Cullen's neck. 'For now.'

Cullen shrugged her hand off.

His phone started dancing on the table.

'Here we go.' He checked the display. 'Crystal bloody Methven.' He put the phone to his ear, eyes closed. 'Good morning, sir.'

'Nothing good about it, ADS Cullen. I need you to come to Niddry Street, immediately. Someone's found a sodding body.'

CULLEN TRUDGED HEAD-ON INTO THE WIND, POWERING UP THE Royal Mile, the shop windows filled with tartan tat. Late March and still the snow was piled up high by the shop doorways. He folded up the collar of his coat and burrowed his chin deep into it, then turned into Niddry Street, a steep decline into the bowels of old Edinburgh. A couple of squad cars sat next to a police van halfway down, the blue and white cordon flapping either side, loud as a whip in the blustery wind.

Acting DC Simon Buxton shuffled next to it, just in his suit jacket, shivering so much that he hadn't noticed Cullen. His hair was freshly cut — shaved at the back and sides, the longer hair on top gelled and flicked back.

'Budgie!'

Buxton looked up, eyes narrow. 'Good morning, Sarge.' His London accent was as out of place up here as his rockabilly pompadour. He slicked a loose strand back with one hand, then gave Cullen a military salute. 'Nice of you to bother showing up.'

'I was looking for you, but all I could see was David Beckham's new haircut.'

Buxton raised his phone in front of him and inspected his hairdo from a range of angles. He blew a loud kiss at the screen. 'Beautiful.' Then he frowned at Cullen. 'For someone who's obsessed with other people's hair, mate, yours is pretty shit.'

Cullen laughed, then walked up to the cordon and glanced at his watch. 'You're keen. Not seen you at work this early since you shat the bed, right?'

Buxton wrapped his arms tight round his shoulders and went back to pacing along the plastic ribbon. 'I got in early to get ahead on that paperwork, but Crystal bloody Methven clocked me. His car stinks of Calvin Klein.'

Cullen grimaced. 'Where is he now?'

'Downstairs.' Buxton handed him the clipboard. 'But you need to sign in.'

Cullen started filling out the form. 'Any idea what this place is?'

'Band rehearsal rooms.' Buxton checked the form like it was the most important thing in the world. When he was satisfied that every box was ticked, he looked back up at Cullen. 'Bands rent the rooms by the month. Huge waiting list, mate. Tried to get on it when I was still a rock star, but we never lucked out.'

'I forgot you were in a band.' Cullen took off his coat and passed it to the shivering Buxton. 'Here, put that on.'

~

CULLEN PULLED THE CRIME SCENE SUIT UP OVER HIS TROUSERS AND tottered back, catching himself on the wall. *Terrific.*

The place felt even colder than outside, colder and damper. These wannabe rockers must've spent a fortune on getting their gear fixed afterwards.

He zipped up the suit and took the inner locus clipboard from the Crime Scene Manager. She seemed awfully familiar but he couldn't remember her name. Hopefully not some drunk office party shag. He shot her a furtive glance, but she had her gaze nailed to the clipboard, checking his signature and nodding without saying a word.

Cullen nodded back. 'You're better off in here. It's freezing outside.'

She grunted something in reply as she took the clipboard off him.

Cullen walked off, following the trail of thick cables running down a stone staircase. A series of arc lights blazed out at the bottom, lighting up a corridor. He stepped through an ancient door into a tunnel that stretched away from him, lamps spaced at regular intervals, the white mould glowing on the walls. He sniffed the air. Damp and putrid, could almost taste the decay. He sped up, keeping his breathing shallow. Past a kink in the tunnel. *The sooner this is over...* He turned the bend and walked right into the back of a SOCO.

'Jesus!' Cullen grabbed the figure in the crime scene suit by the shoulders, arching back in a clumsy shuffle to stop them both from toppling over. Like dancing on ice, just without music. 'Sorry about tha–'

The figure turned around and fixed him with a stare as cold as the corridor. Tall and athletic, even through the puffy white suit. Acting DI Colin Methven, his wild eyebrows sparking through his mask.

'Sir.' Cullen let go of his boss's shoulders and pointed down the tunnel. 'What's happened?'

'Well.' Methven huffed out a sigh. 'Last night, some rock band decided to go for a little wander under the old city. Some sort of sodding dare.' He folded his arms, making his suit crinkle. 'Of course, they found a body and, rather than run up to street level and dial 999, they buggered off. One of their number couldn't sleep, so called it at half past four. Meaning I got the call-out at five. Sodding nightmare. I'd better show you the body, then.' He led the way along the corridor, waving his hand at the ceiling like a tour guide. 'We're not sure, but we think these tunnels run for miles under here. We're probably a good way down the Royal Mile, down towards the Canongate. This place would have been bustling about a hundred and fifty years ago. Open to the sky before they built on top of it. I didn't know it was this easy to get in without paying a sodding tenner for the privilege.'

They passed a SOCO fiddling with the last in the chain of arc lights, just gloom ahead.

Methven clicked on a torch and set off again.

Another boiler-suited figure blocked their way. 'Colin, I was just chatting to Jimmy here and reckons the tunnel joins up with Mary King's Close.' The dulcet tones of Jimmy Deeley, the city's chief pathologist. He stared up at Cullen. 'Oh, young Skywalker. We meet again.'

Cullen groaned as they stopped. 'No new nicknames, please.'

'But I hear you got a promotion. News travels fast on the dark side...' Deeley spread his arms wide and laughed.

Methven shook his head. 'I'm not in the mood.'

Cullen grabbed the torch from Methven and shone it further down. Another SOCO was on their hands and knees, examining something as a colleague took photos.

'On you go then.' Deeley shifted to the side, a cheeky glint in his eye just visible through his mask.

Cullen set off. And stopped dead.

A skeleton was propped up against a side wall, pieces of flesh hanging off the skull. There was barely anything left. From the clothes, it looked like a man — jeans, T-shirt, big work boots.

Deeley's chuckle came from behind them. 'Boy's dead.'

'I can sodding well see that.' Methven swivelled round to glare at him.

'Out of the way.' Another boiler-suited figure pushed through, lugging yet another arc light. 'Here, Cullen, make sure you keep your dinner to yourself this time, aye?' Sounded like James Anderson, the lead SOCO. Total wanker, but at least the Tyvek suit hid his stupid goatee from sight. Anderson rested the lamp on the floor like he was planting the flag on the moon's surface. 'There we — HOLY SHIT!'

In the bright spotlight, words appeared on the wall just above the body, all capitals, all sharp brush strokes, all written in red:

I WILL KILL AGAIN.

2

Methven stared at the writing on the wall, eyes flicking back and forth. 'What the sodding hell?'

'Spooky, isn't it? I think whoever did this,' Deeley waved at the body, 'they're going to do it again.'

Methven shot him a glare in return. Didn't say anything, though.

Cullen shook his head at them, then got out his phone to snap a photo of the message. A ledge above it acted as a drip, stopping the damp getting at it. 'Could've been there for years. Victorian? Edwardian?'

'Hardly.' Methven crouched next to the body, the bundle of bones and clothes. 'Serial killers tend to murder victims from the same historical period. It's at least Sixties. He's wearing jeans.' He frowned. 'His wallet and phone are gone.'

'His phone?' Cullen took another look at the corpse. Just a skeleton, barely any flesh left. 'Must've taken years to get like that. He can't have a phone.'

Methven looked up at him. 'Sergeant, he's wearing a Jeff Buckley T-shirt.'

Deeley cleared his throat. 'Sorry to interrupt such inspired conversation, but by my humble reckoning, the body's been there between twelve and eighteen months. Give or take.' He rubbed his fingers together. 'Very moist down here. Means a body would rot much quicker than in a coffin.' He clicked his fingers, the sound dampened by his gloves. 'Mind that case last year where the boy was shoved in a whisky barrel? Kind of like that.'

Cullen felt a twinge in his shoulder. 'This looks even worse.'

'Course it does. Time has been unkind to this poor laddie.'

Methven scrambled to his feet. 'When do we get answers?'

'I'm afraid anything else will have to wait until I get the body back to my lair. But don't kid yourself — you're going to get more questions instead of answers. There's hardly anything left to give us solid leads. Still, at least we know how he died.' He patted Anderson's arm. 'Show them.'

The SOCO pulled a plastic bag out of an evidence case. 'Cop your whack round this.' Anderson held the bag up to the light to let them see the contents. A bloody screwdriver.

Methven took it off him and stared at it.

'As you can see, it's still got blood on it, though it's very dry and in danger of flaking off. Doubt I'll find any fingerprints on that.'

Methven passed the bag to Cullen. 'Sergeant, I want a list of all screwdrivers sold in the Central Belt. Anything meeting that description in the period in question.'

'You're kidding me?'

Methven gave him another frown. 'Do I look like it?'

Cullen sighed as he took a photo of the screwdriver and passed it back. 'I'll get on with—'

Methven grabbed his arm. 'Sergeant, I'm not sure you've heard, but this is a band rehearsal space.' He jerked his thumb back in the direction they had come. 'Last I heard, the owner hasn't arrived yet, but DC Jain is upstairs with the ones who found the body.'

~

DC CHANTAL JAIN STEPPED OUT OF THE DOOR AND SHUT IT BEHIND her, rolling her eyes. 'I'm working for you again?' The arc lights from below caught her perfectly. No other word for it, but she was stunning, easily a nine in Cullen's book. *Before I settled down and shelved that particular book, of course.* She narrowed her eyes like she could see exactly what was going on in his head. 'Great.'

Cullen folded his arms, then shoved his hands in his pockets. 'Trust me, it's as weird for me as it is for you.'

'Oh, really? You only got that Acting gig because your old boss was kicked off the force.'

'That's not the only reason.' Cullen clenched his teeth, his blood boiling. She always knew how to press his buttons. He nodded over her shoulder. 'Did you get anything from those guys?'

'Nah, just got here. Didn't want to start without an adult present. You'll have to do.' She winked at him. 'They're called Corner. Might be The Corner. Swear the blonde one works in Hollister on George Street.'

'I wouldn't know.'

'You're far too classy for that, eh?' She walked through the door before Cullen could explain.

He followed her into the room, maybe four metres by five. The walls were the same whitewash as the corridor, so he kept his arms tight by his sides. The room was filled with music equipment, leaving barely enough room for the pretty boys to throw rock star shapes.

And they were pretty. Well, two of them were. They sat around as though waiting for a photoshoot to start. One was on a guitar amp, patting his dyed-blond fringe. The other on a chair turned the wrong way round, his lank dark hair and dead eyes giving him an evil vibe way beyond his bad-boy pose.

The third band member leaned against the wall next to a massive drum kit. Shaved head, maybe ten years older and five stone heavier than the other two, and looking like he'd just come in off a building site.

Cullen slammed the door behind him, making them all look over. 'Can I get some names?'

Fringe recovered his cool first. 'Alistair Cameron. You can call me Ally.'

Chantal looked him up and down. 'And what do you play, Alistair?'

Ally stroked the amp he sat on. 'Guitar and lead vocals.'

'The talent, then?'

'Hardly...' The drummer held up a hand until everyone turned to face him. 'Truth be told, I write all the songs. You can call me Roddy. I started The Corner, it's my band.'

Cullen walked over to the kit and didn't stop until he was right in the guy's face. 'Right, Roddy, what's your full name?'

'Roderick Brown.'

Cullen turned his stare on the third band member, his angular jawline just about cutting through his blur of dark hair. 'And you?'

'Gary Moncrieff. Bass and Satanism.'

'You're not the funny one, then.' Cullen sat on the drum stool and got out his notebook. He clicked the pen a few times. 'Now, you.' He pointed the tip at Ally. 'You found the body, right?'

Ally started fiddling with his fringe and shot a glare at the evil one. 'Gary dared me.'

'And you'd walk off the Forth Road Bridge if he dared you?'

'Very good, *Dad*. Course I wouldn't, but we had a bet on who would get us our first gig. Gary blagged us one in Bannerman's.' Ally tugged the fringe behind his left ear and grinned at Chantal. 'We're playing there on Sunday, if you—'

'So.' Cullen got his attention back. 'The dare was to go for a wander down the streets under the Old Town, right?'

Gary's lips curled into a smug grin. 'Pretty much, aye.'

Cullen kept his glare on the singer. 'Go on, Ally.'

'We walked down the... I don't know what it is... the street? We walked down that for a bit. Then we came across the screwdriver and the body.' Ally shrugged like he was trying to pass the whole thing off as no big deal. 'That's pretty much it.'

'Except that you didn't call your discovery in last night.'

Ally stared at Cullen wide-eyed, then threw panicked glances at his two bandmates.

'Don't you agree that seems suspicious?'

'No! Jesus, after we found the body, we just freaked out. We ran off, went to the pub and talked it through. Felt like we'd imagined it, you know?'

Cullen looked at him, letting Ally's panic paint a worse picture of the shit he was in than any words ever could.

The boy seemed to retreat into himself.

'Finding a dead body and going off to the pub isn't suspicious? Do you want to stick with that story?'

More wide-eyed glances. 'Eh, no. No, that sounds way worse than it is.'

'Or it sounds exactly as bad as it is.'

'Hang on, hang on.' The drummer bit his lip. 'Listen, the body looked to have been there for ages already, so there didn't seem to be any rush. Then I tried to go to sleep and...' He swallowed, hard. 'Kept getting flashbacks of that rotten flesh...'

Cullen took in the guy's flat voice, the tired slouch, the deep shadows under his eyes. 'Did you recognise the body?'

Roddy shook his head, looking genuinely mystified.

Ally and Gary shared his expression.

No surprises there. And no way this lot are involved. 'Right. Going to need statements from all three of you.'

The drummer groaned. 'Can we do this later? I've got work and—'

'And I've got a dead body. I need your story on the record. Understood?'

Roddy replied with another dog-tired sigh. 'Fine.'

'How about you two? You got work?'

Ally shrugged, all cool again now that the danger had passed. 'Got a lecture at twelve.'

'Gary?'

'Tutorial at three.'

'Fine.' Cullen walked over to Chantal and leaned in close. 'Get the drummer's story first.' He gave the other two an obvious look, then raised his voice. 'I don't like their attitude, so make it difficult for them.'

'Sure thing.'

Cullen beckoned her out into the corridor, waiting for the door to shut. 'I don't like how they just pissed off after finding a dead body. One, maybe, but all three?'

'Agreed. You expect me to do this on my own?'

'No, I'll speak to Crystal and get Buxton to assist you.'

'Fat lot of good that'll do.'

'You want help or not?'

'Whatever.' Chantal strode back up the corridor, muttering something under her breath.

～

CULLEN TRUDGED DOWN TO THE BOTTOM OF THE STAIRS.

Methven was talking to Anderson, blocking the passage like he was trying to keep him from heading off.

'Sir?'

Methven glanced up, giving the goateed SOCO a chance to escape. Which he took.

Methven called after him. 'Hey! Get back here!' No reaction. 'Anderson, I'm talking to you!'

'My phone's buzzing, sorry.' The SOCO took out his mobile and raced off.

Methven focused his stern gaze on Cullen instead. 'Well, thanks very much. This had better be important.'

'Just spoken to that band.' Cullen shoved his hands in his pockets. 'They're just daft laddies playing games, as far as I can tell.'

'They're not involved?'

'Very unlikely. Chantal's going to take statements, which we'll tick off. I'll need Buxton off Crime Scene Management, if that's okay?'

'Fine. I've stationed some uniforms out front anyway. He looked like he was falling asleep. Can you believe it? No initiative at all...' Methven grabbed Cullen's arm. 'Speaking of initiative, are you keeping DC Jain in check?'

'Do I need to? She's one of the best officers we've got.'

'Is that an appraisal of her skills or her looks?'

'Excuse me?'

'I know your reputation, Sergeant.'

Cheeky bastard. 'Listen, I'm taken and she's best mates with my other half.'

'Right.' Methven stood there, looking anything but convinced. He pointed down the tunnel. 'What do you think "I will kill again" means?'

'It would seem to be the message of a serial killer.' Cullen folded his arms. 'Seem being the operative word.'

'If so, I hope it's one we've already caught.' Methven drew a deep breath, then wrinkled his nose. 'If Deeley's right and the murder took place eighteen months ago, then we'd be due another one, right?'

Cullen caught a whiff of the mouldy stench drifting out through the old door. His eyes started watering. 'That's the standard pattern with serial killers. Again, if we assume this is the work of a serial killer, and secondly if the standard pattern applies in this case.'

Methven nodded, his face pinched tight. 'A whole pile of assumptions there.'

'It's like they've killed during the intervening period.'

'Don't.' Methven sucked in another deep breath. 'Okay. We're going to be working together closely on this, so I need you to keep your cowboy antics to an absolute minimum, understood?'

Cullen felt his eyebrows shoot up. He tightened his hands into fists. 'Sorry, I wasn't aware I'd been naughty again, Dad.'

'Watch your sodding lip.' Methven jabbed a finger at him. 'Bear in mind the big change coming next week. Your position is only Acting, remember?'

So is yours, you wanker.

Cullen clenched his teeth and took a deep breath. Then he smiled. 'What are you saying, sir?'

Methven glanced at him for a second then shared the conspiratorial smile. 'The restructure isn't a hundred per cent cast in stone yet. Just want to give you a heads-up that there are still a few malleable parts.'

'I'll bear that in mind, sir.'

'Best case is we've got a single victim here. Worst case, we've got a serial killer we didn't know about. Either way, I'm afraid that all leave is cancelled until we've got a result on this case. Better safe than sorry, I suppose.'

'Absolutely.' Cullen nodded at his boss. 'I've none planned until May anyway.'

'Sorry, but I have to include weekends.'

A groan escaped Cullen's mouth.

Methven frowned at him. 'Excuse me?'

'Sir. Uhm, it's just that I've got a weekend away booked. Starting tonight.' Cullen ran a hand across his face. 'I suppose I'll cancel that.'

'Absolutely! That's the kind of initiative we need.' Methven clapped Cullen on the shoulder, his face beaming wide. He started up the stone steps to Niddry Street, leaving Cullen to fume in the harsh glow of the arc lights.

Bloody hell, I hope bearing his shit with a grin is worth it in the end...

'Sergeant!' Methven was leaning halfway through the door at the top of the steps. 'Chop, chop! The owner has arrived.'

~

CULLEN GOT OUT ONTO THE STREET, HIS BREATH PLUMING OUT OF HIS mouth like cigarette smoke. He passed Buxton's replacement with a silent nod, the uniform yawning into his fist. Hardly an improvement. He stopped in his tracks and did a double-take.

Christ, that's my woolly coat bundled up on the doorstep!

He jogged back and put it on. *Bloody Buxton.* He trotted downhill after Methven and slowed to step through the front door of the Ghost Tours office.

A skeletal man in his thirties sat hunched over the front desk, bony fingers tapping on a laptop keyboard. He wore a black suit with matching black shirt and tie, his skin as pale as moonlight, looking like a vampire desperate for a blood fix. He looked up so sharply, and with such a severe expression on his face, that Cullen could've sworn he'd just read his mind. He gave them both a grave nod. 'Officers.'

Methven flashed his warrant card with a cold smile. 'DI Colin Methven. This is Acting DS Scott Cullen.' He put his ID away again, but the smile stayed, frozen in place. 'I presume it was you whom I spoke to on the phone?'

The guy eyed him from head to toe, then leaned back and sighed. 'Aye, the name's Paul Temple, and believe it or not, I wouldn't be here at this ungodly hour if we hadn't spoken on the phone.'

Methven glared at the guy.

Cullen rested his hands on the desk. 'How long have you owned this place?'

Temple frowned at him. 'A few years. Why?'

'Well, the body might've been there for as long as two years, so I need a list of bands who rented your rooms in that time, and anyone with access to that corridor.'

'I trust you've got a warrant?'

'We've only just—' Cullen sighed. 'Listen, I can very easily get one. Hopefully we can resolve this right now.'

Temple's frown became even deeper. 'Otherwise?'

'Don't tell me it's not crossed your mind to run murder tours down there?'

'What if it has... Just hypothetically speaking, like?'

'Hypothetically, we could keep that place closed off for a very long time. Or we could have a word with the city council to keep it shut permanently.'

Temple held Cullen's gaze, then dropped it to his desk. 'Well, you're in luck.' He did a few quick clicks on his laptop. 'I've got names and addresses for most band members.' A large laser printer behind him whirred to life, and he reached over to collect a sheet of paper. 'Here.'

Cullen checked the list, double-sided. Maybe twenty-five bands, with four members each on average. All with names and addresses, plus the start and end dates of their tenancies. Only one phone number per band.

Temple cleared his throat with a dry cough. 'That any use?'

'Aye, thanks. It's a start.'

'So, any idea how long you'll take before I can let the bands back in?'

'I'd work towards at least three days.'

Temple's groan sounded like a coffin closing.

Cullen headed back outside, passing the list between his cold hands. He skimmed the list of band members, checking for any familiar names. One Roddy, but it wasn't the lumbering drummer they'd just interviewed.

Methven joined him on the pavement, buttoning up his woolly coat. 'Didn't know you had it in you, Sergeant.'

Cullen took the compliment with a nod. He pointed back at the office, where Temple was already locking up. 'What do you reckon?'

'Cash business. He won't like the police snooping around.'

'You think it's a money-laundering front?'

'There's usually some in these places, but nothing major, and nothing to do with this case.' Methven nodded to himself. 'How does that list look, Sergeant?'

Cullen looked back at the sheet. 'Starter for ten, sir. Assuming the body was someone in a band that rehearsed here.' He waved the page around. 'Trouble is, there's one phone number per band. These guys will mostly be late teens or early twenties, so they would've moved at least once since that time. They don't look like mobile numbers, either.' He folded the list in half, then again, then pocketed it. 'But I'll cross-reference this with the MisPers in that time frame. If that doesn't get us anywhere, the case is in the lap of the forensics gods, right?'

'A good assessment.' Methven clapped Cullen's shoulder. 'I've got another resource on the way from St Leonard's. Should be waiting for you at Leith Walk by the time you get there.'

3

As far as Cullen could see, there was nobody waiting for him in the Leith Walk incident room. The place was deserted, the fluorescent bulbs humming louder than a rock concert. And the heating was off.

Cullen sat at a free desk, facing the window and the view down MacDonald Road. He scanned the list of musicians that gravedigger Temple had given him, then sighed again. *Where do I even start?*

He took out his mobile and speed-dialled Sharon's number.

'What's wrong, Scott?'

Cullen frowned. 'That's a strange way to answer your phone.'

'If you're calling this early, something's wrong.'

'How's your cold.'

'It's not getting any better.'

'Oh, right, sorry. Well... Methven's cancelled my weekend.'

Sharon's sigh was short and to the point. 'Right.' She sneezed. 'Wanker.'

'Me or Methven?'

'I'll let you decide.' An uncomfortable silence stretched out. Sharon laughed. 'Him, of course. I know how the command structure works.' Her turn to sigh. 'I suppose I'll have to see what Chantal's up to at the weekend.'

Cullen sucked in a sharp breath. 'Sorry, she's working for me.'

'Oh for... Methven's only Acting DI. You know, I bet this is because we're both going for the full-time position. Has to be. He's been trying to get at me for months, just chipping away. If it was up to Cargill, Methven would've got it ages ago. Lucky for the rest of us, it's up to Jim Turnbull.'

Cullen felt his mouth go dry. 'He kind of implied that my position after the restructure might be impacted by this case.'

'Oh.'

'What do you mean, oh? Should I be worried?'

'Scott, after Lothian & Borders is put out of its misery on Monday, who knows what joys Police Scotland will bring.'

'Sorry I asked.'

'Sorry, it's this damn cold. Try and forget about it. We'll find out on Monday.'

'You think I've got a weekend to make this DS position permanent?'

'Maybe.'

'Alright, I better go, then. Hope you feel better soon.' Cullen killed the call before it could get soppy, not with a colleague walking in on him muttering something about loving his girlfriend.

A floorboard creaked.

Cullen turned around to check the door and–

'Christ, what's happened to you?' DC Craig Hunter stood in the doorway, six foot three of muscle, every inch the ex-squaddie. He ran a hand over the stubble on his head and strode towards Cullen with a grim look in his steel-grey eyes. 'Seriously, Scott, if you're this broken at seven, this is going to be a long day.'

Cullen glanced down at himself and shrugged off his jacket. 'Craig. What are you doing here?' Then it hit him. 'Hold on, you're Methven's resource, right?'

'Right. That clown sent me down. Told to ask for you.'

'If you're already calling him a clown, I take it you know him?'

'Dealt with him last year. Ally Davenport says he asked for me personally.'

'Sounds like a good thing.'

Hunter scowled at him. 'How do you figure that?'

'If he asked for you, it means he rates you. That's a tick in the box ahead of the big restructure next week.'

'Hardly. Ally hates him. Only going to count against me.'

'Ever the pessimist, mate.'

Hunter held his gaze until Cullen looked away. 'Don't call me that again.'

Cullen laughed. 'What, a pessimist?'

'No.' Hunter narrowed his eyes at him, but there was no trace of humour in them. 'Don't call me mate. I'm not your mate, understood?'

Woah, what's this all about?

Cullen frowned, trying to remember if this was some gag he'd heard Hunter make before.

Hunter stared at him like he'd rather crack his skull than another joke.

Cullen glanced around the incident room. 'Can I get you a coffee?'

'You forgot that I don't like the stuff.' Hunter crossed his bulky arms. 'Let's cut the bullshit. Bring me up to speed on the case.'

∾

CULLEN GLANCED ACROSS THE DESK AT HUNTER, HEADPHONES ON, nodding along to some beat. Between them, a pile of MisPer reports matching their timeframe — eighteen months to two years ago, plus three months either side just in case. Cullen checked Hunter's portion of Temple's list of musicians. Snap, not one name appeared in both.

Hunter pulled his headphones off. 'You could just ask.'

'Right. We're getting nowhere.'

Hunter patted a sheaf of papers. 'Most of these are kids reported missing by their parents, only to turn up five seconds later with not a mark on them. Course the parents rarely bother to tell us. I've got enough here to close six cases. Methven will like that.'

Cullen forced a smile. 'Just in time for the restructure. That should get you the promotion, eh?'

Hunter sighed as he patted the other stack. 'This lot don't quite match the description of your victim. Only set them aside to cover our arses.'

Cullen eyed the messy pile on his side of the desk, wishing

he'd been as organised himself, and as thorough. He hadn't even got beyond the single digits yet. 'How many are you left with?'

'Thirty, give or take.'

Cullen held out a hand. 'Give us half, then.'

Hunter cut him another sharp glance, but after a moment of awkward silence he stuck his earbuds back in. 'Knock yourself out.'

~

'Bingo.' Hunter snapped his fingers. 'I've got him. I think.'

Cullen looked up. 'Go on?'

Hunter shoved the sheet across the desk without making eye contact.

Cullen picked up the page. James Strang, member of a rock band called The Invisibles. Went missing eighteen months ago. He scanned the rest of the information, but couldn't find a single clue. Another quick glance at the info, just to double-check he hadn't missed anything, and he handed the paper back to Hunter. 'Why do you think it was him?'

Hunter grunted, like he resented Cullen for asking, as if Cullen was being deliberately obtuse just to spite him. Or thick as a phonebook. Hunter rolled his eyes, grabbed his screen and spun it around. 'Your skeleton was wearing a Jeff Buckley T-shirt, right? Have a wee look at this magic machine here. It's called a computer. Have you heard of them? Going to be the next big thing, you know?'

Any other day, Cullen would have joined in the banter. But Hunter's tone was off. A hard edge under the apparent silliness. Too tired to explore the root causes of Hunter's bad mood.

Cullen squinted at the screen. 'What am I looking at?'

'It's called Google Images. You know, like a photo album on the Internet? Might even find a pic of you shagging on here.'

Cullen choked. 'What?'

'Rule thirty-four of the Internet. If it exists, there's porn of it. Plus whatever you can imagine. Which in your case must be quite eye-watering.'

What the hell is he on about?

First Methven and now him. Christ, do I need to explain myself to everyone around here?

Cullen took a deep breath and focused on the screen.

One James Strang on stage, screaming into a microphone, wearing a Jeff Buckley T-shirt.

'Okay, so this guy is wearing the same shirt as the dead man. That what you want me to see?'

'Well done, Scott. This was when the band played T in the Park.' Hunter flicked to another tab, to another set of images. 'They played Glastonbury and Reading. Small stages, but that's decent going.'

'So?'

Hunter narrowed his eyes again. 'So, they stopped gigging around the time this Strang guy went missing.'

'Okay. That is promising.'

'Right. Guy went by the stage name of Jimi Danger.'

'Seriously?'

'Deadly. Even spelled Jimmy like Jimi Hendrix. The Danger part, though... I think it's a pun on that Stooges song *Gimme Danger*. That's Iggy Pop and co.'

'Like I'd know who he is.' Cullen scribbled both names down in his notebook, ignoring Hunter shaking his head at his musical ignorance. A step above personal disapproval, maybe. Cullen glanced back at the screen. 'Who reported him missing?'

Hunter shuffled through his stack of paperwork. 'Some boy called Alex Melrose. He's the band's named contact person on that list you got from the ghost tours place.'

'You called him?'

'Thought you'd like to.'

'Be my guest.'

Hunter reached for the landline and dialled the number on the list, then waited. He put the phone back down and frowned. 'Disconnected.'

'Okay.' Cullen flicked through the file. 'It's been nineteen months since this Strang guy went missing, so he probably just changed numbers.' He thought it through for a few seconds, but now it was Hunter who watched him impatiently.

'Mind thinking out loud so I know where you want to go with this investigation?'

Cullen got up and started pacing round. The room was starting to heat up. 'First step is finding out who this guy is.'

'Okay, any idea how we do that?' Hunter held up the file. 'No other info in this bad boy.'

'Right. We could speak to that guy from the ghost tour again.'

'And what do you expect us to do while you're off chasing ghosts?' Chantal stood in the doorway, arms folded over her chest, her posture as challenging as her tone.

Behind her, Buxton's floppy hairdo was bobbing into view as he tried to squeeze past her. He was wearing a beige donkey jacket. Looked like a complete idiot.

'Craig Hunter?' Chantal pursed her lips as she looked him up and down. 'Long time no see.'

Hunter laughed. 'How's it going, Chantal.'

'Been keeping fit, eh?'

Hunter glanced at Cullen. 'Got to do a little something to keep the pounds from piling on when we hit our thirties, right?'

Chantal laughed.

Cullen cleared his throat. And cleared it again. And a third time, until Chantal finally stopped undressing Hunter with her eyes and looked his way. 'DC Jain, nice to see you, too. Have you taken the statements from the band members?'

She gave Hunter a final look, then pulled out her notebook. 'Got them all here.'

'And?'

'Be very surprised if they're the killers.'

'I agree, but I need you to go back for a second round.'

'Oh what?'

'We've IDed the victim. We think.' Cullen pointed at Hunter's screen. 'James Strang. Find out where they were when he disappeared. And can you call James Anderson to see if we've got DNA for Strang on file?'

Chantal sighed, then looked over her shoulder at Buxton, still trapped in the doorway. 'You know you've got an Acting DC for that sort of shite, right?'

Buxton tried to nudge her out of his way, but she stood her ground. 'I resent that.'

'I'm serious.' Chantal was still grinning when she turned back round. 'Look, aren't you making a load of assumptions here?'

Like looking after kids.

'No, Chantal, we're validating assumptions.' Cullen got up. 'There's a huge difference.'

~

Cullen listened to the ring tone again.

'I'm sorry, I can't take your call. You might wish to try Acting DS Scott Cullen or—'

He killed the call.

Bloody Methven. Never there when I need him.

He put the phone away. 'Next left.'

Hunter turned into Niddry Street and hit the brakes. Both sides of the road were rammed with police vans and cars, blue-and-yellow reflectors just catching the morning sun as it crawled up the hill. Hunter navigated their way past and stopped at the bottom of the hill. 'You're a DS now, eh? Come a long way since you were my ADC.'

'Those were great days.'

Hunter flicked the indicator on. 'Were they?'

Cullen gave him a side-look. 'Come on, Craig, what's up? You never reply to my texts and you're acting—'

'I know.' Hunter kept his eyes to the front, speeding up to head along the Cowgate. He skidded to a stop and slammed the car into a parking space, arse first. He killed the engine, unbuckled his seatbelt and got half out of the door.

'Craig!' Cullen grabbed his suit jacket. 'What have I done to piss you off?'

'You really have to ask?' Hunter shrugged his hand away and got out of the car.

Cullen watched him argue with a lorry driver, racking his brain. Thinking through every time Hunter had blown him off over the last two years, and like every other time, Cullen came up empty.

He stepped out on the pavement, willing to give it another try.

Hunter was long gone, pacing back the way they'd driven.

Cullen took a deep breath and started jogging, getting more pissed off with every step.

Whatever I've done to upset him, he's way out of line with this hissy fit. Acting like I shagged his sister.

Cullen rounded the corner back into Niddry Street just in time to see Hunter walk into the ghost tour place. Cullen charged up after him and stomped inside. The bell chimed over the door and neither Hunter nor Temple turned around.

Temple was bright red in the face, ranting with a finger in the air. 'Jimi Danger? Don't come in here and ask me about that prick. Jesus Christ! What a nightmare.'

Hunter had his hands up, like he was deflecting the prods. 'Can you calm—'

'Those pricks left me with a massive unpaid bill. Two grand he and his band owe me! Two. Grand. I kept calling the contact, even went to his flat, but those shitweasels dropped clean off the radar!'

Might explain why Melrose's number doesn't work...

Cullen joined Hunter at the counter. 'You let them wrack up that kind of bill without asking for a deposit?'

'Had a hundred quid off them.' Temple snorted. 'You'd think that a room full of guitars, amps, a drum kit and a PA would stop them, but no. They were on their last warning, those arse candles. I had it up to here.' He cut his hand across his throat like a blade. 'Next thing I know, they've missed six months rent. So I went into their room and would you believe it but their gear's gone. Gone! All of it! Those cock trumpets!' He stood there, sucking in deep breaths like a man who knew a thing or two about anger management. He put his hands up. 'So I did the only thing you can do in that situation. I made sure nobody in this town would book any gigs for them or any other bands they might ever play in.' He uncurled his fingers and forced a tight smile on his face, his thin lips fading back to his deathly white. He stabbed his bony index finger on a notebook on the desk. 'Got their names, though. Their names are mud in this town.'

Hunter snatched up the book and flicked through the first few pages. 'You holding back on us?'

'What? No, that's my personal file. Give it back!'

'Afraid I can't do that. This is clearly relevant to our investigation. I'm sure it just slipped your mind, but we'll have to take it in. You'll have it back next year, unless of course you came by the information in some illegal way.'

Temple tried staring him down, but looked like he knew he was beaten.

Hunter gave him a nod, then handed the book to Cullen.

Addresses and phone numbers not just for one but for all band members. The kind of data strictly protected by privacy laws.

Cullen tutted at the guy, then set off with a glance at Hunter. 'Come on.' He sauntered back towards the car and put Strang's number into his phone.

Hunter caught up with him outside Bannerman's on the corner. 'Who you calling?'

'James Strang.' Cullen held up a finger as he put the phone to his ear. 'Wait a sec.'

Three ascending beeps. 'This number has been disconnected.'

'Another dead end.' Cullen killed the call and leaned against the pub's stone wall. He ran a finger down the open page of the notebook. 'Okay. Temple's also got numbers for the other two.' He dialled the one for David Johnson and passed the book back to Hunter. 'You try Beth Williamson.'

Hunter typed in her number and put the phone on speaker. 'We're sorry, but this number is disconnected.'

Great.

Cullen hit dial on his and put it on speaker, too, not holding out much hope for—

'Hello?' Less a voice than a snarl.

'Hi, eh… is that David Johnson?'

'It's Dave. Who's this?'

'Good morning, sir, this is Detective Sergeant Scott Cullen. I was wondering if I could—'

'The cops? Ah, shite. This about Jimi?'

'Jimi?'

'James Strang.' Johnson sighed, the harsh sound coming down the line with a burst of static. 'Aw, shite, you've found his body, haven't you?'

Cullen frowned at Hunter, saw the same expression on his face and took a deep, slow breath. 'What makes you think that, sir?'

'I'll take a wild guess and say you've got a dead man in a Jeff Buckley T-shirt, aye?'

4

CULLEN STOPPED OUTSIDE THE INTERVIEW ROOM, THE COMFORTABLE one usually reserved for grieving family members. More IKEA showroom than Stasi interrogation cell.

Hunter pointed at the door. 'How do you want to run this, Sergeant?'

Cullen thought it over for a few seconds. 'Play it by ear. We don't know he's done anything dodgy.'

'Yet.' Hunter only needed the one word to make Johnson's guilt sound like a foregone conclusion. 'I'll get things started.' He opened the door and went inside.

Cullen stood in the hallway, rooted to the ground, listening to Hunter mumble his way through the interview preamble. *Need to rein him in a bit.*

'Do I need a lawyer, or what?' David Johnson had a gravelly voice, deep and resonant. Cullen pictured a mountain of a man, with a beer-barrel chest big enough for that voice to reverberate around.

Hunter huffed out a sigh. 'That depends on—'

Cullen entered the room, cutting him off.

Johnson looked up at him for all of half a second before he lost interest again and went back to staring at his folded arms. Spaghetti arms, thin and weak, but adorned with multiple tattoos.

He was squeezed into sky blue skinny jeans, the buttons on his lime green polo shirt done up all the way to his reed-thin neck.

Cullen joined Hunter sitting opposite Johnson.

'DS Scott Cullen has entered the room.' Hunter reached for a glass of water and took a slow sip, waiting for Johnson to look up at him. 'Mr Johnson, this interview is to confirm whether the body we've found is Mr Strang. If at any point we deem you to be a suspect, we shall pause the interview to allow you to consult a lawyer.' He gave a smile, but even Johnson would be able to see through it. 'For the record, Mr Johnson, you're not a suspect at this moment in time.'

Johnson snorted like he couldn't care less. That kind of hard man act usually turned out to be the pose of a scared wee boy, and all it took to dismantle was a tiny bit of pressure.

Cullen narrowed his eyes. 'When I spoke to you on the phone, you seemed to assume this was about Mr Strang.'

Johnson took a sharp breath. 'Just knew it'd be about Jimi, man.'

'And Jimi would be James Strang?'

'Aye, everybody knew him as Jimi, though.'

Hunter raised an eyebrow. 'Were you in Strang's band?'

'Aye. The Invisibles, man.' Johnson tugged at the collar of his shirt. 'I played bass.'

Hunter scraped his chair back and stood up. He started pacing through the small room, eyes locked on Johnson like he was dealing with a prime suspect. *Here he goes again...* 'You don't seem like a rock 'n' roller.'

'Jimi and I are the same height, aye?' Johnson licked his lips. 'Same height as Alex, the guitarist an' all. Jimi reckoned it made us look like a gang on stage, ken?'

Hunter slumped against the wall, looking sorry he asked. 'When was the last time you saw Jimi?'

'Umm, the third of September, two years back.'

'That's very precise.'

'Aye, well, when two cops call you up about an old mate who disappeared, you go over your whereabouts, know what I'm saying?'

'Indeed.' Cullen looked over at Hunter, who gave the slightest of nods, then back at Johnson. 'And you remember what Mr Strang was wearing that night?'

'Those big boots. He used to say it was so if he bumped into racists or homophobes he'd kick the shite out of them.'

'Was Mr Strang gay?'

'Jimi?' Johnson laughed. 'Hardly.' He took a sip from the plastic cup of water in front of him, then licked his lips, again. 'That night, and most nights if I'm being honest, Jimi'd be wearing jeans and his Jeff Buckley T-shirt.'

'And what was Jeff Buckley doing on this T-shirt?'

'It was the cover of *Grace*, the only album the boy released.'

Hunter nodded at Cullen. 'Looks like Strang is our man, then. We are conducting DNA analysis to confirm it, and pending the result, I'd advise you not to leave town.'

'Eh... You think I've got something to do with it?'

Hunter left his perch against the wall and stepped forward, the harsh lights creating shadows in his heavy eye sockets. 'You saying you have?'

'No... It's just. "Don't leave town?" Man... Why?'

'Because we'll need to speak to his friends and acquaintances. If it is him.'

'Right.' Johnson nodded, maybe a bit too eager. But maybe not, maybe he just wanted to help find out what happened to his friend. 'Eh, mind if I have a look at him?'

Cullen swallowed a mouthful of bile. 'There's not much left to see.'

Johnson shut his eyes and rubbed at his forehead. 'Aw, man.'

Cullen sat forward, propping himself on his elbows and examined Johnson closely.

The guy is mostly likely innocent. Might've tried to act all hard at the start, but that's just a reflex to being interrogated by cops. He had nothing to do with Strang's death.

Focus on him as a source, rather than a suspect.

'Alright, then.' Cullen leaned back, making his chair creak like it was going to topple over. 'Can you tell us what happened that night?'

'Long time ago, man, but I remember it like it was yesterday. We were practising, like we did every bloody night.'

'Every night?'

'Swear I should've just taken a sleeping bag to Niddry Street, man.' Johnson rolled his eyes. 'Eighth rehearsal that week, man. Jimi was really pushing us. Boy was driven, and credit to him, things were starting to happen. We were building a following. Did Glasto, Reading, T in the Park. Had a single out on this tiny wee label, but even U2 had to start somewhere, right? Anyhoo, we were supposed to be supporting Biffy Clyro in Glasgow that weekend. They were a big deal at the time. Still are, eh?'

'Do you remember what time you rehears—'

'From six o'clock until nine.' Johnson clicked his fingers. 'Always the same.' More clicking. 'Every night, we went through the set five times, man. Five times. And we did it twice on a Sunday, man. Can you believe it?'

'I can. What about afterwards? Did you go for a pint?'

'Not that night.' Johnson blinked. Maybe he just had something in his eye. Or maybe the memories were hitting him hard, the hard man giving way to a scared boy, then giving way to a sad laddie. 'Jimi stayed behind to fix the intonation on his guitar.' He looked at Cullen then Hunter in turn. 'That means making sure the guitar's in tune with itself. It sounded fine to me, but Jimi... Boy had perfect pitch. So he said, anyway.' His chuckle died in his throat.

'Right. And that's the last time you saw him?'

Johnson reached for the water again and finished the cup. 'It was.'

Hunter was over at the wall, leaning back, arms folded. 'You told the investigating officer at the time you thought Mr Strang might've run away.'

'Aye. And?'

'What made you think that? Had he gone missing before?'

'Not as such.'

'Meaning?'

'No. He hadn't.'

'So why did you speculate about him taking off?'

'Well, sometimes he'd just disappear. Usually before gigs. Poor Beth, she—'

'Beth Williamson, right?'

'Right. She was our drummer. Great drummer.' Johnson smile, wistful. 'But Beth used to get so stressed. Then Jimi started, like, just tearing off after our soundcheck. Nobody knew where the boy went. And every time, poor Beth started worrying that Jimi wasn't going to turn up. He always did, mind.'

'What was he doing?'

'Trying to psych himself up, you know? Jimi Danger and James Strang weren't the same person. You could see him slipping into that persona. He'd put that Jeff Buckley shirt on, part his hair the other way. Then Jimi Danger was in the room, like a howling banshee.'

'Even at rehearsal?'

'Especially at rehearsal. Man, he said to us to never pretend. Live your life like it'll end tomorrow.' Johnson rubbed at his eyes. 'Can't believe it did, man.'

'How was he that night?'

'Late. And drunk.'

Cullen frowned. 'Drunk?'

'That's a big part of Jimi Danger, man. How the boy coped with stress. Used to tan a half-bottle of voddy a night. He told us someone from a label was coming to see us at the Biffy gig... And a big one.' Johnson broke off, tears welling in his eyes, the ice finally melting. 'Every rejection hit Jimi hard. Few months back, he'd just had a big promoter shut the door in his face, so he was getting really nervous. This was the big time and Jimi wanted success more than anything, but...'

'But?'

'Look, Jimi...' Johnson stared at the ceiling, blinking away tears, but they started running down his cheeks. He rubbed at them, eyes shut, then dropped his head. 'It was eating him, you know? All he talked about was getting signed, getting signed, getting signed. He kept pushing us. But... It's hard to describe, man.'

'What happened to this Biffy Clyro gig? You play it without him?'

'Of course we didn't. Christ. Not without Jimi. Had to phone the promoter myself. After that, the band just fell apart. Nobody knew what happened to the boy.'

Cullen leaned back. 'What did you think happened to him?'

'One night... In the pub, just me and him. Jimi was talking about New York. I thought — *hoped* — he'd run away to there.'

Johnson took a few seconds, staring into space, then locked eyes with Cullen. 'Jimi was a stubborn git, right? When he got obsessed with something, he got this look in his eyes. And he got that look whenever he mentioned New York.'

Hunter glanced at Cullen, impatience burning in his eyes. 'Was Mr Strang involved with anyone? Girlfriend? Boyfriend?'

Johnson looked away. 'Not that I knew of, I'm afraid.'

'Any groupies?'

Johnson scowled at Cullen. 'We weren't that sort of band.'

'What sort of band were you?'

'Just... I don't know. It was a hobby for me and Beth. Not Alex, mind. He played guitar. Pair of them formed the band, spent a few months writing songs. Then they found Beth. Anyway, I went to see them play, just as a mate. They were clearly going places, but Jimi was struggling with singing and playing bass at the same time, so I joined.' Johnson frowned. 'Where was I?'

Hunter sighed. 'You still in touch with the other band members?'

'Alex, aye. Lives in Glasgow. Met up with him a couple of times.'

'And Beth Williamson?'

'Far as I know, Beth gave up music. Got married at Christmas time. I don't really keep in touch with her, just send the occasional text, but she rarely answers. That's Beth, alright.'

Cullen picked up his pen and flicked to a fresh page in his notebook. 'Can you give us that number for Alex?'

'Certainly.' Johnson fished out his mobile and read it out.

'Thanks. Did Mr Strang have a job?'

'Worked in a record shop in Stockbridge, place called Captain Plastic. Starbucks now, man, can you believe it?' Johnson shook his head.

'What about friends?'

'No real friends, except me and Alex. The rest were just acquaintances.'

'Not even from this job?'

'Well, that's how he met Beth. The way she told it, he was a bit too cool for school there.'

'Any other musicians?'

'None that I'd count as friends.'

'And what about enemies?'

'Oh, come on, man. Jimi was a good guy.'

'No rivals for that record deal? Nobody Jimi fought over gigs with?'

Johnson drummed his fingers on the desk for a few seconds. 'Nah, he was friendly with a couple of guys on the circuit, but that was to get gigs and...' He frowned. 'Hold on. There were a couple of boys in another band. I thought they were sad wannabes, mind, so I never hung out with them, but Jimi got on with them, though.'

'Can you remember their names?'

'I can't, sorry. I had nicknames for them, mind.'

'What about the band?'

'Oh, right.' Johnson started grinding his teeth. 'Don't think they were in a band. Just a pair of kids.'

'Sure you can't remember their names?'

'Might be Ally and...' Johnson clicked his fingers. 'Gary, maybe?'

In other words, two of the three who'd found the body.

Cullen hid his interest by making a note. *The first useful lead.* 'So, he just had two friends outside the band, then?'

'Well, they weren't friends. They thought Jimi was a rock god. Look, there were a couple of bands he was friendly with online. Helped us get gigs.'

'Anyone spring to mind?'

'Well. Expect Delays for one.'

'As in, the band in the charts?'

'Them. We did a few gigs with them. Always went fine.'

'What about any flatmates?'

'Jimi lived in a shared flat in Gorgie, just by Tynecastle. Didn't mix with his flatmates, though. Never came to any gigs. The way he tells it, they used to get annoyed by how drunk he'd get. And he made a racket recording demos on his four-track.'

Cullen stared at the almost-blank page. Two missing band-mates and two possible friends, now on their way to being megastars. He made eye contact with Johnson. 'So nobody had a serious grudge against Mr Strang?'

'Tell you, Jimi was sound. Everyone got on well with him.'

'So there's nobody he'd done over or let down?'

Johnson shrugged. 'Not that I can think of, sorry.'

Cullen got to his feet. 'Right, we'll likely be in touch again, Mr Johnson. Please answer the phone when it rings.'

Johnson looked up at him. 'What about his family? Aren't you going to ask me about them?'

Cullen cringed as he sat down again. *Schoolboy error.* 'Yes, of course... I was about to let DC Hunter discuss them with you, but if there's anything you'd like to tell me personally, go ahead.'

Hunter was looking at Cullen with the same surprise in his eyes as the interviewee.

Johnson shrugged and went back to gazing at his hands. He started wringing them again, like coiled serpents. 'Jimi was from a wee town called Dalhousie but—'

'Dalhousie?'

'Aye. You know it?'

'I'm aware of it.' Cullen scrawled on his notebook. 'Go on.'

'Jimi never talked about it much, though. Never talked about anything personal, even towards the end when he was getting plastered most nights. As a friend I should've...' Johnson fell silent with a heavy sigh. 'All I know is that both of his parents were alive and well back then, but other than that, I can't help.'

'Thanks for your time, we'll be in touch.' Cullen felt a buzz in his pocket. He nodded at Hunter to close things off, then checked his phone. A text from Methven:

MEET ME IN THE CANTEEN. NOW.

5

'ON YOU GO.' CULLEN HELD THE CANTEEN DOOR FOR HUNTER. THE queue snaked almost to the door. 'Wait here.'

'Sarge.' Hunter looked away.

Cullen walked round the canteen, scouring for wild eyebrows. No sign of Methven. He checked the message again. *Bloody hell.* He hit dial and put the phone to his ear. Methven had already bounced the call. *Bloody, bloody hell.* He walked back to join Hunter in the queue, five places forward, but another ten behind. 'No sign of Methven. Typical. Might as well get something to eat. Takes forever to get served here.'

Hunter just raised an eyebrow, eyes front.

What the hell is his problem?

The queue moved again, letting them get to the first fridge. Hunter reached for a bottle of water, ignoring Cullen's sideways glances so much that he knocked a bottle of Pepsi to the floor. Looked like he was going to leave it until he clocked Cullen's glare. He sighed as he crouched to pick it up and put it back. 'Alright, you seem like you want to talk. Did that interview get you any insight?'

'A bit.' Cullen grabbed a tray. 'Apart from knowing Expect Delays, and the reference to the two bandmates from The Corner, who also happened to be the ones to find the body. Bit of a coincidence, wouldn't you say?'

Hunter just stared at the boring range of foods steaming behind the glass counters.

Cullen sighed. 'You're probably right. That lead will most likely turn out to be just another dead end.'

Hunter shook his head. Cullen couldn't work out if was at him or the choice of food. Hunter headed back to the fridge and returned with a pair of boiled eggs and a salad box. 'And I take it you want me to do it?'

'I was going to ask Chantal, but if you don't mind.'

'Keep me busy, I suppose.'

A baby had started screaming.

Cullen looked around but couldn't see one. 'Why do people do that?'

Hunter shook his head like a disappointed teacher. 'Still a ray of sunshine, then? You hate people bringing their kids in?'

'Doesn't it—'

'Afternoon, Scott.' Barbara smiled at him, her lank hair held back in a net. 'Usual roll for you?'

Cullen glanced at Hunter's eggs, salad and water. 'No, trying to be a bit healthier.'

'Oh, aye? What's wrong with my food?'

'Nothing.' Cullen dropped his gaze to the counter to dodge her stare. 'Just trying to avoid too much bacon and mayonnaise, that's all. Give me a ham roll and a coffee, please.'

Hunter raised a hand. 'Coffee for me too, please.'

Barbara shouted the order over her shoulder, then leaned in close. 'You heard anything about these cuts, Scott? There was a bit in the paper this morning about getting rid of non-police resources. That means me, doesn't it?'

Cullen smiled. 'You're hardly going to be replaced, are you?' He thumbed at Hunter. 'Can't see Craig here making such good coffee.'

'I've worked as a barista, you cheeky fu—'

Barbara held up an index finger. 'I've warned you lot before about your language.'

Hunter bowed his head. 'Sorry.'

Barbara scowled at him as she dumped Cullen's roll on his tray, the plate clunking off the wood. 'You should be ashamed of yourself. A grown man — a policeman no less — with a mouth like a toilet.' She handed them their coffees like she had never seen such degeneracy.

'I'll get this.' Cullen handed over a tenner and took the change.

Hunter was scanning the room for a table, avoiding Barbara's drill-like stare. 'There, one by the window.' He strode through the busy canteen.

Cullen followed, watching for Methven. No sign of him. *Bloody hell.* He plonked his tray on the cheap Formica and pulled out the chair. 'Now you see why there's always a massive queue down here.'

Hunter shot a glance back at the food counter. 'Barb-wire Barbara never shuts up.'

Cullen laughed. 'Just because she told you off for your potty mouth.' He took off his jacket and sat down. 'You hearing any rumours up at St Leonards?'

Hunter bit the top off a hard-boiled egg and sat chewing.

Cullen watched him for a moment. 'Well?'

'I've not heard anything.'

'Sure?'

'Why, what have you heard down here?'

'Nothing much, and I never believe any of it until it's set in stone.' Cullen bit into his roll, the English mustard biting him right back, right into his sinuses.

Hunter laughed. 'Before I forget.' He pulled his phone out of his pocket. 'Left a message for the cop who caught the MisPer back in the day.' His eyes darted up.

A strong hand grabbed Cullen's shoulder. 'Sergeant.' DS Bill Lamb. Athletic and with eyes as unrelenting as his grip.

Cullen got up to shake hands. 'How you doing, Bill?'

'Brand new, Scott.'

'I can see that.' Cullen reached over to stroke Lamb's top lip. 'Where's the old moustache?'

Lamb swatted Cullen's hand away with a laugh. 'Left it back in East Lothian. Didn't fancy it anymore.'

'You mean Angela didn't?'

Lamb's laugh turned into a sigh. 'Aye, she said it aged me. Now I'm in my forties, I've to take better care of myself. Age is a harsh judge, and a younger wife even harsher. Not that you have to worry about either...'

Cullen gestured at Hunter. 'Have you guys met?'

Lamb squinted at him. 'Aye, long time ago. You were seconded to Haddington for a bit, right?'

'Six months.' Hunter pointed at Cullen. 'Just before this clown here was my Acting DC.' He scraped his chair back and got up. 'Anyway, I've got some admin to do. See you later.' He grabbed his tray and left them to it.

Lamb watched him go. 'He's a live one, that's for sure.' He clicked his fingers. 'Oh, I just remembered why I wanted to talk to you. You seen Angela?'

Cullen frowned. 'She's on maternity leave, isn't she?'

'Yeah, I know, but she came in with me today to show young Jamie off to your old lot.' Lamb tapped his nose. 'While I had a meeting with Jim Turnbull.'

'Oh aye?'

'Don't be getting excited, Scottie boy. It had nothing to do with you.'

Cullen laughed like he didn't care either way. He looked around and spotted Angela over in bollocking corner, right next to Chantal and a couple of other female officers fussing over her new baby.

Lamb followed his gaze. 'Ah, mystery solved.'

'How's fatherhood?'

'Good.' Lamb let out a heavy sigh. 'We've been lucky with wee Jamie. He sleeps like a log and I'm not talking about one with a chainsaw in it.'

Cullen laughed. 'Going to make an honest woman of Angela?'

'You'd better believe it. That's the other thing she's showing off, a giant rock of an engagement ring. Cost me half my savings. Getting hitched next summer.' Lamb looked into the middle distance. 'How's your other half doing? We'll need to get the pair of you to the wedding, of course. Maybe she'll catch the bouquet?'

Cullen raised an eyebrow. It didn't wipe the smirk off Lamb's face, so he raised a fist. 'Watch it, Bill.'

Lamb snorted. 'Come on. Grab your coffee and come meet my wee one.'

Cullen replaced the lid on his takeaway cup and followed Lamb over, scanning the room for Methven as he went. Still no sign of the bugger. As per usual.

Angela Caldwell got to her feet with a squeal of delight and grabbed Cullen in a bear hug. 'Scott!' She let go and looked down at him, her few inches of height advantage aided and abetted by some platform shoes. 'You're looking well.'

Cullen shrugged off the compliment. 'I don't feel it.'

'Six months as an Acting DS, eh? Maybe you'll finally stop moaning about not getting promotions.'

Cullen shrugged again.

Angela went to retake her seat, but Lamb swooped in and grabbed her around the waist to pull her on his lap. Her shriek turned into a giggle as she twisted around to kiss Lamb.

Christ, Bill, you're in a canteen.

Cullen pointed at the baby. 'How's wee Jamie?'

'I love him to tiny wee bits.' Angela wriggled off Lamb and stood next to Cullen, beaming at the little thing. 'When I found out I was pregnant, I doubted I'd ever be maternal. Now, I just can't stop thinking about him.'

'You are coming back, right?'

'Of course.' Her smile dimmed, from neon light bulb to energy-saver wattage. 'Can't afford to be a lady of leisure, much as I'd like to be.' She looked up at Cullen. 'I'm sure Sharon will be the same.'

'Mm.'

'Oh shit.' Angela put a hand to her mouth. 'Have I touched a nerve?'

Cullen shook his head, but avoided eye contact. 'Don't worry about it. She's not in today anyway. Day off, and she woke up with a stinking cold. You could head up to the flat if you want?'

'Maybe.' Angela took Jamie from Lamb. 'Do you want to hold him?'

Cullen raised his hands and stepped back. 'No, thanks. I'm not great with kids.'

'Really?'

'I've no idea what to do with them.'

Chantal leaned over and took the baby. 'No need to be a dick about it, Scott.'

'I'm not being a dick.' Cullen glanced around. Nobody seemed to notice. Or care. He looked back at Chantal. 'I just don't want them thrust in my face, that's all.'

Chantal grinned. 'See what you just said there? That's commonly known as being a dick.'

'Right, that's it. Back to work.' Cullen pointed at Chantal, then at the door. 'Off you go.'

'Yes, boss...' She collected her things, a cheeky grin all over her face.

Cullen smiled at Angela and the rest of the table. 'Nice seeing you all.' He bent down to shake the baby's hand.

'Cullen!' Methven was standing at another table, hands on hips. 'Where the sodding hell have you been?' He pointed at him, then threw his thumb over his shoulder and disappeared out of the canteen.

～

CULLEN FOLLOWED METHVEN INTO THE MEETING ROOM, THE DI still a few metres ahead of him. 'Sir, I—' He glanced around. Buxton and Hunter sat back like they were in a pub. Cullen frowned. 'Where's Chantal?'

Methven glowered at him. 'Was she not with you?'

'Aye, was. You didn't say you needed to speak to her as well.'

Methven dismissed him with a wave. 'Text her.'

Cullen took a seat across the desk from Methven, sandwiched tight between Hunter and Buxton, and feeling increasingly like one of the bad boys here to get their knuckles rapped by the headmaster. He got out his phone and texted Chantal.

Methven got up and walked over to the whiteboard. 'Nice of you to join us.' He uncapped a pen and started scribbling. 'DC Hunter was just briefing me that we have a positive ID. When were you going to tell me this?'

'I was looking for you in the canteen, sir.' Cullen pocketed his phone and shot a glare at Hunter. 'But our ID isn't a hundred percent yet. It's a starter for ten. We obviously can't get anyone to confirm it's Strang, so we'll need to make sure Anderson checks DNA, dental records and so on.'

'Are you on top of it, Sergeant?' Methven didn't so much ask the question as spit it.

'Absolutely.' Cullen leaned forward, at least looking like he was taking the initiative. 'I discussed it with DC Jain before lunch. She's been looking into it.'

Methven gave him a curt nod, then shifted his gaze to Buxton. 'And you've been doing what exactly?'

'Going through missing persons reports, sir.'

Methven shut his eyes. 'Constable, DC Hunter went through them first thing.'

'Oh.' Buxton drew a hand through his hair and scratched the back of his head. 'Nobody told me.'

'I see.' Methven watched him for a second, then arched his wild eyebrows at Cullen. 'So what's the plan of attack, Sergeant?'

'Well, we need to—'

The door swung open and Chantal waltzed in with a smile as loud as her voice. 'Anderson's just confirmed it's Strang.'

Methven's eyebrows shot up even higher. 'He's positive?'

'Totally.' She perched on Methven's chair. 'Strang's DNA was on file. Got done for a breach of the peace in his student days. Anderson's matched it against the blood on the screwdriver and... his flesh.'

'Excellent work, Constable.' Methven beamed at her as if he had personally selected her for the task. 'Excellent.'

Cullen let him enjoy his self-delusion, but the smile showed no signs of fading. 'So, where does that leave us?'

Methven's smile faded to another glare. 'You tell us, Sergeant.'

'Well, we now know it's a murder and we know who the victim is. Problem is, we don't have many suspects.'

'So?'

'So let's start with the band who found the body. Chantal?'

'They check out. Back then, two were still at school in St Andrews. The night Strang disappeared was a Saturday. Ally, the singer, was so drunk he had his stomach pumped. Got the hospital records coming down. His pal with the black hair was out with him.'

'You've got that on the record?'

'I've got a list of three names of people who can back it up.' Chantal folded her arms. 'Why?'

'Well, it's just that we spoke to someone who was in Strang's band who told us Ally and Gary hero worshipped him.'

'When were you going to tell me?'

When you were twatting about with Angela's baby in the canteen.

'I'm telling you now.' Cullen held her gaze, his temple throbbing. 'Can you speak to them again, please?'

'Will do.' She took out her notebook and scribbled something. 'Anything else I should ask?'

'If they were in St Andrews, fine. I don't like the fact they knew him and have kept something from us.'

'I'll speak to them.'

'And the drummer? Roddy, is it?'

'He's proving a bit trickier. He's ten years older than the other two. Reckons he was with his mates in Ibiza. I've got a list of names and numbers to call if you think that's a wise use of time.'

'I do.'

'I don't.' Methven was staring at Cullen. He raised his hands, palms out. 'Your call, *Sergeant.*'

As in, my promotion is on the line.

No pressure.

Cullen looked around. The other three avoided his gaze. *Time to nail my colours to the mast. No turning back now.* He nodded at Chantal. 'Call them, please.'

'Okay.' Her eyebrows flashed up.

'Thanks.' Cullen glanced at Hunter, then back at Methven. 'DC Hunter and I spoke to David Johnson, the guitarist in Strang's band. He gave us a few leads, specifically the record shop where Strang worked and the student flat where he lived. Craig, Chantal, can you follow up on them?'

Hunter twisted around on his chair to look at Chantal, who was still standing just inside the door. She gave him a blank look. Hunter turned to Methven. 'That's not going to be easy. The shop shut last year.'

Methven sighed, like he was on to more of Cullen's ineptitude.

Cullen clenched his teeth as he cut a sideways glance at Hunter. 'I know the shop closed. Find the owner and ask them about Strang and any other staff who might remember working with him. It's hardly rocket science, is it?'

A muscle twitched in Hunter's jaw. 'Right-o.'

Methven watched them for a moment, then huffed out a loud sigh. 'What else?'

Cullen frowned. 'We're still awaiting the post mortem and

forensics. In the meantime, we need to track down the other two bandmates.'

'Excuse me?' Methven's eyes bulged. 'You haven't spoken to the entire band yet?' He looked around the room. 'Leave.'

It took a few seconds for anyone to react.

'All of you. Out!' Methven pointed at the door, his finger trembling. 'Not you, Cullen.'

Cullen sat back down, a furious blush creeping up his neck.

Hunter was the last one out, the door shutting with a click.

Methven slammed his fist on the desk. 'Sergeant, this is out of control.'

'Sir, I didn't get a chance to get an update from the team. I was up in the canteen looking for you, but you weren't there.'

'I waited for you. Quite some time, but there was a baby. I've been stuck in meetings all morning, first with Alison, then with Jim and the powers that be. They're concerned that we're dealing with a serial killer.'

'We're not.'

'We may be.' Methven took a deep breath, then flexed his hand. 'Sergeant, you're focusing all of your efforts on people Strang knew, but the writing was *literally* on the wall. *I will kill again.* I don't get the impression that you're worried we're dealing with a serial killer.'

Cullen took a big breath, held it to a five-count, and breathed out again. 'Do you want me to get someone to search the records for similar murders spanning the past, what, ten years say?'

'That'd be a start. For all we know Strang wasn't the first victim but the last, or any number I could pick out of a hat for you.'

'Just to satisfy your action bias.'

'My what?'

'It's a natural tendency to take action, to do something even if there's no benefit. Like in football when the goalkeeper jumps left or right to save a penalty, although it's been proven he'd be more likely to make a save if he stayed near the centre.'

'You sodding know my thoughts on football.' Methven stared at him, unblinking. 'What are you implying, Sergeant? That I want you to jump around like some brainless monkey in padded gloves and a clown suit just to make me think you're doing something? Initiative for the sake of not seeming clueless?'

'I'm sorry if I gave you that impression. All I meant to say was that—'

'I know what you meant to say. Have you got a list of screwdriver sales?'

'Eh, not on me, no. Chantal was—'

'Come on, Sergeant. This isn't good enough. It seems like DC Jain is doing all of your work for you.'

'Look, with all due respect, we'd know if there was a serial killer stabbing his victims with screwdrivers and scrawling "I will kill again" over his crime scenes.'

Methven sighed like he was tired being the voice of reason. 'Sure, Sergeant, if it had happened in Edinburgh. Or, should I say, on the surface level of Edinburgh. Then we would know about it, yes. I'll even concede that we might've heard if it had happened in Glasgow.' He paused, leaning so far over the desk he breathed stale coffee breath in Cullen's face. 'But what about London? Berlin? New York? Tokyo?'

'Alright.' Cullen made a note on his pad. 'I'll get Buxton on it.'

'Really?' Methven rocked back on his chair. 'He isn't the sharpest tool in the box, is he?'

'He's a good officer.'

'Mm, or just a tool.' Methven got up and walked back to the whiteboard and added more arcane scribbles.

Whatever he says, he's exactly like that goalkeeper, cluelessly jumping around in the hope of making an accidental save.

Methven stopped staring at his hieroglyphics and nodded to himself. 'What are you doing to find this Alex Melrose?'

Cullen went back to his notes. 'I was going to speak to the band's drummer.'

Methven uncapped his pen. 'His name?'

'Her name. Beth Williamson.'

'What? Can women play drums?'

Cullen held his gaze. *Are you serious?* 'Well, sir, they tend to wear trousers.'

'Oh, yes, of course.' Methven covered his blush with a cough. 'Um, eh, I didn't mean are they physically capable. It's just that I've never actually seen—'

Cullen tried to hide his smile. Tried and failed.

'What's so funny, Sergeant? What if she's dead, too?'

'Look. We've got an ID on the victim and we've spoken to one of the other band members. Next, I'll track the others down as soon as we're done here. Okay?'

Methven recapped the pen. 'Someone needs to brief Mr Strang's parents.'

'You're the Deputy SIO, right?'

'And I'm up to my sodding ears in work, Constable.'

'Sergeant.'

'What? Oh, right. Yes. Look, is this Jimi Dangerous from Edinburgh?'

'Dalhousie. My home town. And the name's Danger, not—'

'Whatever. Take ADC Buxton and break the news to his parents. And see what you can find. I'll steady the ship here.'

6

At some point during the endless talks in cramped offices and crowded canteens, it had rained out here in the real world, leaving the cloudless white sky above them looking polished and hard. Cullen lowered his eyes to trace the narrow band of asphalt that stretched out for miles ahead, glistening in the March light. It hurt Cullen's eyes; at least, that's what he told himself when he stopped looking outside and pulled out his phone to call Sharon.

Buxton glanced over, still in no mood to talk.

Sharon answered the phone with a sneeze.

'I was calling to ask how your cold is but that answered it.'

Another loud sneeze. 'I feel rotten.'

Rotten.

Cullen closed his eyes. The rotten body of Jimi Danger stayed. He took a slow breath. 'Right, I'd better not catch your cold, then.'

'Always thinking about yourself, eh?'

'Who'll look after you if I'm ill?'

'Who, indeed?'

'Can I get you anything?'

'Nah. Angela came round with the baby. Brought along some soup, so I'm fine.' Another sneeze. 'Are you driving?'

'Heading to Dalhousie.'

'Without me?'

'Well, yes, but it's a coincidence. This case. The victim's from Dal and Methven got me to break the news.'

'Oh.'

'Yeah, this day keeps getting better.'

'Angela said she bumped into you at the station. Scott, we need to have a serious conversation about your attitude to kids.'

'Right.'

'Look, I need to lie down. Talk later.' And she was gone.

Cullen put his mobile back in his jacket pocket.

Buxton reached over and stabbed the radio. Music boomed out of the speakers. Cullen flinched as he turned it down. 'Christ, that's enough to make you deaf.'

'What?' Buxton bobbed his coiffured head to the dance beat, eyes trained on the road.

Then it hit Cullen. It was Expect Delays. He turned the radio off.

'I was listening to that.'

'They're a bunch of wankers.'

'Christ, what's up with you?' Buxton glanced over at him. 'You know, I supported them at Bannerman's a few years back.'

Cullen frowned. 'What?'

Buxton laughed. 'My old band. Must be, what, six years ago now? Yeah. We had one of them rooms on Niddry Street, too. They were like gold dust, but somehow we nabbed one. Practiced there four times a week at the start. Expect Delays were just down the corridor. Our drummer blagged the gig. Swear, they were in there all the time. We didn't last long at that pace, though. Things fell apart and it was just a storage space for our amps and drums.'

'What were they like?'

'Complete clowns.' Buxton snorted. 'This was just before their first single came out. The way they were talking, it was like the Beatles releasing *Sergeant Pepper*.'

'Did you play a lot of gigs?'

'Anything we could, mate. And I mean anything. Weddings, christenings, bar mitzvahs.' Buxton laughed. 'Not many of them in Edinburgh, mind. Best gig we did was the G2 in Glasgow. That was mental. They reckon there were about a thousand people there.'

'So, if things were going well, what made you break up?'

'Take your pick.' Buxton shrugged. 'Apathy, lack of success, the singer getting knocked up by the guitarist while she was going out with me.'

'Oh.' Cullen winced. 'That's rough.'

'It's belittling, mate.' Buxton floored it to overtake a van indicating for the Kinross services. 'Like my current situation. I think I've got the record for the longest Acting DC tenure in Lothian & Borders' history. At least you know you're in CID after Tuesday.'

'Specialised Crime Division.'

'Whatever. You know you're going to be in the Edinburgh Murder Investigation Team, though.'

'Major, not Murder. You do read the emails, right?'

'Piss off.' Buxton slowed to let a pair of Audis get on the motorway. 'Look, you have the certainty of a detective job after the restructure. I don't.'

'I can see how that's far worse than your girlfriend getting knocked up by your bandmate.'

Buxton burst out laughing. 'You prick.'

'Do you want me to speak to Cargill or Turnbull?'

'You're more likely to cock it up, aren't you?'

～

'DOWN HERE.' CULLEN POINTED AT THE JUNCTION TO BROUGHTY Terrace, one of Dalhousie's better housing estates.

Buxton turned off and pulled into the first free parking space. 'Pretty swanky round here.' He killed the engine. 'Sure beats Hammersmith, mate.'

All Cullen could see were plain driveways and even plainer cottages. And no sign of the Family Liaison Officer. 'Come on.' He got out onto the street and set off. 'My parents live two streets that way. Used to play round here as a kid. Used it as a shortcut home from high school.'

Buxton climbed out of the car and slammed the door shut like that settled it. End of debate. 'You know these people?'

'Nope.' Cullen led Buxton over to the address. An old stone cottage set back from the road. Most of the front garden was tarmacked over, a silver Ford Focus parked on the left, the right reserved for another car.

Cullen chapped the door. 'You okay to lead? Good experience and all that.'

Buxton shook his head. 'Trust me, I've had more than my fair share of telling people their kid's dead. But fine.'

The door opened and a woman peered out at them. 'Hello?'

'Police, ma'am.' Cullen held up his warrant card. 'Need a word inside, if you don't mind?'

~

NORMA STRANG SAT WITH HER FIST CLENCHED AROUND THE HANDLE of a coffee mug, now backlit by the dying sunlight in the enormous conservatory at the back of the house. Her face was in shadow and she stared at them in silence, still clinging to the coffee mug. She held her chin up high and met Cullen's gaze with just a slight twitch under her eyes. She took a deep breath, then held it with tightly compressed lips, her eyes never leaving Cullen's, but from the back of her throat a tiny moan escaped, the dying sound of hope. 'That's what I expected.'

Cullen sat on the white settee, cradling his mug in his hands. 'Is your husband around?'

'George is at work, but he should be— God, that's bright!' She squinted at Buxton, stood by the doorway. 'The other lights, please.'

Three reading lamps flickered on at once, bathing the room in a soft glow.

'George should be back in the next hour or so, depending on how many meetings he had today.' Norma picked up her coffee mug again and swigged it in one swift motion. 'Where did you find Jamie?'

'In Edinburgh.' Buxton sat next to Cullen on the sofa. 'Near the rehearsal rooms where his band used to practise.'

'And you're sure it's him?'

Buxton nodded. 'A DNA test confirmed it.'

The tears started somewhere deep inside her with a deep, suppressed sob, and soon filled her eyes. Norma had the good grace to nod at him with a sad smile as she took a paper tissue from the sleeve of her cardigan and dabbed her eyes. Just like that, she was back in control. 'Can I see him?'

'I wouldn't recommend it. Your... The body is in an advanced state of decomposition.'

'Oh, dear God.' Norma ran a trembling hand through her hair, leaving strands of grey standing up. 'I won't even be able to have an open casket funeral.' Her eyes misted over, but this time she blinked the tears away and a hard resolve steadied her shaking hands. 'How did he die?'

Cullen took a sharp breath. 'We believe he was murdered.'

She nodded absent-mindedly. 'I want to help you find who did this.'

'Thank you. Can you think of anyone who may have wished to harm James?'

She shook her head, no hint of hesitation. 'We went through this with the police when he first went missing. Jamie was a lovely laddie. Very warm, very popular, lots of friends. He just lived for his music, always playing that guitar. Learned it at the school and we got him his first proper one at thirteen. He would spend hours at it. Used to be a right bugger to get him to do his homework. Still did well enough to get into Edinburgh. That was our Jamie alright, capable of focusing at just the right time.'

'What did he study?'

'Chemical engineering. He was the only one from his school who went there. Even then, there weren't many people left in the town that he was friends with. They all just drifted apart over time.'

'Why was that?'

'You should know.' She looked straight at him. 'You're the same.'

'I'm sorry?'

'You're a Dalhousie laddie, aren't you? I very much doubt you've looked back since you moved away.'

Cullen couldn't remember her, but it had been over a decade since he'd left. Plenty of time for people to change beyond recognition. And she had a point. 'I meant was there a specific reason why he cut his ties with Dalhousie?'

Norma seemed to think it through, then slowly shook her head. 'Just liked his Edinburgh life more. He was much more at home there. Him and his music.'

Buxton shifted on the couch. 'Was there anyone your son fell out with in Dalhousie?'

Cullen wanted to punch him.

But it did the trick. Norma started nodding. 'Aye, now that you mention it.' She gave Buxton an intense stare. 'There were a few aggressive kids around back in his school days. Jamie was bullied for a while.' She bit her lip at the memory but then dropped her gaze to the tissue balled up in her hands. A smile twitched at the corners of her mouth. 'Actually, the bullying was never that serious. Jamie was just a very sensitive flower, only comfortable with his books and guitars. He was never one for sport. Didn't come into his own until he moved through to Edinburgh.'

Buxton got out his notebook and wrote something into it, then glanced up at Norma. 'What did you think happened to your son?'

'Well...' She avoided his gaze. 'Like I said, Jamie was very good at cutting himself off from people if he'd had enough of them. Sadly, that included us. He hadn't been home in months, then he was reported missing... We'd not had a row as such, but we hadn't spoken on the phone for... At least a couple of weeks. Maybe more.'

'I see. What happened to his belongings? Guitars, CDs, computers, that sort of thing?'

'Most of his stuff was in Edinburgh. Your colleagues went through it all at the time, but they gave it all back. George drove through for it. Didn't seem to be of any use in finding him. It's just sitting upstairs.' Norma looked at the ceiling. 'I'm afraid I've turned his old bedroom into a bit of a shrine.' She smiled at him. 'If you think it might help, I can show you the room.'

'That'd be great, Norma. Thanks.'

~

Halfway up the stairs, Norma stopped to frown.

The front door opened and a male voice called from the far side of the house. 'I'm home!'

Norma glanced at the door. 'That's George, James's father.' She brushed past them, padding down the stairs. She stopped, holding a hand to her head, torn between what to do. 'Go ahead. His room's first on the right.'

'Thanks.'

She glanced over her shoulder at Buxton and narrowed her eyes. 'I know precisely everything that's in there.' Then she set off to the sound of her husband's light-hearted whistling.

Cullen followed Buxton up. 'What the hell was that about?'

'Search me, mate. Better ask if there's anything you want to nick.' Buxton opened the door and went in.

James Strang's bedroom was a cross between a museum and a mausoleum. He had the same posters from ten years ago that most kids born in the Eighties would. Jeff Buckley, Iggy Pop, Muse and the classic, doe-eyed, black-and-white Kurt Cobain shot. By the window looking across the back garden was one with a similarly me-against-the-world vibe, some guy wearing a T-shirt that said: "Who the fuck is Mick Jagger?" A Marshall stack lurked next to the single bed, black with gold controls. A powder blue Fender Telecaster rested on a stand in front of it, shining like it had been polished in the last week.

Buxton nudged Cullen, then nodded at the guitar. 'That is beautiful. Always wanted one.'

'Thought you played bass?'

'I can play guitar as well.'

Cullen waved his hand at the walls. 'What do you think of that lot?'

'All the posters and stuff? Weird.'

Cullen crouched down to sift through the tall CD rack opposite the amp. Next to it, a stack of LPs teetered on top of a turntable. 'Surprised someone younger than us isn't purely into streaming.'

'All the hipsters are into vinyl these days, mate.' Buxton slicked back his fringe. 'Got a record player a couple of months back...'

'Why doesn't that surprise me.' Cullen took a closer look at the records for a clue on how James Strang became Jimi Danger. They matched the posters on the wall, though a few jumped out. On the one hand there was Massive Attack, Portishead and Underworld. On the other, Joni Mitchell, Bob Dylan, The Beatles, Scott Walker, Neil Young.

'This boy must have been gay.'

Cullen shot him a glare 'What?'

Buxton waved his hand around. 'The posters are all blokes. He wasn't a teenager. He was in his twenties and he didn't have a single picture of a woman up.'

'He wasn't.' Norma Strang was standing in the doorway, hands on hips.

Cullen walked over, palms up. 'I'm sorry. DC Buxton shouldn't have said that.'

'Why? He just spoke his mind, and I just stated a fact. My son wasn't gay, but it wouldn't have been a problem if he had. Or would it?'

'Eh, no, of course not. Not to me, anyway. I just thought you might have misunderstood DC Buxton's remark as an intended insult.'

'Why?'

Cullen swallowed. 'Neither. I just wanted to err on the side of caution and—'

'Norma.' Buxton stepped between them. 'How is your husband?'

She smiled at him. 'Thank you for asking, Simon. He's... He's okay. I suppose. Another officer turned up and he's helping him. I was only getting in the way.'

Another officer?

Cullen looked back into the hall. A floor-to-ceiling window looked out onto the street and a squad car gleaming in the sun. Hadn't even heard them arrive.

Norma sat on the bed and cast a sad look around the room. 'You know, I often wondered about my son being gay, but he had a couple of girlfriends I knew about.'

Buxton sat on the desk chair. 'Were any of those girlfriends serious?'

'Not serious enough to bring home and introduce to us.'

'What about not serious?'

Laughing, Norma wagged a finger at him. 'Now you mention it, aye. There was one girl. I think her name was Jane. He only mentioned her a couple of times.'

Buxton took out his notebook and made a note. He glanced around the room for a moment, then looked back at Norma with a conspiratorial smile. 'These are all the possessions Jamie had with him in Edinburgh?'

Norma started nodding but stopped herself. 'Actually, there

were a few things he'd left here, some of his more embarrassing CDs, I think. They're up in the loft. I could fetch them?'

'Oh, that's very kind, but I don't think that'll be necessary for now.' Buxton prattled on and Cullen stopped listening.

Can't believe how calm she's being. Then again, she's an Angus wifie. They built them differently up here. My mum would be the same if anything happened to me or Michelle.

'—journal or diary?' Buxton was still smiling at her.

Cullen snapped out of his thoughts.

'You know, that's a good question, Simon. I wonder why I never thought about it myself, but my gut feeling is no. I don't think Jamie kept a journal. I never saw one lying around anyway.'

'Might've been an online journal, or some notes he kept on his laptop.'

Norma thought about it with a deep frown. 'Well, if he did, your colleagues didn't find it. At least they didn't mention it to me and they handed back his laptop after just a few days. Never asked about it again, mind.'

Cullen noticed the machine on the desk. Quite dated now, a black and red brick compared to the sleek silver MacBook Sharon had just bought. A trip to Charlie Kidd, their Forensic IT Analyst. 'Do you mind if we take this in as evidence?'

'I don't suppose it would make a difference if I did mind, would it?' She returned her attention to Buxton. 'Will you make sure he returns everything, Simon? I'd be very sorry if any of Jamie's things were to get lost. It's all I have left of him, you know?'

Cullen ignored her and stopped listening. He closed the laptop lid and hefted the computer off the desk, heavier than he'd thought. He spotted a pile of unmarked CDs behind where the screen had just been. He put the laptop back down and inspected them, blank CD-Rs with two words scribbled on each of them in permanent marker: The Invisibles. Demos, most likely.

The only thing we know about what the band sounded like was what David Johnson told us.

Cullen cleared his throat and waited for Norma to tear herself away from Buxton's fascinating description of how evidence is collected, bagged, tagged... 'Do you mind if I take these CDs as well?'

She dismissed his question with a casual wave. 'Fine. George put them on his computer a long time ago. Alex was going to send me some other songs he had.'

'Alex Melrose?'

Norma smiled. 'Ah, Alex. He's a lovely laddie. He was very pally with Jamie.'

'You knew him?'

'Only after Jamie went missing. He reported it. Met up with us when we came through to speak to the police. He used to call me up every now and then to talk about my boy. Part of it was his way of coping, I imagine, but he was sure something had happened to him.'

'Did he say what?'

'I didn't ask.'

'Norma, we're struggling to get hold of Alex. Just wondering if you could give us his phone number?'

7

CULLEN SET OFF TOWARDS THE CAR AND POINTED BACK AT THE house. 'What do you think?'

'Seen his type a lot in the music scene.' Buxton plipped the locks but didn't get in. Just stood there, hands in pockets, thinking. 'Introverted guy, obsesses over his guitar, listens to loud music, then becomes a rock star when he's pissed on stage.'

'Maybe.' Cullen leaned back against the car and folded his arms. He dialled Alex Melrose's new number. It rang and rang, and kept ringing.

He's maybe not interested in taking an anonymous call.

That, or he has a different reason for not answering his phone. Like James Strang's.

He pocketed his mobile. 'I don't like not being able to get hold of this Alex Melrose guy.'

'Reckon he's a suspect?'

'Why call in a MisPer if you'd killed them?'

'Exactly. So why do you care?'

Cullen thought it through for a few seconds. 'It's a loose end and I like them even less than your haircut.'

Buxton smoothed his floppy fringe down with a tender hand. 'Get over it, mate.'

'Look, do me a favour and head down to the local station. See if they know anything about Melrose or Strang or anything.'

'Bloody hell.' Buxton narrowed his eyes at him. Then a leery grin crept onto his face. 'Why, what are you doing? Hooking up with an old flame, Shagger?'

'I wish.' Cullen checked his phone again. 'I'm taking my parents out for dinner.'

~

'He does know Sharon and I were supposed to be coming up tonight, right?'

Cullen's mother took a sip of wine, arching her thin eyebrows over the rim of the glass. No point in disagreeing with her. 'You know your father, Scott. He's very much like his son. And he's just very busy right now. The company's got a lot of deals going on, so he's called a way a lot. This is no slight on you and Sharon, not that she's here to take offence.'

'I told you she's got a cold. It's not like she chose her day off to get sick.'

'I understand, of course I do.' The restaurant's low lighting just about showed the cheeky glint in her eye. 'It's almost like sometimes unforeseen things happen that disrupt our best-laid plans.'

'Fair enough, point taken. Now I suppose you'll ask me to take all the food you bought for the weekend home with me?'

'You know me too well.' She threw back her auburn curls with a throaty laugh. 'Aye, the fridge is full to bursting. I even bought some of that high-protein peanut butter you keep going on about. You'll definitely have to take that with you.'

'Oh, the things I'll do for you.'

She laughed again, then glanced around to make sure she hadn't offended any of the other diners. 'Here.' She reached under the table and pulled out a hessian shopping bag. 'Take it.'

'Not now.'

'Come on, Scott. You'll forget otherwise.'

'Right.' Cullen took the bag, hiding it under the table. He sneaked a look. Various jars and cartons. 'Thanks.'

'This is just a rain check though. When are you next off?'

'May, but we're going to Crete.'

'So not until then?'

'Sorry, Mum. I did tell you I'm an Acting DS now, right?'

She gave him a pointed look, half stern, half proud. 'No, son, you did not. I worry about you. You had too much pressure on you even before that promotion.'

Cullen dodged her usual concern with a casual head shake. 'It's not a promotion, not yet. It's just interim, but I'm not letting it go without a fight. Besides, Sharon wants a new house and I've got a lot of responsibility, people reporting to me... Takes time to become efficient in a new role, but I'm still young and—'

'Who's having the pizza?' The waiter arrived with their food — a pizza drowning in oil and cheese for his mother.

'That'll be me.' His mother thanked the waiter with a beaming smile.

'Sir.' The waiter dropped a tuna salad in front of Cullen, the promised handful of pine nuts being three at most. 'Enjoy.'

Mum lowered her gaze at his plate, and the smile dropped from her face. 'Well, I hope you do have enough energy, because you won't be getting any from that.' She made it sound like he was eating out of a bin.

'Trying to be healthy. Thought you'd be pleased.'

'You know what would be healthy? Speaking to your sister.'

Cullen dropped his knife and fork. '*Knew* this was coming.'

Mum daintily cut into her pizza. 'And have you got in touch with her lately?'

'It's up to Michelle to get in touch with me. I've tried loads of times, as you well know.'

'Scott, your sister lived in Edinburgh for a whole year and you didn't meet up with her once. It's not like you live out in the countryside. You're on the Royal Mile, for crying out loud. And now she's working in Glasgow, I don't see how you'll ever cross paths.'

Cullen picked his cutlery up and ate a forkful of tuna and lettuce. 'Michelle's ignoring me. She even unfriended me on Schoolbook. That's just petty.'

'Will you try again, please? For me? I think she's hurt.'

'She shouldn't be so bloody precious.' Cullen shook his head, the old anger surging. 'I didn't do anything wrong, didn't say anything Dad wouldn't have said.'

'I'm not sure he'd agree with that, Scott.'

'Really?' Cullen ate one of his trio of pine nuts. 'How is the old bugger, anyway?'

'Ach, you know your father. He won't stop playing his games, always up to something. And I'm not talking about computer games. At least he's finally stopped playing that infernal Play-Station.'

'He's like a scheming teenager hiding his secret life from his overbearing mother.' Cullen held up his palms, taking the sting out of the remark. Then he frowned. 'Listen, do you know a James Strang?'

'I know his parents. Norma and George, right? Oh, that's the laddie who disappeared, isn't it? They were devastated by it.'

'You know about that?'

'Of course. The whole town does. Is that why you're here?'

Cullen rested his cutlery down. 'Found his body in Edinburgh. Can't really talk about it, though.' He took a drink of his lemonade. 'So, if everybody knew he'd gone missing, what's the word on the street?'

His mother smiled. 'Am I a witness in this case?'

'No, but truth be told, I could do with any clue right now. We've got nothing on him, and the guy was three years younger than me, so I don't remember him from back in the day.'

His mother leaned over the table and patted his hand. 'Leave it with me. I'll see what I can dig up.'

$\sim$

CULLEN LET THE WAITER PICK UP HIS PLATE, A PUDDLE OF GREEN pesto goop at the bottom. 'Thanks.' His chair back vibrated. He reached for his suit jacket draped over the backrest. It buzzed again and he got his phone out of the pocket. He gave his mother an apologetic smile and pulled it out to check the screen. Two texts from Buxton:

'DONE YET?'

'CHOP CHOP, GEEZER! DALHOUSIE COP SHOP IS SHUTTING!'

Chasing me up when I'm at dinner with my mother? Cheeky bastard.

'Stop texting, Scott, or I'll confiscate your phone.'

'Sorry.' He dropped the mobile back into his pocket. 'I need to get back to Edinburgh.'

'No time for a coffee?'

'Wish I did.'

'Well, don't worry about it.' She pursed her lips like she didn't mean it.

Cullen put two twenties on the table and got up.

His mother smacked his hand. 'You put that away, Scott Cullen. This is my treat.'

Cullen shook his hand in mock agony, then smiled and leaned down to kiss her on the cheek. 'I promise we'll be back up again soon.'

She returned the smile, but there was a slight twitch at the corners of her mouth. 'Well, just make sure you keep that promise. I really do miss spending more time with you.'

'Sure will. Night, Mum.' Cullen walked through the restaurant, a tight knot in his stomach. He opened the door and got out into the cold night air, the noises of the restaurant fading away. The old town looked exactly as he remembered it, the same shops, the same restaurants, and probably the same people.

The sooner I get back to Edinburgh, the better.

Even dealing with a dead body is preferable to this.

Buxton was in the squad car, a heavy din blasting through the closed doors.

Cullen opened the car door and let Buxton's drone blare out onto the street.

'Scott Cullen?' Across the road, a plump woman in her early thirties was pointing at him, rooted to the spot. Then she charged towards him, finger outstretched like a knife. 'You arsehole!'

A car swerved out of her way, horn blaring away down the street.

But she kept charging towards him. 'You arsehole!'

'Excuse me?'

She flew at him, her hand coming at his face in full swing. He managed to grab her wrist before it landed. Squealing, she wriggled free of his grip. 'Piss off, Scott Cullen!'

Cullen let go, jumping back to dodge the next slap. He reached for his warrant card and held it out in front of him like some magical shield. 'I'm a police officer. Clear off or I'll arrest you.'

She cut a long, sharp look at Cullen, eyes like daggers, then marched off in the direction she'd come from.

Who the hell is that?

8

CULLEN GRABBED THE "OH SHIT" HANDLE ABOVE THE PASSENGER SEAT as they hit the Forth Road Bridge with that familiar thump. Bright lights ahead, the black waters of the firth below, further glowing dots to the left as Edinburgh expanded along the coast, almost joining up with South Queensferry. The metal banister was rushing past him, a blur in the bright wash of the headlights, then another thump and they left the bridge. Up ahead, a black obelisk towered over the carriageway, a fancy new hotel.

Cullen leaned back in the seat. His phone buzzed in his pocket. He checked — a text from his mother:

'Nice to see you Scott. Mind and call your sister!'

Buxton glanced over at him. 'Trouble at mill?'

'Nothing much. Did you get anything?'

'What?'

'At the station.'

Buxton grumbled something unintelligible.

Cullen turned the stereo off. 'What?'

'I got Sweet Fanny Adams, mate. That Strang geezer kept a low profile.'

'And Alex Melrose?'

'Nothing much. They'd never heard of him, like I suspected. I did a check of all the usual. He was still posting on Schoolbook after Strang went missing. Looks like he kept plugging away at music.'

'Anything specific?'

'That's the thing. His posts are blocked, but I've sent him a friend request. Let's hope he's still alive enough to respond.'

'Si, I did that a couple of years ago and got into deep shit for it. Promise me you'll not mention it to Methven.'

'Wasn't planning on it.' Buxton shook his head, then hung left to stay on the A90 towards Edinburgh. He hurtled past a trundling white Hyundai.

'You want to slow down?'

'Eh?'

'You're pushing the speed limit again.'

Buxton checked the speedometer. 'Just going eighty, gramps.'

'It's a seventy zone.'

'Come on, there's nobody about.'

'Hate to tell you, Si, but you're a policeman. Slow down.'

'I need to get back in time for a date.'

'Oh, for... Who's the lucky lady?'

Buxton hauled the car into the right lane as a wall of traffic emerged from the side road. 'Blind date. My flatmate set up.'

'Sure it's not with her?'

'Not tonight.'

'You okay about it?'

'Don't want to think about it. In fact, stick a CD on, will you?'

Cullen reached into the back seat for his bag. The stack of James Strang's CDs was on top. He picked one at random and slid it into the player. He turned up the volume and a harsh blend of squalling guitars and pounding drums filled the car. Then strange vocals cut in, far too loud in the mix, switching between talking and shouting. He put his hand on the volume knob, but something held him back. Something about the band's dynamic, maybe. Listening to a dead man pour his soul out. He let the music wash over him, his contact lenses dry in his tired eyes.

'She can sure play.'

'What?' Cullen looked at Buxton. 'What did you say?'

'Beth Williamson. She's a really good drummer.'

'You know that Methven actually asked me if women could play drums?'

'Seriously?'

'Do you even have to ask?'

'Suppose not.' Buxton laughed. 'Tell you what, though, while you were wining and dining your mum, I found some photos of her online. She was a wild one. Shaved head, tattoo on her neck.'

'You didn't think to tell me that until now?'

'Eh? I texted you.'

'What? No you didn't.' Cullen got out his phone. He pulled up Buxton's texts. Shite, there it was — a load of picture messages, all held up by Dalhousie's ancient mobile network.

Sure enough, Beth Williamson was an archetypal rock chick. Frayed Guns 'n Roses T-shirt, tight leather trousers, dyed red hair. And a green dragon crawling from her left wrist to her right ear.

'Got it.' Cullen flicked through some other shots, looked like professional gig photography, all dry ice and harsh lighting. 'See what you mean about the tat.'

'Be great for her job prospects.' Buxton laughed, but the sound died in his throat. 'I found her on Schoolbook too. Got an address for her in Dalkeith.'

~

CULLEN RANG THE BUZZER AND STEPPED BACK. BETH WILLIAMSON lived in a new-build beige executive home, four or five bedrooms of debt in a sprawling dormitory town just south of Edinburgh. The sort of place Sharon would kill to even look around. Low lights in a couple of rings, curtains drawn. Probably to shield the inhabitants from the group of teenagers cruising the streets on BMXs, boys and girls in skater pants and knee-length baggy T-shirts.

The door opened and a young woman of medium height, slight build and long blonde hair peered out. She wore comfy black leggings and a soft cashmere jumper, stretched wide over her massive bump. 'How can I help?' The sort of accent that cost a fortune at one of Edinburgh's many private schools.

'Hi, looking for Beth Williamson. She in?'

'Yes, she is.' She frowned. 'Can I ask who are you?'

'Police. DS Scott Cullen.' He showed his warrant card. 'This is DC Simon Buxton. Could you get Beth, please?'

She gave them an uncertain nod. 'Sure...' She swallowed. 'I am Beth?'

Cullen caught Buxton's frown. *Talk about a change...* 'We should probably do this inside?'

~

'JESUS.' BETH SAT AT THE END OF A LONG DINING TABLE, PATTING HER belly. 'What a way to go.' Her accent had slipped and there were at least some glimpses of the old rock chick. 'What a way...'

Cullen was at the opposite end, Buxton halfway along. The monochrome prints of cityscapes on the beige walls looked to have come with the frames. A light flashed on through the French windows, trapping a black cat in the spotlight. It froze, then sprinted across the small patio towards a patch of lawn where it took a final leap and was swallowed by the dark.

Buxton gave her a smile and pointed at her bump. 'How far along are you?'

She glanced down at her belly. 'Just over eight months, but I'll be honest — I'll be glad when he's out.'

Buxton laughed. 'I can believe that.'

'I wondered what happened to Jimi. All the time. It's why I gave up music.' Beth fiddled with her wedding ring. 'Who am I kidding? I'd fallen out of love with it. I still liked writing songs, but the gigs... And Jimi made us practise every single night. I was knackered at work and something had to give. I was managing a record shop. It's where we met. And...' She gave a wistful look. 'The shop closed last year. My husband works at Alba Bank and he got me a job there.' She motioned at her bump. 'I'm on maternity leave. I suppose it's all worked out okay in the end.'

Cullen caught her rubbing her neck and throat, where the mouth of the dragon tattoo used to erupt into flame. *Must've cost a fortune to remove, not to mention the sheer pain...*

Buxton cleared his throat. 'How did Mr Strang get on with the staff and customers? Any problems?'

Beth raised her eyebrows at him. 'Not that I remember.'

'Anyone there we should be speaking to?'

'Not off the top of my head. Look, I can give you the owner's number. I mean, the assets were liquidated, but he might have kept some paperwork. Might have a better idea.'

'That would be excellent, thanks. Was there a Jane there?'

'Who?'

'Jane. According to his mum, that was his girlfriend's name, no?'

'Never heard of her.' Beth shook her head, two dainty pearl earrings catching the low light. 'Jimi didn't have a girlfriend, at least not one that I knew of. He always picked a new groupie after each gig.'

Cullen cocked his head to the side. 'David Johnson said you weren't that sort of band.'

'He's not wrong. We weren't that sort of band, but Jimi was *definitely* that sort of guy. Tried it on with me once as well. Early on, but I was having none of it. Don't shit where you eat, right?' She laughed, giving a glimpse of the rock 'n' roll drummer, still alive and well behind the yummy mummy façade.

'Do you know the names of any women Jimi was involved with?'

'Nah, David or Alex might, but I wasn't in the habit of tracking Jimi's bed-hopping.'

Buxton reached for his notebook. 'Alex Melrose?'

'Aye, our ex-guitarist.'

'You still in touch with him?'

Beth frowned at his impatience. Or maybe she was just thinking hard. 'I've *tried* staying in touch with him, but the thing about Alex is that he's evasive at the best of times. Nothing malicious, mind, just completely unreliable. He's a very good guitarist, but talk about flaky. That was how Jimi described him.'

Buxton nodded as though he'd expected nothing else. 'Do you have a number for him?'

'I do, actually.' Beth reached for the giant Samsung on the table and fiddled around with it for a moment before pushing it across to Buxton. 'Here you go.'

He peered at it, eyebrows raised, pen at the ready. He dropped both with a sigh. 'Thanks, but that's the one we've already got.'

~

CULLEN WALKED THROUGH THE DIMLY LIT HOUSING ESTATE IN silence, the misty drizzle hanging in the cold night air, hazing the street lights. 'Thoughts?'

'Well. She's a changed girl. Must've hurt like buggery to get that tat removed. I had one on my—'

'I mean about telling a different story to Johnson. He claimed Strang wasn't a shagger.'

'Do you reckon she's hiding something? Maybe she was at it with bad boy Danger.'

'Maybe. Maybe not.' Cullen got in the car and gazed out at the deserted street.

'Where do we go from here?'

'Good question. One to pass up the command chain.' Cullen pulled out his phone and rang Methven.

Bounced to voicemail.

Cullen sighed and called Chantal instead. 'Hi, it's Scott. Is Crystal there?'

'Nope. Think I saw him disappearing with Turnbull and Cargill. Why, what's up?'

Cullen cursed under his breath. 'Nothing, and that's exactly the problem. You got any news for me?'

Chantal was quiet for a moment, her hard breathing the only indicator that she was still there, probably struggling to keep her temper under control. 'I've been looking into this infernal... Hang on. Methven's just walked into his office.'

'Put him on.'

'Piss off. Call him yourself.' She killed the call.

Cullen huffed down the dead phone line. He dropped the mobile onto his lap, closed his eyes and counted to ten. Then he opened them again and called Methven.

'What is it, Sergeant?'

'Good news, sir. We've found Beth Williamson. She's alive and well, and we've just spoken to her.'

'That's a relief.' A harsh burst of static stung Cullen's ear. 'Okay, I've been strategising with Jim and Alison all evening about how to put a positive spin on our lack of progress once the story breaks in the media, but this sounds like we might finally be getting somewhere.'

Cullen glanced at Buxton. 'So, do you want us back at the station in the morning?'

'No.'

'No?'

'No. I want you back here now.'

9

BUXTON STOPPED OUTSIDE THE INCIDENT ROOM FOR A LEISURELY stretch. 'You fuck off, eh?'

'It doesn't work with your accent. And no, I don't drink coffee at this time.' Cullen got his wallet out of his coat pocket. 'Get me a tea and one for Methven and Chantal. Oh, and something for yourself, sweetheart.'

Buxton made big eyes at him. 'Thanks, sugar daddy.' He snatched the tenner from his hand and wandered off, whistling that bloody Expect Delays tune.

Cullen opened the door.

'Scott!' Chantal's voice, from behind.

He shut the door again and swivelled round. 'What's up?'

'Come here.' She waited until he joined her by an interview room door. She opened it a crack.

Roddy Brown sat at the desk, head in his hands. The drummer's massive frame seemed to shrink inside the black hoodie.

Cullen shut the door. 'Christ, Chantal, what have you been doing to him?'

'Interviewing him.' Chantal flicked through her notebook. 'How many of his idiot mates would it take to convince you that he was really in Ibiza when Strang died?'

'Three?'

'Well, I've got seven.'

'Well done. You can let him go.'

'Thanks.' She opened the door again and gave a thumbs up to the uniform inside, then shut it again.

'Remind me never to get on your wrong side.' Cullen gave her a smile, but it bounced off her glower. 'What about the other two?'

'Remind me to stop flirting with intel sources.' Chantal rolled her eyes. 'I swear that Ally kid's going to send me a dick pic.'

'You phoned him?'

'Right. Had to get his approval to release the hospital information. Got it an hour ago. Turns out he was getting his stomach pumped at Ninewells in Dundee.'

'And Gary?'

'According to the records, he was with him in hospital.'

'Okay, so they're in the clear.' Cullen nodded slowly. 'Anyone else?'

'Follow me.'

~

'I HAD A WORKSHOP OUT DUNBAR WAY.' JOHNNY BURNS KEPT scratching at his shaved head, rasping it like sandpaper on wood. 'Those screwdrivers were designed for musicians, right? The guitar companies and amp companies, they all put these custom screws on, so I made a load of screwdrivers so the bands could fix everything themselves.' He stopped scratching. 'Problem is, musicians don't like paying for things. As I found out to my cost.'

Chantal ran a hand through her hair. 'Explain?'

'Well, I went bust, didn't I?' Burns folded his arms and looked away. 'They all moan about file-sharing, but they didn't want to buy my screwdrivers. So they can get to—'

'And this model is definitely one of yours?' Chantal pointed at a photo from the crime scene.

'Damn right. Designed for an Eighties Tele. Did these weird screws, man. Course they won't tell you that when they're selling the guitars. Sound amazing, but when the bloody thing's out of tune with itself, you have to pay through the nose to fix the intonation.'

'Well, it was used as murder weapon.'

'Seriously?'

'No, sir, we've just got you in for a joke.' Chantal shook her head. 'We need a list of stockists.'

'Well, that's not going to be difficult. It's just me. I only sold direct from my workshop. Probably why I went bust. Took a massive loan for all that equipment and none of those pricks bought them.' Burns took the photo. 'This specific model was only on sale between February and August of 2012, just before I went bust.'

'Can get a list of customers, then?'

'Well. I've got a list, but I've been having problems with my computer. The files are on an old one which broke a while back. I've not had the inclination to repair it. Just got a new one, you know?'

Cullen leaned over to Chantal and whispered: 'Get Charlie Kidd on it.'

She shot a micro-glare back. 'Does the name James Strang mean anything?'

'Oh aye. He was one of the few customers I had. Bought a complete set of Fender and Marshall screwdrivers.'

Cullen slumped back in the seat. *Another dead end.* 'Thanks for your time, sir.'

~

'KEN RIORDAN.' HE SHOOK CULLEN'S HAND, THEN CHANTAL'S. 'Pleasure, pleasure.'

Chantal pointed at the interview chair. 'Have a seat.'

'Alright if I stand?' Riordan put a hand to his lower back. 'My lumbago's playing up again.'

'That's fine.' Chantal looked over at Cullen and rolled her eyes. Then smiled at Riordan. 'So, we spoke earlier about James Strang. Did you manage to find anything?'

'Well.' Riordan screwed up his face and started fiddling with his spine. 'There's a wee bit of an issue with all that documentation from Captain Plastic, god rest its soul.'

'What kind of issue?'

Riordan's forehead creased tighter and tighter. 'Well, I put it all in ARGH.' He panted, hard. 'Oh, you bugger.' Then he stood up tall. 'Christ, that's got it.' He shook off his shoulders. 'I'll have that seat now, thank you very much.' He planted himself behind the table and leaned back. 'Feel brand new.'

Chantal shot him a bullet of a glare he didn't catch. 'What was this issue?'

'Well, I put all that stuff into storage when the company folded, right?' Riordan shifted around on the seat, grinning. 'Only, the archive company's through in Glasgow. And they lost my boxes on the M8.'

'Lost them?'

'Bloody nightmare. Happens more than you think, apparently. The van door wasn't shut properly and they flew out at seventy miles an hour. I mean, you're welcome to search the streets of Livingston and Bathgate looking for my IN THE NAME OF THE WEE MAN!' Riordan shot to his feet like he'd been tased. He stuck his hands to his back. 'That's bloody agony!'

Chantal gave him a second to crack his spine. 'You okay?'

'Thought that was it, you know?' Riordan was grinding his teeth. 'Mind if I...?' He lay back on the desk, feet dangling inches from Cullen's face. 'This should fix it.'

Cullen got up and moved away. 'So you lost the documentation?'

'Not my fault, but yes. Scattered all over West Lothian and North Lanarkshire.' An almighty crack. 'Oooh, that's it.'

'Do you remember Mr Strang?'

'Not much. Like I say, I know the name.' Riordan looked over. 'This the guy who's been killed? The one in the papers?'

Cullen frowned at Chantal. 'Not that I'm aware of.'

'Right.' Riordan lay down again and his back cracked again. 'I mean, when you called us, I had a wee think about the boy. You might want to check with Beth, but all I can remember is that he was in early every day. At least half an hour before his shift. Sometimes came in when he wasn't working.'

'What was he doing?'

'Just wanted to listen to the new music. Used to get stock in on a Monday and new releases on a Thursday night. Used to put these big DJ headphones on and listen to the stuff in peace. Always wanted to see what was hot, you know? Oh and bore people about his band.' Riordan grimaced. 'You have spoken to Beth, right?'

'We did.'

'Some change, eh?' Riordan laughed. 'I mean, she used to frighten the bejesus out of me, man. That tattoo. I'm working at HMV now, and she came in one day. Couldn't believe it. Could not believe it. Some change, eh? Said the tattoo removal cost her a grand. Suppose she's got the money now.'

'How close were they?'

'Beth was pals with everyone. Even though they were in a band together, they didn't seem like great mates.'

'Okay. Did Mr Strang have any enemies there? Rivals? Might be customers who annoyed him. Anything like that.'

'That boy annoyed everyone. Had such a snooty attitude towards his music. I mean, I'm no saint, but that boy... Beth had to tell him to stop being such a spanner to the customers. Then again, some of them like it, right? You don't obsess about collecting LPs if you're not a wee bit damaged.'

'But nobody springs to mind?'

'Sorry, no.' Riordan held out a hand. 'Gonna help us up here?'

10

'Well, we're getting somewhere, I suppose.' Cullen walked into the incident room, holding the door for Chantal. 'Just not any closer.'

Hunter was sitting by the door. He looked up at them, then back down again.

Methven was over by one of the whiteboard walls.

Chantal drew a hand through her jet-black hair and refastened her scrunchy. 'Want me to follow up with Beth?'

'Not sure what it'll give us.' Cullen walked over to the board to take a closer look at Methven's work.

The DI pinned up a photo: James Strang, taken from a magazine article. He had surrounded the shot with an assortment of other pictures, memos, notes and newspaper clippings, but no connecting arrows. Yet.

Not far from full-on conspiracy nutjob.

The photos were dated, taken over the course of two years, but Strang had aged considerably in that time. Lines appeared on his fresh face, hair started greying at the temples, then shaved close to hide it. His face was long and thin, his brown hair spiked up in most of the pictures, the sides shaved ever closer as the grey took over. Still he was a good-looking guy, in a fey way.

Methven continued doodling on the wall, oblivious to Cullen. And there it was — the first connecting line, between Strang and

Beth Williamson, full-on rock vixen, not expectant mother. Then one to Dave Johnson, a portrait shot, him pouting at the camera.

Cullen wandered back over to Hunter. 'How's it going, Craig?'

Hunter deadpanned him, kept his gaze on his notebook. 'Methven and I caught up with Deeley. He's finished the post mortem. As you'd expect, there's hardly anything left of the body, but he found a match on the screwdriver in Strang's flesh.'

'It's definitely the murder weapon?'

'Without a doubt.' Hunter pinched the bridge of his nose. 'Long story short, the blood on the screwdriver handle matches Strang's DNA on file and the flecks of blood on the T-shirt. There was very little to perform an autopsy on, so Deeley couldn't give us much else.'

'To be honest, that's more than I expected.'

'Well. I caught up with Anderson too.' Hunter scratched his chin. 'Come with me.' He threaded his way through the desks to the wall not far from Methven and pointed at a photo of a pair of blue jeans, blown up to life size. Dark stains lined the bottom of the jeans. 'These scuff marks show the body was dragged from somewhere. Remember that bodybuilder case back in the day?'

'Won't forget that one in a hurry.'

'Whatever. It's like that. These aren't usual signs of wear and tear. Besides, there are traces of blood in the fabric. He wasn't killed where he was found.'

'Wait a sec. The steps are stone, so the trail would've been visible. Somebody should've seen something, right?'

'That would be a good point if it wasn't complete bollocks.'

'Craig, I swear I'll—'

'Chantal and I visited the room Strang's band used. It's the one furthest down, near that door. Our killer lucked out. Assuming he was killed in that room, all he or she had to do was scrub the bottom step, not the entire staircase. Since nobody apart from the murderer and the bands sharing the room had any reason to be down there, nobody would've noticed the clean-up.'

Cullen thought about it. 'Can we check with the other bands who rented their room?'

'On it. Still nothing from the dude.'

'The dude?' Chantal frowned at Hunter's choice of words. 'He's got a name.'

'Well, whatever. Either way, he hasn't called me back.'

'What about the original cop?'

'Got hold of his sergeant. Off today for a funeral. Back in tomorrow.'

'Okay.' Cullen nodded. 'Anyway, what you said makes sense. They might've checked these band rooms, but they thought Strang ran away. Wouldn't have been looking for bloodstains or other telltale signs that a dead body was dragged out of the place.'

Chantal arched her pencil-thin eyebrows. 'Doesn't mean they shouldn't have noticed, though.'

Cullen took a deep breath to summarise his thoughts. 'So, we've got a few assumptions left to validate. First, we're assuming he was killed in his rehearsal room and dragged down to the catacombs. Second, that our killer cleaned up after themselves.'

'Fair assessment.' Hunter blew up his cheeks. 'Either way, we have no suspects.' He turned away from the wall to head back to his desk but stopped short. 'Oh, that's a sight for sore eyes.'

Buxton lumbered towards them with four coffee cups on a tray. He handed Cullen and Chantal one each, then looked at Hunter apologetically. 'Sorry, mate. I didn't know you were here.'

Hunter gritted his teeth. 'Right.'

Cullen shoved his cup at him. 'Here, take mine.'

Buxton motioned at the photo of the jeans with his cup. 'What about the guys in the band with him? Johnson and Melrose?'

Hunter frowned, sipping his coffee and staring at the photograph as if that would help him figure out what the hell Buxton could possibly be talking about. 'What?'

'You just said we had no suspects. What about Johnson? Seemed shifty.'

Hunter walked to the mind map he had pinned up next to the photo. 'We've only got five direct connections. His parents are two, the others are the three bandmates. We've got nothing implicating either of them.'

Cullen took Hunter's mind map. 'There's another one. Jane, his alleged girlfriend. His mother told us.' He looked at Buxton. 'Si, can you follow up with Dave Johnson about her?'

Buxton closed his eyes. 'Try not to forget.'

Cullen glanced from one to the other, then back at the mind map. 'The three bandmates are possible but unlikely.'

'You're just discounting them like that?'

'No. We urgently need to speak to Melrose.'

Hunter paused. 'I've tried, but we can't get hold of him. Guy's disappeared into thin air.'

Cullen sighed. 'I've got another number, but he's not answering, so—'

'Is that suspicious?' Methven was looking up from the latest line on his conspiracy board.

Cullen looked around the group, blank faces looking back at him. 'For all we know, Melrose might be on holiday, or maybe he's got himself yet another new phone number.'

Methven pursed his lips, looking rather sceptical. 'But even without your speculation we know he's at least got two mobile numbers. That's suspicious in and of itself, wouldn't you say?'

Buxton shook his head. 'Not these days, sir. But I called Tommy Smith in the Phone Squad while I was getting the coffees.' He handed one to Methven. 'Reckons we'll get something tomorrow.'

Methven gave an impatient huff as he tore off the lid. 'What do you think, Sergeant?'

'I don't think he's a suspect yet. Nobody's mentioned any antagonism between Melrose and Strang. In fact, he was speaking to Strang's mother, helping her deal with the loss of her son from the sounds of it.'

'When was he last in touch with her?'

'She didn't exactly say, but it's been a while.'

'So he could be another victim!' Methven thumped his coffee down on the nearest table, splashing brown liquid everywhere. 'This could be the work of a serial killer!'

Cullen glanced at the rest of the team. 'That's a bit of a stretch, sir.'

'Look!' Methven pointed at the wall of photos. 'I WILL KILL AGAIN. What if the "again" is Alex Melrose? What if the "I" is Alex Melrose? Sergeant, I want this on the top of your radar tomorrow.'

Cullen frowned. 'The top of our what?'

'Sodding hell.' Methven dismissed him with an impatient wave. 'Just get it done.' He looked back at the board. 'Did you get anything from the parents?'

'We spoke to his mother.' Cullen nodded. 'Other than the potential lead on this mysterious Jane, well, we haven't got much. Just some interesting personal background stuff if you want to make a bit of money on the side by writing a biography on him, but that's it.'

'Well, that's work, I suppose.' Methven checked his watch. 'Okay, that's all for tonight. We've made progress, but tomorrow's another day.' He nodded at the group. 'Dismissed.'

The others turned away from the whiteboard and headed to the door. Cullen got up to follow.

'Not you, Sergeant.'

Cullen gave Methven a tired look. 'Sir, I'm knackered. Wouldn't mind getting home. Can't it wait until—'

'Who is Richard McAlpine?'

'My ex-flatmate.' Cullen swallowed. 'Why?'

'Oh, I'll tell you why. He ambushed me in Tesco when I was fetching a sandwich. How come he was asking me about a serial killer on the loose in Edinburgh?'

'Sir, that has nothing to do with me.'

'If I find out that—'

'I'd never tell a journalist about an ongoing investigation, even if... Shit.' Cullen pulled out his phone and checked the Edinburgh Argus website.

Front page, top headline:

CAPITAL SERIAL KILLER THREAT

Underneath it: the photo of the body and the wall.

Edinburgh living under threat from murderer who WILL KILL AGAIN

Cullen closed his eyes. *Ken Riordan's murder victim in the papers...*

Methven sighed. 'I would ask you to stop it, but it's obviously too late.'

Cullen nodded but kept his eyes firmly shut. 'I'll have a word.'

～

CULLEN WALKED INTO THE KITCHEN AND SPOTTED A CARTON OF MILK on the counter. *Bloody hell, Sharon...* He took a deep gulp. And spat it straight in the sink. Sour and warm. He stared at the white splotch in the metal basin, then turned on the top and washed down the drain. He rinsed out his mouth and straightened back up.

Then he spotted a handwritten note on the breakfast bar:

GONE TO BED. PLEASE DON'T WAKE ME UP.

-SHARON X

Cullen headed for the bedroom, brushing against something soft and furry. Fluffy darted out from under his feet, baring a set of prickly fangs in his tiny pink mouth.

'Shhh. Sharon's asleep. We don't want to wake her.'

Cullen reached down and picked up the cat. Fluffy resisted slightly, still annoyed but still, he let him. Cullen tickled him under the chin, making him purr in spite of himself. 'See, I'm not so bad.' He put the cat back down and the wee guy scurried off.

Cullen smiled to himself, then got out his phone and called Rich.

Voicemail again.

Somebody else giving me the cold shoulder? Surely not.

The *Big Issue* was on the sofa, half of Expect Delays staring up at him from the magazine's front cover. They were still living the dream — or trapped in the belly of the beast. Just a matter of perspective. He didn't know if they'd made enough to never work again. Maybe they'd have to retrain when it all fell apart.

He went through to the bedroom, stripped down to his boxers and got under the covers. As ever, Sharon was lying with her back to his side, so he snuggled up to her, burying his face in her hair, breathing in her scent as something deep inside him stirred.

And then Sharon stirred, though not quite for the same reason. 'Don't get any ideas, big boy.'

DAY 2

Saturday

11

CULLEN FOUND HUNTER IN THE EMPTY CANTEEN. 'MORNING, CRAIG.'

Nothing in return, just carefully chewing toast.

Cullen sat across from him and ate his porridge in silence.

Buxton slammed himself into the chair next to Cullen, cracking his plate off the table. 'I don't know why you keep banging on about it.' He had enough bacon and sausage to fight off a bastard of a hangover. 'Are you jealous?'

'Jealous?' Chantal sat opposite and laughed, shifting her chair slightly closer to Hunter. 'Si, get over yourself.'

Cullen swallowed another spoonful of grey slime. 'What's up?'

Buxton couldn't answer, his mouth filled with fried meat, so Chantal did it for him. 'He pulled out of a date last night.'

'Wish I'd never told you.' At least, that's what Cullen thought Buxton said through the mush. 'And I didn't pull out.' He wiped a hand across his face, smearing brown sauce. 'I was in here till half ten, wasn't I?'

'Still think it's a dick move.' Chantal dug her spoon deep into her muesli.

'What is?' Methven took a seat at the end. Wearing jeans and a pink jumper.

Cullen pointed at the knitwear. 'Don't think I've ever seen you out of a suit, sir.'

The hint of a grin twitched at the corners of Methven's mouth.

'Wipe that smirk off your face, Sergeant. This, I'll have you know, is a cashmere pullover I bought on my holiday last month. Magenta happens to be the gentleman's colour of the season in the Alpine region, not that you'd know of fashion.' He took his time to stare at each of them in turn. 'What is wrong with you people? No man has worn a suit at the sodding weekend since nineteen fifty-eight.'

Buxton frowned at him. 'What about at a wedding?'

Methven stared at him. Then he closed his eyes and shook his head. 'Constable, I meant people don't wear suits when they go to work at the weekends. Are you planning on going to a wedding today?'

'I've got one tomorrow, sir.'

'You had better clear that with DS Cullen then, hadn't you?'

Buxton ground his teeth. 'Sir. Sorry, but I don't usually work on a Sunday.' He looked at Cullen. 'Can I go?'

Cullen put a fresh spoonful in his mouth and raised his eyebrows at Methven.

The DI folded his hands across his magenta cashmere. 'Fine, you can attend. But on one condition. You find Alex Melrose today.'

Buxton smiled like he was taking that as a victory. 'Thanks, sir.'

Methven reached down and slapped that morning's *Edinburgh Argus* on the table. 'And someone needs to speak to Rich McAlpine.' He jabbed a finger at the front page, last night's speculation about a serial killer being on the loose now etched in black ink. 'Sergeant?'

'He's not answering my calls.'

'Well, go and find him.' Methven paused. 'Did you speak to the other band?'

Cullen frowned. 'Which other band?'

'Try to keep up, Sergeant.' Methven rolled his eyes. 'The rooms are shared by various bands. The band who shared the room with The sodding Invisibles. We want to know if they found any telltale signs of a sodding body being moved!' He shifted his ire to Chantal. 'Well?'

She finished chewing. Took her time with it. 'Tracked them down last night, got a call from the bass player first thing. Works nights in Sainsbury's. They do still use the room. Guy sounded *baked.* I checked them out on YouTube. Total stoners. Anyway, he says they never saw anything.'

'Do you believe him?'

'No reason not to. And they've got an alibi for the night in question, too. Played at some festival near Rotterdam. Sending me through their travel documents. Or at least he promised to.'

'Purple sodding buggery.' Methven looked over at Cullen. 'Missed my sodding triathlon, and now I've got to deal with this sodding nonsense.'

Cullen frowned at him. 'You expected something from them, sir?'

DCI Jim Turnbull walked into the canteen and stopped in his tracks, hands on hips. He roared at them with a voice even bigger than his rugby player shoulders. 'Colin, my office. Now.'

Methven tossed the paper at Cullen. 'Get this sorted.' He got up and raced off after Turnbull.

'All this over a cold case...' Chantal shook her head. 'Although, I'm starting to think there's something in the serial killer angle.'

Cullen raised his eyebrows at her. 'Have you found a matching MO?'

'Well, no, but—'

'Seriously, Chantal.' Cullen waved at the doors, still swinging. 'Crystal doesn't need any encouragement. You saw the spaghetti web he's drawing in the incident room. He's this close to snapping. Until we've got evidence this is a serial killer, please keep it to yourself.'

'Right.'

Hunter's phone blasted out some high-energy disco. 'Sorry. Better take this.'

Buxton smirked at him. 'That your boyfriend?'

'Hardly.' Hunter marched off, phone to his ear.

Chantal leaned in to Buxton. 'He's not gay, is he?'

'No idea.' Buxton sliced a sausage in half lengthways. 'He does moisturise, though.'

'Jesus Christ.' Chantal's spoon rattled off the side of the bowl. 'I'm stuck here with a pair of cavemen.'

Cullen held the spoonful in front of his mouth. 'Don't bring me into this.'

Hunter stomped back over. 'Here, Scott, that's the original

investigating officer. He's back in today, down in Leith. Some guy called Willie McAllister.'

Cullen groaned. 'His legend prevails.'

~

'You know this guy?'

'For my sins.' Cullen pulled away from the lights at the foot of Leith Walk, passing the Wetherspoons, its early morning drinkers already smoking outside. 'Worked for me on a case a couple of years back.'

'He worked *for* you?'

'Not for long. I had to move him on pretty fast.'

'But you were just a DC, then, right?' Hunter scratched his head. 'What were you doing in charge?'

'He was seconded and the DI told me to manage him.'

'I can feel his pain.'

Cullen pretended not to have heard the jibe as he parked outside Queen Charlotte Street Station, a stone fortress in the heart of Leith. In the grey morning light, the thick columns out front looked just like flexed fingers. In the mist above, the bird shit made the ridged roofline gleam like a row of white knuckles. The building was about as inviting as a clenched fist. With a sigh, he unbuckled his seatbelt.

Hunter frowned at him. 'What's up?'

'Just that...' Cullen nodded at the police station. 'Come on.'

~

'You're lucky.' McAllister sat on the interviewer's side of the table, arms folded, waiting. 'Not long till I'm out of this game, boys.' With his bloodshot eyes and sallow skin, the veteran cop looked like he might not even hang on for another two minutes, never mind another two months. He waved at Hunter to sit opposite. 'Be my guest.'

Cullen took a seat on the same side of the table and gave a curt nod.

McAllister turned to Hunter. 'Heard they made him a sergeant.'

'Acting DS, for now.'

'Well, congratulations all the same.' McAllister rested his hands on the table. 'Due my date from Personnel any day soon. Can't wait to be shot of this place. The people they're promoting these days...' He sneered.

'I hear you.' Hunter got out his notebook. 'So, James Strang.'

'What do you want?'

'Chapter and verse.' Hunter held up McAllister's MisPer report. 'Particularly the details you didn't be bothered to put in this.'

'Rightio.' McAllister retrieved his own notebook, battered to within an inch of its life, then put on a similarly vintage pair of reading glasses. Still he had to hold it at arm's length. 'Where do I start?' Said to himself rather than them.

'Just wonder why you're investigating a disappearance from Gorgie from down here?'

McAllister cut him a sceptical sideways look. 'That what you want to ask me?' He sighed. 'I was covering a maternity at St Leonard's. Got posted back down here not long after, which suits me fine, seeing as I live just up the road in Lochend, eh? Anyway, this laddie phoned up to report his mate going missing.'

'Got a name?'

McAllister squinted at his handwriting. 'What the hell does that say? Alex something.'

'Melrose.'

'That it? Oh, aye. Christ, my writing is shocking.' McAllister looked thoughtful for a moment, then flicked through a few pages. 'Anyway... What do you want to know? I mean, I spoke to some people who knew the laddie.'

'Who?'

'The boy Melrose, for starters. Then some lassie called Beth or Bess or something.'

'Beth Williamson?'

'Aye, her. Said she was a drummer?' McAllister laughed. 'I mean, a lassie drumming? Seen it all now.' He went back to flicking through his notebook. 'Took a birl up to sheep-shagger land to speak to the boy's family. Knew less than heehaw about their boy. Such is the way these days, I suppose.'

Cullen frowned at him. 'They were all you spoke to?'

'Standard practice, son. You'd know if you'd done any proper policing recently. Shouldn't even have gone up to Dalrymple.'

'Dalhousie.' Cullen ground his teeth. 'Are there any open leads you didn't close down?'

'What are you trying to say?'

'Just that...' Cullen gave him a searching look. 'We're wondering if there was anything you didn't have the resources to check into at the time. It's a murder case now, so we have—'

'Nothing springs to mind.'

Cullen looked him up and down. 'The mind is the bit I'm worried about.' He nodded at the notebook. 'What about in there? Any loose ends.'

McAllister shut the book with a loud snap. 'Nope.'

∿

CULLEN MARCHED OUT INTO THE COLD, IGNORING THE POLITE uniform who held the door open for him. He barged past two pedestrians, making them swerve out of his way as he headed straight towards the car. 'What a joker.'

Hunter laughed. 'You should start a fan club. Or maybe McAllister will start one for you when he retires.'

Cullen slumped back against the pool car and folded his arms. 'We're getting nowhere.'

'Oh, get over yourself. It's not like your career is resting on this case.'

'What's that supposed to mean?'

Hunter shrugged and got in the passenger seat.

Cullen got behind the wheel but didn't start the engine. 'What exactly are you saying, Craig?'

'Whatever happens on Monday, happens.'

Cullen gripped the wheel tight. 'You know something, don't you?'

Hunter let out a slow sigh. 'Last night, when Crystal went apeshit, Buxton and Chantal cleared off. I got a text from my brother and, as I was reading it, I accidentally overheard you and Methven.'

Cullen watched his knuckles turn as white as the bird shit on the station's rooftop. 'What did you make of it?'

'Guy's an arsehole.'

'That's not what I meant.'

Hunter looked straight at him. 'I'd be shit scared if I were you.'

Cullen glanced away, his guts bubbling. He started the engine. 'We need to get hold of Alex Melrose.'

'You say that like I've killed—'

A sharp knock on the window. McAllister leered into the car with his droopy eyes.

Cullen buzzed down the window. 'What's up?'

'I found something in my notes.' McAllister held up a faded Post-It. 'Must've fallen out of my notebook. This lassie came in with Melrose when he reported it. Never saw her after.'

'His girlfriend?'

'Maybe. Just tried calling here there, but the phone's off the hook.' McAllister handed Cullen the Post-it. 'Name's Marta Owenson. Think she lives in Niddrie. Might be worth a shot?'

12

'YOU'RE SURE THIS IS IT?' CULLEN SQUINTED THROUGH THE windshield. The March downpour blurred the street, the wipers going hard at it but struggling to clear a gap for long. Years after the infamous slums were cleared, Niddrie was now full of starter homes that looked like they came from an IKEA catalogue. Wooden panelling adorned navy blue gables jutting out of white-harled boxes.

Hunter peered down at the Post-It then up at the top floor of a white terrace. 'According to this.'

Cullen killed the engine and the glass flooded within seconds. He dragged the collar of his suit jacket over his head. He yanked the door open and jumped out, straight into an ankle-deep puddle. 'Bollocks!' He slammed the car door shut and sprinted through the pelting rain, his shoes squelching. When he squeezed under the tiny overhang, his jacket felt as if he had taken a shower in it. He pressed the doorbell marked Owenson. He turned around, looking to see what was keeping Hunter.

Hunter sauntered towards him underneath a massive golf umbrella, the rain popping off the top like a snare drum roll. He stopped next to Cullen and shook it off. 'No answer?'

Cullen pressed the doorbell again. 'If she's in, you can lead.'

'Oh, you're letting me, this time? How gracious of y–'

A burst of static from the intercom cut him off.

'Hello?' Female voice, frail, and like it wasn't coming from upstairs but halfway to the moon.

Hunter leaned close to the speaker. 'Marta Owenson?'

A long pause.

'Aye?'

'This is the police. We need to ask you a few questions.'

'What about?'

'Alex Melrose.'

An even longer pause, then the voice was back even frailer. 'Top floor.'

Hunter collapsed the brolly and headed inside. Stuck behind him on the narrow staircase, Cullen followed, trying not to look at his flexing buttocks. *Those trousers are surely too tight to be street legal.*

Hunter stepped over to an open door and rested his brolly against the wall. 'Sure you're okay with me leading?'

'Just don't make an arse of it.'

The door opened and a Slavic-looking woman stared out at them with the hungry eyes of a junkie three days past the last fix.

'DC Craig Hunter and this is DS Scott Cullen.' Hunter held up his warrant card. 'Are you Marta?'

Her eyes looked almost feverish as they flickered between them. 'I'm Marta, aye.' Broad Fife accent. 'Come in. Flat's getting cold.' She stood back and ushered them in, then pushed the door closed behind them and padded through to the living room, wrapping her cardigan tight around her skinny frame.

The flat was baking. And heaving with nervous energy. Three kids scuttled around the place, screeching as though the toys they were throwing at each other were heat-seeking missiles. All looked younger than five, the youngest still crawling, dressed in nothing but a nappy.

Cullen shrugged his soaked jacket off and stood by the door, keeping away from the kids.

Hunter perched on the edge of a battered green sofa and got out his notebook. 'We gather you know an Alex Melrose?'

Marta sat in a tatty armchair and shivered. She drew a woolly blanket over her bony legs and fixed her piercing gaze on Hunter. 'What's he done now?'

'Nothing. We just need to speak to him.'

'Two detectives only get involved if he's done something.'

Hunter forced a smile on to his face, if not into his voice. 'Just need to speak to him.'

'Well, I've not seen him in months.' Marta looked away as if to prove the point, but then she blinked a few times like she was trying not to cry. 'He was the love of my life, that boy. Can't believe he left me.'

'Mind if I ask why?'

'I do.' She blew out her hollow cheeks and let out a quivering breath. 'Truth is, I don't know.'

'Nothing to do with your kids?'

Marta glanced at them scooting in and out of the room, oblivious of the cops in their midst. She gave another thin breath then shook her head.

Hunter dropped his voice even lower. 'Was it because of the drugs?'

'What?' Marta glanced at him, then averted her eyes again. 'I'm not going to answer that.'

'Come on, I know heroin addiction when I see it. And you're not on methadone, either, because those track marks are fresh.'

She hauled her sleeves down to cover her wrists. 'You wanting me to help or what?'

'Look, we're not here to take your kids away from you. Just need to speak to Alex. We need to find him to ask about a friend of his. Neither of you are under suspicion of any crime.'

Marta looked over at her kids, who were still shrieking, still hurling toys at each other and still unharmed. She sighed with what sounded like relief and resignation all at once. 'Last chance saloon for me with my boys.'

Hunter waited.

'Fine, it was my habit.'

Hunter looked her straight in the eye. 'Was Alex into drugs too?'

'Just a bit of blow...' She glanced away again. 'Alright, he smoked the H a couple of times with me, but he wasn't into it. Kept going on at me to give it up. I even went on methadone, trying to wean myself off the skag. But it's not the same. You know how hard it is to spend all day, every day inside my head? Eh?'

'Are the kids his?'

'Two before, one after.' Marta smiled. 'Wee Xander, my middle one, he was born when I first met Alex. Hence the name, eh?'

'Did Alex ever want to become their father?'

'He did, aye. In the end, though, he couldn't deal with... with me being the way I am.'

Even now, Cullen knew her plight would haunt his dreams. 'Marta, sorry to interrupt, but we really need to speak to Alex. Have you got his phone number?'

She blinked at him like she couldn't remember who he was or what he was doing in her living room. Then she sighed like it didn't matter. 'He lives in Glasgow now.'

'And do you have a number?'

'Aye, but I called him a month ago and it was disconnected.'

Hunter got up to show her his phone. 'Is that the number you called?'

She peered at it. 'That's the one. Keeps doing that. Every six months, a new phone.'

'When was the last time you spoke to him?'

'Eh, well.' Marta got up as if she had been waiting for the question. 'He sent me a CD a few weeks ago.' She lumbered over the piles of toys, patting one of her sons on the head, and rummaged around in a set of drawers.

She came back and handed him a Jiffy bag.

Cullen opened it. A silver CD-R, the black writing smudged. ROCK YOUR WORLD. There was a letter folded inside the clear cover. A quick scan showed it was impersonal, all about his music. Nothing to suggest Alex and Marta had ever met, let alone been an item.

But he'd put his address on the note. West End, not far from Glasgow University.

≈

THE RAIN WAS DRIVING FAST AND LOUD ON THE M8, THE WIPERS were swishing back and forth full pelt. Another wave of brake lights ahead, bleeding into red blurs in the torrential downpour, and Cullen slowed, like he kept having to. He looked over at Hunter in the passenger seat. 'Call Crystal, will you?'

'Crystal?' Hunter frowned as he reached into his pocket. 'Oh I get it. You're still full of the bantz.'

'Stick it on speaker.'

Dial tone drilled out of the car's speakers. 'DI Methven?'

Cullen ignored the tone, kept his eyes on the road, hands on the wheel. 'Got an address for Alex Melrose.'

'Really? DC Jain couldn't find one.'

'We got it off an ex-girlfriend.'

'And? Is he alive?'

'Don't know yet. The address is in Glasgow. We're heading there now, if that's alright with you, sir?'

'You're asking my permission?'

Cullen clenched his teeth. 'I thought you'd want to do this by the book.'

'Just sodding go through there.' Methven snorted. 'I don't have time for this.'

'Shouldn't we speak to Strathclyde CID?'

'Is Melrose under suspicion of murder or other serious offences?' Methven was jingling change in his pocket, loud enough to hear down the phone line. 'Well, Sergeant? Is he likely to be under surveillance by Strathclyde?'

The rain spattered on the roof, the wipers swished on the windscreen, above the steady rumble of the engine. 'Not that I'm aware of.'

'Then just get on with it. I want this Melrose guy found, am I clear?'

'Crystal clear, sir.'

'Goodbye.' Methven ended the call.

Hunter put his phone away. 'What the hell's up with him?'

∾

CULLEN SLOWED TO A CRAWL, COUNTING OFF THE HOUSE NUMBERS along Loudon Terrace. Might as well be Edinburgh, going by the look of the terraces, the Victorian architecture, the sandstone and the pissing rain. 'There we go, twenty-seven.' He slotted the car into a roadside space two houses down and reached onto the back seat for the umbrella. 'My turn.'

'Wanker.' Hunter got out into the deluge and disappeared.

Cullen opened the brolly and got out. Hunter was shivering on the pavement and got up close, making them walk to twenty-seven like an old couple, huddled close.

Hunter broke off, pushed the front door open and headed straight inside. The entrycom system dangled by the door.

Cullen followed him inside, into gloom, punctuated by flickering lights, the pungent stench of piss and dope. Hunter's footsteps rattled up the spiral stairwell and Cullen trudged up, shaking the brolly off. Felt like half the North Sea came off.

At the landing, Hunter knocked on flat six's door and waited.

Cullen collapsed the umbrella. 'Just like the old days, this. Though I don't remember you—'

Something hit Cullen between the shoulders. Maybe a baton, maybe a boot. Pain flashed down his spine and legs like an electric shock. Next he knew, he was on his knees, then someone grabbed his right arm, locked it behind his back and pushed him face-down.

'You are under arrest!'

13

ALL CULLEN COULD SEE WITH HIS CHEEK PRESSED INTO THE WET ceramic tiles was a pair of arms in dark sleeves leaning on Hunter's back. Even with all that martial arts he did. Krav maga or some bollocks. Hunter lay perfectly still. No hint of a struggle, but also no fear in his eyes. Just calculation.

Cullen took the cue, making his voice sound as even as possible. 'We're police.'

'Are you hell.' A harsh Glasgow accent, male and aggressive, coming at him in a hiss.

'I'm DS Scott Cullen. My warrant card's in my pocket.'

'Likely tale. Returning to the scene of the crime, are you?'

Hunter bucked like he'd been hit with a taser, then spun on to his back, knocked the black sleeves aside with one forearm. He hooked the guy's neck in the crook of his other arm, pulling the head in close to his chest as he bridged his hips and rolled over to land on the guy's stomach in full mount. Then he raised his arm, fist locked and loaded as he released the guy's head to let him see the trouble he was in. He looked at the guy leaning on Cullen. 'Looks like we've got ourselves a standoff, pal.'

Cullen's cop snapped out a baton. 'You're outgunned.'

A tense silence settled on the stairwell.

Cullen cleared his throat with a wet cough. 'We're Lothian & Borders CID. Check my pocket.'

'I'm not rummaging around in your trousers, you pervert.'

'Coat pocket!'

'And take my eye off your mate over here? Think again.'

Cullen took a deep breath. 'Get. Off. Now. Or I'll get my chief constable to hand your arse to you.'

Another pause.

Then Cullen felt the grip slacken.

'Show us your credentials, then. But nice and slow, eh?'

Cullen raised himself up onto his elbows and fished his warrant card out of the inside pocket of his sodden jacket. He held it up and it was snatched from his hand.

With a grunt, the guy handed it back and finally got off.

Cullen did his best to stand up without letting on in how much pain he was in. A dull ache between his shoulders made him wheeze as he straightened up.

All he could make out in the flicker of the failing strip light was an overweight man in his late thirties, rough face and bald head. Looked like a real nasty bastard too.

Hunter climbed off his guy — younger, thinner, hairier.

Baldie got right in Cullen's face. 'You should've told us you were coming. Could've saved us all a lot of hassle.'

'My DI approved this.'

'Mine will be spitting teeth.' Baldie held out a hand. 'DS Damian McCrea.' He nodded at his colleague. 'And that's DC Davie Lucas.'

Hunter merely scowled at them. 'DC Craig Hunter.'

Lucas pointed at Hunter with pleading eyes, like a lap dog disgusted at his master for letting him get hissed at by the neighbour's cat. 'Damo, he can't do that to me. He can't just assault a cop.'

'Leave it, Davie.' McCrea ran a hand through hair no longer there, then turned to face Cullen. 'What are you doing on our patch? There's a protocol for a reason, don't you know?'

Cullen ignored the second question. 'We're looking for an Alex Melrose.'

'Why?'

'We're working a murder case. He—'

'You what?'

'You do understand English, right?' Cullen held his gaze until

McCrea glanced away. 'Mr Melrose reported someone missing nineteen months ago. Someone whose body we just found, with a screwdriver stuck in it. We've tried getting in touch with Melrose, but no joy.'

'Disaster for Scotland.' A sigh like he couldn't care less. McCrea straightened his black leather jacket, slick and shiny from the rain. 'You pair need to come back to the station.'

Cullen pointed at Melrose's door. 'I'm going in there.'

'You want me to take you down again?'

Hunter barked a laugh at him. 'Like to see you try.'

Lucas shrank back but McCrea just shook his head. 'Look, lads, just follow us. That's all I'm asking.'

Cullen stood his ground. 'Why? Is he dead?'

'I need to clear everything with my DI. Until then, I can't let you in there.'

Cullen glanced at Hunter but merely got a shrug in response. End of the road. He turned back to McCrea and nodded. 'Alright, I need to run this past my own DI.'

'Fill your boots.'

∾

'MY SHOULDER'S BLOODY KILLING ME.' CULLEN WAS MASSAGING IT IN the passenger seat, trying to rub some feeling back into the numbness that was his entire right side. 'What the hell is going on here? Why are Strathclyde CID at his flat? He's either been murdered or a murderer himself, right?'

Hunter was behind the wheel. He shrugged like he didn't care either way. Then he looked out of his window and sighed, his breath steaming up the glass. 'You're still quick to make assumptions, Scott.' He turned around to face Cullen. 'This could be anything. Assault, drugs, money-laundering. Maybe we've waltzed into an observation.'

'I'm getting a bad feeling, though. You know that Methven thinks a serial killer got to Strang, right?'

'The "I will kill again" stuff, right?' Hunter laughed. 'You and him are welcome to each other.'

Cullen looked out into the dreary rainscape and considered their options.

Cagey Strathclyde detectives are probably indicators that we've just walked into a murder investigation, or there's been some other violent crime.

Behind door one — Melrose is dead, a screwdriver jammed into his gut, "I WILL KILL AGAIN" scrawled on the wall above his rotting body.

Behind door two — Melrose is a serial murderer, and our new friends from Strathclyde CID have caught him. Or they're still hunting him.

Or there's a third door behind which something else entirely is going on...

Cullen glanced at Hunter. *And God only know what's happening behind his eyes.*

Even if we focus on the first two options, Methven could get us access, at least in theory. Run it up the ladder, get Turnbull or White-head to reach across to their opposite numbers in Strathclyde.

And get ignored, no doubt.

Maybe merging the whole lot so there's just one person in charge of all the detectives wasn't the worst idea in the world. Just two days too early.

Bugger it.

Cullen tried Methven's mobile.

Answered straight away. 'I'm in a meeting. Have you found Melrose?'

'Not quite, but—'

'Call me when you find him.' Click.

An old Ford Escort rattled to a stop next to Cullen's window, a silvery blur in the rain. Cullen buzzed his window down just enough to see what was going on. Rain blasted in, drenching him. Lucas sat there, giving him a two-finger salute out of the passenger-side window, then beckoning them to follow.

Cullen closed the window again. 'Lucas wants us to drive after them.'

'Shall I?'

'Not like we've got a choice.'

Hunter put the car in gear and drove off. 'When did they even stop making Escorts?'

'Jesus Christ, Craig. Wankers to the left, arseholes to the right. I really am stuck in the middle with you, mate.'

'Told you before. Don't call me mate.'

Cullen glared at him. 'What the hell is up with you?'

Hunter just stared straight ahead. 'Mind not talking to me? I'm driving.'

~

UP AHEAD, THE STRATHCLYDE ESCORT INDICATED LEFT, THE YELLOW light flashing in the same hypnotic rhythm as the windscreen wipers. The car meandered through the bendy roads of Glasgow's sprawling motorway network and took the turning marked Govan.

The place was nothing like Cullen remembered from TV crime dramas and documentaries of Glasgow's post-war ghettos. New apartments and boutique hotels lined the street, alongside designer bars and hipster cafes. In the distance, bright floodlights shone down on Ibrox stadium, home of Rangers, or what was left of them.

'Changed days round here.'

Hunter grunted. 'My brother's ex bought a flat just down the road. Cost a packet.'

'Oh, Craig, how come every silver cloud has a black lining with you?'

Hunter took the next right and squeezed the car into the space beside the Escort.

McCrea waited on the tarmac. 'See you've brought your brolly. Pair of wallies.'

Cullen put the umbrella back in the car. 'Sod this. Where the hell is Alex Melrose?'

'I'm not telling you out here. Come on inside.'

Cullen put his mobile to his ear again, but this time Methven didn't even answer his call. Just bounced it to voicemail. Cullen slipped the phone back into his suit jacket. 'After you, then.'

~

MCCREA BENT OVER THE DESK TO SIGN THEM IN, HIS FIST CLENCHED round the pen like he'd just learnt to write.

The waiting room was filled with the bruised and damaged of southern Glasgow, looking that bit worse than Edinburgh's walk-in crowd.

Cullen tapped McCrea on the shoulder. 'Enough. What's the story with Melrose. This is a complete waste of time.'

McCrea looked up with a face like a dog licking piss off a nettle. 'I don't have to tell you anything. Glad to finally witness your moaning in person.'

'What's that supposed to mean?'

'Your reputation precedes you.' McCrea started walking away. 'In here.' He pointed inside a vacant interview room. 'Back soon.'

Cullen went into the room, a cramped space that felt like a funeral parlour's anteroom. *If this is where they speak to the families of murder victims then... Christ.* Cullen sat at one of four plastic chairs grouped around the rickety Formica table, pockmarked with countless cigarette burns.

Hunter stayed standing, leaning against the wall, arms folded, foot tapping, staring at the door. 'You met those pricks before?'

'Never.'

'The bald one seems to know you.'

The door to the room across the hallway opened and two men left in a hurry, one a lawyerly type in a suit, the other a sullen-looking model sort in shades, the collar of his parker pulled up tight around his designer stubble.

Cullen frowned. 'That's Mike Robertson from Expect Delays.'

Hunter leaned over but looked out of the door too late. 'You sure?'

'I'd recognise that comb-forward anywhere. Wonder what he's doing here?'

'He's helping us with our enquiries.' The door closed behind Cullen with a bang. 'Well, well, well. If it isn't the Sundance Kid.'

14

CULLEN STUMBLED TO HIS FEET, HIS HEART RACING AS HE TOOK A step back from the desk. His blood thumped in his ears.

WHAT THE HELL?

He got sacked, didn't he?

DI Brian Bain sat with a grin like a spreading wound and stared Cullen straight in the eye. 'Bugger me, Sundance. I wish I had that effect on half the boys I have under arrest in this station.'

Calm down, you arse.

Cullen retook his seat, trying to get his heart rate back down to double digits.

'You're still an arsehole, then?' Bain rocked back on his chair, rubbing his top lip. His trademark moustache was gone. And he looked younger, the old familiar frown lines ironed out, giving his face a hard tightness. His grin spread almost to his ears, pulling bloodless lips thin over grey teeth. 'What's up, Sundance? Bit weird seeing your old boss? Looks like you've missed me, the way you're staring at me.'

'Hardly a day's gone by that I don't miss our time together. Eighteen months of misery and belittlement.'

Bain laughed. 'Thought you'd have heard I was back in Strathclyde.'

'You seem a lot more relaxed than when I last saw you.'

Bain kept his smug grin in place. 'Course I'm more relaxed

now. I'm away from that wanker Turnbull and his little pit bull. Besides, I'm getting married again.'

McCrea smirked as he sat between them. 'Wee Thai lassie. Should see the—'

'Shut it.' Bain slapped McCrea's arm.

'Mail order, right?'

'Don't be so crass.' Bain sneered at him. Then he dropped his eyes to the table. 'I'm in love, Sundance.'

'You don't know the meaning of that word.'

'Oh, really?' Bain looked up at him and just like that the smug grin was back, stronger than ever. 'Well, I'm not quite the swordsman you are, Sundance. Your better half still into other birds?'

'Shut up.' Cullen felt his fingernails dig into his palms.

'Oh, by the way, I went to see Alan Irvine in Bar-L a few weeks back.' Bain crossed his legs. 'Said to congratulate you on getting your stripes. Might stop you moaning. Course, that's Irvine's old role you're Acting DS in, right?'

'He was guilty.'

'Not gone to court yet. As you should know.'

'Speaking of criminals, how's your son?'

Bain's smile died as though he'd been hit in the face with a mallet. 'Right, let's get down to business.'

'Too close to home?'

Bain clenched his teeth and took a deep, hissing breath. 'Let's start with what the hell you pair are doing through here.'

Hunter was sitting back, watching as if he was at the cinema. All he was missing was a bucket of popcorn.

Fat lot of use he is.

Cullen cleared his throat. 'We found a body down an old close under the Royal Mile. A rock star in the making. Died nineteen months ago, give or take. Alex Melrose reported him missing.'

A flicker of amusement danced across Bain's face as he leaned over to McCrea and whispered something in his ear.

Hunter smiled. 'We've shown you ours. How about you show us yours?'

Bain laughed. 'Heard yours doesn't touch both sides at once.'

Hunter shot to his feet. 'What did you say?'

Bain stared up at him in silence for a moment. Then burst out laughing.

'Enough!' Cullen hit the table with both hands, almost collapsing the rickety old thing. 'Tell us what the hell's going on here. Now.'

Bain exchanged a look with McCrea, grinning wide. 'Don't know about you, Damo, but I am absolutely shitting myself.' He leaned back on his creaking chair. 'Well, Sundance, now you know what it feels like to be kept in the dark. I lost count of the number of times you went off on your lonesome, then pulled a rabbit out of a hat.'

'Melrose. Tell me now, or we're leaving. And five minutes later DCI Turnbull will be on the phone to your boss.'

'Ooooooh.' Bain raised his hands, twiddling his fingers and trembling with fear. Then he dropped the act. 'Listen to me, you pricks. I'm in charge of the murder investigation. Me.'

'Melrose has been murdered?'

'Damo, didn't you tell him?'

McCrea glanced away. 'Thought you wanted the circle tight on this, no?'

'Tight as a choirboy's arsehole.' Bain rubbed his top lip. 'Sod it. In the wee small hours of Thursday morning, uniform got called to Melrose's flat. Neighbour thought he smelled gas, couldn't get an answer. Pair of palookas had to break the door down. Didn't find any gas leak, mind, but they did find Melrose. Dead.' He reached into a folder on the desk and pulled out a crime scene photo. 'A stabbing, and a vicious one at that.'

Cullen's mouth was bone dry. 'Ours was stabbed, too.'

Bain imitated him with a pathetic whine. 'Ours was stabbed, too.'

Cullen took a deep breath and a few seconds to calm down. 'Was there a message?'

'A message? Have you lost it, Sundance?' Bain laughed. 'Hold on, don't you think for one second that you can steal my case. Message, my arse.' He leaned forward. 'Bit of a coincidence you finding your body the same week his mate gets stabbed, eh?'

'You know what I think of coincidences.' Cullen tapped the folder. 'Let me see your file.'

'No danger. We're keeping the cases separate.'

'I take it you don't read the *Edinburgh Argus* anymore?'

'You know I'm a red-top guy, Sundance.' Bain sniffed. 'Why?'

Cullen opened his phone and navigated to the Argus's website. Last night's story had bloomed to seven pieces. 'Talk on the street is we're dealing with a serial killer.'

Bain stared at the screen. 'That's shite, and you know it.' He stood up and brushed dust off his shoulder. 'If a serial killer is behind these crimes, I might need to co-opt your investigation into mine. Need to make sure we leverage all opportunities here, don't we?'

Cullen snorted. 'You sound like Turnbull.'

A flash of anger lit up Bain's eyes. He blinked and it was gone. 'Nice speaking to you, Sundance. Don't be a stranger.'

'I want to see the crime scene.'

'Aye, good one.'

Cullen held his gaze for a few seconds. 'Fine, I'll get out of your hair, but only if you let us have a quick look at your case notes. Promise.'

'Sod it.' Bain pulled a wad of paper out of his file and tossed it to Cullen. 'Here you go, Sherlock.'

Cullen flicked through the pages. A body covered in blood, a kitchen knife still in his gut. A small bedroom, rock star posters everywhere. No bloody message, but the photos were of the body, not the walls. 'There wasn't a message?'

'What do you expect?' Bain looked at him like he had just lost the last remnants of respect for Cullen's intelligence. 'It's a murder scene. The photographer obviously focused on the body.'

'I really need to see the crime scene for myself.'

'Not going to happen. That's an active crime scene and you're not on the case. You'd know that if you were a professional.'

'What's Mike Robertson doing here?'

Bain froze. 'What?'

Cullen pointed at the door. 'I saw Mike Robertson over the way there.'

'He was supposed to meet up with Alex Melrose.' McCrea snorted. 'Melrose never turned up.'

Cullen forced his fingers to relax, then took a deep breath and counted to ten. 'How did they know each other?'

McCrea huffed. 'According to Robertson, they know each other from the music scene in Edinburgh. Robertson was helping him get a job in a studio.' He stopped short as if he had said too much, then pointed a finger at Cullen. 'I better not see anything about this on Twitter. Be bad if him being in a police station leaked to the public.'

'I don't use Twitter.' Cullen stared at Bain. Like staring at a brick wall. 'One last time. I need to see that flat.'

Bain didn't even glance at him as he stuck his file under his arm. 'Right, Sundance, that's me off. Have a good trip back to Edinburgh. Don't forget to send a postcard.'

'This isn't over. I'm going to speak to Cargill and Methven as soon as I get back.'

Bain stopped in his tracks. 'Say a big hello to them from me.' He walked to the door, waving over his shoulder. 'Oh, and we're taking over your case. See you here tomorrow. Seven on the dot.'

15

AT LEAST THE RAIN HAD STOPPED. CULLEN GOT IN THE POOL CAR AND turned the heating on full blast. The hot air started hitting his chilled face.

Hunter got in the driver side and turned the heating down.

'Craig, I'm freezing.'

'Aw, diddums.'

Cullen reached over and turned it on again. 'Seriously.'

'I'll fall asleep at the wheel in this heat.' Hunter said it like he meant it.

Cullen angled the vents at himself and let the feeling return to his numb cheeks. 'How's that?'

'It's just great, Scott.'

With a sigh, Cullen got out his phone and called Methven.

'I'm sorry, I can't take your call. You might wish to—'

Bounced my call again. Bloody hell.

He stabbed out a text with his thumbs:

'URGENT, NEED TO SPEAK. MELROSE IS DEAD.'

Then he called again. And Methven bounced it again.

'Bloody hell!'

Hunter took his eyes off the road, the still-wet urban landscape of south Glasgow rushing past them in a blur of grey. 'What's up?'

'He keeps bouncing my calls.' Cullen stuffed his phone away. 'What did you make of that?'

'You seem to leave a trail of very angry ex-colleagues.'

'Aside from him.' Cullen looked down at the Clyde bubbling below, soon replaced by modern office blocks. 'Victim one, Edinburgh. Nineteen months later, victim two, Glasgow. Two members of the same band dead.'

Hunter raised his eyebrows, but still didn't look round. 'So you're coming round to Methven's way of thinking?'

'No.' Cullen gripped his knees to give his hands something to do. 'There can't be someone killing a band.'

'Can't there?' Hunter grunted as he overtook a coachload of schoolkids, the facing side filled with faces pressed up against the glass. 'You thinking what I'm thinking?'

'What, taking Beth Williamson and David Johnson into protective custody?'

'Not that, no.' Hunter pulled in front of the coach and let a Mercedes whizz past. 'I was thinking you should call Chantal or your English mate and get them to drag Methven out of whatever meeting he's in.'

'Oh. Right.'

Cullen called Buxton.

'Sorry, I can't take your call right now. Please leave—'

Cullen killed it. 'Bloody hell!'

'Buxton? He'll be in the bog. Guy seems to spend half his life having a dump.'

Cullen prodded Chantal's contact number.

'What do you want?' Sounded like she was eating.

'Can you see Methven?'

Sounded like she swallowed. 'He's in Turnbull's office.'

'Get him out of there, will you?'

'No.'

Cullen sighed. 'Chantal, I'm ordering you. It's urgent.'

'Scott, come on. Can't I get—'

'Alex Melrose is dead.'

'Jesus Christ.' Sounded like she scraped a chair back and walked through the canteen. 'That prick made me go to Starbucks for coffee for them. Now you're at it.' She knocked on a door.

A muffled voice called out: 'Not now!'

She opened the door anyway. 'Sir, Cullen wants to speak to you.'

'Fine.' Methven huffed down the line. A door slammed behind him. 'Sergeant, this better be important.'

'You see my text?'

Another huff. 'No. I'm busy.'

'Alex Melrose is dead.'

'Purple sodding buggery.'

~

CULLEN KNOCKED ON THE SAME DOOR. NO ANSWER. HE OPENED IT and stuck his head into Turnbull's office. Empty.

Where the hell are they?

He scrolled through his messages, checking if he had missed an update from Methven. Nothing, so he tried calling him again.

'I'm sorry, I can't—'

This is becoming ridiculous.

Cullen left the office.

'Scott?' DI Alison Cargill was at her desk, hunched over a laptop. Face pinched tight, her pink blouse the same colour as her face. She looked up and gave him a hard stare as she closed her laptop. 'What's up?'

'Looking for DI Methven?'

'He was in with Jim. Haven't seen him since.'

'I need to speak to him about the Strang case.'

'Okay.' Cargill reached for her desk phone and hit a button as she put the handset to her ear. She muttered something. Then waited. 'At my desk. Now.' She hung up, combed her fingers through her bleached crew cut and nodded behind Cullen.

'It's just as I said, Jim, a serial killer.' Methven strutted into the room, leading Turnbull like a smitten teenager. 'Two deaths, same band. It fits.'

Turnbull stopped by Cargill's desk and smiled at Cullen. 'Excellent work, Scott.'

'Thank you, sir.'

'Come into my office. You too, Alison. This case is growing arms and legs.' Turnbull walked into his office and took a seat at the head of the meeting table. 'Please.' He gestured at Cargill and Cullen to take the two other chairs.

Methven followed them in and wheeled the desk chair over to sit next to the boss.

Turnbull didn't even look at him as he nodded at Cullen. 'So, Scott, correct me if I'm wrong. James Strang got stabbed in the tunnels under the Old Town nineteen months ago. Now you've found a second stabbing victim, one Alex Melrose, the man who reported Strang missing.'

'Spot on, sir. And Strathclyde are invest—'

'Strathclyde?' Cargill made the word sound like an insult. 'It'll all be water under the bridge soon.'

'Fantastic.' Turnbull sat back and started rolling up his left sleeve, his arm as hairy as a dog's back. 'Come Monday, we'll all be one happy family. Unfortunately, the criminal fraternity doesn't respect police restructures.'

Cullen cringed. 'Problem is, sir, the SIO is DI Bain. He said they're—'

'Right. Well. That puts a different complexion on things. Do I need to pick up the phone and speak to his boss?'

'Keith Graham.' Cargill had her laptop out, tapping away at the keyboard. 'He's a good guy. You can probably do a deal.'

'Not so sure.' Turnbull sighed. 'Bain and Graham go back a ways. Pulled Bain out of the trash, if rumours are to be believed.'

Cargill looked up from her computer. 'You know they'll try and merge the cases, Jim.'

'He said they were. Told me to get through for tomorrow's seven o'clock briefing.'

Turnbull sighed, sounding like all the energy left him with a single long breath. 'And a live murder trumps our cold case.'

Cargill shut her laptop again. 'Are we sure these cases are linked?'

'They were in the same sodding band, and coupled with the message...' Methven tossed that morning's *Argus* on the table, the ominous message making his point. He looked at each of them. 'And now the killer has killed again, like he said he would.'

Turnbull snatched the paper off the table. 'Have you got to the bottom of who leaked this?'

'Scott?'

'Not yet, sir.'

'I told you to—'

'Scott, do you know this guy?' Turnbull held up the paper. 'Rich McAlpine?'

'I do. Went to school and uni together. He's not answering my calls.'

Turnbull tossed the paper in the recycling. 'Well, I don't want to be seen to pressure them, but have a word, eh?'

'I'll head over as soon as we're done.'

'Good man.'

Methven smoothed down a stray eyebrow. 'Sir, I told you this had all the hallmarks of a serial killer case.' He nodded over to the recycling bin. 'That message, for starters. And now we have a second victim. There may be more.'

Cargill shook her head. 'Could just be a coincidence.'

Methven scowled at her. 'I don't believe in coincidences.'

'Nor do I. But sometimes—'

'Alison, the victims were in the same band, and both were killed by similar means a year and a half apart.'

Cargill leaned back on her chair, arching her razor-sharp eyebrows at Methven. 'Serial killers aren't notorious for taking out rock bands.'

'But they do select their victims. Why not pick a band? Why not? A year and a half later, our killer hasn't stopped feeling the bloodlust, but now he knows he's got away with it, so he strikes again.'

'At the same time as body number one is found? Come on.'

Methven huffed at her. Didn't have anything to say, though.

'Okay. I'm not having those clowns taking over our case.' Turnbull shook his head. 'I'll speak to Keith and we'll sort it out.'

'Like I said, he told me—'

Turnbull cut him off with a raised hand. 'You're only to listen to direct orders from myself, Alison or Colin here. Sergeant, you of all people know that DI Bain has unfinished business with us. Don't let his shenanigans distract you. Treat this as a separate case until I tell you otherwise, understood?'

'Understood.' Cullen smiled, though his head was starting to spin at the thought of getting sucked back into Bain's vortex of chaos. 'If this is a serial killer, shouldn't we put the surviving band members in protective custody?'

'That would be wise.' Cargill gave Methven a pointed look. 'Colin, get some officers on it straight away.'

Methven glanced from Turnbull to Cargill. 'This is my—'

'*Colin.*' Cargill glowered at him like she was sending him straight to bed.

Methven bit his lip. 'Okay.'

'Alright.' Turnbull clapped his hands. 'Alison, we've got an empty flat in Leith. The drug dealer's one?'

'On it.' Cargill got up and left the office.

Methven watched her leave, waiting for the door to bang shut before focusing on Turnbull. 'So, where does that leave my team, Jim?'

'Keep investigating Strang as a standalone. Usual belt and braces approach. Just remember, the new Chief Constable of Police Scotland is currently the Chief of Strathclyde.'

'Does that mean what I think it does?'

'Just get me a result by tomorrow night, Colin.' Turnbull pointed at the recycling, where the *Argus* was sticking out like a warning sign. 'And get this story shut down before it gains traction. I don't want to give them any more ammo.'

16

'I JUST DON'T KNOW, SI.' CULLEN STARED OUT OF THE WINDOW. Stuck on Leith Street and the constant tramworks. He looked over at Buxton behind the wheel. 'It's Bain. What can I say?'

Buxton set off, bumping up on the pavement to round a bus. 'So, what are we doing now?'

Cullen picked the *Edinburgh Argus* off the dashboard. 'Getting this off the front page.'

'Easier said than done.'

'Sod it.' Cullen sat forward as Buxton cut down Calton Road, descending into the bowels of the Old Town. 'You been busy this morning?'

'Busy, but...' Buxton clicked his tongue. 'Chantal and I spoke to three people who worked at the record shop. Sexy stuff, eh? Getting nowhere.'

'What about his flatmates?'

'You need to ask Chantal about that.'

'Right.' Cullen took out his phone, then put it away again. She could wait. 'Tell me you've been doing something else.'

'Course. I've been searching for any stories on the band. They were getting somewhere. Bastards.'

Cullen gripped on tight as they rattled over the cobbles. 'Jealous?'

'Damn right. Rather be snorting coke and shagging groupies

than being stuck in traffic with you at the weekend.' Buxton laughed as he pulled up at the roundabout by the Scottish Parliament, his head scanning the other two exits. 'Anyway, found a few articles about the band, all written by the same guy. All in the *Argus*. Even did one the last Invisibles gig.'

'So this is why you're so keen to chum me.'

'Never understood what that meant.' Buxton pulled off, cutting between the Parliament building and the Palace of Holyroodhouse and heading towards the darkness under the Salisbury Crags. 'Some geezer called Sonny Bangs.'

'Sounds like Lester Bangs.'

Buxton laughed as he stopped at the next roundabout. 'Get you.'

'My old man was a punk.'

'You're a punk.' Buxton shot off, avoiding getting stuck behind a trail of cars. 'The article was a puff piece, full of gushing praise for the band. And the picture... Man, it showed Strang in full-on Iggy Pop mode. The guy cut his chest open onstage with a broken beer bottle.'

'Seriously?'

'No, I'm joking.' Buxton took the next right, homing in on their target. 'Sounded like the gig was packed, people standing on tables and all that.' He drove past Dynamic Earth and pulled up outside the Scotsman building, opposite the Edinburgh Argus office. The three of them looked like space stations dropped from orbit into old Edinburgh. 'That paper devoted a whole page to an unsigned band's gig review. Can you believe it?'

'You think this Sonny Bangs guy's connected to them?'

'Maybe.' Buxton killed the engine, the rumble replaced by the drum pattern of rain on the roof. 'He was touting the band as the next Expect Delays. Here.' He reached into his coat pocket for a print and tapped a picture of Strang smashing a guitar, like on the cover of The Clash's *London Calling*. 'Remember that blue Fender in his bedroom?' He moved his finger to another photo, where Strang was playing another blue guitar. 'That's this one. Worth at least a grand.' Then back to the other photo. 'The one he smashed was a cheap one, probably bought for a tenner from Cash Generator or something. Makes smashing up your gear to be like Jimi Hendrix almost affordable.'

'All very interesting, Si, but does it get us anywhere?'

'Absolutely, just bear with me. According to the gig review, the last song — remember, this was the last song James Strang ever performed — was one of those noise jams. Went on for ages. Strang was shouting, "They took all the money and all the fame." Then he smashed the guitar and cut himself.'

Cullen looked over at the Argus office and played the scene through in his mind. 'Think there's something in it?'

'Definitely sounds suspicious. And Dave Johnson said something about Strang getting depressed about music. He was probably just angry with the world for denying him the adulation he felt he deserved.'

Cullen's phone buzzed in his inside pocket. He reached for it and glanced at the screen. A text from Rich McAlpine. Finally.

'PISS OFF'

Charming.

Cullen rang Rich's number, not expecting an answer, and not getting one.

Nobody's taking my calls anymore.

He closed his eyes and rubbed them one-handed until orange and yellow sun spots flashed through his head. Then he counted to ten, opened his eyes again and typed out a text:

NEED TO SPEAK. NOW.

Cullen stared at the screen until it went dark. 'Sod it.' He put the phone away and looked back at Buxton. 'Let's kill two birds with one stone.' He got out of the car. Holyrood Road was one large puddle. He stuck to the pavement, picking his way through smaller puddles towards the Argus, the sharp March wind cutting right through his suit, still damp. He pushed through the revolving door into foyer, concrete, chrome and glass. The building teemed with activity, the Sunday edition heading to the presses, last-minute football reports, probably half the news desk working on their case.

At the reception desk, a young Asian man looked up from his screen. He wore a sharp suit and an even sharper beard. The guy smiled. 'Good evening, sir, can I help?'

Cullen produced his warrant card. 'DS Scott Cullen. I'm looking for Rich McAlpine.'

'One moment, please.' The receptionist checked on his

computer, then dialled a number, topping up the smile as Buxton joined them. 'Got a Scott Cullen for you... Oh. Okay.' He put the phone back down, and the smile slipped to a frown. 'Sorry, sir, he's not available.'

Cullen glanced up the staircase beyond the reception desk. 'He's here, though?'

'I can't say.'

Bloody hell. Cullen went back to scratching his stubble. 'Okay, how about Sonny Bangs?'

The guy chuckled.

'I'm serious.'

'Oh, okay.' The receptionist peered at his computer screen again. 'Sorry, sir, got nobody of that name here.'

Cullen pulled out Buxton's article. 'He wrote this about eighteen months ago.'

'Yeah, but he's not on the system.'

'Can you at least try to—'

'We got a problem here?' A grey-haired man in a charcoal suit descended the staircase like he was coming down from the heavens.

The receptionist smiled at him. 'Eck, this guy's a cop.'

Eck stopped by the desk and snatched Cullen's ID out of his hand. 'Oh, you?' He laughed like there was some kind of joke in the name. 'We ran that big story on you. You're that hero cop, right?'

'Whatever. Are you in charge here?'

'Alexander Spence. I'm the editor.'

'Just need to speak to Sonny Bangs.' Said out loud, it sounded so ridiculous.

'Oh aye?' Spence handed back the warrant card with a wry smile. 'Lad doesn't work here anymore. I let him go in the last round of cuts. Sure you'll hear similar war stories on Monday.'

'Eh?'

'Only reason the police are restructuring is to get rid of people. Same as here.' Spence smiled at Buxton. 'You'll just be collateral damage.' He laughed. 'Look, my circulation's in free-fall. Another rounds of redundancies last week.'

Cullen gave him a blank stare. 'You got a phone number for Sonny?'

Spence ran his tongue around his teeth and took a deep breath through flared nostrils, not breaking eye contact once. 'This about the Strang case?'

'Just need a word with him.'

'Look, if you come upstairs, I'll put you as an anonymous source. You won't get into shit. It'll be fine.'

Cullen clenched his teeth. 'Is Rich McAlpine here?'

'Take that as a no?' Spence grinned then nodded at Buxton. 'What about you?'

'No, mate.'

'I just need to speak to either Rich or Sonny.'

'Not going to happen, pal. I've got all seven days under mine and a Sunday edition to put to bed. So piss off.'

∿

CULLEN LEANED BACK IN THE CAR. 'STAY HERE.'

Buxton gave him a puppy-dog look, adding a pout for good measure. 'Really?'

'This guy is a mate.' A lorry trundled past and lifted up Cullen's jacket. 'Was a mate.' He shut the door and trudged along Portobello High Street. Even in the few months he'd been away, the place had gone slightly upmarket. One fewer greasy spoon, one more hipster bar. He walked up to the glossy black door and rang the buzzer.

At least he's got the intercom fixed, finally. Wonder how long that's been working for again.

Bloody hell, I haven't been back since I moved out. Can't even remember the last time I saw Rich.

The buzzer sounded. 'Yo.'

'Hi, Tom. It's Scott.'

'Who?'

'Very funny.'

'Up you come, mate.'

Cullen trudged up the stairs, his footsteps echoing off the bare stone walls.

The number of times I climbed these steps, off my face at half three in the morning. And that time Tom found me asleep halfway up and—

Tom opened the door to their old flat, guitar rock pounding

out from behind him. He'd lost a ton of weight, almost a shadow of his former self.

Cullen looked him up and down, his face straight. 'Hi, mate, I'm looking for Tom?'

'Aye, very funny.' Tom patted his flat stomach. '5:2 fasting, mate. It bloody works.'

'I can see that. My old boy's been doing it, too. Seems to be the latest craze among middle-aged men. You look knackered, though.'

'I'll take that as a compliment.' Tom stood aside. 'In you come.' Cullen walked in and started shrugging off his damp jacket. 'Where's the coat rack?'

'Gone. It was getting too cramped in here and we hardly have guests anymore.'

'How come?'

'Can't speak for the others, but I've been working in London a lot. Big project down there in Corporate.'

Cullen threw his jacket over the back of a wooden chair. The hallway was still doubling as a living room. 'London, eh? Alba Bank branching out?'

'If only.' Tom laughed. 'Nah, we've always had a presence down there, nothing like RBS or Lloyds, but let's just say it needs some TLC at the moment.'

'Meaning a disaster?'

'That's an understatement.'

Cullen's old bedroom door was shut, some illegible name and bullet points scribbled on a note. Looked like a set of warnings or conditions for entry. 'What's that all about?'

Tom whispered: 'New guy's a bit of a weirdo. Don't think I'll renew his lease.' He collapsed into a chair, sounded like enough force to crack the wood. 'Anyway, what brings you back?'

'Rich. The clown's bouncing my calls.'

'Has he lost his phone again? Left it behind when he had to scarper from some bloke's flat after his boyfriend found them at it, am I right?'

Cullen shrugged. 'You tell me.'

Tom gritted his teeth and opened his laptop. 'Ask him yourself.'

'He in?'

'Probably. Haven't seen him, but I've been working all afternoon.'

Cullen laughed. 'Cheers.' He walked to Rich's door and knocked, bitter experience having taught him to never barge in without an invite.

'Come in, Tom. I'm not bumming anyone.'

Cullen opened the door and walked in.

Rich was sitting at his desk, laptop open but obscured by his shaved head. He turned around, and gawped, wide-eyed. 'Shit!' Then he spun around again and slammed his laptop.

Cullen chuckled. 'Porn?'

'Hardly.' Rich scratched his stubbly head. 'I'm writing a detective book.'

'A novel? You?'

Rich looked away, cringing. 'Turns out writing about the real world is much easier than writing about a fictional cop.'

'Try living that life.' Cullen laughed. 'If you put the stuff I've seen in a novel, you'd be locked up. Couldn't make it up, mate.' He sat on the bed. 'Feels like everybody makes money from policing except for the police.'

'You poor thing. Tell you what, I'll give you a kickback if I ever get published.'

'Answering my calls would be a start.'

Rich held his gaze for a few seconds. Then narrowed his eyes. 'You warning me off about doing my day job or something?'

'You don't even have to ask what it's about, do you?' Cullen got up and walked over to the window. Outside, Portobello thrummed with life. A group of teenage girls stood by the bus stop opposite, all dressed up and giggling. 'My orders are to get you to stop. Rich, I'm just asking you to play nice.'

'Coming from you...'

'Where did you get that photo anyway?'

'No comment.'

'Come on, Rich.' Cullen walked over to the desk and stood over him. 'That was a photo from a crime scene. You shouldn't have it. We've not had a chance to brief the press about that message.'

'Eh, DCI Turnbull gave a statement this afternoon.' Rich shoved his hands in his pockets. Seemed to shrink away from Cullen. 'Had some of his heavies hassle me. Boy with mad eyebrows. Now you're here playing good cop to his bad cop, right?'

'This isn't part of your novel. This is the real world, Rich. There are consequences when an investigator breaks the law.'

Rich curled his lips into a smile. 'You're in the shit, aren't you?'

'Who gave you that photo?'

'Scott, I'm not disclosing that.'

Cullen took a slow breath. 'You're worrying the public, Rich.'

'Wait, are you saying there's no serial killer?'

'Not that we know of.'

Rich folded his arms on his skinny chest. 'Heard there's a second body in Glasgow.'

'Who the hell is leaking this to you?'

'It's true, then?'

'No. There's been a murder in Glasgow, sure, but it's not connected.'

'Officially or at all?'

'Rich—'

'Oh, Eck is going to love this.'

'Alexander Spence? I was just talking to him.'

Rich closed his eyes. 'Tell me you didn't mention me.'

'Why? You're messing with *my* job. Don't like it up you, do you?'

Rich opened his eyes again. 'Don't even joke about that, mate.'

'Then answer my question.'

'Fine.' Rich sighed. 'Spence is kind of the boss's boss, but aye. I work for him.'

'I need you to have a word with him.'

'This is in the public domain, Scott.'

'I'm talking about the Glasgow angle. The serial killer shit. Need you to back off on that.'

Rich looked over at the window. 'The best I can do is to leave it until Monday morning. Then I've got to publish.'

'I appreciate that.'

'Don't think it's a favour, but you do owe me one.'

Cullen laughed. He retrieved the article from his jacket pocket and handed it to Rich. 'You know this guy?'

Rich looked at the clipping. 'Sonny Bangs?'

'Seems to know a fair amount about Strang. Might even be a

mate. This article reads like, I don't know, someone inducting U2 into the Rock Hall of Fame, although it's just a gig review of a local band.'

'Christ, this is Strang?' Rich stared at the inset picture. 'He cut himself with a bottle?'

'You should be all over this, Rich. Let's call this your favour.'

Rich put on a sombre voice. 'From the big time to dungeon death. The story of the Old Town Serial Killer victim.'

'Rich, I'm warning you...'

'I know, too many syllables. What about just "Old Town Killer"?'

'This isn't a serial killer.'

'Bullshit.' Rich folded the article and slid it underneath his laptop. 'Trouble is, Sonny Bangs was let go in the last round of job cuts.'

'So you know him?'

'Alan Stephenson. Good guy. Think he lives in Midlothian somewhere. Penicuik or Rosewell. Somewhere like that.'

'Cheers for that.' Cullen reached over for the document print.

Rich kept a hold of it. 'Tell you what, I'll chum you to his house.' A grin twitched at the corners of Rich's mouth. 'After all, I've still got Alan's mobile number.'

17

'I WAS RIGHT.' IN THE REARVIEW, RICH PUT HIS PHONE AWAY AND grinned at Cullen from the back seat. 'Penicuik.'

Cullen kept his eyes on the road, pretending not to notice Rich's sulky look. Or Buxton's. *No doubt expecting to be left in the car again.* 'The *Argus* seems decimated, Rich. Still don't understand why you moved back from London.'

'I wanted to write a book. My own. That job lets me keep the fridge full while I work away on my first international bestseller. It's much cheaper to live here on London money.'

'Not so cheap on Edinburgh money.'

'That room in Tom's flat is cheap enough and I still get paid the same, so I'm happy, even though he's a wanker.' Rich grinned at Buxton. 'You met him?'

'Couple of times.' Buxton was still staring at his phone. 'Decent bloke.'

'Mm.' Rich locked eyes with Cullen in the rearview. 'Never thought I'd say this, Skinky, but I miss you.'

'Not enough to tell me how you got your hands on a crime scene photo.' Cullen took a left towards Penicuik. 'You should've run it by me.'

'You'd have told me not to use it.' Rich huffed, turning away to look out of his window. 'Eck loved it. Highest circulation in months. Had him dreaming of the glory days again.'

'Speaking of which, you remember Strang from school?'

Buxton looked over, frowning. Didn't say anything.

'Dalhousie Grammar, eh? Same year as your sister, right?'

Cullen gritted his teeth. 'No idea.'

'Well, I bet she'd remember. Him going on to become a big rock star and all. How is Michelle, anyway?'

'Don't ask.'

Rich turned his head back around to frown at Cullen. 'Why?'

Cullen kept staring at the road, at the queue of traffic waiting to turn right into the Tesco car park. 'Because I haven't seen her in years.'

'You're such a twat, Skinky.' Rich gripped Buxton's shoulder. 'You should see his sister, mate. I mean, I'm as gay as a window, but... Michelle's *fit*.'

'*Rich.*'

He burst out laughing. 'Never stops winding you up, mate.'

Buxton shook Rich's hand off. 'How can a window be gay?'

Rich rolled his eyes. 'Where did you find this guy, Scott?'

'I know.' Cullen took a tight corner, shifting gears down. 'Take it you and this Stephenson guy are close?'

'Had a few good nights with the guy. He helped me out when I started at the paper. Got chatting on a night out, good laugh. He worked the news desk and the gig reviews thing was a freebie because he was into music. Sade at the SECC. Morrissey at the Barrowlands. Album reviews. But he liked unsigned bands, wanted to help them out.'

'He ever talk to you about The Invisibles?'

'No, but...' Rich was looking out of the window. 'See, when Strang went missing, Alan wanted to turn it into a big thing. Eck was behind him, supporting him all the way, but when Strang didn't wash up dead as expected, well. Eck lost his raging hard-on.'

'That gig review seemed like he was trying to build them up. Was he mates with someone in the band?'

'Don't know him that well, Scott.'

'Guess I'll have to ask him myself.'

CULLEN KILLED THE ENGINE AND TURNED ROUND TO RICH. 'JUST SO we're clear, I'm leading in here. Okay? But, given that he's your mate, you step in any time he starts putting up walls, okay?'

Rich shifted in his seat. 'Fine.'

'Meanwhile, I'll just be playing with myself.' Buxton sat there, yawning, thumbs tapping the screen of his phone.

'What else is new?' Cullen got out of the car and headed up the drive. The sun hadn't yet set but the dusky half-light gave the terraced bungalows soft edges. Light filtered through the thin curtains, music through the door. The dull thud of hardcore punk. 'Sounds like he's in.' He knocked on the brown front door and waited.

'Forgot to say—'

The door opened and a skinny guy leaned halfway out, bulbous eyes struggling to focus on them. His T-shirt had John Lydon scowling at a camera in the late Eighties, long after his punk heyday as Johnny Rotten. 'Rich, man, what's up?' His accent was somewhere in the south of England. Less gruff than Buxton's Cockney, but not far off.

Cullen flashed his warrant card. 'Mr Stephenson?'

'Yeah?'

'I need a word.' Cullen pointed over his shoulder. 'Inside, please.'

Stephenson stared at him, then his eyes bulged even further and he glared at Rich. 'What the hell, man?'

'You wrote this article.' Cullen showed The Invisibles concert review. 'And you wrote about James Strang's disappearance.'

Stephenson's eyes flickered from Cullen to Rich and back again. 'You found him?'

Rich stepped over and patted Stephenson on the arm. 'Better do this inside, mate.'

∾

'WHAT A MESS.' STEPHENSON LEANED BACK IN HIS ARMCHAIR AND looked around his lounge. What had been furnished as a family room, smart oak furniture and a leather three-piece, had descended into bachelor squalor. Crushed beer cans and half-empty bottles of spirits littered every corner. The coffee table was covered in a pile of pizza boxes, next to a neat stack of foil take-away cartons covered in mould. Stephenson cleared his throat, his eyes almost popping out of his head as he stared up at Cullen.

Rich motioned at the mess. 'You been okay, mate?'

Stephenson reached down for a can and opened it with a spray. 'Wife left me.'

'Sorry to hear that.'

'Really?' Stephenson took a noisy slurp from the can. 'Not worked properly since I got made redundant. Picked up some agency work here and there, but that dried up.' He belched on the last word and waved his hand around. 'The house is on the market, but I doubt we'll get what it's worth. Savings are all gone.'

Rich bit his lip. 'Must be hard. Another round of cuts pending.'

'It's a bloody disgrace, man.' Stephenson took another swig from the can. 'Even the lucky ones who got to stay in the job, people like you, you'll be working twice as hard for the same money.'

Rich grimaced. 'For less, actually.'

'Shite.' Stephenson's large eyes slowly going out of focus. His whole life was circling the plughole. 'Why are you here again?'

'James Strang...'

'Jimi Danger... The Invisibles were a great band.' Stephenson sat up in his armchair. 'Most of the stuff I had to cover — David Byrne, Tracy Chapman, Bryan Ferry — it was all tedious shit for the readers. But I loved what that band did. My sort of noise. Even paid my way in. And I never paid my way anywhere.'

'You knew Strang well?'

'Ish. Kid was a trier, that's for sure. Used to pester me for gig reviews and features. Had a lot of front, I'll give him that. Problem was, the geezer was living the life of a rock 'n' roll star without the income.'

Cullen leaned forward on the sofa. 'You mean drugs?'

'God no. It was drink with Jimi.' Stephenson raised his can. 'Welcome to the club.'

Cullen slid the review out of his pocket and held it up. 'That concert was a week before Mr Strang went missing. As far as we can tell, he was killed around the time he went missing, possibly even the same night. Did he mention anyone he'd had a falling out with?'

Stephenson frowned at the clipping. He looked away and took another long slurp of beer. 'Not really.' He stared at the clipping, his drunken eyes slowly focusing. 'When he came onstage that night, he was shitfaced.' He pointed at the photo. 'That bottle of Jack Daniels he was sipping on stage, well. It didn't last long until he smashed it and cut himself.' He squinted at the photo. 'I must've seen them play ten times in the previous year, but I'd never seen him act like that.' He took another deep drink from his can. 'Jimi had got worse over the last few months. Angrier. Started with him smashing his guitar, which any clown can do. Then he started cutting himself on stage. Went way over the top. I mean, Iggy Pop did it in the Seventies, before AIDS.'

'You got any idea why?'

Stephenson drained his beer's foamy dregs. 'See when I wrote this piece, I got the train through to Glasgow with the band. Not long before that last gig. They were playing and they let me interview them. And I mean interview *him*. The others didn't get a word in edgeways. As we got close to Queen Street, Jimi started talking about a record deal. He reckoned they were offered a contract from someone, someone pretty big. Sony, EMI, Universal, can't remember. One of those sub-labels they have that look like indies. The rest of the band, they started trying to jump in, trying to get him to stop. But Jimi, he was shitfaced. Kept talking. Reckoned they'd had a lawyer go through the deal and so on, reckoned they were close to signing.'

Cullen waited, but Stephenson reached down for another can. Acting like the story was over. 'But?'

Stephenson opened the can. 'But something happened. No idea what. One minute they're about to sign a two-album deal, the next the deal's dead.' He took a swig. 'If you ask me, Jimi sort of imploded after that.'

Cullen closed his eyes. *Why the hell didn't I hear about this from the band?*

18

CULLEN SWUNG INTO HOLYROOD ROAD AND PULLED UP OUTSIDE THE Argus office. He swung round and grabbed Rich by the arm. He nodded at the gleaming office. 'You got something in there that you're not sharing with me?'

'No. I'm going to speak to Eck, see if I can get some work for Alan Stephenson.' Rich tried to shrug him off but Cullen's grip was too strong. 'Mate, what are you playing at?'

'Remember our deal?' Cullen fixed a hard stare on him. 'Nothing until Monday.'

'Yeah, yeah. You got what you wanted.'

Cullen let him go. 'Very Christian of you.'

'Yeah, yeah.' Rich got out into the night and marched over to the door in the flicker of Cullen's indicator.

'Tenner says he's writing that up, mate.' Buxton was still looking at his phone. 'How about you? You get what you wanted?'

'Sort of, but I definitely feel a lot better about my career prospects over his.' Cullen frowned. 'You beat your high score yet?'

'Hardly.' Buxton reached over and plugged his phone into the stereo. Music blasted out of the speakers, indie rock, raw and noisy but still somehow it had a tune. Sounded like it had been recorded in a bathroom, though, with the shower running.

Cullen turned it down a notch. 'What's this?'

Buxton showed his mobile. Concert footage filled the screen, looked like it was recorded on a phone, Jimi Danger grinning like a demon. 'Took me ages, but I found it.'

'What?'

Buxton snorted. 'This is The Invisibles' single. Called *Gone-away*. Looks like just five hundred seven-inch singles pressed. Not even on Spotify or Apple Music. This is the only recording I could find on YouTube.'

Cullen set off, tailing a car back to the centre, his thumbs drumming the steering wheel in the same tom-heavy pattern Beth Williamson was beating on the recording. 'Reminds me of something.'

'Tell me about it.' Buxton sighed. 'While you and Rich were in his flat, I spent all that time listening to this. Still can't figure it out.'

Cullen's phone rang. He answered it and put it through the car speakers, killing The Invisibles' racket. 'Aye?'

'Is that how you address a senior officer now, Sergeant?' Methven's irritated hiss burst out with a sharp blast.

'Sorry, sir, I'm driving.' Cullen bit his tongue. 'How can I help?'

'This lengthy voicemail you just left, something about a failed record deal?'

'Right?'

'Have you got anything to back it up?'

'Just what Alan Stephenson told us.'

'That's it?'

'Me and DC Buxton are going to speak to the rest of the band.'

'I see.'

'You don't think I should?'

'I didn't say that.' Methven huffed out a sigh. 'Look, I'm stuck in a session with Alison and Jim. DC Hunter has secured the other two at the safehouse. Speak to them. I expect a full briefing later.'

'Sir.'

Cullen hung up. 'Wanker.'

～

CULLEN TURNED THE FINAL CORNER INTO THE GENTRIFIED docklands of Leith and parked outside a converted warehouse. He got out and pressed the buzzer for flat eighteen.

'What?' Hunter sounded annoyed.

'Craig, it's Scott.'

A long sigh. 'What the hell do you want?'

Cullen gave Buxton a shake of the head. 'Just let me in.'

Another sigh, then the buzzer sounded.

Cullen headed inside. While the area's industrial heritage was preserved on the outside, inside the old rusty machinery had been traded for shiny hardwood floors, overhung by polished-glass mezzanines. All for its up-and-coming drug lords. He set off up the glass staircase, each step like he was walking on thin air. Set off a minor attack of vertigo.

Hunter was outside a second-floor flat, arms folded like a bouncer. And giving Cullen the up-and-down like one as well. 'You got a new lead?'

'Maybe.' Cullen nodded at him to step aside, but Hunter stood his ground. 'Just need to chat to them.'

Hunter unfolded his arms and stood up tall, his extra couple of inches looking down on Cullen. 'Need to call this in to DI Cargill.'

Cullen shot Buxton a look. 'Seriously?'

Hunter just stared at him, his eyes blank. Then he laughed. 'Of course not.' He opened the door and led in, his footsteps clicking off the hardwood. He opened a door and stood aside. 'Here you go.'

Cullen stepped into the living room. A uniformed officer stood outside a pair of patio doors at the far side. Gave Hunter a nod, then went back to looking out of the window. The large open-plan space was divided into smaller areas: a high-spec kitchen, the black-marble counter gleaming under the spotlights; six leather-and-chrome chairs around a concrete dining table; two armchairs and a sofa around a TV playing a golf tournament from some-where hot and sunny. No sign of anyone they were protecting, though.

Buxton walked alongside Cullen. 'Shame to waste it on a safehouse.'

Hunter picked up a remote and killed the golf. 'Used to belong to that Edwin guy. Can't remember his surname. Big dealer.'

'I know who you mean.' Buxton sat at a dining table. 'Didn't Wilkinson take him down?'

Hunter frowned at him. 'Who?'

'Never mind.' Buxton sighed. 'Have you lost who you're protecting?'

'Don't give up the day job, Si.' Hunter marched across to the doors and walked outside without waiting.

Buxton brushed his hand over the concrete table. 'Cracking surface for racking up lines, isn't it?'

'Don't get any ideas.' Cullen sat at the other end of the table. The chair didn't make a sound.

The doors opened again and Hunter came back out, followed by Beth Williamson, looking tired and pissed off.

She slumped on the sofa with all the grace a heavily-pregnant woman could muster. 'He's kicking like he's at Murrayfield. And Olly's on a boy weekend. Knew I shouldn't have let him.'

Cullen nodded at her with what he hoped would pass for sympathy. 'Olly's your husband, right?'

'He's in Cheltenham for a cricket match. Back tomorrow night.' She winced, then stroked her belly again. 'You can't do this to me.'

Cullen frowned. 'Do what?'

'Keep me here.'

'This is for your own safety. DC Hunter has briefed you, right?'

'Of course he has, but it's stupid. There's no serial killer.'

Hunter took a seat in an armchair next to Beth, his forehead creasing. 'Can I get you anything?'

She smiled back. 'No thanks. Just wish this baby would arrive.'

Behind Cullen, a door opened and the gurgle of a flushing toilet filled the room. David Johnson stood in the doorway, rubbing his hands on his jeans. 'What's up?'

Cullen pointed at the table. 'Take a seat.' He waited, eyes flitting between Beth and Johnson. 'As you know, police in Glasgow have found the body of Alex Melrose. We believe he was murdered on Thursday night. You're here for your own protection. DC Hunter is personally guarding your front door, this is the safest place for you to be right now.'

Beth's hollow laugh echoed through the large room. 'Unless Dave is the killer.'

Johnson looked from Hunter to Cullen, his face twitching. 'I told this boy here, I was at work on Thursday.'

'We're not treating you as suspects.' Hunter gave a cold smile.

'My colleague has been going through your movements and you're both in the clear.'

Beth folded her arms. 'Okay?'

Cullen held her gaze, long and hard, until she looked away. 'I'm wondering when you were going to tell us about your record deal?'

Beth's eyes bounced to Johnson, who looked up at the ceiling.

Cullen got up and walked over to the middle of the table, resting his hands on the cold concrete as he leaned over to Johnson. 'I understand your band was offered a record deal. Came close to signing it, too.' He shifted his glare to Beth. 'Wonder why you're playing at mummies and daddies instead of driving a Rolls Royce into a swimming pool.'

Beth took a deep breath. 'That's unbe—'

'Beth.' Dave leaned back and sighed. 'Fair enough. We were offered a deal, aye. Pretty tasty one. Two albums, plus an option for a third if the first two sold well. Big advance, plus guaranteed two hundred quid a week wage, plus a nice per diem.'

'Per diem?'

'Daily spending money. For when we were on tour or in the studio. And Jimi said we'd be doing either most days.' Johnson snorted. 'The lawyer was cock-a-hoop about it. We were just about to sign the papers when the deal disappeared from under our feet.' He clicked his fingers. 'Just like that.'

Cullen looked at them both in turn. 'What happened?'

'Search me.' Johnson ran a hand across his forehead. 'I didn't get involved in that side. Alex and Jimi dealt with it all.'

'You know anything else, Beth?'

She was staring at the floor at Hunter's feet. 'I just turned up, hit the drums, that's it. The other stuff was boring.'

Cullen waited until she finally raised her eyes to meet his. 'How big a deal are we talking?'

'Dave told you. Two albums. Four singles.'

'I meant how much money?'

She looked away again. 'Can't remember.'

'Five figures?'

'More.'

'So six. Are we talking a hundred grand or nine hundred?'

Johnson sighed, rubbing his hands together like he was grabbing a stack of notes. 'About six, if I remember correctly.'

Cullen raised his eyebrows. 'Six hundred thousand pounds?'

'We had to pay for recording and stuff out of that. That's how Jimi explained it, anyway.'

'Which label was it?'

Beth glanced at Johnson, then back at the floor. 'He probably mentioned a name to us, but I can't remember.'

Dave shook his head, keeping his gaze firmly nailed to the wooden floor. 'Same.'

'So someone was going to give you over half a million quid and you can't remember who?' Cullen cleared his throat, making Dave look up and nod. 'How did the deal dying make you feel?'

Johnson winced, his hands twitching. 'Shouldn't we be doing this at the station, you know, with lawyers?'

'There are four police officers here, Mr Johnson. This will stand up in court if I need it to.' Cullen just kept staring at him. 'Are you trying to tell us you were involved in Mr Strang's death?'

Johnson's twitchy fingers froze. 'No. No, of course not.'

'But you don't know which label it was?'

'Like Beth said, the other two dealt with all of that. We played drums and bass.'

'So, you never even met a representative?'

'Course we did. We met a whole bunch of them. They even came to see us at T in the Park, bought us booze and stuff, took us out for dinner. I could name ten people, but I couldn't say which label we were going to sign with. The main guy was this sleazy fat bastard. Jamie. English. You know the sort. Had a real oily voice.'

Cullen nodded along. 'And what did Jimi and Alex make of him pulling the deal?'

'No idea.'

'They didn't tell you?'

'No, they were pissed off, but...'

'They blamed each other.' Beth picked up a pillow and started squeezing it. 'When they told us, they each said it was the other's fault. Things escalated and...'

'They had a fight.' Johnson leaned back in his dining chair. 'Really battered each other.'

Cullen looked over at Hunter and Buxton, both with their eyes wide, then back at Johnson. He breathed through his nose, trying to keep calm. 'Why didn't you mention this before?'

'It... It didn't seem relevant.'

'WHAT THE—'

'I'm sorry!' Dave flinched. 'Look, Jimi... Jimi and Alex were great mates, but they were at each other's throats all the time. Alex was a bit of a, I don't know.' He glanced at Beth, but she was still staring at the floor, trancelike. 'Alex was a bit of a drifter, always doing casual jobs, never settling into anything long term. Musically, he was great, but...'

'But he was unfocused.' Beth kept staring at the floorboards. 'He'd forget where different sections of the songs started. Drove Jimi bananas.'

Cullen raised an eyebrow. 'Bananas, how?'

'He just got angry with him. Kept shouting at him.' She glanced up at him and he caught a glimpse of something honest in her eyes before they clouded over again. 'Our sound was quite dynamic. Loud, sure, but we had some very pretty bits in our songs. Quiet bits. The structures were very complex.'

Buxton laughed. 'So Alex would crank up the volume in the wrong section?'

'That's about the size of it.' Beth shrugged. 'Jimi found it hard to sing a sweet song with a Marshall turned up to eleven behind him.'

'Did this ever happen on stage?'

'Not as much as in rehearsals but when it did, Jimi would go ballistic.'

Cullen returned to his seat. 'Fractious relationships tend to snap at some point. Did Mr Strang by any chance blame Mr Melrose for the deal falling through?'

Beth and Dave exchanged a quick look.

'No.'

'Maybe.'

They clamped their mouths shut.

They're rattled.

Cullen let them sit in silence for a moment. *Let them figure out for themselves how close their backs are to the wall.* 'For the last time, do you know why the deal fell through?'

Beth glared at Johnson. 'Like we've already said, twice, we don't know.'

Cullen shifted his focus to Johnson. 'You know, I find that hard to believe. Touring, gigs, six hundred grand... This was going to be your freedom. You weren't pissed off it fell through? Didn't want to know who'd screwed you? Or how?'

'We're happy where we are now, detective.' Beth stroked her belly. 'I certainly am. Like I told you, I was getting bored of it. I was thinking of quitting anyway. That happening, really, it was a blessing in disguise.'

'Did Alex blame Jimi?'

'No.' She threw the cushion away. 'Maybe. I can't remember.'

'Enough to kill him?'

'No.' Beth stabbed a finger at Cullen. Her accent was all coarse again. 'Jimi and Alex were best friends. Jimi disappearing like that really cut him up.'

Cullen gave her another one of those doubtful nods. 'You mentioned a lawyer, right? Looked over the deal.'

'Jimi just told us that. Him and Alex met the guy, lived through in Glasgow, I think. Me and Beth never met him.'

'Didn't even know there was a lawyer.'

Cullen sat back in his chair and studied the pair of them, each one getting a few seconds attention. 'You expect me to believe neither of you questioned why a deal that could have changed your lives forever fell through at the last minute?'

Dave glared at him. 'Jimi blamed the label, said they were corporate pricks. He wasn't wrong, but it is what it is and we've moved on. End of story.'

Cullen got up and nodded at Hunter, then Buxton, then walked out of the apartment.

Another bloody dead end. Which means there's only one place left to go.

19

'RIGHT, WELL.' BUXTON PUT ON HIS WOOLLY COAT AND SHOVED HIS bag over his left shoulder. 'See you Monday.'

'See you.' Cullen scanned the incident room. No sign of Chantal, and Methven wasn't here either. 'Wait, aren't you in tomorrow?'

Buxton finger-combed his floppy hair, checking his reflection out on his phone screen. 'Got a wedding tomorrow. Two good friends of mine getting hitched. Fife, of all places.'

'You cleared that with Crystal?'

'He was fine about it.'

'Crystal signed off on that during a major investigation?'

'Yup. I forwarded the email.' Buxton stretched out with a yawn. 'I'll be thinking of you when I'm drinking Stella tomorrow.' He gave a mock salute and flicked his hair back again. 'Right, I'm off. Enjoy your spiral into depression. I always get a little uncomfortable watching you crywank until it bleeds.' He sloped off with a final leer.

Cullen stood alone in the incident room. *Should really just piss off home myself.* He got one arm in his coat, when Chantal came in, sitting at her desk.

Cullen shrugged off his coat and sat. He made brief eye contact with Chantal, but she went back to typing. 'You seen Methven?'

'That all I'm good for?' Now she looked up.

Cullen bit his tongue. 'Just need a word, that's all.'

She closed her eyes. 'Right.'

'How's it going?'

'Slow.'

'Tell me you've found a suspect among Strang's workmates.'

'God, you're getting desperate.' She laughed. 'Afraid not. Even figuring out who was working at that record shop back then is next to impossible. They were all hired as casual labour, so documentation is light, to say the least.'

Cullen wheeled a chair up to her desk. 'Can you check something for me?'

She groaned. 'What?'

'Ask them if Strang told them who the band were going to sign with.'

'Wait a sec.' She rummaged through her notebook. 'Right, the people I've spoken to... Nope, they were all bored shitless by him. Said he was a tedious prick, just zoned out when he was talking about his band. Thought he was as successful as Bono, but he was only as interesting as him.'

'Not a fan?'

'Hardly.' Chantal turned a page. 'Got nowhere with the list of friends Johnson and Williamson gave us. I split the list with Buxton, but he's buggered off somewhere. Anyway, I've covered the lot. All for nothing.'

'How about the flatmates?'

'Same, but I'm missing about half of them.'

'Anybody mentioned this Jane girlfriend his mother told us about?'

Chantal dropped her notebook to the desk. 'No.'

A floorboard creaked over by the door.

Cullen swung round and saw the back of Charlie Kidd. 'Stop right there.'

Kidd swung round, eyes closed. 'Evening, you prick.'

'Nice to see you too. What's up?'

'Just finished with this.' Kidd walked over and dropped a laptop on the desk next to Chantal. 'Someone needs to give it back to his folks.'

'Get anything off it?'

Kidd frowned at the machine. 'Not really. Spent a bit of time focusing on his Facebook, Myspace, Google+ and Schoolbook accounts.'

Cullen grinned. 'Was Jimi Danger too dangerous for Twitter?'

'Maybe.' Kidd winced. 'Either I can't find his profile or he doesn't have one.

'You find anything anything useful?'

'Nope. This Strang boy just spammed people about gigs and CDs and Bandcamp, whatever that is. Not so much as a single personal message.' Kidd set off towards the door. 'I'll give you a shout if I find anything, Chantal.'

'Thanks.

Cullen leaned back on the chair and rubbed his face. *So bloody tired.* 'Christ, what did I ever do to piss him off?'

'Being a wanker?'

'Charming.'

'I went to see—'

'Are you going to be here long, Sergeant?' Methven stormed into the incident room, struggling to tear off his black coat.

Cullen tried to cover a yawn as he nodded at Methven. 'Another few hours, sir.'

'Remember the Clear Desk Policy.' Methven waved at Buxton's desk, covered with photocopies.

Messy bastard. 'I'll clear up before I leave tonight, sir. Just need a word.'

Chantal chose that moment to dart off out of the office, all dressed up for home.

'Sergeant, I'm on my way out.' Methven checked his watch. 'I've missed a sodding dinner party and Mrs Methven isn't too pleased with me.' He headed off, but stopped at the door. 'By the way, I appreciated your latest update, but your texting could do with a little more clarity. Am I right in thinking that this band were offered a record deal and it was subsequently rescinded. Is that correct?'

'So it would seem. The two surviving members don't remember who it was with.'

'You believe them?'

'I don't know, sir.'

'Hmm. Interesting.' Methven paused, then nodded to himself.

'Do you think this missed shot at fame might be connected to Strang's or Melrose's deaths?'

'Don't know. Strang was feeling under a lot of pressure towards the end. The record deal was part of it.'

'Do you reckon it could have been like Elliott Smith?'

'Elliott who?'

Methven rolled his eyes. 'The American singer-songwriter, another musician who committed suicide by stabbing himself in the chest.'

'I thought we'd ruled out suicide?'

'Well.' Methven stared at Cullen as if he had gone mad. 'I was at the post mortem, Sergeant. I spoke to the pathologist.'

'I know. Hence me asking what he made of it?'

'It was Sweeney, not Deeley.'

'Okay, what did she reckon, then?'

'That suicide was highly unlikely. Given the forensic evidence we subsequently obtained, vis a vis the stains on the jeans, it was upgraded to impossible.'

Cullen took a deep breath. 'I see...'

Methven squinted at him. 'There's always a but with you, isn't there?'

'What if we kept that post-mortem report to ourselves? We could just not mention it to Bain. That would clearly separate the cases and leave us in charge of the Edinburgh side.'

'No! No games. However Bain runs his show in Glasgow, we do things by the book through here.'

'You know Bain will play games, sir. He'll find some easy suspect and frame them, and we'll have to stop him from—'

'Okay...' Methven paused, his face lighting up. 'You're probably right, Sergeant. While I don't like to play that way, I'll think it over. Now, do you mind if I get home?'

'Okay. Speaking of Bain, what's the latest?'

'I strategised with Jim and Alison and... Well, we had a conference call with DI Bain and his superiors. This wasn't my idea, you understand?' He cleared his throat, then gave Cullen with an awkward smile. 'Sergeant, I need you to go through to Glasgow.'

'Are you kidding?'

'No, I'm not.' Methven leaned in close. 'You're a DS now. I

expect you to follow orders. You're to report to Govan police station at seven a.m. tomorrow.'

Glasgow.

How the hell am I supposed to manage Chantal and Buxton and Hunter forty-odd miles down the M8?

'Shouldn't I focus on Edinburgh?'

'DC Jain can cover. After all, we've pretty much run out of road on the very few leads you've found here.'

'So, what, I'm Bain's resource now?'

'No, no. I just want you to validate that there is a connection between the cases, that we really are dealing with a serial killer.' Methven looked him up and down like he was about to say more. Instead, he stormed off, checking his watch as he went. 'I'll be in touch.'

Cullen slouched back on his chair, the moan of the backrest sounding about as cheerful as his voice. He looked out of the window but saw only his own miserable reflection.

≈

CULLEN SHUFFLED DOWN THE ROYAL MILE, STRUGGLING TO DO anything other than yawning and putting one foot in front of the other. He turned into the entrance to World's End Close and stopped dead.

A teenager was pissing against the bins just by the stair door.

'Hey!'

The ned tucked himself in and hurried off without a word.

Cullen just stood there, shaking his head, counting the number of times he'd done the same thing. Then he carried on his way to the main door and managed to match key to lock. He yawned his way up to the top of the stairs and unlocked the flat door.

Fluffy looked up at him, his yellow eyes a reminder that there were more important things in life than people pissing against your door.

Cullen knelt down and tried to stroke him. 'Hiya, Fluffy.'

The cat took a step back. 'Miaow!'

'What are you? A guard dog trapped in the body of a fat cat?'

Fluffy reared up and rubbed his chin against Cullen's finger.

'He's sensitive about his weight.' Sharon's voice came from the bedroom, followed by a weak cough.

Cullen headed through, squinting to see her in the dim light.

Behind the mound of duvet, her wave was as weak as her cough.

Cullen walked over, kissed her on the forehead and sat on the edge of the bed. 'How are you doing?'

'I've been in bed all day, choked with this bloody bug.' Her hair was lank and greasy, her breath as stale as the air. 'I feel terrible. I'm shivering. That's not good, is it?'

Cullen frowned at her. 'Could be 'flu.'

'I already told you I've got the 'flu.'

'Not what most people call a cold. The actual 'flu 'flu, as in influenza.'

'Pedant.' Sharon laughed, then a coughing fit took over. She raised her head to catch her breath. 'I'm supposed to be back in on Monday.' She grimaced. 'This is the worst possible time to be sick.'

'Take it easy. The most important thing is to get well. People die of 'flu every year.'

'Thanks. You know just what to say.' She dropped her head back on the pillow. 'It's a good thing I don't depend on your emotional support. While you were at work, I substituted one ginger for another.'

Cullen touched his hair. 'I'm hardly ginger.'

'I'm just joking. You're clearly strawberry blonde.' She smiled at his feigned outrage. 'Fine, dark blond.'

'My hair's brown. It's just my stubble that's a bit ginger. Why I never do Movember. Happy to pay for the privilege, mind, but nobody wants to see my moustache.'

She studied him for a moment. 'Have I ever told you how sexy being sensitive about your colouring is?'

'Uh, no, I don't think you have.'

'That'll be because I don't find it.'

Cullen laughed. 'What have you been up to today?'

'Just reading. Chantal came round for a bit.'

'Right.'

'Oh, come on, like you've never skived off yourself. You don't need to keep an eye on her all the time, you know? She's a good cop.'

'I know, but... Crystal.'

Sharon patted his hand like a child's. 'The joys of management. Remember when you reported to me. Bain was a nightmare for knowing exactly what everyone was up to, especially you.'

Cullen winced. 'Speak of the devil...'

'What?'

'You'll never guess who I bumped into today.'

'Oh no.' Sharon heaved a huge sigh that turned into an even bigger yawn. 'Bain? Is he working again?'

'Got it in one. Up to his old tricks again, only now he's heading up a Strathclyde murder squad. Like a phoenix rising from the ashes.'

'More like a cockroach crawling from a turd.'

Cullen's laugh caught in his throat. 'Thing is, I've got to head through to report to him tomorrow.'

'Seriously?'

'Seriously, but right now I'm absolutely starving. Can I get you anything?'

'I'm fine.' Sharon yawned again, then turned to her side and was asleep before Cullen could disagree.

You look about as fine as I feel.

DAY 3

Sunday

20

Seven a.m. in Glasgow.

Bloody hell.

Cullen closed in on Govan police station, the sandstone cold and grey in the early morning light. He caught a flash of purple drew in the rear-view mirror.

A sporty Ford Mondeo followed him in, then parked a couple of spaces away.

Bloody... whatever. Just suck it up.

Bain got out of the Mondeo, beaming at Cullen. 'Didn't expect you to show your pretty face, Sundance.'

Cullen rubbed his ginger stubble, cursing himself for forgetting to shave. 'Just following orders.'

'What the Nazis said, and remember where that got them.' Bain grinned at him like that was meant to be funny. 'When you're coming through tomorrow, bring us a tray of donuts from that Krispy Kreme at Edinburgh Park, would you?'

'You serious?'

Bain burst out laughing. 'Of course I am. As you well know, I look after my team.' He reached into his car and brought out a cardboard tray of takeaway coffees. 'See?'

Cullen shook his head. 'The Krispy Kreme queue was backed out all the way to the M8 and the sun's only just up.'

'This country...' Bain looked over at Cullen's bottle green Golf, seventeen years old and unwashed for the past sixteen. 'Your piece of crap here might die before you reach the front of the queue. Would've thought a DS's wedge would get you a proper motor, no?'

Cullen started walking to the front doors. 'I'm here to review your case files, that's it.'

'Aye?' Bain squinted at the glass as the low sun turned it into a mirror. 'Little birdie called to say you're seconded to my investigation.'

Cullen opened the door, avoiding his leer. 'Not what I was told.'

'I don't care, Sundance.' Bain walked through, both hands busy holding the coffees. 'You're shadowing McCrea while you're through here.'

'I'm not under your orders.'

'Sundance, Sundance, Sundance.' Bain plonked his coffees on the front desk and started rummaging round in his pockets. 'You're an ADS, I'm a DI. Means you do what I tell you.'

Cullen clenched his teeth.

'And what I'm telling you now is that you're shadowing McCrea.'

'How about I get familiar with the case files while you have a word with Methven?'

Bain looked Cullen up and down. 'I always hated the way you would do absolutely anything to avoid taking orders.' He pointed with a devilish grin. 'Open the door for me.'

∽

CULLEN LOOKED UP FROM HIS PAPERWORK AND DID ONE OF THOSE yawns that went on and on. He checked his watch. *One o'clock.* He checked through his notebook again — five pages of notes from three of eight case files. And nothing of any use.

McCrea swung by, carrying two mugs, wafting a burnt instant coffee smell about. He handed one to Cullen with a sneer, a few words dripping out of the side of his mouth.

Cullen pulled out his earbuds. 'Come again?'

'The gaffer told us you were a fiend for the coffee.'

'Thanks.' Cullen clenched his teeth and took a sip. It tasted as burnt as it smelled. 'Good stuff.' He drained the mug in one and handed it back.

McCrea took it with a confused frown, then shrugged and slurped his own coffee like he couldn't taste how bad it was. 'How's it going?'

'Getting there. I suppose.'

'Want to run anything by me?'

Might kill a few minutes. Cullen flipped back to the first page. 'Here's what I've got. The body of Alex Melrose was found by uniform responding to a noise complaint. Pathologist thought Alex Melrose was stabbed in the kitchen of his flat and left to bleed out. The kitchen knife found at his feet was the murder weapon.' He looked at the summary notes he'd made of the post mortem. 'The pathologist ruled out suicide, right?'

'Right.' McCrea took a loud slurp, like he was trying to goad him. 'I attended. Doc reckoned there were none of the tell-tale signs. Wrong angle of entry. None of the hesitation wounds you'd get with a self-inflicted stabbing. No markers anywhere on the body from previous attempts.'

'That it?'

'Nah. The wounds on his wrists were almost certainly defensive wounds, suggesting he was attacked. Thing is, if he'd done it himself, surely the boy would've lifted up his clothes? The knife went through his T-shirt and cardigan.'

Cullen tapped the folder. 'There's no mention of that in here.'

'Aye?' McCrea sniffed. 'Must've slipped my mind.'

'Look, are you trying to piss me off, or are you just incompetent?'

'Take your pick.' McCrea shrugged. 'Look, we found the bread knife in the bin, so it's—'

'Thought it was at his feet?'

McCrea leaned his heavy gut over the desk and snatched the PM report. 'Ah. Right. I see what the problem is. That's the first draft.'

Cullen leaned back on the chair and rubbed his face. 'Alright. So what actually happened?'

'Like I say, the knife was in the bin.' McCrea took another slurp of his coffee and licked his lips. 'We found blood traces at the victim's feet, hence the confusion. The knife was part of a set he had in the kitchen. John Lewis's finest from about ten years ago.' Another slurp of coffee, another lick of the lips. 'They didn't find any fingerprints or DNA apart from the victim's.'

Cullen scratched his stubble. 'Odd.'

'It is and it isn't. Could be a professional job. We just don't know yet. But the fact the knife was in the bin, well. The flat's a bomb site. Those bloodstains were covered in pizza boxes. Should see the state of it, man.'

'I tried to, remember? But you arrested me.'

McCrea laughed. 'That was class. Thanks for the reminder. You've brightened my day already. That why they call you Sunshine?'

'Sundance.' Cullen stared at him until the daft grin faded from his lips. 'And they don't. Only Bain does, and God knows why he thinks it's still funny.'

'Right. Still, could be drugs.'

Cullen held his stare for a second. 'Okay, why?'

McCrea reached over for the blood toxicology report. 'You have read this, right?'

'Next on my list.'

'Now who's incompetent?' McCrea started flicking through the document. 'Says here, we found traces of cannabis and another opiate in Melrose's bloodstream.'

Cullen snatched it off him and started leafing through. *Melrose was on smack? That didn't gel with Marta Owenson's account. According to her, Melrose ended their relationship because of her heroin addiction. She said he smoked heroin, but only once or twice. It must've escalated, as per usual.*

Then again, never trust a junkie, even a recovering one.

Cullen shut the report and dumped on the desk. 'Heroin?'

'Eh?'

'The opiate found in the victim's blood — was it heroin?'

'We think so. The doc reckons he mostly smoked the heroin, though, rather than injecting it.' McCrea perched on the edge of the desk. 'That said, we found his works. Hypodermic needle, strap, spoon, lighter, the whole shooting match. Didn't find any gear, though.'

'No heroin?'

'None.'

'Hold on a minute. If Melrose is an unemployed junkie, how could he afford a flat in the West End?'

'Ooh, get you.' McCrea's eyebrows crawled up his bald head. 'The West End, eh? Our rough-talking visitor from Edinburgh's filthy docklands has heard about the posh bit of Glasgow.'

'I actually know that area fairly well. Full of students and young professionals. Besides, the knife is John Lewis's finest, as you pointed out. That's not a cheap lifestyle for a suicidal junkie.'

McCrea avoided Cullen's glare. 'You can go off people, you know?'

'Right. If you found his works, why did you think he chased the dragon rather than mainlining?'

'Listen to you. Sounds like you've just read *Trainspotting* while listening to Spacemen 3.' McCrea tapped his forearm. 'There were very few track marks on the boy's arms, but we found a shitload of tinfoil. I'll let you work the rest out.'

Cullen looked up at the ceiling. 'What other leads do we have?'

'We?' McCrea slurped the last of his coffee and put his empty mug down. 'Not a lot. It's nowhere near as bad as your half of the case, mind.'

'Our case.' Cullen took a deep breath and focused on him again. 'Have you any suspects?'

'Few irons in the fire, aye. Nothing to trouble you with, but we're not doing too badly.'

'Mind if look round the flat?'

McCrea scanned around the office, like he was looking for Bain. 'Don't see why not. The scene of crime boys have finished up. Just waiting for the gaffer to give us the nod.'

Cullen looked over at Bain's office. His voice rasped out, even through the closed door. 'He told me I should head over there as soon as you were free. Must think I need a babysitter.'

'He's not wrong.' McCrea grinned as he hopped up to standing. 'Grab your coat, then.'

⁓

CULLEN STEPPED UP ONTO THE LANDING AND WAITED. *GOT ALL THE way to Melrose's flat without being assaulted this time.*

McCrea unlocked the door, spun around and threw a punch at him. But he held his fist back at the last second, grinning like a moron. 'Come on in. Make yourself at home.'

Cullen followed him in, taking a pair of gloves out of his pocket and snapping them on.

The place was way smaller than Cullen had imagined, more like a bedsit than a flat and as narrow as a coffin. Only two rooms, by the looks of it. The door to the tiny bathroom hung open, the cistern silent. Everything else was crammed into a single room. Three kitchen units squashed in next to a sofa-bed, a small desk covered in books and mail.

Cullen checked the walls, but there was no message from a serial killer, there or anywhere else.

And McCrea was right — the place was a bomb site. Like Alan Stephenson's house in Penicuik, just a year or so down the line, should he ever start smoking heroin. The old pizza boxes made cramped space seem even more claustrophobic, not to mention the crumpled clothes and empty bottles littering every available surface.

'We found him in that...' McCrea walked over to the doll's house kitchen, overlooking the communal drying green out back. A roll of tinfoil lay on the kitchen counter. 'That's why we think he was a smoker.' He dropped his hands to his hips. 'Time was, this whole area would've been bedsits like this, but the block was bought up and turned into bigger flats. No idea why this is still here. I thought they'd all been gentrified.'

In the corner next to the other window, a teetering pile of well-thumbed paperbacks leaned back against the wall. Mostly older fiction, classics like *Naked Lunch, Crash, Lolita, The Master and Margarita, Crime and Punishment.* Next to it was a neater stack seemingly made up exclusively of rock biographies, the likes of Julian Cope, Joe Strummer, Morrissey, David Bowie, John Lennon and, on top of the pack, Ian Dury. The afternoon light caught a golden guitar resting against a small amp.

No stereo, not even a small TV.

A netbook poked out from under the music magazines on the desk.

Cullen stepped over a few pizza boxes on the floor and pushed the magazines aside with the end of a pen. 'You got anything off the computer?'

'Like what?'

Cullen glanced around at McCrea. 'Tell me you've had it looked at?'

'The gaffer warned me you could be a bit of a cock. Normally, I'd be tempted not to believe him, but I'll start siding with him if you keep that up.'

'I'm serious. Forensic Investigations should've had this.'

McCrea gave a defensive shrug. 'Bit of a kibosh on spending ahead of the restructure, big man. We live in a time of austerity. Might not seem like that in Edinburgh.' He pronounced it like an insult. 'Anyway, the eggheads are analysing Melrose's mobile. That's enough.' He glanced around the room like even he wasn't all that convinced of what he was saying anymore.

Cullen sighed, loud enough to get McCrea's attention. 'When we discovered our body, there was a message written on the wall behind it. Said, "I WILL KILL AGAIN". Nothing like that here?'

'Oh aye, under those posters. Took us a while to find them there, mind.' McCrea waved his hand round the room. The walls were covered in gig posters for bands Cullen had never heard of, interspersed with the occasional one for The Invisibles.

Cullen stepped closer to one of them. 'Oh, really?'

'Of course not, you twat.'

Cullen dropped his gaze, feeling the heat rise up his neck. A stack of flyers sat next to Melrose's computer, promoting a band called The Ferocious Butterfly. He picked one up to read the tour dates. The flyer said the band was playing Glasgow at two p.m. today, a venue called Stereo. Another check of the wall and Cullen found a couple of gig posters for them.

Cullen held the flyer up for McCrea. 'You know if he was in this band?'

'Found a web page for them. Sure enough, Alex Melrose plays guitar, aye. Gaffer didn't want me to dig too deep down that rabbit hole.'

'Bet he didn't. You spoken to them?'

'Emailed them, but nothing back.' McCrea shrugged. 'Couldn't find any contact details, eh?'

'Not even on the victim's mobile?'

'Ever seen a junkie's phone? It's all just numbers. Secrets and lies, man.'

Cullen took another look at the flyer. 'I suppose we should go to this gig, right?'

21

McCREA DROVE THROUGH CENTRAL GLASGOW AND ITS CHESSBOARD road network, rows and rows of Victorian tenements either side. All so familiar and yet so alien, like being driven through some distorted version of Edinburgh, everything reconfigured and enlarged.

Cullen shifted in his seat. His stomach rumbled but he ignored it. 'You ever heard of a lunchtime gig?'

'Nope. They're usually in dark rooms in the evening, before bouncers chuck everyone out at ten for a club night.' McCrea took a sharp left turn onto a long street, busy with traffic. 'Glasgow's a funny city, though. Neds and gangs and high finance musicians all squeezed in. And just think how many big bands have come out of Glasgow. Primal Scream, Texas, Hue and Cry, Franz Ferdinand, Chvrches.' He pulled into a parking bay. 'That's us.'

Cullen craned his neck to get a better view.

A bohemian pub, right next door to a much earthier boozer. McCrea was right — the city's arts and underside sitting cheek by jowl.

'Right, let's see if this lot know Melrose, then.' Cullen got out of the car to lead the way to the venue's front door.

A giant blocked their way, six foot five but lanky. He looked down at them in turn, sniffed and held out a hand. 'Five quid.'

McCrea reached for his police ID.

Cullen stepped in front of him. 'Here. I'll get it.' He handed the doorman a tenner.

'Thanks, dude.' The doorman stamped the back of his hand.

Cullen held the door for McCrea. 'What was that about?'

'What, you want to pay for a gig?'

'Don't want to get a reputation.' Cullen followed him in.

Stereo seemed to be nothing but a single long, plain room, but it was absolutely rammed, full of skinny boys and girls with trendy haircuts being all ironic as they took group photos. Way too busy for a Sunday lunchtime.

Stab me now.

Cullen nudged his way to the bar, squeezing between two girls in matching Hello Kitty dresses. He waved like a deranged maniac to catch the barman's attention, a miracle given the thickness of his glasses.

The guy came over and leaned on the bar. 'What can I get you?'

Cullen raised his voice over the incessant chatter: 'Looking for The Ferocious Butterfly.'

'You press or something?'

'Something.'

'Comedian.' The barman rolled his eyes. 'They're playing two sets today. Just between them now.'

Cullen glanced over at the stage, but it was empty. 'Any chance I can speak to them now?'

'Wait till the end. Like everybody else.'

Cullen reached into his pocket for his warrant card, but his stomach rumbled again. 'Can I get a bacon roll?'

'This place is vegan?' The barman folded his arms. 'No meat or any other animal products.'

Cullen cringed. 'Okay, uh, what have you got?'

McCrea barged in with a wide grin. 'Two falafel burgers. Chips with both.'

The barman passed the order through to the kitchen. 'Anything to drink?'

Cullen peered past him at the selection of bottled lagers, feeling like they had come all the way over from Germany to visit him.

Be rude not to, right? And at least three American craft beers on tap.

It's lunchtime, I'm a cop, and there are witnesses. Including McCrea.
'Pint of Coke. No ice.'

McCrea nodded. 'Same.'

'It's organic cola. That okay?'

'Whatever.' Cullen glanced back at the jumble of instruments on the small stage. Still no sign of the band. 'Sure I can't speak to them backstage?'

The barman looked up from pouring. 'Sure.'

The crowd roared as the band returned, three heads bobbing over the top. A trio, but they didn't look like they belonged in the same city as each other, let alone the same band.

The singer was so skinny his bass guitar seemed heavy enough to topple him. The drummer was a bodybuilder with a samurai bun, his hair tied up tight and shaved around the sides. Off to the left, the keyboard player seemed to be hiding behind her instrument, just a black denim jacket and a heavy fringe on show as she stared down at her keys.

Cullen took his pint of cola and handed over a twenty just as a screech of feedback erupted from the PA.

'Thanks for staying around for our second set.' The Ferocious Butterfly singer adjusted his mic stand. 'This song is called *The Girl in Morrisons Didn't Give Me Cashback*. It's about a girl in Morrisons not giving me cashback.'

The drummer counted to four on his sticks and launched into a slow beat, accompanied by soothing wash of electric piano chords.

The singer started playing a jagged rhythm on his bass. 'The girl in Morrisons didn't give me cashback...'

⌇

'HERE!' THE BARMAN HANDED OVER THEIR FOOD AND MCCREA started wolfing it down without looking.

Yet another acoustic dirge blasted out from the stage. The drummer was now singing, the keyboard player was playing electric guitar and the singer was standing behind the kit, thumping a floor tom with sticks as he wailed.

Cullen took his plate and stepped away from McCrea's feeding frenzy. *Absolutely starving, but I'm not a bloody animal.* He lifted the lid and inspected the burger — it looked healthy, perfect for his new regime. He spooned relish on the burger and tried the Cajun chips. Had to take a long drink of cola to dowse the heat. He tipped the yoghurt relish on and bit into the burger.

The song ended and applause burst out around the room.

'Thanks, you've been great.' The singer started applauding the crowd. 'If anyone's interested, we've got some CDs and T-shirts on sale at the door. And our album's on Spotify and YouTube.'

Whistles filled the room as the band left the stage.

Cullen finished his burger and put the plate down. 'What did you think?'

'Shite.' McCrea was eyeing Cullen's spare chips. 'Mind if I...?'

'Fill your boots.'

The band walked back on stage, thankfully not for an encore, just to pack up their gear.

Cullen set off towards them

McCrea grabbed his wrist. 'Give them five minutes.'

'They'll get away.'

'Five minutes won't hurt.' McCrea shoved Cullen's last chips in his mouth and wiped his fingers on his trousers, leaving five streaks of relish on the dark fabric. He swallowed before he could've finished chewing and pointed at the crowd lining the stage. 'Look at those idiots waiting to speak to them.'

Cullen turned back to the bar and waved at the barman. 'Another cola, plea-'

'Hey.' McCrea grabbed Cullen's shoulder and spun him round.

The singer lugged a guitar case through the crowd towards the front door, the crowd parting.

Cullen set off and caught the skinny chancer just by the door, grabbing his shoulder. 'Excuse me, sir, need—'

The singer spun round, swinging his case like a club.

Cullen ducked it, then stepped forward, catching him in a bearhug as the singer's own swing pulled him off balance. 'Police.'

The guy reared back, his shoulder muscles like thin steel wires under Cullen's forearms. 'Let go, you bastard!'

'Stop resisting.' Cullen hugged him tighter, hissing into his ear. 'Now.' He felt the guy slacken off. 'Now, like I said, I'm a cop. What's your name?'

'James Preston.' His voice was choked with aggression. Or with

Cullen's arms. Either way, he wasn't giving up. 'It's nothing to do with me!'

'What isn't?'

'Whatever you're here about.'

'Need a word about Alex Melrose.'

'Not talking about that prick.'

~

THE BACK ROOM WAS FILLED WITH CRATES AND BARRELS, BLEACH NOT quite masking the stench of stale beer. Easily the least glamorous place Cullen had ever been in, and one of the coldest.

James Preston sat on an upturned crate, his nostrils flaring as he hugged his arms around his skinny body. His sweaty T-shirt making even Cullen shiver just from looking at it. 'What the hell's going on?' Spoken through clenched teeth.

'Like I told you at the door, I just want a word with you about Alex Melrose.'

'Useless prick.'

'Go on?'

'You saw that shambles just now, right?' Preston waved a hand at the closed metal door back to the bar, then refolded his arms. 'Prick's gone off the radar. Couldn't bother himself to turn up to our last two practices. We had to choose between cancelling this or playing as a three-piece. In the end...' He shivered, then started rubbing his upper arms. 'In the end we sorted out our songs so they could be done without his guitar. You saw that last one, I had to drum so Kegsy could play the guitar part. Shambles, man, shambles.' A bitter shake of the head, his lips twisting up. 'Sod it, man, they're better for it. We're better off without that prick.' He pressed his lips together, the colour draining quickly. 'Alex is dead to me.'

Cullen narrowed his eyes at him. 'He's dead full stop.'

'What?' Preston's mouth hung open.

Cullen let him sit in silence, let the icy cold motivate him to be a bit more transparent in his answers.

Instead, McCrea sniffed. 'Found Mr Melrose's body on Thursday. Stabbed. Murdered.'

Preston stopped rubbing his arms. 'Shite.'

'You didn't know?' McCrea raised his eyebrows. 'Now, isn't that interesting? No, wait, that's the wrong word.' He scratched his bald head. 'I meant, isn't that completely unbelievable?'

Preston glared at him. 'You honestly think we'd have played a gig if we'd known? This is a disgrace.'

'What is?'

'Why has it taken you so long to tell us? We were his *friends*.'

'You just called him a prick.'

Preston seethed in silence.

Cullen cleared his throat, his breath frosting in the cold air. 'Look, you can help us by answering our questions about Mr Melrose. We do that here, or we take you down to the station. You choose.'

'What's to say?' Preston got off the crate and started pacing back and forth. 'Alex was a good lad, you know? He was a bit older than the rest of us. Been in another band before and done well, so he used his contacts and that.'

'What kind of contacts?'

'Got us gigs. Found this label who was interested in signing us.'

'Was there anything in the offing?'

Preston stopped pacing to glower at Cullen. 'You know, that police station must be warmer than this.'

Cullen didn't even shake his head. Just kept staring. 'The sooner you answer, the sooner you leave. Was there anything in the offing?'

Preston went back to pacing. 'Nothing concrete. It's all just stuff Alex was putting together. Some boy in London sounded like he wanted to put out a single. A thousand copies in pink vinyl, that kind of thing.'

Cullen played it through. Sounded low key.

Preston froze. 'Hold on, do you think someone killed him?'

McCrea rolled his eyes. 'What part of "he was stabbed to death" is hard to follow?'

'Christ.'

'Try to keep up, eh? Did Mr Melrose ever go missing before?'

'Yeah, no, I mean, not turning up wasn't an isolated incident, but he never stood us up for a gig before. You got any idea who... killed him?' He looked from McCrea to Cullen, then shivered like someone had walked over his grave. 'You can't think I did it? Christ, I'm a pacifist.'

'Really?' Cullen raised his eyebrows. 'The sort of pacifist who swings guitar cases at cops?'

'What do you want to know?'

'Where were you on Wednesday night?'

Preston sneered at him. 'I was in Newcastle. Plenty of witnesses for that. Me and Kegsy did an open mic night at the uni. Audience of about a hundred. Playing another show there next Tuesday. Trying to get people interested.'

Cullen glanced at McCrea and caught a reflection of his own suspicion cooling off. *Time to change tack.* 'Did Mr Melrose ever talk much about his time in Edinburgh?'

'Never.' Preston hissed a plume of breath. 'Why?'

Cullen gave the answer a slow, thoughtful nod. 'What about his last band?'

'No, I mean, yes, he talked about tours and gigs and stuff. Never anything specific. Said they fell apart when he split up with his girlfriend.'

Cullen raised his eyebrows again, but this time in genuine surprise. 'Is that what he told you?'

'Isn't it true?'

Cullen held up a copy of the morning's *Sunday Mail*, a photo of James Strang inset at the top right. 'That's the singer of his old band. He disappeared nineteen months ago. Found his body last week too.'

'Jesus.' Preston darted forwards and snatched it out of Cullen's hand. 'You think it's connected?'

'Was Mr Melrose a drug user?'

Preston shrugged. 'He didn't really mention it.'

'Didn't really or didn't at all?'

'No comment.'

McCrea took a threatening step towards him.

Preston took a step back and wrapped his arms tight around his scrawny torso. 'He liked to smoke, aye.'

'Cannabis? Heroin? Crack?'

'Cannabis, man. Jesus, what do you take him for? There's no way I'd be in a band with a smackhead.'

MrCrea stabbed a finger at him, stopping just short of

touching Preston. 'Melrose had traces of heroin in his blood-stream, meaning he didn't just smoke weed. Are you trying to tell me you didn't know?'

'Alex would get us a half Q of resin every so often, that's all.' Preston was staring at the concrete floor. 'That's not dealing, is it?'

'Did he sell you the drugs?'

Preston became even smaller. 'Look, I like a smoke, man. Helps me sleep. That's it.'

Cullen came at him from the side. 'Where did he work?'

Preston sniffed. 'He didn't.'

'Was he a dealer?'

'No way, man. No way.'

'Did he bring any friends to gigs?'

'Never. Kept himself to himself.'

Cullen pulled back a little to avoid losing him, gestured for McCrea to do the same. 'Thank you. You mentioned a girlfriend. What was her name?'

'There was a lassie, aye.' Preston looked up at Cullen like a grovelling dog, grateful that the shouting had stopped. 'Used to come to our gigs. Wee Rowan, her name. Lived down in Pollokshaws.'

'A current girlfriend?'

'Aye? What did you think I meant?'

22

'SHE'S IN THAT ONE THERE.' McCREA NODDED OUT OF THE DRIVER'S window as he pulled up on the kerb and killed the engine. The residential street was lined either side with rows of identical three-storey buildings in muddy concrete breezeblocks. 'Top floor.'

Cullen looked from the building to McCrea. 'How did you–'

'Magic.' McCrea tapped his nose. 'Police ju-ju.'

'You had a first name and an area, and you managed to come up with a full name and an address. How?'

'Connections.' McCrea got out of the car.

Cullen hurried after him, catching him at the front door and blocking his way. 'Come on, tell me.'

'Kiss my hairy arse.' McCrea leaned to the side, trying to reach the buzzer panel.

Cullen sidestepped him and leaned against it with his back.

McCrea sighed. 'You are such a persistent arsehole.'

'It's one of my many endearing qualities. Now tell me.'

'Fine, I texted a boy I know in the Serious and Organised Crime Agency. Their drugs database covers all their leads and sources and God knows what else. Rowan plus Pollokshaws gave us this. Voila.'

'Right, so it's probably not her, then.'

'Piss off.' McCrea's lips twitched. 'Alex Melrose is a known associate of hers.'

'Wait? He's known to SOCA?' Cullen glared at McCrea. 'Why am I only hearing about this now?'

'Weren't you listening to all that shite Preston was saying? Melrose was dealing to his bandmates. And not just them, either. Boy didn't have a job, but lives in a nice part of the West End? Even a bedsit there should have been way out of his league.' McCrea stared at him for a good few seconds, then nodded at the front door. 'Now, can I get us inside?'

~

ROWAN TAYLOR STOOD IN HER DOORWAY, A TOTAL MESS, HER EYES struggling to stay open let alone focus on her visitors. She was thin, almost skeletal-looking with her shaved head, skinny black jeans and baggy grey jumper pulled up to the elbows. Didn't say anything, just raised an eyebrow.

'DS Damian McCrea of Strathclyde Police.' McCrea held up his warrant card, then jerked his head at Cullen. 'This is DS Scott Cullen of Lothian & Borders. We need to speak to you about Alex Melrose.'

Rowan reached for the door. 'I've nothing to say to you or *Alex.*'

'That's just as well.' McCrea gave her his cold smile. 'The boy's dead.'

Her eyes bulged. 'What?'

Cullen gave a discreet cough. 'We're investigating his murder. We'd like to come inside, if that's okay.'

Rowan blinked hard at him, then turned around to lead into the flat. 'I need the toilet.' She shuffled off, scratching at the raw track marks on her arms.

McCrea followed her, then positioned himself outside the bathroom door as she closed it behind her. 'Don't be too long in there.'

Cullen left him to it and took a look around the rest of the flat. More rooms than Melrose's bedsit, but a stripped mattress in the middle of the living room was the only furniture. He headed back to McCrea's sentry post outside the bathroom. 'I keep expecting Sick Boy or Spud to show up.'

'Wrong city.' McCrea chapped on the door. 'Come on, Rowan,

we're waiting.' He shook his head. 'You know *Trainspotting* was filmed through here, right?'

'Is that because Glasgow's still as much of a dump as Leith in the Eighties?'

McCrea laughed.

The bathroom door slid open and Rowan looked out with red eyes. 'What's so funny?'

'Nothing.'

Rowan turned her back on him and padded along the corridor to the living room, her bare feet slapping on the wooden floorboards. She knelt on the mattress like she was meditating.

McCrea leaned against the door. 'Alex Melrose is your boyfriend, right?'

'Not really.' Rowan sighed, her gaze locked on the naked mattress and its many stains. 'Just a fuck buddy. Helped me get my gear.'

McCrea twisted his lips into a sneer. 'You let him have sex with you in exchange for drugs?'

Rowan closed her eyes. 'It's nothing like that.'

'So money changed hands?'

She looked out of the window at the overcast sky. 'I'm not telling you nothing.'

McCrea shook his head, a sad look in his eyes. 'There are programmes you can go on to get off drugs, you know?'

'I'm fine as it is.' She hesitated. 'Thanks for asking, though.'

McCrea approached her, taking slow steps. 'Rowan, someone stabbed Alex at his flat on Wednesday night.'

Her eyes shot up to meet his. She held his gaze for a few seconds, then she crumpled as though made of paper. 'Stabbed?'

'Afraid so. Do you suspect anyone?'

'No, of course not. I don't know anyone who would...'

McCrea stood over her, waiting for her to finish the sentence, but she kept her silence. 'Anyone who would've lent him money and wanted it back? Maybe his dealer?'

She gave him a shrug.

McCrea glanced at Cullen.

Big mistake. Cullen took over, getting in Rowan's eyeline. 'Did Alex smoke heroin?'

A frown dug into Rowan's pale forehead. 'A bit.'

'What about injecting?'

'Not so much.'

'But he did?'

'Hmm.' Rowan hugged her knees tight. 'Can't believe he's gone.'

Cullen crouched in front of her, just off the mattress. 'Listen, Rowan, if you want us to find his killer, you have to tell us where he got his drugs.'

Rowan reared back like he'd slapped her in the face. 'You think I'm stupid?' She sneered at Cullen. 'He's not really dead, is he? You're just playing me.'

McCrea shook his head. 'He's dead, Rowan. His body's in the mortuary. Going to be there for a while. Months, until who killed him's defence team can do their own post mortem.' He stepped over to the window, shrouded by the dull light. 'I spoke to his mum on Friday. She's keen to bury her son but I just can't let her do that, not until we close this case. I mean, she can do a memorial service, but it's not the same, is it? She wants to know her boy's safe.'

Rowan wiped a tear from her cheek. 'I don't know anything.'

McCrea huffed a deep sigh. 'Really?'

'He just got my drugs, that's it.'

'In exchange for sex, right?'

Her eyes strayed back to the mattress, but she kept her mouth shut. She glanced up at McCrea. 'Fair enough, that's how it worked.'

'I see it now.' McCrea nodded like he was getting the full picture now. 'Started like that, but he got you to have sex with other men in exchange for more drugs, right?'

'No!' Rowan threw her hands up. 'It was nothing like that. Alex was a good guy.'

'A good drug dealer more like, and I've yet to meet one of those.' McCrea folded his arms across his chest. 'Who did he score from?'

Rowan looked away again. 'I don't know.'

Cullen got up and walked across to stand behind Rowan, bang in the middle of McCrea's line of sight.

McCrea shot him a wink.

What the hell does that mean? Is he doing this on purpose, switching back and forth between good cop and bad cop to–

'Rowan, let me tell you a wee story.' McCrea stretched out, pressing his palms against the sides of the dormer window. 'We went to see this band at lunchtime, in town. They were good, you know? Well, I enjoyed them, my colleague here didn't. Anyway, the singer told us that Mr Melrose had a girlfriend.'

Rowan avoided McCrea's penetrating stare.

'All he gave us was a first name and a district of this fair city. The area was Pollokshaws. The name?'

'Rowan.' Her voice was a whisper.

'That's right.' McCrea crouched down in front of her. 'You're very well known to the authorities, Rowan. I just need a name and a location and...' He clicked his fingers. The sharp sound echoed round the bare room. 'Luckily for you, you're of peripheral interest to us, and it can stay that way.' He paused. 'But if you don't help us with our inquiries, and if I was to report that back to my pals who provided me with your ID, well... I suspect they'd have to add a prostitution charge to your file.'

Rowan winced. 'I'm not a whore.'

McCrea looked down at her for a moment, then winked at Cullen. 'Do you believe her, Sergeant?'

Cullen folded his arms, uncomfortable with the power play. The woman was clearly vulnerable and McCrea was hitting her with one cheap shot after another.

Instead of taking Cullen's negative body language as a cue to quit the games, McCrea doubled down on it. He stepped forward and knelt on the edge of the mattress, his knee creaking. 'My colleague from Edinburgh doesn't know how we operate through here. He'd be perfectly happy to hand you over to SOCA. I'm afraid those boys and girls will listen to an eastie beastie more than we do around here.' He leaned in close, his voice a wet hiss. 'If you speak to me, Rowan, I can protect you. It has to be now.'

She mouthed something Cullen couldn't hear.

'Shug McArthur?' McCrea straightened back up with a beaming smile. 'Big Shug?'

Rowan looked up at him, her voice a broken rasp. 'That's what Alex told me. But please don't tell Shug. *Please?*'

'Course.' McCrea patted her on the arm, ignoring her pleading. 'And do yourself a favour. Get off the drugs.'

∽

Cullen looked over at McCrea on the driver's seat, a smug grin on his face. 'Eastie beastie?'

'I had to improvise.' McCrea was texting, not even bothering to look at Cullen as he lied to him.

'Who are you texting?'

'Eh?' McCrea looked up at him, pretending to have missed the question. 'I'm texting a mate.' He pocketed his phone. 'I'm thinking this *is* drug related, after all. Silly bastard probably took on a debt too many, used it to get his end away with her upstairs but forgot to pay for the gear.'

Cullen unclenched his fists and let go of his frustration with a long sigh. *He's not worth it.*

'Would need to be a fairly big debt to be killed over, mind.' McCrea clicked his tongue a few times. 'Or our friend Alex pissed off someone big.'

'Like this Shug McArthur?'

'Kid's got form, aye.'

Cullen looked back out at the block of flats. 'What about the lack of forensics at the crime scene?'

'I told you.' McCrea went back to typing on his phone. 'It's a pro job. Wipe everything clean, leave no loose ends.'

'Wouldn't a pro make it look like suicide? Or frame someone else? Maybe Rowan?'

McCrea finished his text, sent it and stuck the phone in his pocket. Then he looked across at Cullen. 'Well, perhaps this pro left just enough dangling threads to let us poor cops get tangled up in them. Pros know how we work. They know that soon enough the case will wither on the vine.'

Cullen could see the logic. 'Yesterday, we spoke to Melrose's ex-girlfriend in Edinburgh. Another junkie. She was smacked out of her head, with a troupe of kids she's lucky to still have.'

'Boy's clearly got a type, eh?'

Cullen shook his head. 'So, what now? Speak to this Shug?'

McCrea barked out a laugh. 'You don't do intelligence through east, do you?' He waved a hand around the rough street. 'Shug is the big man around here. We can't just waltz along and interrogate him about some dead junkie.'

Cullen blew out his cheeks, then let the breath go slowly. He closed his eyes and leaned back against the headrest. 'Drive the car into the next wall, will you? Must be better than this, right?'

Another laugh. 'I'm growing to quite like you.'

~

'CAREFUL, SUNDANCE, IF THE WIND CHANGES YOUR FACE'LL STAY LIKE that, and then we're all scubbed.'

Cullen looked up at Bain. 'That joke is so old, I'm surprised you went anywhere near it. Don't you prefer them young? Young and from Thailand?'

The muscles in Bain's jaws tightened, but he kept his temper in check. For once. 'Sundance, this is a drugs murder. Pure and simple.'

'Tangentially, maybe, but I take it you're not seriously interested in what I think?'

Bain made a cry-baby gesture. 'Poor Sundance.'

Cullen shook his head. 'Look, I don't buy it. There's no drug angle to our case, right?'

'Right. My drug killing isn't connected to your stabbing.'

'Why am I here, then?'

'Just playing games, Sundance.' Bain looked down at him with a coy smile. 'You're here on the off-chance that this is all one case. Which it's not. But if it is, I'm taking over your side.' He leaned in close. 'I'm like the mountains, Sundance. I've got a hell of a long memory. That bitch Cargill took over my case six months ago, and that's not happening again. Ever. So I'm giving her a taste of her own medicine.'

Smashing.

'So, what do you want me to do?'

Bain snorted. 'We're raiding Big Shug's house and McCrea needs cannon fodder. Suit up.'

23

CULLEN SQUIRMED IN THE PASSENGER SEAT AS MCCREA DROVE. IN the back, two other male detectives muttered to each other, excluding him from their strategy talk. Cullen turned to McCrea, mouthing the words to a Deacon Blue song playing on the radio. 'What's the plan?'

McCrea turned the radio down. 'You do what I tell you.' He paused. 'But like I said, I kind of like you, so I'll be polite and say please when I tell you what to do.' He smirked, but Cullen didn't give him anything in return. 'We've got a uniform squad plus six detectives and an Armed Response Unit in place.' He pulled a set of photographs out of his inside pocket and tossed them onto Cullen's lap.

A4 black-and-white shots of a shifty-looking man in a tracksuit.

'Who's this?'

McCrea grinned. 'Should've read the file on Big Shug.'

The pair on the back seat laughed. 'Good one, Damo.'

If you'd given me the file, you prick...

Cullen took the ridicule like a big boy and carried on with a smile. 'Just so we're clear, this is Big Shug?'

'Jesus H Christ.' McCrea pulled up at the lights, shaking his head. He reached across and tapped the photo. 'This is Malky

Nicholls. He's been messing with us for years but somehow he's always kept himself clean.'

'I thought you were after Big Shug.'

'And we're never going to get Shug.' McCrea pulled off again, sighing at the heavy traffic. 'In the name of the wee man...'

'How does Nicholls fit into all of this?'

McCrea hit the indicator as if swatting a fly, then swung through a roundabout. 'I sent a couple of lads to speak to Marta Owenson in Edinburgh this morning.'

'You should've got that approved by us.'

'Yeah, yeah, whatever.' McCrea cruised down a potholed road into a residential area chock-a-block with run-down grey tenements. 'She told my lads that Nicholls is Melrose's supplier. Has been for years. Used to meet him at Harthill services. Money left in a bag on the forecourt, drugs left in trap two with an "Out of Order" sign on the front.' He reached into his pocket again and passed Cullen a sheet of paper. Like the bloody TARDIS in there. 'Gaffer got our warrant approved while we were on the way back from Rowan's.'

Cullen checked it out. Malcolm Robert Nicholls. An address with a G42 postcode. Through in Edinburgh, that'd be out in East Lothian, twenty-five miles away. Glasgow just sprawled and sprawled. 'You'd better hope Nicholls doesn't have any bent coppers in his pocket.'

McCrea snorted. 'Nicholls is small fry. Medicates kids with a bit of weed, then gives them a wee taste of heroin before referring them on to one of Big Shug's specialists. Now he's fingered in a murder, he's gubbed.' He turned right, into a car park encircled by six multi-storey tower blocks. A row of souped-up boy racer cars and white vans. He pulled up and waited for the Escort's engine to die. 'Ready to rumble?'

'Chomping at the bit.'

McCrea was out first, leading Cullen and his two gimps over to a gunmetal grey van. Eight bored officers stood around, yawning, backs resting on a brick wall daubed in layers of graffiti.

McCrea clapped his hands. 'Gather round, lads!' He pointed at something off to his right. 'Malky Nicholls stays in the next street over. You should all know what he looks like.' He held up the photo anyway. 'We've got a constable dressed as a postman outside

Malky's house to give you a reference point. Think of it like a setter and we're hunters. Cullen and I are serial alpha.' He nodded at the two who had driven out with them. 'Willie and Jim, you're serial beta. Alpha will be entering the house. Beta will establish a perimeter. It's like a jungle in there so be wily, alright?'

Grunts and nods.

McCrea divided the other cops into support units of four each, like picking sides at playground football. 'Alphas, we're waiting for serial beta to establish the perimeter before we enter the address. Then it's the usual protocol. Switch on your Airwaves and listen to each other.' He clapped his hands again. 'Alright, move out.'

They left the police van behind and jogged down the street. Cullen's heart pounded as they cut through a narrow vennel on to a long road lined with two opposing blocks of colourless flats, six storeys high. Exterior corridors ran down the length of the buildings' narrow balconies connecting the front doors. Going by the layout of the doors, the flats would be maisonettes, two floors with only one way in or out.

The fake postie was on the third floor, twitchy eyes monitoring the street below. Two uniformed officers ran ahead of the pack, sprinting to the far end of the building. One stood guard outside, while the other darted into the main stairwell. Another two covered the bottom of the steps.

Cullen followed McCrea to the nearest staircase, two officers behind him, and they thumped up, snapping out batons as they went. McCrea led out onto the open corridor.

The postie stood outside a door two-thirds of the way along. Reinforced steel, a drug dealer's best friend.

A burly officer nudged past Cullen, hefting a battering ram the size and shape of a metal fence post. He got in position and swung the ram back, then held it cocked and gave a thumbs up.

McCrea stepped next to him and hammered his fist on the door. 'Mr Nicholls? Open up! It's the police!'

Silence.

Then a muffled voice shouted back. 'Piss off!'

McCrea took a deep breath. 'Mr Nicholls, we have a search warrant!'

'He's not here!'

McCrea stepped aside. 'Bugger this.' He nodded at the officer with the battering ram. 'Open it up.'

The guy fired the ram against the door, metal smashing on metal with a deafening CRACK. Cullen felt the thud in his chest. The door held, though. Unfazed, the officer swung the ram back and hit the door again, and again, and again, working up a ferocious force. Still the door held. Then the hinges creaked. One last go and the door burst open, falling back into the flat.

People spilled into the corridor, scrawny bodies everywhere, blocking the way, trying to scramble out of the front door, shouted insults flying through the air like shrapnel.

Cullen was first in, ducking and weaving, following the burnt-marshmallow stench of cooked heroin through what felt like a zombie apocalypse.

A familiar tracksuit charged up the staircase at the rear of the flat.

'Nicholls! Stop!' Cullen dropped his shoulder and bulldozed through a skinny guy with razor blades for cheekbones, shouting back over his shoulder. 'Nicholls is heading upstairs!'

'Help! Cullen!'

Cullen spun around.

McCrea was wielding his baton at three men who had boxed him into a corner. He caught one on the side of his thigh, hard enough to drop him to his knees with a guttural groan. But another brandished a flick knife.

Cullen charged at him, barrelling into his back and pinning his arms to his sides in a tight rugby tackle. He drove the guy's forehead into the wall, then stepped back to catch his knife hand on the rebound. He twisted it up his back, making him double over with a high-pitched squeal. As the blade dropped to the floor, a uniformed officer took the third man down with a hit to the back of the neck. The guy's eyes rolled back in his head — he was knocked out before he hit the ground.

Cullen tightened an arm bar on his thug. 'Are we clear?'

McCrea passed his assailant to another uniform, who crouched down, knee between the guy's shoulder blades. Breathing hard, he scanned the corridor, still heaving with panicked energy, but nobody was posing any danger. He nodded. 'All clear.'

Cullen snapped cuffs on the disarmed knifeman's wrists and pushed him over to another uniform. He shouted over the mayhem of uniforms struggling to control a flat full of wired junkies. 'Upstairs!' He took the steps one at a time, keeping a tight grip on his baton, craning his neck to scan the upper level as he climbed. The landing was deserted and eerily quiet above the clamour of the drug den. Three doors, all closed.

Cullen pointed two fingers at his eyes, then one finger at each of them.

McCrea took point as Cullen checked.

First, a bedroom. Empty.

Second, a bedroom. The floor was covered in bare mattresses, like Rowan's living room but spread out.

Finally, a bathroom, empty.

McCrea frowned at Cullen, hands on hips. 'He can't have just disappeared. You definitely saw him?'

'Definitely.' Cullen threw another glance in the first bedroom. The master, by the looks of the built-in wardrobe in the corner. 'In here.' He crossed the beige carpet and looked inside. Empty. Just the carpet giving way to bare floorboards at the edges. 'He can't have just disappeared into smoke.' He walked over to the windows. Painted shut. Besides, it was a long drop.

'What's that?' McCrea was in the cupboard, screwing his eyes up at something.

Cullen joined him.

McCrea shone a torch up at the ceiling. A recessed panel in the top corner. 'A hatch.' He bit his lip. 'Was he armed?'

'I didn't see him that well.'

McCrea went back to the top of the stairs and shouted down. 'I need two uniforms up here.'

Footsteps thumped up the steps and two burly uniforms clattered into the room, both out of breath but grinning.

McCrea pointed at the one who had swung the battering ram. 'You're going to lift Cullen up.'

Cullen shook his head. 'I'm not going up there.'

McCrea passed the torch to Cullen. 'I'm ordering you.'

'And I'm refusing.'

'I'm serious.'

Cullen clenched his teeth, then extended his baton again. He wanted to snap it against McCrea's neck.

The uniform joined Cullen in the wardrobe, then went down on one knee. Cullen stood in front of him, then balanced himself against the walls as he was lifted up. The uniform swayed with the effort. Cullen took a deep breath and pushed the hatch up.

He didn't need the torch. Whatever was up there was glowing, a pale-blue light.

He stuck his baton up through the hole. And waited for the gunshot.

Nothing.

So he hauled himself up in one swift movement and looked around.

The long room looked like it might cover an entire floor of the building, lit up by double-rows of strip lights shining down on raised beds lined with tinfoil. Like a snooker hall, only the lamps weren't illuminating bright green baize. Same colour, different thrill. Cannabis plants.

Cullen twisted around to call down to McCrea. 'He's got a hydroponics setup.'

Something moved in the corner of his eye. A boot smashed into his face. He dropped through the hatch like a dead weight, collapsing his carrier underneath him. They landed hard in the confined space of the wardrobe. Cullen took a knee in the stomach that made him retch. Blood leaked through his clenched teeth as he tried to steady his breathing. 'Someone's up there.'

McCrea grabbed his arm, yanked him back on his feet. 'Is he armed?'

'No idea.' Cullen wiped his sleeve across his bloody mouth. 'But I'm not going back up.'

McCrea pulled his Airwave from his pocket and shouted into the clunky police radio. 'McCrea to armed response squad: get up here now!'

Cullen leaned back against the wall, dizzy, and watched it all happen.

Four guys with guns charged into the room and took up position under the hatch. Shouted warnings. One vaulted another up, his pistol drawn. Then he disappeared and other was hefted up.

24

BAIN SAT AT HIS DESK WITH A DEEP FROWN AS HE TWO-FINGER TYPED on his laptop. He glanced up, then down again. He did a double-take and exploded with laughter. 'What the hell happened to you, Sundance?'

Cullen blinked to snap out of his daze. 'I caught your suspect. Found a nice little hydroponics factory to boot.'

'Same boot you got clattered with?'

Cullen touched two fingertips to his swollen lip. 'Aye, very good.'

McCrea perched on the edge of his boss's desk, like a little dancing monkey waiting for the organ grinder to start playing. 'We got Nicholls and a shitload of known users and pushers shooting up in his flat. Thing is, we had to use the ARU to get Nicholls.'

Bain flinched, like he knew a bollocking was heading his way. 'Was Nicholls armed?'

McCrea looked over at Cullen, like he was trying to deflect the blame. 'It was Cullen here who—'

'He hit me.' Cullen dabbed at his lip again. 'I didn't know if he was armed or not.'

Bain closed his eyes. 'Was he armed or not?'

McCrea fumbled around for a better answer, eventually waving a hand at the bruise spreading across Cullen's jaw. 'We've got a shitload of drugs in there. He couldn't flush that many kilos of smack. But he assaulted a police officer.'

'Good work, Sergeant.' Bain leaned back to stretch. 'Are you sure he killed Melrose?'

McCrea nodded. 'One hundred per cent.'

'Excellent.' Bain went back to his laptop.

'You've been burnt by this—'

'Careful.' Bain stabbed a finger at Cullen, then gave him a thin-lipped smile. 'We know Nicholls was Melrose's dealer, and Melrose owed him a ton of money.'

'And that's it?'

Bain shifted his attention to McCrea. 'A word in private, Sergeant.' He got up and led McCrea out of the room.

Cullen slumped down in Bain's desk chair and picked at the frayed fabric on one of the armrests.

Fed up with this shite.

His shite. Bain, always trying to pull a little trick.

He sneezed and gasped.

Felt like that kick had broken his nose.

Bain sauntered back into the room, followed by McCrea and half of their squad. Bain stopped, spreading his arms wide to hold back the troops. 'Careful, we've got a biological hazard on our hands.' He pointed at Cullen, his familiar shark grin on his face. 'You shouldn't be here if you've got a cold, Sundance. Don't want you spreading your germs. And you with your sickness record...'

Cullen clenched his teeth. 'It's just some dust from your manky old furniture into my nose.' He took a few deep breaths to calm his nerves, then got to his feet. 'Anyway, looks like you've got every-thing under control here now, so I'm heading back through to Edinburgh.'

'No, you're not, Sundance. You're my resource.' Bain grinned at him with more malice than a boot to the face. 'You're seconded through here.'

'You've got your guy. He's not our guy, meaning my second-ment's over.' Cullen gave a mock salute and walked off. 'See you later.'

Bain grabbed his arm. 'You're staying here, Sundance.'

Cullen barged past and walked towards the door.

'Stop! That's a direct order!' Bain grabbed his arm, desperate like a spurned lover. 'You're staying here. You and McCrea are interviewing Malky.'

'No.'

'No?' Bain looked at Cullen, long and hard, then he nodded. 'Alright. You've made your bed, so I'm going to make you lie in the wet patch.'

'Classy.'

Bain snarled at him. 'This is nothing compared to what I'm willing to do to mess you up.'

Cullen looked him up and down, then laughed. 'You're lucky to still have a job, you bullying wanker.'

'Excuse me?'

'You heard.' Cullen pointed at his throbbing jaw. 'This is on you. I got kicked in the face because of your botched raid. You ordered me to be cannon fodder. Now get out of my way. This secondment is over.'

Bain glared up at him, sticking his chin out like he was asking to get punched. 'You can't speak to a superior officer like that.'

'After the way you treat people, you honestly think you can make something of this?'

Bain pulled his lips back over his clenched teeth. 'Insubordination is written all over your record. Always trying to be the hero, heading off on some wild goose chase, and now those chickens are coming home to roost. And don't you dare point out that's a mixed metaphor, you smartarse. I'm going to take your shitty attitude and shove it so far up your a—'

A knock on the door.

Bain spun around.

Methven was squinting at him. 'Sorry I'm early, Brian. Just wanted a quick word before the session, but I seem to have caught you in the middle of something.' He paused. 'Everything alright here?'

Bain forced a saccharine smile on his flushed face. 'All hunky-dory, Col.'

Methven nodded slowly. 'I just need a second to brief Cullen about the headway we've made through in Edinburgh.'

'Be my guest, Col.'

Methven led Cullen out and set off down the corridor. 'Well?'

'I don't think our case is drug-related. Bain thinks his is, but I'm not so sure.'

'I know how slapdash he can be.' Methven sighed. 'I've been clearing up after him for the last year. I'm meeting with DI Bain and DCI Graham in ten minutes. Anything I should know?'

'I meant to text you but I never got round to it.'

Methven dismissed the excuse with a wave. 'Anything I should know?'

'Strathclyde are now suggesting the deaths of Strang and Melrose aren't related. Hasn't stopped Bain trying to use the potential link as a way to take over our case. And he's trying to bust open a drug ring.'

Methven nodded and went back into the incident room. 'Brian, where are we on the Melrose murder?'

Bain looked at him, cool, calm, the consummate professional. 'Alex Melrose appears to have been killed over drug money. We've got strong leads and a suspect to interview, which I believe is more than you can say about your lot.' He said it with a smile, but there was no humour in it. 'We know Melrose was a heroin user. Smoking and injecting. Found his works in his flat, along with enough Bacofoil to roast a hundred turkeys.'

Methven glanced at Cullen. 'What's your assessment?'

Cullen shrugged. 'According to his fuck buddy — her words — he was procuring drugs in exchange for sex.'

'Scott's right.' McCrea wandered over, hands in pockets. 'Melrose sourced his drugs from Hugh McArthur, aka Big Shug. Malky Nicholls is Melrose's direct supplier. The boy owed him a fortune according to my sources in SOCA.'

A frown flickered on Methven's forehead. 'Do you agree, Sergeant?'

Cullen frowned. 'First I'm hearing about this debt.'

'Rowan mentioned it.'

'Aye, I mean your SOCA information.'

'Gaffer, we should send this clown back to Edinburgh. He can't keep up with our case.'

Bain nodded.

McCrea smiled at Methven. 'Sorry, don't think we've met. DS Damian McCrea.'

Methven shook his hand but didn't look at him. He focused on Bain. 'Brian, I've seen you go for an easy collar a few times.'

Bain let out a sigh. 'I don't like your tone there, Col.'

'Persuade me we're dealing with mere coincidences here. Because Strang and Melrose weren't just in the same band, they were also murdered in much the same way. Aren't you ignoring rather a lot here to make this about some drug deal gone sour?'

Bain tutted at him. 'Col, DS McCrea has a contact in SOCA. They have a link between Nicholls and Melrose. Supplier-dealer relationship, big debt owed. Stands to reason.'

Methven nodded. 'Well, I think we should keep this open while you investigate.'

Bain sighed. 'Stop looking for ghosts, Col. There's no serial killer here.'

'And I'll be happy to agree, just as soon as you've managed to explain away those coincidences to my satisfaction.'

'We're dealing with two separate cases.' Another sigh from Bain. 'But if you insist they're one and the same, maybe you could be the winner here. You could work for me. Might learn a few things.'

'You arrogant—'

'Gents, sorry I'm late.' DCI Keith Graham marched into the incident room. Shifty, short, his mid-blue suit hanging off him. 'Now, where are we?'

'Just a second.' Methven nodded at Cullen to follow him out to the corridor again. He closed the door. 'Has he got anything?'

'Not that I know of.'

'Good, I've had enough of Bain's poison to last a lifetime.' Methven paused, nodding to himself. 'Right, I'll head back in there and make sure the two cases are not treated as one, given your certainty that there is no connection.'

'That's not—'

'Thanks for your efforts, Sergeant.' Methven opened the door again. 'I appreciate you've been putting in the hours, so go home, spend some time with your better half and get an early night. Big day tomorrow.'

'Sir, that's—'

Methven walked into Bain's office and closed the door in his face.

25

Sharon sat at the breakfast bar in her dressing gown, eating ice cream straight from the tub.

Cullen walked up to kiss her, but she pulled away. 'I'm not after your ice cream.'

'I don't want you to catch this cold.' She transferred the tub to her other hand. 'And I've had to fend off one greedy ginger.'

The cat jumped onto the counter and started sniffing the air.

Sharon looked at both of her gingers with a coquettish smile, then dug the spoon back into the golden swirls of ice cream. 'Mmf mmmmf little bugger.'

Cullen snatched the spoon out of her hand and stole a mouthful. 'Ah, that's nice.'

Sharon snatched the spoon back and used it to fend him off. 'Not tonight, Scott. I feel bleurgh.'

Cullen grinned. 'Don't worry, I just want your ice cream. Really need that after today.'

'Why? Was Glasgow that—'

'Bleurgh.' He patted his swollen lips. 'Glasgow was bleurgh.'

'Bain?'

'Bain. Tried to avoid him and largely succeeded. Got stuck with his new understudy, though. Two steps forward, one step back. Thought we were making some headway on the case, until I got kicked in the face.'

'That's not how that expression goes. It's kicked in the teeth or
—' She fell silent as she focused on his busted lip in the low light.
'Oh, Jesus.' She reached for his lip but pulled back as she saw him
flinch. 'Shit, sorry. Is it sore?'

'Of course not. I'm a man.' He gave her a hard look, then
laughed. 'No, it hurts like a bastard, but the sacrifice paid off. We
made a few arrests, so Bain got what he wanted and I got to go
home.'

'Like murder arrests?'

'Nah, drugs.'

Sharon thought it over with another spoonful of ice cream.
'Dope?'

Cullen looked at her. 'No, heroin.'

'I know that look.' Sharon pointed the spoon at him. 'You're
suspicious, right?'

Cullen scowled. 'I've worked for Bain too long.'

'Did you tell Methven?'

'Didn't have to. He came through to Glasgow and got the same
impression. When I left, he was getting ready for a big ding-dong
with Bain and his boss.' He pulled out his phone and checked for
messages. Nothing from Methven, so he texted:

WELL? WHAT HAPPENED?

'Scott?'

'Mm?'

Sharon cocked her head to the side. 'You just drifted off there.'

'Oh. No word from Crystal. He's still having kittens about there
being a serial killer on the loose. Two members of a band
murdered, so he's put the other two in a safehouse, but now Bain's
stuck his size three in the door, trying to muscle in on our turf
before Monday. Shit, tomorrow.' Another deep sigh. 'It always
comes down to politics, doesn't it?'

'Crystal knows Strathclyde are going to run Police Scotland.'

Cullen sighed. 'Don't say that... Having Bain as a boss again?
One day of that was enough. Normally, I'd have just let him get on
with making an arse of himself, but...'

Sharon arched an eyebrow. 'But?'

'Well, I still think our cases are related, but now we're in the
middle of a turf war with Bain, instead of trying to solve a double
murder together.'

'So, what are you going to do?'

Cullen shrugged. 'I'm certain our case isn't drug related, so until Bain or his boys dig up something to prove me wrong, I'm keeping well away from him and that bloody city.'

Sharon nodded slowly, her eyes glazing over as she poked around in the tub. Looked like her thoughts were flatlining.

Cullen sat next to her and rubbed her back. 'You okay?'

'Mm?'

'Eating ice cream in your dressing gown?'

She blinked a few times, then spooned the last of it out of the tub and ate it. 'It's just the dregs of that flu. And ice cream makes me feel good.' She got up, chucked her spoon in the sink and stuffed the tub in the bin underneath, then looked at him with tired eyes. 'Big day tomorrow.'

'Only if you're feeling better.'

'Yes, nurse.' Sharon yawned. 'But it's a big day whether I'm there or not.'

Cullen smiled. 'Pedantic to the last breath, eh? Or aren't you that sick after all? What have you been up to anyway? You can't have cuddled the cat all day.'

'Not *all* day.' She reached down to stroke Fluffy. 'Chantal came round for a bit at lunchtime. Poor thing. While you've been annoying Bain in Glasgow, she's been at the mercy of Methven.'

Cullen folded his arms over his chest. 'I would've thought she'd be relieved to be rid of me for a day.'

Sharon leaned against the counter and humoured him with a smile, then. 'She's not that bad, Scott. I think she's just on edge about the restructure, like the rest of us.'

'Wait, Chantal thinks she'll get a DS position? Really?'

'What, don't you think she's good enough?'

'More like she's not ready. Not that I'm the best judge, but she's... Well, she's green, isn't she?'

'And you're not?'

Cullen caught Sharon's pointed look and glanced away. 'Okay, so I've worked out an hour of what you were doing. What else?'

'Chantal was here for more than an hour, but don't tell Crystal.'

'As if. Besides, it's me she should be worried about.'

Sharon dismissed him with a snort. 'Get over yourself, Scott.

She's more worried about her romantic life than about her ginger boss.'

'Ha ha.'

'She's joined a dating website.'

'Her?'

Sharon frowned as she stuck the kettle on, speaking with her back to him. 'What do you mean her? Think she's too pretty to be single?'

Cullen got up and wrapped Sharon in a big hug, nuzzling her neck with his stubble until she relaxed into him and started laughing. 'Jealousy doesn't suit you. Of course I can see that Chantal's pretty, but she's not my type. I'm just surprised she's still single. Didn't she get off with Budgie on a night out?'

'Don't be crass. Really makes me wonder if you're ready for...' Sharon pulled away from Cullen's embrace and stepped away from him.

'Ready for what?'

She fixed him with a stare that made him fear for the worst. 'Scott, I think I'm pregnant.'

26

'PREGNANT?' CULLEN STARED AT HER, MOUTH HANGING OPEN. FELT like he was falling right through the kitchen floor. 'I don't like children.'

She looked at him as if that was the worst thing anyone had ever said.

He raised a hand. 'I mean, I don't like other people's children. You... You said you *think* you're pregnant. How pregnant are you?'

She took a deep breath, her eyes never leaving his. 'I'm like two thirds pregnant, Scott. What the hell do you think? I think I'm one hundred percent up the duff.'

Cullen's brain broke down. He couldn't process it.

Pregnant? How can she be pregnant?

How can I become a father?

How can this be happening?

How—

'Scott, we need to discuss this.'

'How?'

She sighed. 'I talk to you and you listen. You talk to me and I listen.'

'No, I mean, how can you be pregnant? We're normally so careful.'

'It must have been in the bath at Budgie's birthday party.'

'But we used—'

'Did we? You were so pissed you tried to do it in the sink first.'

'You remember that?'

'Yeah, but only that. The rest is a bit of a blur.'

'Shit.' Cullen rubbed his face, furious with himself. 'Shit, shit, shit. I can't remember.'

Sharon shook her head at him. 'How the hell can we—'

The kettle started rumbling as it neared the boil and she turned to plonk tea bags into mugs. She stared into space as the kettle clicked off, then poured the water into the mugs. As she turned again to take the milk out of the fridge, Cullen stared at her belly, mystified, nervous, scared of what was growing in there.

My child.

My stupidity.

My drunken stupidity.

Sharon mashed the teabags in the cup. 'What are you thinking, Scott?'

'Is why you've been avoiding...'

Sharon blushed but her tiny nod confirmed it. 'I've felt so crap over the last few days. I've also started getting morning sickness and...'

'Have you... done a test?'

Sharon dumped her teabag in the bin and blew on her tea, her eyes obscured by steam. 'Chantal brought a couple of home tester kits round.'

'*She* knows?'

'Well, if she doesn't then she *really* isn't ready for that promotion.' Sharon laughed. But it died on her lips. 'I need to get it confirmed by a doctor, but three brands of pregnancy kit all agree.'

Cullen took a shallow breath, his mind in chaos.

She stared back into the depths of her teacup. 'You'd make a good dad, you know?'

'Me? I really don't think so...' He felt a frown flicker across his forehead, then saw that Sharon had seen it too and tried to relax his face. Tried and failed. 'I don't know, Sharon. I just don't know. When I'm ready, maybe.'

'This is a huge thing, Scott.' She reached for his hand, her palm hot from the teacup. 'You need time to get used to it. We both do.'

He bit his lip. 'Did you plan this?'

'What? Of course not.' She pulled her hand back like he'd bitten it. 'Christ, do you *honestly* think I'm capable of that?'

Cullen looked away from her disgusted look. 'No. Sorry. I don't know why I said it.'

Her eyes were huge with anger. 'Are you?'

'Genuinely. I take it back.'

'Which bit?'

'All of it. Accusing you of getting pregnant on purpose. I'm sorry. I wouldn't have said that if I'd thought about it properly. I'm just confused, just not thinking straight, just...'

Sharon shook her head, rage still etched deep on her hard face. 'Never accuse me of anything like that again. Okay?'

'Don't get pregnant again.' Cullen held his hands up. 'That was a joke. Instinct. Sorry.' He rubbed his face. 'I'm sorry. I'm all over the place. I'm not taking this at all well. And... And I just don't know what to think.'

The anger on her face gave way to disappointment, less intense but just as deep. 'So, what do you want to do?'

He looked at her, trying his best to hold her steady gaze, and failing yet again. 'How are you so calm?'

'I'm not.' She kept looking at him, her gaze not wavering for a second. 'One of us has to hold it together. Whatever we do about this, we need to think about it carefully.'

He frowned at her. 'What do you mean, whatever we do?'

'Well.' She averted her gaze. 'We don't have to keep it.'

The room went quiet. Just the sound of the blood rushing in his ears.

Cullen shook his head. 'Your mum will never be alright with you having an—'

Sharon cut him off with a sharp look. 'Scott, this isn't about my bloody mother. And anyway, I spoke to her and she was okay ab—'

'What?' Cullen felt a surge of anger. 'Chantal? Your mum? Why am I the last to know about you being pregnant?'

'For God's sake, Scott, this isn't just about you, you know? In fact, it's hardly about you at all. You got your usual thirty seconds of fun. The rest is for me to suffer.' She counted it off on her fingers. 'Morning sickness, weight gain, stretch marks, back ache, swollen ankles, constant fatigue, mood swings, labour pains, anxiety attacks, sleep deprivation. A year's maternity leave with a little monster who won't let me sleep, then listen to you moaning about shit and...' She stuck her fists on her hips and stared at him. 'And that's if it all goes well. I'm *scared*, Scott. I don't know what to do.'

'That's probably the first time ever.' He reached for her hand and wrapped it in his. 'How pregnant are you?'

'One hundred per cent.'

'I meant the amount of time.'

'Six weeks, I think.' She looked down at her flat stomach. 'I'll have to see the doctor to confirm it.'

'Okay, so we've still got plenty of time to decide.'

'I guess so.' Sharon withdrew her hand to reach for her cup and took a sip.

Cullen watched her, wondering if it was an excuse to get away from him, a displacement activity betraying emotional withdrawal.

Get over yourself.

He gave her a reassuring smile. 'I just want to make sure we're doing the right thing. Having children is a huge step. It needs to be planned, not something that just happens to you. I've seen too many people stumble into parenthood when they weren't ready. When they're lucky, it only breaks their relationship. When they're not, it messes up their lives, and their kids...'

Sharon frowned. 'You don't think we're ready?'

'I don't know. I'm lucky my parents still love each other, warts and all. Countless friends of mine can't say the same. It can be worse to stay together for the sake of the kids, heaping a miserable family life on them, not to mention watching a marriage fail right in front of them.' He started pacing the kitchen. 'What do you want to do?'

She sat down with her tea, staring at the floor. 'I think I might like to keep it.'

He nodded to himself, still going back and forth. 'Okay, I mean, I'm not against it. We just need to think it through.'

'We need to *talk* it through.' She gave him a stern look that made him stop his pacing. 'Together.'

'Agreed, but I need space to think first. I need to go to my cave like in that book you made me read.'

She looked at him for a few seconds, then sighed. 'That's the only thing you took away from it?'

Cullen shrugged. 'This is... massive.' He went back to his pacing. 'My head's full of shit right now. I'm working with bloody Bain again and by this time tomorrow I might have lost my job. I need perspective.'

'Well, I need to talk about it.'

'So talk.' Cullen caught his breath. 'I need to cook. You've got a captive audience.' He marched to the sink and refilled the kettle. 'Pasta okay?'

'Again?'

'You're eating for two and all that.'

She folded her arms. 'Can you be serious about this for once?'

'I'm trying.' He got a tub of fresh pasta from the fridge, then started gathering sauce ingredients from the cupboard — herbs, onions, garlic, passata. He peeled the onion and started chopping. He heard a sniff and glanced around.

Sharon was crying.

Cullen dropped the knife, returned to her side and held her tight. 'Listen, we'll be fine. We'll talk it all through, okay?'

'Okay.' She wiped a tear away, dropping her gaze to her hands as she started kneading them. 'I love you, Scott.'

He lifted her chin. 'I love you, too.' He kissed her, tasting her salty tears, feeling terrible and wonderful at once. 'You know, whatever we end up doing, I'd rather go through this with you than anyone else. Okay?'

The cat bleated from under the kitchen counter, his yellow eyes staring up at him. They both laughed.

'Seriously, though.' Cullen took her back in his arms. 'We'll work it out together if we're keeping this or not. And I'm not talking about the cat.'

She cuddled into him, a smile in her voice. 'He's staying.'

∿

BUT WHEN IT CAME TO SIT DOWN AND EAT, CULLEN COULDN'T SAY A thing. He pushed his empty plate away and yawned. 'I'm going to bed.'

She didn't say anything, didn't look at him. Just poked at her half-eaten food.

'Sorry it was only pasta, again.'

'Mm.'

He frowned. 'Look, is there something else bothering you?'

She gave him a withering look. 'Well, you're not talking about it.'

'I know.' He got up and put his plate in the sink.

She didn't even blink, just stabbed a fork into a pasta parcel.

'Night.' Cullen felt her piercing eyes on his back all the way to the bedroom.

Should've shut the kitchen door.

Should've not been a bloody idiot.

When will I ever learn?

He took off his clothes and dumped them on the chair, got into bed and closed his eyes.

And it was all he could think about.

The little thing growing inside Sharon. Our mistake. My mistake. Our responsibility.

It'll change my life, that's for sure. But how?

Will it force me to grow up, settle down, take on responsibility, or just break me?

Break us?

Break our child before he or she's even born?

I just don't know.

DAY 4

Monday

27

Alex Melrose's corpse lay on the floor of his tiny bedsit.

Marta Owenson and her army of children danced around it like they were performing some shamanic ritual, wailing like banshees, their faces contorted into feral grimaces.

Then Marta leaned over her ex-boyfriend, her hand dead still as she dipped a paintbrush deep into his open chest, then dripped a blood trail across the floor as she walked over to the wall, where she wrote big, bright red words on the wall.

But Cullen couldn't read them.

Cullen jerked awake, panting hard, his sweat-soaked T-shirt clinging to his heaving chest.

Just a dream.

Bloody hell.

He took a deep breath and looked around the bedroom, waiting for his eyes to adjust to the dusky half-light filtering in through a gap in the curtains.

Sharon snored next to him.

He couldn't remember her coming to bed. And he didn't want to lie back down and slip back into that dream.

As the grey morning crept in through the window, he knew he should've talked to Sharon last night, rather than withdraw into himself.

He watched her sleeping next to him.

Soon there'll be three of us in this bed.

Shit, there already is.

He shivered.

Whether it was that thought or the cold, he didn't know.

He glanced at the clock. 5:42. Hardly any sleep at all, but it'd have to do.

Time to get up.

Shower. Shave. Then judgment day.

～

A PALE SUN HURRIED UP THE SKY IN THE EAST AND CULLEN STEERED his Golf into Leith Walk station's underground car park, yawning his head off. He almost clipped the wing mirror on the gate.

Probably should've walked.

He descended into the deep shadows of the garage and pulled to a stop.

A few spaces down from him, Buxton was peeling stickers off the panda cars, removing the words 'Lothian & Borders', leaving only 'Police'. Hunter was working his way along the line from the opposite end.

Cullen got out with another yawn. 'What the hell are you pair up to?'

'Crystal's orders.' Buxton ripped away at another sticker and it came off with a snap, loud and reverberating under the low concrete ceiling. 'Outsourcing this would cost a packet, so he's got constables doing this kind of shit.'

Cullen shook his head. 'So who's doing your day job — the cleaners?'

Hunter raised an eyebrow at him. 'They'd do a better job than you.'

Buxton laughed. 'Same goes for you and me, mate. We're all stuck in first gear on this murder case.' He started on the next sticker. 'A couple of my mates on the beat are unstitching the lettering from their uniforms.'

Hunter grunted. 'Don't know what's worse.' He stared down at himself. Part of a sticker had got stuck to his hairy forearms. He tried to ease it off. 'I got called in at five to do *this*.' He gave up and tore it off.

Buxton watched him for a moment, then turned back to Cullen. 'Got any gossip?'

'The jungle drums are dead. You?'

'My mate in the Met reckons Turnbull is getting a DCS gig down there.'

Cullen frowned. 'He's just a DCI, though, right?'

'Just passing on what I hear.' Buxton walked to the car next to Hunter and picked away at the sticker, frowned at it as though he could read the future in the curled-up plastic. 'What'll happen to you, Scott?'

'Hopefully, I'll get made a full DS.' Cullen sounded about as uncertain as he felt. 'God knows they need more.'

Hunter sighed as he started at the other end of the sticker from Buxton. 'Aye, I've heard whispers to that effect.'

'Really?' Cullen cleared his throat to get rid of the catch in his voice. 'Who's the source?'

'Methven was blabbering away on his mobile as he came in. Don't think he saw me. Saying you're a shoo-in for one of them.'

Butterflies started flapping deep in Cullen's gut. 'Did he say anything else?'

'Aye, he asked what the date was.'

Cullen checked his watch. 'First of April.'

Hunter look him up and down, a cold sneer on his face. 'April Fool.'

'You...' Cullen clenched his fists. 'Craig, I thought we were mates. What the hell did I do to you?'

'You don't know?'

'No!'

'Then you're the wanker.'

Cullen threw his hands out wide. 'That's it? That's all you've got?'

Hunter just stared at him, unblinking. After a moment, he turned away and walked off. 'You're not worth getting pissed off about.'

Cullen watched him go. 'What the hell's got into him?'

'He's a funny one, mate.' Buxton shrugged. 'Doesn't exactly open up, does he?'

~

CULLEN TOOK HIS BOWL OF MUESLI FROM THE CANTEEN COUNTER and walked away.

Methven sat in the far corner, spooning cereal into his mouth like there was no tomorrow.

Cullen headed across and sat down next to him, getting a grunt by way of greeting. 'Morning, sir. I tried calling you.'

Methven spoke with his mouth full of bran flake mush. 'I know.'

'So why didn't you answer?'

He gave Cullen the side-eye as he took a sip of tea. 'Because I'm extremely busy.'

Cullen coughed into his hand. 'I can see that.'

'Excuse me? Did you say something, Sergeant?'

'No, sir. Why are Buxton and Hunter peeling stickers off squad cars?'

'Because I asked them to do it. Nice to know that at least someone listens to me around here.'

Cullen frowned. 'What do you mean?'

'Exactly what I said.'

Cullen gave him a tight smile. 'How did it go with Bain and Graham last night?'

'We agreed that these are not necessarily linked cases. All we have is both victims knew each other.'

'And their killers used a similar MO.'

'Indeed. But it fits into their drugs case.'

'So, you're giving up on the serial killer angle?'

'Not as such.' Methven glanced away. 'Mr Johnson and Ms Williamson are back home, but they're checking in on an hourly basis.'

Cullen nodded. 'So how do we progress?'

'Sergeant, that's asking me how to do your job.' Methven gave him a harsh look, then took another spoonful of cereal. 'We've got a dead body in an old close, no forensics and no promising leads. We're giving it another couple of days, then marking it as a cold case.'

Cullen swallowed a spoonful of muesli. 'You were all over the serial killer angle at the weekend.'

'Which we've contained. Unless we find evidence to the contrary, we assume the message of the wall was just a sick joke.'

Wish you'd been this reasonable on Friday.

Methven got up. 'Please be on time for the briefing.' He strutted through the busy canteen and, through the chatter, his heels struck the floor with a loud dick, dick, dick.

Cullen took a deep breath and returned to his muesli.

Chantal left the servery and walked through the canteen carrying her breakfast roll. Hunter followed and took one look at Cullen before leaving the room.

Chantal took a seat across from him. 'Morning, boss.'

'Morning.' Cullen leaned over his cereal to make sure nobody else heard his question. 'Any idea what's up with Hunter?'

'None.' Chantal shrugged. 'He seems nice enough, only acts like that around you. He was a squaddie, though, so maybe you trigger PTSD or something.'

'You shouldn't joke about that.'

'You shouldn't dismiss it as a joke.' She bit into a breakfast roll, pretending not to notice his discomfort. 'Heard you had an eventful day yesterday.'

'The drugs raid? Aye, they got a good haul. Hope they get a conviction as well.'

'I meant you telling Bain to go fuck himself.'

'What?'

Chantal gave him a pointed look. 'Bain's been on the phone to anyone who'll listen. Methven took me aside on his way out of the canteen just now. He's raging. Bain wants you on a disciplinary.'

Cullen rubbed his eyes. 'You really think *Bain* has the balls to do someone over *swearing*?'

Chantal shook her head. 'Not the point. A, he's your superior. B, you have an authority problem, and everybody knows it. C, he's Strathclyde now, so his complaint will fall on sympathetic ears.'

Cullen frowned at her. 'I'm not that bad, am I?'

'I'm not the one you need to convince, but you don't half make it difficult for yourself sometimes.' Chantal laughed. 'Great entertainment for the rest of us, though.'

'Glad to be of service.'

'You back in Glasgow today?'

Cullen sighed. 'No. Can't tell whether I'm coming or going.'

'You coming is the problem, especially when the condom bursts.'

'Jesus Christ!' Cullen glanced around. Nobody seemed to have heard. He lowered his voice to a hiss. 'Keep that under wraps, okay?'

Chantal winked at him. She laughed at his blush. 'Can't imagine you as a father.'

'Me neither, which is why I'm so scared.'

'Let me guess, you're being a wanker to Sharon about it?'

'Obviously.' Cullen wanted to talk to someone about it, but not to her. Never her. 'You get anywhere yesterday?'

'I'm bored shitless. Looking for people, taking statements? This case is a waste of time. If Methven didn't have such a hard-on for the serial killer...'

'He seems to have lost that overnight.'

'I heard. Typical.' She sighed. 'But no, we got nothing from the friends or his flatmates. Same story with the useless slacker idiots he worked with. Actually, I tell a lie.' She got out her notebook. 'One of his flatmates told me that Strang was seeing a psycho-analyst.'

'Seriously?'

'Not that it did him much good. Slashing his chest open with beer bottles?' Chantal took a hearty bite out of her roll. 'Anyway, I tried getting hold of the doc, but he's out of his office. It was the weekend, I suppose. I meant to chase him this morning, but Crys-tal's had me unpicking thread from uniforms.' She closed her notebook and got up. 'Anyway, back to Crystal's sweat shop.'

'Give me the psychoanalyst's number, I'll give him a ring.'

She sat down and tapped something into her phone. Cullen's phone thrummed in his pocket. 'Good luck with that. See you.' She walked off through the canteen, yawning into her fist.

Cullen checked his phone. Dr Dougal Simpson, and a landline number. He tapped the number and put the phone to his ear.

A male voice, but Cullen couldn't make out any words, so he stuck his finger in his other ear to block out the noise in the canteen. 'Hello? Dr Simpson? Can you hear me? This is—'

Dr Simpson talked right over him, like he hadn't said anything.

Then it beeped.

Voicemail.

Cullen sighed. 'Dr Simpson, it's Detective Sergeant Scott

Cullen of Lothian and— of Police Scotland. Can you give me a call back, please? It's an urgent matter. Thanks. My number is—'

∿

CULLEN ENTERED THE INCIDENT ROOM JUST AS THE GENERAL chatter died down. Not the last in, with a few other latecomers still finding their seats in the rows of plastic chairs. He spotted an empty one in the third row, between Sharon and Buxton. He sat down with a smile, but only Buxton returned it.

Sharon just locked eyes with him, the kind of intense glare that meant they really needed to talk, then looked to the front of the room.

DCI Jim Turnbull stepped up to the lectern and cleared his throat. The current Lothian & Borders logo filled the screen behind him. 'Can I have your attention, please?'

A few chairs squeaked as the last arrivals hastily sat down.

Then silence.

'Morning. Right now, briefings such as this are happening all over Scotland. This is a bright new dawn for our proud service.' Turnbull clicked a button on the small device in his hand, making the logo shrink down and move to the top of the screen. Below, two arrows appeared that pointed at two boxes. 'The first big change is that Edinburgh City is now separate from Lothians & Borders in the Police Scotland East structure. This will create more local accountability as well as national consistency.' He pressed his clicker again.

The boxes made way for a slide entitled "The Future of CID".

'As you probably know, CID will be split into two sections as well, meaning that some of you will transition to the first-response CID units in the Divisional areas, such as the new Edinburgh City. Most officers in this room, however, will move into the central Major Investigation Team structure in SCD.' He clicked and the screen went blank. He sighed, then pointed his clicker behind him and clicked again.

A headline appeared – Edinburgh MIT Structure.

A line of text flew in from the left to sit atop an empty space, sure to be filled with the department's new hierarchy.

Cullen had to read the text twice to take it in. Detective Superintendent Jim Turnbull. His breath caught in his throat.

If Turnbull could be promoted...

Turnbull nodded to himself. 'I will head up the Edinburgh MIT, reporting to DCS Carolyn Soutar, head of the nationwide MITs. The bulk of officers from the Torphichen Street, St Leonard's and Leith Walk CID units will merge under my command. Longer term, we will be based either here in Leith Walk or up in St Leonard's, but we will occupy desk space in both locations until the strategic decision has been made.' He pressed his clicker again. 'My number two will be DCI Alison Cargill.'

Another promotion.

Cullen's pulse rose in time with the next click.

More text appeared, this time three names.

'In this new structure, there will be four DIs. One position has yet to be filled.' Another click. 'For now, DCI Pieters will take the grade of DI alongside DI Alistair Davenport from St Leonard's and DI Colin Methven from Leith Walk. Congratulations, Colin.'

Sharon swore under her breath, loud enough for Cullen to hear.

Turnbull pressed the clicker again and a name flew in to the row below the DIs. 'At the DS level, Bryan Holdsworth continues in the Admin Officer role.' Another click and Sharon's name appeared. 'Sharon McNeill will report to DI Pieters.'

More swearing from Cullen's left.

Turnbull ploughed on. 'Brian McMann from St Leonard's will report to DI Davenport.' Another click. 'DS McKern will be taking early retirement, effective immediately, to be replaced by DS Bill Lamb from East Lothian. Welcome to the team, Bill. And finally, the fourth new DS will be—'

He clicked but nothing happened.

Cullen closed his eyes, trying to calm his breathing.

Click.

He opened them just in time to see the last name appear on the screen...

'Chantal Jain will assume an Acting DS tenure.'

What the hell?

Cullen sat there, mouth hanging open. He looked from the screen to Sharon then back at the screen.

My extra stripe has gone.

And no-one bothered to brief me in advance.

Turnbull pressed his clicker again. 'Now, moving on to the DCs.'

The screen changed, and another diagram with downward pointing arrows appeared to illustrate which DSs would be in charge of which DCs.

Cullen saw his own name, directly underneath Chantal Jain.

28

IDIOT.

You actually thought they awarded results.

Cullen barely took in the rest of Turnbull's presentation, the droning voice as much background noise as the rain splashing the window.

All that talk of wanting a promotion, deserving a promotion, DS this and DS that. Should've kept your bloody mouth shut. Now you've let them humiliate you, and publicly.

Cullen looked around the room, trying to see who was pointing at him and laughing.

But it was worse. Way worse.

They ignored him, their eyes focused on the screen.

Why did you think your tenure was going to be made permanent? You kept talking up your style, how you get results without toeing the line.

You're not a cowboy, you're a clown, and soon they'll all be laughing at you when Chantal has you—

Turnbull cut into his thoughts, looking directly at him. 'I appreciate this will be a disappointment for some of you.' He looked around the room.

So much for being a rising star.

Turnbull continued as if he had read Cullen's thoughts. 'In times of austerity like this, we can't all climb to the top at once. All

I ask is you behave in a professional manner. These are straitened times and, while you may not be among those who got their stripes on this occasion, you are all valued for the contributions you make to our wonderful service.' His eyes settled on Cullen again. 'Dismissed.'

Cullen sat back, watching Turnbull walk out of the room, followed by Methven rushing out of the door after his new master.

Cullen got up, ready to follow.

Ready to punch him or scream at him or—

Sharon grabbed his arm. 'We need to talk.'

CULLEN FOLLOWED HER THROUGH THE NOW-DESERTED CANTEEN TO A table at the far end. And just sat down, still raging. Everything inside was way past boiling point.

'You okay, Scott?'

Cullen frowned at her. 'I'm very far from okay.'

'So talk.'

Cullen picked up a half-torn sachet of brown sugar and, ever so slowly, continued the tear, dusting the table top with sugar. 'I'm reporting to Chantal now? Seriously?'

'She's a good cop.'

'She's—' Cullen raised his hands in apology. 'Fine, maybe she is. What do I know? Maybe Chantal deserves that promotion.' He poured the rest of the sugar out and sifted it into a pattern. 'What I'm so pissed off about is that nobody told me.' He looked up at her, his left nostril twitching, tears stinging his eyes. 'I worked for Methven for six months. Six months. I've spoken to that tit every five minutes over the last four days working on this stupid case. Put up with Bain and Glasgow and him...' He went back to rearranging the sugar. 'I'm just a name on a spreadsheet to him.'

'Scott, I saw the draft list for the DS promotions last week, and your name was on it.'

'Really?' Cullen sat back, mouth hanging open. 'You didn't think to tell me?'

'Not my place.'

'You're my girlfriend and it's not your place?'

'I thought it'd be a nice surprise.' Sharon sighed. 'Look, we had a meeting, the DIs and a few others. Cargill, Methven, Davenport, they were all arguing. The room was baking and I started feeling sick and... Well, I know why that is now. I went to the toilet and threw up. When I was gone, they must've swapped you as DS for Chantal as Acting DS. Saves them pension money.'

'So Methven knew?' Cullen clenched his jaw and brushed the sugar away onto the floor. 'That wanker.' He took a deep breath. 'This is what I get for all the hours I've put in? For letting others take the credit for my results?'

'Scott, there'll be other opportunities.' She reached out and stroked his tense arm. 'I'm sure they just had their hands full with the enforced retirements and making sure the St Leonard's officers were properly briefed to avoid formal grievances with HR.'

'So what? They didn't have two spare minutes to brief me? Didn't brief you, either, did they?'

'They did.'

'What?'

She looked away, her lips twitching. 'Turnbull called me yesterday while you were through in Glasgow. He was very courteous. Said he regretted that I couldn't get the DI position just yet. I was going to tell you, but...'

'The baby. Right.' Cullen took another deep breath.

When it rains, it pours. And when it pours, the rain burns.

'What did he mean, "just yet"?'

'There's a job application process starting—'

'There you are!' Chantal barged in, smiling bright and broad. 'DS Jain... Can't believe it.' Her smile faded as she caught Cullen's glower. 'Oh, you heard Craig Hunter got booted back to uniform?'

Cullen looked right through her.

Great. He'll be even more pissed off now.

When it pours, it floods.

Chantal switched the smile back on and looked at Sharon. 'You'll still get that final DI vacancy, won't you?

Sharon shrugged. 'I doubt it. It'll be someone Methven or Cargill wants to bring in from another force or someone from Strathclyde to watch over us...'

Sharon tried to explain the situation to Chantal, but he wasn't listening. He just wanted Chantal to piss off so he could speak to Sharon.

Just want to apologise for the way I reacted last night, for clamming up like that.

You daft arsehole. She loves you, you love her. Why did having a child freak you out?

Because I'm not ready?

If you believed in a higher power, you'd see this as a test, a chance for personal growth and development.

But I don't believe in any higher power.

You've changed so much since you've been a full DC. Surely you can get past this as well, right?

Wrong. I've changed so little when it comes to my bloody ego. That row with Bain yesterday proves it. My head said stop, but my ego said go, go, go. And now it's telling me to run.

He caught himself.

You're in your thirties. Act like a man.

No, you need to grow up. Forget all about that promotion until it's in black and white. Until then, look on the bright side — almost six months as Acting DS will look good on your record, like detachments to murder cases helped you become a detective.

And remember why you do this job. Not to make more money, but to make a difference to a society in which you'll soon have to raise a child.

'—Bill Lamb.' Chantal pouted, snapping Cullen out of his thoughts. 'Weird seeing him again, eh?'

Sharon seemed as surprised as Cullen. 'Was Bill at the briefing just now?'

'Yeah, stood at the back, him and Stuart Murray.' Chantal wolf-whistled. 'The things I'd let Murray do to me...' She bit her lip and flicked up an eyebrow.

'Shag him and blank him?' Buxton joined them at the table, his shoulders sagging.

Chantal pressed her lips together, focusing on her coffee cup. She looked back up with a warm smile. Buxton gave a dark sigh. So Chantal smiled at Sharon. 'Crystal Methven did well out of the restructure, didn't he?'

'Of course he did.' Buxton was looking right at Cullen, but he wasn't broadcasting any clear message. 'He's a sneaky two eight six eight.'

'A what?'

Buxton grinned at her. The boy couldn't hold a grudge for

long. 'Type it on your phone. Like an old Nokia or something. Doesn't work with an iPhone.'

Chantal pretended to hold a mobile in her hand and fiddled with her fingers, her eyes going out of focus. 'Aunt?'

'Methven isn't a sneaky aunt.'

She burst into laughter. 'Oh, that's good.'

'Chantal, that's your boss.' Sharon gave her a stern look. 'You're a DS now, so you need to start acting like one.'

Chantal choked her laughter with a cough. 'Right, sorry.'

Cullen folded his arms, making eye contact with Sharon before looking at the rest of them again. 'Can you guys give us a minute?'

Chantal tutted at him. 'That's no way to treat *your* new boss, is it?'

'Want me to call you a two eight six eight?'

She raised to standing and leaned across the table. 'Briefing in ten minutes. Okay, Scott?' Then to Buxton. 'Simon?'

'Right.' Buxton set off before her.

Cullen just nodded, then watched them leave. 'I should've expected it, really, but whatever. We've got much more important things to think about now.' He turned to her. 'So, how do you feel about–'

'DS McNeill, I need to brief you.' Turnbull now, standing in the middle of the deserted room, Lamb just behind him.

Sharon got up. 'Sorry, Scott. Later.'

Cullen nodded, but she wasn't paying attention to him anymore. He kept staring at the doorway, even after they had all disappeared. Just kept staring into empty space. The smell of frying onions started overpowering the cleaning chemicals.

If only my head was that easy to clear.

With a hefty sigh, he got up to go to his first briefing with his new boss. Chantal Jain. Jesus wept.

His phone started ringing. *That'll be her, chasing me up already.* He pulled out his mobile. ID. Didn't recognise the number, but he took the call anyway. 'Morning.'

'Hello, is that Sergeant Cullen?' Sounded like a flustered old man.

'Yes, this is Detective Ser... This is Scott Cullen. How can I help?'

'Oh, I'm glad I caught you. It's Dr Dougal Simpson.'

'Right?'

'I'm James Strang's psychoanalyst? You asked for a call back? Said it was urgent?' The guy sounded as if he had won the lottery – an urgent request for help in a police matter.

'Right, right.' Cullen reached into his coat pocket for his notebook and pen. 'Thanks for getting back to me. I need to—'

'Can I just stop you there. I'm happy to help with James's situation, but patient confidentiality will prohibit me from discussing his personal situation.'

'We found his body on Thursday.'

'... Oh.' Simpson's bluster dwindled to a whisper. 'He was murdered?'

'I'm afraid it appears that way, yes.'

'Oh my. Where had he been all that time?'

'Does that mean you'll help?'

'I... yes, I mean... I'll see what I can do. What can I do?'

'Can I drop by today?'

Simpson hesitated, sounded like he was driving. 'Normally, yes, but listen, I'm en route to the airport. Flying to a conference in Copenhagen today. Can we do this another time?'

'This is pretty urgent, I'm afraid. We're dealing with the possibility that Mr Strang was killed by a serial killer.'

You wanker — playing Methven's card.

Simpson sighed. 'Oh my.'

'Look, we can do this formally later, but if there's anyone that Mr Strang spoke to who he might—'

'Listen, I stopped seeing Mr Strang about eighteen months ago. He just stopped coming. I billed him for missed appointments, of course, but they were never paid. At least I've solved that mystery...' He chuckled.

'So you saw Mr Strang right up to his death.'

'It would appear to be that way, yes. Oh look at that bloody traffic. I suppose I can tell you a fair amount of stuff. James discussed the stress of being a musician. Of touring, recording, constantly on the hunt.'

'Did he mention a record deal?'

'There was a fair amount of bile devoted to finding a record label, yes.'

'What about losing that label?'

'Well, quite. For a moment, James had— Oh heavens, I'll never get there in time. James had hope. He felt positive about the future.'

'And then the record deal was cancelled?'

'Right. He never mentioned why. Just vented spleen over the actuality of it.'

'Did he mention any women in his life?'

Simpson hesitated. 'He did, yes.'

'Did he mention this girlfriend by name?'

'Listen, Sergeant, I'm really not comfortable revealing—'

'Was her name Jane?'

Simpson took a deep breath, then exhaled noisily into the phone. 'Seeing as how you already know about her. Yes, Jane. The trouble is, James had slight issues with reality. I was never convinced that Jane was real, but you seem to know her, so—'

'What do you mean, she wasn't real?'

'Are you a fan of Lou Reed?'

'Not really.'

'Well, James was. In Lou Reed's work, you'll notice that a certain Jane is a recurrent motif with him. Both in his solo work and in the Velvet Underground. "Sweet Jane", for instance. Of course, such thematic preoccupations are by no means rarities. Just think of the mystified gypsy theme in Bruce Springsteen's oeuvre, so perhaps Jane was just a muse to James, a figure of a more ethereal—'

'Do you think she existed?'

Simpson cleared his throat. 'Well, as I was about to explain, that may not be important here, but was is certainly important is that James believed she did.' He sighed, either at having to explain his theory to an educational subordinate, or at the traffic. 'James mainly talked to me about his difficult childhood and how it left him with serious unresolved tensions between his ego and his unconscious.' Another sigh. 'Let me make this simple for you. James grew up in an environment that didn't make room for his sensitive nature, which later in life led to anger issues. As you should know, anger in females tends to turn inwards and manifest itself in the form of depression. In males it tends to express itself through violence.'

'And in Mr Strang's case?'

'His GP prescribed anti-depressants and I was comfortable with the type and the dosage. Until he went back to self-harming. And to seeking out violence with strangers in pubs and bars. Occasionally even with specific individuals.'

'Ever mention any names?'

'We used codenames, I'm afraid. Like with Jane. It allowed James a personal distance from his issues, which in turn allowed him greater analytical self-reflexivity.'

Cullen gripped his phone tight, getting impatient. 'Could you be more specific?'

'Yes, I, um, I suppose you're right. James mainly talked about people in his home town, people he grew up with, people he hated with every fibre of his being, first and foremost a certain Black Matt.'

'Black Matt?'

'That's the codename, yes. I understand that he bullied James at school. A traumatic formative experience. There was more of a similar nature later in his life. I encouraged him to make peace internally, but James wanted to confront him.'

'And did he?'

'I'm afraid I don't know.'

'Do you know if he talked to anyone else about this?'

'He talked about his family, but I don't think he spoke to them much. He never mentioned any friends, other than his band members.'

'He didn't give you any names for any friends?'

'Codenames. It didn't matter to me who specifically he was talking about, but it mattered gravely to James that he explored the issues he had with them.'

'So, he never gave you any clues who this Black Ma—'

'Hang on!' Simpson clicked his teeth. 'Yes, I completely forgot. After Mr Strang stopped attending, I got a call from a young gentleman, flatmate of his. I believe his name was Aidan. Can't remember the surname. He said that James had moved out about three months before he disappeared. Can that be right?'

News to me, but wouldn't his mother have mentioned that? Great, I'll have to call her next and—

'Sergeant? I hope that helps. I really must go now. Bye.'

Click, and Cullen was holding a dead phone in his hand.

～

CULLEN WALKED INTO THE INCIDENT ROOM, BUT CHANTAL'S DESK
was empty. He got out his phone and called her. As he listened to
the ringtone, he scanned across her desk, spotting a print-out
covered in scribbles.

The list of flatmates.

He killed the call and picked up the sheet.

What did Dr Simpson say this flatmate of Strang's was called?
Aidan something? Nothing, nothing, nothing, there. Full name and
phone number. Aidan Collins.

He typed the number into his mobile and put the sheet back
down.

Chantal walked in through the door, yawning into a coffee.

He froze. But she hadn't seen him yet, too busy talking to some
guy in uniform, her eyes all over him. Jesus, it was Craig Hunter.
Arms bulging out of the T-shirt.

Cullen turned around, head down, and went deeper into the
room, circling round the desks until he ducked through the doorway. He charged down the corridor, weaving his way through a
pair of plainclothes detectives he didn't recognise, then hit dial.

'Hello?' Male voice, forty-a-day deep.

'Is that Aidan?'

'Who are you?'

'Detective Constable Scott Cullen. Aidan Collins?'

'Uh, aye. What do you want?'

'You're a friend of James Strang, right?'

'No, well, yeah, but friend is a strong word. We shared a flat,
but he was a nightmare. Noisy, drunk, aggressive, you name it, so
we kicked him out and got someone else in. Why? What's he done
now?'

'When was this?'

'About two years back?'

'Did you stay in touch?'

'No, well, yeah. Sorry, this is a bit confusing. We didn't stay in
touch and I've no idea where he went, but we kept getting his mail,
so I returned to sender.'

'Did he leave a forwarding address?'

'Just his parents, but I'm not writing on every letter. Just stuck "no longer at this address". I mean, I'm not a postie, am I?'

'I don't know. Are you?'

'Very funny.' Didn't sound like he was laughing. 'What's he done anyway?'

'Anyone come looking for him?'

'No?'

'What about anyone called Simpson.'

'Oh, the shrink? Aye, well, few months after Jimi moved out, these bills turned up. Then red ones. Turns out he was seeing a shrink. Imagine how bad he'd be if he hadn't?'

'So Mr Simpson came to your door?'

'Aye, just pitched up. Reckoned he was due about a grand in unpaid bills. But I had no idea where Jimi went.'

'Okay, Mr Collins. Thanks for your time.'

Cullen hung up and stared at the door opposite.

Another dead end. That guy knows nothing.

His phone rang in his hand. He checked the screen and groaned. 'Hi, Chantal. How can I help?'

'By being on time for my first briefing. We're waiting for you.'

29

CULLEN STOPPED OUTSIDE THE MEETING ROOM AND WAITED, listening. Quiet. Meant they were waiting for him. He opened the door and stepped through like he was on time.

Chantal stood in the far corner, her dark brown skin almost black against the stark white of the projector screen behind her. Her new team sat in front of her – Simon Buxton and an empty chair. She greeted Cullen with an arched eyebrow. 'Nice of you to join us, Constable.'

Cullen sat, gripping the table edge hard. 'Sorry.'

'Okay, DI Methven's put me in charge of the Strang case, so I need to get up to speed on where you were. You've hit a wall, haven't you?'

Cullen folded his arms and smiled at Buxton. 'Si, give us a minute?'

Buxton couldn't get out of the room fast enough.

Cullen waited for the door to click shut. 'Have you got a problem with me?'

She sighed. 'No. Have you got a problem with me?'

'Why would you think that?'

'You're fifteen minutes late, Scott. Come on. Don't take the piss.'

'Sorry.' Cullen couldn't hold her eye contact. 'Just finding this whole thing a bit hard to take.'

'You and me both.' She switched off the screen and sat next to Buxton. 'Scott, you're a friend. You can talk to me.'

Cullen stared at his feet. His shoes needed shining. And taking the layer of grime off. 'It sucks being back on the bottom rung of the ladder.'

'I get it. Must've been hard to take, especially coming from Crystal?'

'That's the thing, Chantal.' Cullen looked up at her. 'It didn't. It came from Turnbull.'

'What?'

'The first I heard I was no longer a sergeant was in that room this morning.'

'Oh.'

'Oh, indeed.'

Chantal looked genuinely sorry. 'That shouldn't have happened. I'll speak to Methven about it.'

'I'd rather fight my own battles.'

'Stop being a wanker.'

Cullen sighed. 'If only I could.'

She laughed at him. 'Seriously, Scott. That's bullshit. Crystal should've briefed you. I need to have a word.'

'Don't. Please.' Cullen took a deep breath. 'Look, I don't have any issues working for you. It's about twenty percent that I'm not doing that job anymore, but mostly... I'm really pissed off that I had to find out in a conference room in front of everybody like that.' He huffed out a sigh. And actually felt better for it. 'But I'll get over that. I just need time. And I'll have a word with Crystal when I don't want to smash his head off a bloody wall.' He caught a smile off her. 'When did you hear anyway?'

'Methven told me this morning. First thing.'

'Sharon thinks it was switched.'

Chantal frowned. 'So, you expect me to say no to a promotion?'

'Of course not. Look, we'll solve this case. We work well together. It'll be fine.'

Chantal flashed him a bright smile. 'I'm glad to hear it.'

'Alright then. Do I need to go back to Glasgow?'

'Methven said since your role has changed, the secondment is no longer valid.'

'It's hardly a secondment if it's just a day.'

Chantal got up and flicked the screen on again, then stood staring at it. 'My instinct is to tell Methven this is a cold case, and move on.'

'Your decision, Detective Sergeant.' Cullen held up his hands. 'Joke!' He took out his notebook. 'Look, I spoke to Strang's therapist, Dr Simpson, and—'

'His therapist?'

'Yeah, gave me something and I spoke to his ex-flatmate. There may be something we should check out.' He found the right page. 'Might be a dead end, but you never know. Simpson said someone from Strang's past bullied him, someone Strang referred to as Black Matt.'

Chantal took a sharp breath. 'That's a bit racist.'

'I don't think he meant it literally. From what I understand, Strang talked about him the same way he talked about Jane.'

'The mystery girlfriend?'

'Simpson wasn't sure she existed. Might have been some fancy notion of a muse. Or a codename like Black Matt.'

Chantal nodded. 'Possible, I suppose. This is from school?'

'Right.'

'And Strang's from your home town, right?'

'Yeah, why?'

'How about you drive up and speak with his family again? Find out if they've heard of this Black Matt? Maybe talk to some people who knew Strang back in the bullying days?'

Cullen frowned. 'You trying to get me out of the way?'

'Scott, you've had some bad news. I know you were forced to work the weekend instead of meeting your parents, so why don't you take some time off?'

Cullen glared at her. 'I'm not taking time off now.'

'Okay, how about you follow that lead, see if it gets you anywhere. That or I send you back to Bain.'

~

CULLEN STOMPED DOWN THE CORRIDOR AND TURNED THE CORNER. Right into Buxton, splashing hot coffee over Cullen's mucky shoes.

Cullen stepped back. 'Sorry, mate. You okay?'

Buxton sighed, a deep frown peeking out under his floppy fringe. 'No.'

Cullen hesitated at his sullen tone. 'What's up?'

'Just found out my tenure's up in two months. No chance it'll be renewed.' Buxton stared at his feet. 'Back to uniform.'

Cullen didn't know what to say, so he reached for a couple of platitudes. 'You'll get there eventually. Just be patient.'

'You might've lost your stripes, mate, but at least you've got a tenure.' Buxton gave Cullen a sad nod and wandered off, looking about as lost as a detective could be in a police station.

'Scott!'

He turned around, quickly wiping the frown off his face, but not quickly enough for Sharon to miss it.

'You okay?'

Cullen shook his head. 'We need to talk.'

'Finally.' She grabbed Cullen's hand and led him to the stairwell. 'Through here.' She walked down to the landing between the floors, their clipped steps echoing off the walls. 'What's wrong?'

'Chantal sent me to Dalhousie.'

'What? Why?'

'She said I should take some time off after a busy weekend. I think she's sidelining me.'

Sharon leaned back against the naked concrete wall. 'Oh.'

'I'll get over it. It's just hard to take all at once and—'

She blinked. 'Jesus, Scott.'

Cullen frowned. 'What?'

'With everything we've got going on, this is what you want to talk about?'

He swallowed. 'I... I'm sorry. Like I said, it's just...' He trailed off, feeling about as shit as he could possibly feel as a healthy man with a good job and a beautiful girlfriend who wanted to have his child and raise it with him in a loving relationship and start a happy family.

He had to stop thinking about it if he didn't want to throw up in his mouth.

Sharon took one look at him and knew what was going on in his head. 'It's alright, Scott.' She took his hand in hers. 'We'll be okay.'

'This is all too much. Everything. Right now, I just...'

She stroked his hand. 'Then let's take it one step at a time.'

'First, I got demoted.' He glanced at her. 'I suppose I'll just have to take that one on the chin, right?'

'Try to remember you were never actually promoted. It was just provisional. No guarantees, and I kept telling you not to get your hopes up.'

'Wouldn't listen, would I?' He tried a self-deprecating smile on for size.

She smiled back. 'Look, Scott, I got promoted without first being an ADS, but I was just in the right place at the right time. It's a different place now. Jim Turnbull has to trim his budget in half. It's not all about getting results anymore, it's about making ends meet.'

'I need to play the long game here, right?'

Sharon gave him another smile, but this time it was bittersweet. 'You do. We all do.'

He looked down at her hand in his and gave it a gentle squeeze. 'What did Turnbull say about your promotion?'

'Are you changing the subject?'

He smiled. 'It's what I do.'

'Well, it's between me and him.'

'What?' He frowned. 'You won't tell me?'

'No, you arse. I meant the vacant DI position is between me and Bill Lamb. Unfortunately for me, Bill's got four years on me as a sergeant, plus he was an Acting DI about three years ago. We've got to go through an assessment centre. Then we'll see.'

'I take it you didn't tell Turnbull about... you know?'

Sharon looked away. 'It's nowhere near twelve weeks, Scott. Anything could happen.'

'So, other than Chantal, who else knows?'

'My mum. That's it.'

Cullen smiled. 'Right, so your dad, my parents, your sister and half of Edinburgh?'

Sharon pulled her hand back and slapped his shoulder. 'She *can* keep a secret.'

'Believe it when I see it.'

'Scott, we need to talk about it.'

'I know. I've been thinking about it a lot.'

'And?'

'And I just don't know what to think.'

'I could have a... a you know what.'

Cullen looked away. 'I can't believe we were so careless.'

'You mean me, don't you? You think I was careless, don't you?'

Cullen reached out and took her hand back in his. 'It's not your fault. If anything, it's mine. When the dick is hard, the mind is soft and all that.'

She pulled her hand away again. 'Jesus, Scott.'

'Sorry, but you know what I mean, right?'

'I'm worried I do. You don't want the baby, right?'

Cullen squeezed his eyes shut. He looked at the dull grey walls, felt they were squeezing in on him. 'Look, pregnancy has always been like an STD to me. Like as bad as AIDS. Now it's real and it's in my life, I just don't know what to think.'

Sharon's glare made him regret his phrasing. She looked away again. 'I think you should maybe spend the night at your parents.'

He held his breath. 'Are you chucking me out?'

She grabbed his arm, forcing him to face her. 'I'm not chucking you out, Scott. My flat is our home. Both of ours. It's where we live, together. And Fluffy. And this thing I've got in my...' She glanced down at her belly, then back up at Cullen, her eyes big and round. 'What I mean is you should speak to your mum about it.'

Couldn't bear looking into those eyes. He felt so small.

Sharon cleared her throat.

Has she been crying? Bloody hell, Scott, get over yourself. Look at her and—

'Scott, Chantal has a point. You've been pushing yourself so hard to get that promotion and it never came. Take a break. See the wood for the trees.'

Cullen still couldn't look at her.

It's probably true. Something's not right with me. Maybe I do need to talk to somebody. I've always been able to share problems with mum.

All that shit I got up to as a teenager, and she never judged me for any of it.

He took a lungful of air through his nostrils. 'Okay. I'll get my head straight. Sorry, this isn't great timing—'

'Don't say that.'

'I don't mean the pregnancy. I mean my... Demotion, whatever.

I need to make time to deal with it.' He finally managed to look at her. 'I love you, Sharon.'

'I love you, too, Scott. If I'm going to have kids, it's going to be with you.'

'Same here. I just don't know if I'm ready, that's all.'

She smiled. 'Nobody's ever ready at this stage, but hey, we've got eight months to get ready.'

30

Cullen pulled up outside the Strang's house. Back in Dalhousie, with its grey granite. Back in the world of shoe leather.

Grow up, you arsehole.

He got out and walked up the drive. The house looked empty, the front windows dark. He knocked on the front door.

It shot open. George Strang peered out, screwing his eyes up. 'You? Have you found my son's killer?'

Cullen took a step back. 'Not yet, sir. I'm afraid I need to ask some further questions.'

Strang scratched the grey stubble on his chin. Sounded like he was rasping iron filings. 'Better come in then, Sergeant.'

Cullen didn't correct him, just followed him into the living room. The mantelpiece was now filled with sympathy cards, like some shadow version of the boy's birthday.

Strang caught Cullen's look. 'My wife is sorting out the arrangements at the funeral director's office.'

'I'm sorry to miss her. You know you won't—'

'—get the body until you shower catch who did this to our boy?' Strang shook his head. 'Aye, we know. It's just a small ceremony. Something to help us get over his...' The unspoken tragedy in the air like a hanged man.

Cullen walked over to the sofa and took a seat. 'Mr Strang, does the name Black Matt mean—?'

'What?' Strang hovered over the armchair opposite, froze in place, his face twisted into bitter fury. 'Is that some kind of joke? Matt Black?'

'No, no...' Cullen decided to let it go for now. 'Never mind.'

'Don't you never mind me, son. What are you looking for?'

'Well, someone mentioned that to me. Black Matt. It was a nickname your son gave to... to someone.'

'A bully?'

'Possibly.'

'Christ.' Strang took his seat, slumping down hard enough to make the mechanism crack. 'He had no end of shite at that school, I tell you. Tried to hide it from me and his mother, but his sister knew. She told us.' He shook his head. 'We didn't have the money then to send him to Dundee High. Otherwise I would. My wife... She wanted to send him to another school, but Arbroath? Really? Or Montrose? Talk about out of the frying pain and into the fire...'

'Can you think of any of your son's friends who might be able to help me find this Matt?'

'There's Mark, of course. Mark...' Strang frowned with the effort to remember the guy's surname. 'Used to be on the school football team with him.'

'And this Mark—'

'Agnew! Mark Agnew.'

'Thanks.' Cullen didn't recognise the name but noted it down. 'Anyone else?'

Strang stared into space, his face screwed up. 'There was another laddie...' He clicked his fingers like that would help. 'What was his name?' One final click and he looked at Cullen. 'Paul.'

'You know his surname?'

'Sorry, I can't remember.' Strang shook his head. 'I know both those laddies' parents, but just enough to speak to in Tesco. I think the Agnew boy works in Dundee.'

Cullen added it to his note. *Thank God I don't have to go to London or trace the guy through a foreign police agency.* He looked up at Strang with a patient smile. 'I gather James moved out of his shared flat in Edinburgh?'

'That's right.'

Cullen pointed at the ceiling. 'Your wife said you went through to get his stuff so you could store it in his bedroom upstairs?'

'So?'

'Well, I don't understand. There was three months between—'

'James moved out of that flat, but he was staying in this other place in Leith. I got a call from his landlord, saying he was going to chuck my boy's stuff out and would I... You know. So me and my brother went through and collected his things. Filled Davie's van. You can imagine how hard that must've been for us, aye?'

'I can. Was James staying on his own?'

Strang nodded. 'The landlord said James was the main tenant, but there a lassie called Jane staying too.'

Cullen took a slow breath. 'Your wife mentioned a Jane the other day.'

'Right.'

'Thing is, we've not had any luck catching up with Jane.'

Strang frowned. 'Are you saying we've made her up?'

'No, sir. I just need to get in touch with her. Did you get any paperwork from the landlord?'

'No. It wasn't that kind of arrangement, if you get what I mean. Cash left on the radiator, no questions asked.'

'You still got a number for this landlord by any chance?'

'It's not something I kept, no.' Strang hesitated. 'Lost my phone six months ago down at the harbour. So the number's lost to the North Sea, I'm afraid.' His forehead twitched. 'McKay! That's it!'

'Sorry?'

'James's other school pal. Paul McKay. Don't have an address for him either. My daughter might know. Audrey. She lives just down the road.'

∾

CULLEN KNOCKED ON THE DOOR. NO ANSWER. A CURTAIN TWITCHED. Could just be a cat. He kept a focus on it as he tried her mobile.

Straight to voicemail.

Cullen hung up and scanned the other houses. A small terrace made out of grey brick, all with the same bath towel front gardens, lace curtains drawn tight over every window.

He turned away and called Control.

'Sorry for any inconvenience caused, but due to the ongoing exercise to merge Police Scotland into one strategic telephony platform, the switchboard is unavailable. Please try again later.'

Cullen killed the call with a sigh. *Time to head down to the local cop shop and do the graft myself.*

∼

DALHOUSIE POLICE STATION WAS A NEW GLASS AND CONCRETE building out by the equally new ring road. All hard angles and dull greys under the overcast sky. Back when he was growing up, the shopping centre and supermarket surrounding the cop shop were all fields. And as far as he was concerned, they should've stayed that way. Now little boxes spread up into the hills towards the dual carriageway between Dundee and Aberdeen.

Cullen got out his brand new Police Scotland warrant card, Detective Constable Scott Cullen back in black and white.

I'd got so used to being DS Scott Cullen, the A for Acting always silent. And I liked it that way.

He stared at the card and something clicked in his head.

As soon as Sharon or Lamb get the final DI position, there'll be another Acting DS tenure.

Hope, at last.

He got out of the car and walked over to the station.

'Skinky?' Someone stood in the doorway, blowing on an Aberdeen F.C. mug in one hand, a cigarette burning in the other. Richard Guthrie. Jeans and a navy polo shirt, despite the weather. 'Scott bloody Cullen.' He put the smoke in his mouth and held out his hand. 'What are you doing here?'

Cullen shook his hand, unable to avoid grinning. 'Just up here on a case.'

'Still in Edinburgh?'

'For my sins.'

'Last I heard, you went to uni in Edinburgh, never to be seen again. Now I, eh, work here.'

'After you started working the rigs. Are you a cleaner here, or something?'

'Something.' Guthrie laughed. 'I'm a cop.'

Cullen felt like he was back in school. 'How you getting on here, Goth?'

Guthrie sighed. 'Not heard that one in a long time.'

'You've grown out of all that Marilyn Manson shit, though, right?'

'Never.'

Cullen could still picture him, though he was carrying a few extra stone from his emaciated days. 'I take it your colleagues don't know about you wearing makeup?'

'That's strictly after-hours fun these days.' Guthrie finished his cigarette and stuffed it into the bin. 'So what does Police Scotland bring to you?'

'Just back here. You?'

'Just back from our briefing in Dundee.'

Cullen checked his watch. 'It's eleven. Ours was at seven.'

'So was ours, but I went for a breakfast after to digest it.' He burped into his hand as if to prove he wasn't quite done digesting yet. Then took a slurp of coffee. 'Big changes. I've been shunted here to run North's Local CID for the rest of my life.' He sighed, failing to mask his disappointment. 'What about you?'

'Edinburgh MIT.'

'You sound tired, Skinky.'

'Been busy, mate. Eighth day in a row. Running a murder case.'

Guthrie frowned. 'Running it? You're a DI?'

'Long story.' Cullen glanced away, his face saying don't ask as clearly as if he had spoken aloud. 'Any chance I can get a desk?'

∼

THE DESK SERGEANT YAWNED INTO HIS FIST, EYES SCREWED UP. TOO tired for a Monday morning. Cullen swiped his warrant card through the reader and the door clunked open.

Guthrie set off down the corridor, then into a small room, rammed with desks in the corner. Looked like two of them were free. Guthrie took one, covered in boxes of files, some empty burger wrappers, three half-empty Coke bottles.

Cullen pointed at the chaos. 'You can work like this?'

'Not very well.' Guthrie sat down with a smile. 'Anyway, I don't remember the boy. James Strang?' He frowned. 'He's a Dalhousie lad?'

'Was.' Cullen pulled up a chair and sat next to him. 'He lived in Edinburgh. I'm supposed to be digging into Strang's past. We've come to a dead end in Edinburgh, so I was hoping to find something here that kick-starts us again.'

'You need any help?'

'Looking for an Audrey Strang.'

'Oh.'

'What's up?'

'She's a bit...' Guthrie cringed, like he was looking for the right word. 'Challenged? You must remember her from school.'

'Can't say I do. Went round to her flat, but she either wasn't in or wasn't answering the door.'

'Bet that happens a lot with you.'

Cullen laughed. 'Aye, very good.' He looked around the office. The place smelled of mushrooms, with no obvious explanation. 'So I need to do some checks on the PNC, but Control's switchboard is down.'

'You want a hand?'

'I can search the PNC myself.'

'I mean with your case?'

Cullen arched an eyebrow at the messy desk. 'Aren't you busy?'

'This is just paperwork. Wouldn't mind a break from it for a few years.'

Cullen laughed. 'Look, I just need to speak to a few people. That's it.'

'Mate, I'm the only DC in Dal. My DS is in Dundee and I hardly ever see her. And she's hardly going to check on me today of all days. She didn't even brief me about the announcement, can you believe it?'

'Easily.'

'Well, it's bloody boring work around here. I keep praying for a murder.'

Cullen shook his head. 'Careful what you wish for.'

'So, who else are we looking for?'

'Mark Agnew?'

'I know Mark. He's at work today.' Guthrie grabbed his suit jacket. 'Come on, let's go pay him a wee visit.'

31

THE GREY CLOUD COVER TORE OPEN ABOVE THEM AND BRIGHT SHAFTS
of sunlight lanced the slick black asphalt.

Cullen glanced across at Guthrie. 'You know Mark well?'

'Aye, Mark's a big shot at a new games company.' Guthrie was
driving close to the speed limit, his gaze locked on the city up
ahead, lurking down by the river. 'Indignity Design.'

'Seriously?'

'I know, right? Shite name.'

'No, I'm surprised that he works for them. They're massive. I
see the adverts everywhere. News stories about how many billions
they've made.'

'They're not *that* successful.'

Cullen laughed. 'You jealous?'

'Me?' The first buildings of Dundee flashed by outside, post-
war council houses surrounding a group of football pitches. 'Here,
Skinky, remember when we played there. You scored this mental
goal. Pushed past half the team. It was like Maradona.'

'And now you're deflecting.'

'Piss off.'

'You are jealous, Goth.'

'Not I'm not.' Guthrie was blushing. 'I was shite at computing,
anyway. Sure Big Tom Jameson could've worked there.'

'Maybe.' Cullen glanced out at the shiny glass building beyond the window, Indignity Games written over the front doors in huge, bold letters. 'But you're telling me they haven't made it big?'

'All window dressing, mate. I was reading this book the other week, boy going on about how we all tell a story to the world. Hiding who we really are.'

'Sounds a bit deep for you.'

'Aye, well, when you're on the rigs for a fortnight at a time, watching dodgy Norwegian streams of football and porn soon gets old. So I started reading. History, mainly. But of philosophy. Wish I'd got into that stuff at school, then I'd not be a bloody cop.'

'I was into all that stuff, Goth. And I'm a bloody cop.'

Guthrie gave him the side-eye. 'Fancy a pint tonight?'

'If I'm still around.'

∾

THE RECEPTIONIST SMILED. 'MR AGNEW WILL JUST BE A SECOND.'

Cullen stepped back. Guthrie was twatting about on his phone, his tongue poking out of his mouth like he was working on a particularly hard colouring book.

The building buzzed with chatter. A pair of female hipsters argued by a whiteboard, drawing over each other's diagrams. The place had the feel of money. High ceilings, airy spaces, entire walls made of glass, the crisp April sunshine lighting up the interior like a jewellery showroom.

Large posters in chrome frames, familiar from big-budget adverts on Sky Sports. *Dawn of Heroes* was a roleplaying game, full of over-muscled barbarians and under-clothed female warriors. *War Games* was one of those shooting games that seemed popular with just about any age group — killing people with guns, killing buildings with tanks, killing boredom with killing, killing and more killing. But *Indignity* itself took pride of place on the wall, two rows filled with gaming awards that looked like they were polished daily. A sure-fire success formula where you play a gangster and do what you want — killing people, stealing cars, selling drugs and doing God knows what else.

A man approached them from the far side of the reception hall, tall and angular in his too-small grey T-shirt, skinny black jeans and oversized NHS glasses. His hairstyle fit him even worse

— dyed black and slicked back as if he was on a Scorsese film set. But he walked without swagger, his skinny shoulders stiff and straight, his body practically immobile apart from the long legs. 'DC Cullen?' He held out a hand. 'Mark Agnew.'

Cullen shook it. Felt like he'd crush it. 'Got somewhere we can speak?'

Agnew flashed a shy smile at Guthrie before he nodded at Cullen. 'Come through to my pod.'

HIS POD TURNED OUT TO BE A CIRCULAR ROOM ENSHRINED IN THREE sides of glass. The single solid wall was made of red brick and dotted with framed stills from *Goodfellas*, *Casino* and *The Departed*, with *The Lord of the Rings* sticking out like a sore thumb.

Agnew stepped up to a glass desk and started walking on a treadmill. 'Pull up a pew.' He gestured at some chrome bar stools.

Cullen perched on one of them while Guthrie stayed standing, frowning at the uncomfortable setup.

Agnew's feet hammered off the treadmill as it wound on with a deep drone. He thumped the space bar on the keyboard and his screen woke up. Under the desk, a custom-built PC flashed away like something from a Star Trek film, just missing the lens flare. Then he folded his arms and kept walking. 'Speaking to a real-life police officer is pretty cool.'

Guthrie's frown deepened. 'Mark, you speak to me every Friday in the Ferry.'

'You're not a real cop.' Agnew inclined his head at Cullen without making eye contact. 'This boy's on the telly. Caught a serial killer.'

Cullen settled back in his chair and folded his own arms, deciding that playing along might get some results. 'I believe you're friends with James Strang.'

'Jimi.' Agnew shook his head with a rueful smile, but still without making eye contact. His walking pace quickened. 'I was friends with him at high school, but we lost touch. You know how it is. We just drifted apart during uni.'

Cullen glanced at Guthrie. *I know what you mean, mate.*

Agnew didn't catch the look. 'Jimi went to Edinburgh, but I

went to Abertay. It's not the best, but their games course was the best in the UK. Still is, I think. Anyhoo, we saw each other a fair amount in first year, but... We mostly just emailed after that. Haven't seen him in a *long* time, likes.' He looked round at Cullen, his forehead creasing. 'Why the sudden interest?'

Cullen stared straight at him for a few seconds. 'He's been murdered.'

Agnew's eyes bulged. 'My god. When?'

'Approximately nineteen months ago, but we only discovered the body last week. In Edinburgh.'

Agnew still hadn't blinked, but his walking pace had slackened off a bit. 'Jesus, why are you speaking to *me*?'

Cullen said nothing, just looked him up and down. He got out his notebook and started flicking through it like he had pages of questions. 'Did Strang ever mention a Jane to you?'

Agnew relaxed a little, even cracked a shy smile. 'No, I can't remember any specific names.' His walking pace was back to normal. 'Always had a bird, did Jimi. Changed every time I spoke to him.'

'But not a Jane?'

'Afraid not.'

Cullen flicked to another page, keeping his tone casual. 'His mother mentioned a Paul?'

'Right.' Agnew nodded. 'Paul McKay. Far as I know, Jimi and Paul haven't spoken since school. Still see him in the boozer every so often.'

'So he's still in Dal?'

'Still stuck there. I mean, I could live anywhere and I chose the best house in the town, but...' Agnew scowled. 'I think your old man built it for me?'

'Sounds likely.' Cullen flicked the page, ignoring Agnew, trying not to give him anything. 'Does the name Black Matt mean—'

'What?' Agnew stopped walking. 'What did you say?'

Cullen raised an eyebrow at him.'

Agnew's eyes went out of focus, but it looked like he was trying to remember, rather than lie. 'I had a flurry of emails from Jimi about a year and a half ago. Shite, that's when he disappeared isn't it?'

'Correct. What did he say?'

'The emails were...' Agnew started walking again, his face pinched tight. Seemed like he wasn't trying to hide anything, just looking for the right word. 'They were odd. Cryptic. Before that, he was always on about his band and the music. Used to spam me a lot about gigs, but I never had the time to go. I told him to stop sending me that shit and he took it personally. Then there was radio silence for a few months, until he started up again with this bizarre stuff.'

'What do you mean by bizarre?'

Agnew picked up a foam stress ball from his desk and started squeezing it. 'It was like he was writing some sort of dark poetry, you know? He mentioned Black Matt. No idea why, but it stuck in my head. Must be my creative side, you know?'

'Do you still have those emails?'

'Let me check.' Agnew tapped on his computer. 'Here we go. I'll just print them for you.' He clicked his mouse and left the room without another word.

Guthrie watched him go, smiling as the glass door slid shut and the treadmill wound down. 'Boy's a character. You suspicious of him, Skinky?'

'Not really.'

Out in the open-plan space, four people approached Agnew on his way back from the printer, looking for approval for something or other. Clearly a big shot here.

Guthrie was crouched by the treadmill. 'This is mental. How can he work at the same time?'

Cullen pointed at the posters on the wall. 'He's making a mint by glorifying the sort of shit we deal with every day.'

'He didn't make those movies, mate.'

'No, but computer games based on movies based on the shit we deal with.'

Guthrie shrugged. 'Can't say I've ever dealt with a serial killer.'

'You're still a pedantic bastard, aren't you? Well, I have.'

Guthrie stood up and placed a foot on the treadmill. 'You think that's what we're dealing with here?'

'Not likely.'

Agnew swung the glass door open and held out some pages. 'Sorry it took so long. Printer was out of paper.'

'Don't worry about it.' Cullen took the paper and started

flicking through the emails. Eighteen messages in total, the history cut off. He found the latest one:

I COULD HAVE PAID IT FORWARD, BUT INSTEAD I'LL PAY IT BACK
   I could have moved forward, but instead I'll paint it black

MATTE BLACK WALLS
   Black Matt steals time
   Time will get us all
   When is our time up?
   When is up down and down up?
   When do I go under the waves?

UNDER THE WATER
   Let me drown
   I'm not waving
   I'm going down

I FAILED, BUT TO SUCCEED IS TO FAIL FULLY.
   In failing, I failed to fail.

IN THE END, I WAS REDUCED TO IT.
   Stealing what wasn't mine, taking what didn't belong to me, coveting my neighbour's wife.

BETRAYAL IS THE HARDEST PART.
   Dishonesty, theft, hiding.

CULLEN SHUFFLED THE SHEETS INTO A STACK AND PLACED IT ON THE glass desk.
   This is either the work of a broken mind or the result of long-term narcotics abuse.

He looked up at Agnew. 'Any idea what that means?'

'None. I mean, it freaked me out when I got it. I tried to make sense of it, but... I just gave up.'

Cullen sighed. *I'll lose hours to examining these garbled lines of pseudo poetry. Like being back at university.*

Guthrie was staring at the last email. 'Did you reply to this?'

'No. The last thing I asked him was how the record deal was going.'

'Record deal?'

Agnew picked up a sheet and waved it in Guthrie's face. 'He mentioned it here. Sounded like a typical Jimi fantasy, about how he was going to become a big shot.'

Cullen took the page. Two months before the disappearance. *Could be something. Could be nothing.* 'No other mention of a deal?'

Agnew shook his head. 'Afraid not. It all went quiet.' He stared at his movie posters. 'When is the funeral?'

Cullen collected the sheets. 'You'll need to discuss that with Mr Strang's parents.'

32

'No, Si, it's M-C-K not M-A-C-K.' Cullen gripped the phone tight as Guthrie swerved through a roundabout, ignoring the articulated lorry he really should've given way to. Or at least seen.

'Right, you jocks need to sort your surnames out, mate.' Buxton sighed. 'You having a nice jolly up there?'

'Not really.' Cullen watched Dundee's post-industrial hellscape give way to the Angus hills. 'How's it down there?'

'Hate to say this, but Chantal's even worse than you are, mate. Shouldn't have... Well, I had no way of knowing she'd be my boss one day and oh, here we go. Got an address for a Paul McKay in Dalhousie. Ferry Road, number eighteen.'

'Cheers, Si.' Cullen grinned. 'What did you mean, you shouldn't have?'

'Speak later.' And he was gone.

'Back to Dal, Goth.' Cullen put his mobile away and held up the stack of emails. 'What do you make of these?'

Guthrie glanced at them, then looked back out at the road. 'Gibberish, mate. Guy was cracked.'

Cullen bit his lip. 'Looks like it, doesn't it? But I still can't put it all together. It's backed up Strang's record deal. And it falling apart. But then he sends this shite.'

'And then someone murders him. Doesn't make any sense.'

Guthrie slipped into the fast lane and overtook a lumbering Citroen. 'You're sure it was murder?'

'Someone wrote I WILL KILL AGAIN on the wall above the dead body.'

Guthrie shrugged. 'Could've been Strang himself. Just to add some rock-star mystery to his suicide. Desperate for posthumous fame, know what I mean?'

Cullen frowned. 'In his own blood?'

Guthrie shrugged again.

'Goth, you watch too many stupid films.'

～

CULLEN LED GUTHRIE UP TO PAUL McKAY'S BUNGALOW, A MID-Seventies harled thing set back from the road by a patch of over-grown weeds. Looked like nobody'd taken care of the place since it was built. 'You know Paul McKay?'

'Bit of a piss artist.' Guthrie tried the doorbell. 'Always find him feeding pound coins into a puggy in the Ferry. Picked him up for fighting a few years back.'

'Fighting in Dal is like breathing anywhere else.'

'It's a lot better now, mate. People just get tanked up at home, you know how it is. Can't remember the last time I had to fish out someone's teeth from a gutter.'

Cullen winced. 'Christ.' He glanced at the closed curtains in the main window, then gave the bell another ring. 'Know where McKay works?'

'Not sure he does. Bit of a grey-market employee, if you catch my drift. Selling fags off the rigs, that kind of thing. His folks died in a car crash a few years back, inherited this place. Only child. Think he got a good chunk of compo. And he's been feeding it into the puggies of Dalhousie ever since.'

'Right.' Cullen took one last look at the curtains. 'Let's get back to your station.'

～

CULLEN TOOK A SEAT AT A FREE DESK. NO SHORTAGE OF THOSE. THE open-plan office was quiet, just a couple of officers lurking by the coffee machine, talking in low voices.

Guthrie leaned against the wall, mobile pressed to his ear. Judging by his body language, he was flirting away with someone, and if that someone had seen his body language, it would've been game over there and then.

Cullen shook his head and spread the emails out across the desk. The older ones were filled with gossip about old school friends, par for the course. Then Strang started talking more and more about himself, the bragging becoming borderline narcissistic. Agnew, the bona fide success of the pair, barely mentioned anything about co-owning one of the most-successful video games companies in the UK, if not the world. Unlike Strang, he didn't have to keep harping on that he was a success. Agnew was busy being one.

Cullen was getting a sense of how Strang's mind worked, so there was no point putting it off any longer. Time to focus on the poem.

I COULD HAVE PAID IT FORWARD, BUT INSTEAD I'LL PAY IT BACK

WHAT WAS HE PAYING BACK? THERE WAS THAT SAYING ABOUT 'PAYING your dues' in music. Playing crappy venues to learn the trade. Called them toilet venues in the press. Like the Beatles in Hamburg and in The Cavern back in Liverpool, two sets each night.

Was that what Strang meant?

Paying it forward was American. That film Sharon made Cullen watch a couple of years ago. It meant being good to strangers, paying favours first, instead of getting them in return. A modern twist on karma, only in this life.

But Strang was saying he hadn't paid anything forward, and he was going to pay something back. Or pay someone back?

I COULD HAVE MOVED FORWARD, BUT INSTEAD I'LL PAINT IT BLACK

. . .

PAINT IT BLACK WAS ONE OF THE FEW ROLLING STONES SONGS Cullen's dad would allow in the house. Was Strang into the Stones? Wait, that poster on his wall: 'Who the fuck is Mick Jagger?'

Cullen googled it on his phone. It was Keith Richards, the Stones guitarist.

Does that mean anything?

Take a step back.

Wikipedia told him that *Paint it Black* was about a girl's funeral. Could it be Jane's funeral? Could she have died and that explained his cracked mental state? Or was it someone else's? Or was it just a broken mind reaching for a reference?

He could spend hours decoding some hidden meaning when, most likely, it was just used because it rhymed and fit the meter.

MATTE BLACK WALLS
Black Matt steals time

WHO OR WHAT WAS BLACK MATT? NOBODY SEEMED TO KNOW. BUT Strang had talked about him to his analyst. If it was a real person, rather than some abstract concept, how the hell did they steal time?

TIME WILL GET US ALL
When is our time up?
When is up down and down up?
When do I go under the waves?
Under the water
Let me drown
I'm not waving
I'm going down

DROWNING...

Jeff Buckley died from drowning. Officially, it was ruled a lethal accident, but some suggested it was suicide. Strang wore his T-shirt the night he went missing, and he was still wearing it when his corpse was found. And he had a poster of Buckley in his room. Maybe Strang didn't kill himself, but this showed he'd considered suicide. Maybe. Or was it just some morbid hero worship.

IN THE END, I WAS REDUCED TO IT.
  Stealing what wasn't mine, taking what didn't belong to me, coveting my neighbour's wife.

DID HE HAVE AN AFFAIR WITH SOMEONE? BETH WILLIAMSON? SHE'D told them Jimi had tried it on with her, but if she was to be believed, nothing had happened between them. Unrequited love, maybe.

As for the obvious candidate, the mysterious Jane, nobody could even validate her existence, never mind some affair with Strang.

Wait a sec.

My neighbour's wife.

Marta Owenson, Alex Melrose's girlfriend.

She was a heroin addict. Maybe Strang was bewitched by that rock 'n' roll thing. The gritty allure of heroin. Live fast, die young, leave a good-looking corpse.

Until we find you a year and a half later, your body rotting away to a skeleton…

Cullen blinked away the flashback.

Could Strang have slept with Marta?

Could Melrose have killed Strang in revenge?

Stabbing someone with a screwdriver seemed desperate, a real crime of passion. Or an accident when a fight among friends went ugly?

I FAILED, BUT TO SUCCEED IS TO FAIL FULLY.
  In failing, I failed to fail.

· · ·

Hints of Samuel Beckett's existential mantra here: 'Ever tried. Ever failed. No matter. Try again. Fail again. Fail better.' Or it was all just mumbo jumbo.

What a mess. Cullen looked around the office.

Guthrie put away his phone, shaking his head at something. He caught Cullen's look and trudged across the room. 'My date just cancelled on me. Tell you, Skinky, I could do with a pint.'

'Later. I've got to see someone first. I'll give you a call.'

33

CULLEN PARKED OUTSIDE HIS PARENTS' HOUSE IN THE COLD GREY dusk. One look at the dark windows was enough to tell him they weren't in. The Invisibles blared out of his stereo; he was trying to get inside Jimi's head. Trying and failing. All he was achieving was reasserting his hatred of guitar music. He got out his phone — no messages. From anyone.

Out of sight, out of mind.

Should I call Chantal to give update her on...

Well, on what exactly?

With a tired sigh, he decided to let the boss do the calling. He reached over and took out the CD, swapping it for an Ólafur Arnalds record Tom had lent a few months ago. Heartbreakingly beautiful Icelandic piano music.

Really should give this back. Or buy my own copy.

He turned the volume up and let the haunting music resonate deep in his stomach.

The baby.

Sharon's promotion.

She hasn't called to say whether she got it. Then again, I haven't called her. I hope she's okay.

Never mind hope – ask her.

He got out his phone again and made the call.

'Scott?'

'Aye, just calling to see how you are.' A car trundled down the street, slowing as it passed him, then shooting off. 'Any news?'

'Nothing yet.'

'How you doing?'

'I'm okay.' She sounded tired. Not quite yawning yet, but not far off. 'How're you?' Distracted too, like she was reading emails while talking.

'The case is still, well. In the toilet.' Cullen ran a hand down his face. 'I'm starting to feel better about... This whole...' He sighed. *Try again.* 'I'm starting to get in the headspace of being able to think about becoming a dad.'

She gasped. 'Oh, Scott. I'm glad.' Her voice betrayed a smile. 'You coming home tonight?'

A slow breath slid out of his mouth. 'Still got some leads to chase up in Dalhousie tomorrow, so I'll stay at my parents tonight.'

'Oh, well, good luck.' She sounded disappointed. 'See you tomorrow, then.'

Click.

Cullen stared at his phone.

Shite.

I really should've offered to come home and support my pregnant girlfriend. Help her with the stress of the promotion hanging over her. The stress of the human life growing inside her. She shouldn't be dealing with it alone.

His thumb hovered over the call icon. A door slammed. When he looked over, a light was on in his parents' house.

Must've just got back from work.

Cullen put his phone in his pocket, grabbed his overnight bag from the passenger footwell and got out. He could hear their voices as he reached the front door and rang the bell.

Mum opened the door, still dressed for the office. She looked him up and down. 'Scott?'

'You got a room for the night?'

∾

'—NOT BEEN THE SAME SINCE THE ENGLISH PREMIER LEAGUE started.' Cullen's old man slumped in his chair. 'The Scottish game died that day, I tell you.'

Cullen took another sip of beer, tangy and sweet. *Need to check the can is still in date.* 'You watching the game tonight?'

'Aye, Liverpool are on, I think.' Dad's gaze shifted to the TV, Sky Sports News playing on mute.

'I thought Aberdeen were on?'

'Like I can be arsed watching that shower. Haven't you been listening to me?'

Not really.

Cullen yawned, too tired to give much thought to what he was saying and hearing. His dad's greyhounds were lying on their sofa in the living room, absolutely conked. As ever.

Cullen smiled at them. *I know how you feel, lads.*

'The game's a joke now. And we'll never qualify for a World Cup again.' His dad stared into his beer glass, shaking his head like it was a personal tragedy. 'The Euros is twenty-four teams in 2016. Still don't fancy our chances with that shower.'

'Ever the optimist.'

'Before you were born, Scott, we thought we'd win the bloody World Cup. Can you imagine that?'

Cullen yawned again and finished his beer. Left a bitter taste and a gassy bloat in his gut. 'Right.'

Dad finally relented. 'Never mind.' He finished his own glass. 'How's Sharon? Shame you couldn't come up for the weekend.'

'Shame you couldn't come out for dinner with me and Mum.'

'I'm a busy man, Scott.' Dad sighed. 'Too busy. You should come and join me.'

'Cullen and son, house builders. Not for me.'

'You should think about it. I'll put you on the board. You can take over from me when I retire. Won't be too long now.'

'Dad.' Cullen gave him a tired look. 'We've been over this.'

'The police that much fun, eh?'

'No, but...' Cullen fell silent.

But what?

Stuck on the bottom rung of a slippery career ladder with no guarantees of ever earning enough to support a family...

How much fun is that?

Maybe he's right. Maybe it's time to reconsider my options. Maybe—

'Dinner's ready.'

Cullen got up and walked through to the dining room.

Dad caught his arm and blocked his path. 'I'm serious, son. Think about it. You'll get a very nice salary. Move up here, start a family. Dalhousie's a great place to raise kids. You should know.'

Aye, ask James Strang's ghost...

Cullen shrugged off his hand. 'I'll think about it.' He smiled. 'Thanks, Dad.' He entered the dining table and sat in his old spot, halfway down, right between his parents at either end. No Michelle to kick under the table, though.

Mum dolloped lamb stew onto a bowl and passed on to Cullen. 'Just as well I had the slow cooker on this morning, isn't it?'

'This looks good.' Cullen blew on a spoonful until the steam let off, then tried it. Rich and tender, the sort of food Sharon hated. 'Mmm, tastes good, too.'

The greyhounds stood in the doorway, sniffing as if their noses agreed. Dad raised a finger and they both settled down on all fours, watching for any scraps from the table.

Cullen took a sip from his wine glass. 'This is nice.'

'Only the best for my boy.' Dad frowned, then topped Cullen's glass up from the bottle. It might have been Cullen's imagination, but it was like he pointed it so the expensive label was facing him. 'So, how is the police, then?'

Cullen smiled. 'Mum, he's offering me a job.'

Dad raised his hands. 'Just trying to help my boy, that's all.'

'David...' Mum gave him a stern look. 'You know that's not called helping, right?'

He folded his arms. 'Oh, really?'

'It's meddling.'

'Come on, Liz... What if he needs a bit of a leg-up to—'

'We've talk about—'

'I got demoted back to DC.'

Silence. They both stared at him.

Cullen sighed. 'I'm okay, it's not a cancer diagnosis.'

'Aye.' Dad nodded. 'My point exactly. It's hard making it in the world, my boy. Hence me offering you a foot on a different ladder. A better one.'

'David...'

Cullen bit back his anger. 'Thanks, Dad.'

Dad's phone rattled on the table. He put on his glasses to inspect it, craning his neck back. 'Never a moment's bloody peace.' He got up and stretched his back. 'I'll take this through there.' He waddled through to his reclining chair. 'Tony, what now?'

Mum looked after him, eyes narrowed. 'Sorry, Scott. You know he's not very good at this sort of thing.'

Cullen stared into his glass. *One day it'll be me leaving my son or daughter to talk to Sharon while I escape to the living room.*

'I know that look.'

Cullen glanced up. 'What look?'

'It's not just the job.'

Cullen rubbed his ear. 'I'm fine.'

'I know when you're lying to me, Scott James Cullen.'

All three names. Bloody hell.

Cullen took a deep breath, followed by an even deeper gulp of wine. 'Sharon's pregnant.'

Mum frowned, her mouth hanging open. Then it resolved into a beaming smile. 'That's wonderful!' She raised her glass. 'Another grandchild to love and cuddle and...' She paused and the frown was back. 'I thought you weren't going to have children?'

Cullen drained his glass and reached for the bottle. 'Wasn't planning on it.'

'Oh, Scott, have you been a silly boy again?'

'Again?' He closed his eyes. 'I've never got anyone else pregnant, Mum.'

She smiled. 'That's not what I meant. Just that... Well, you have a tendency to...'

'Thanks.' He shook his head at her. 'Why does everyone always blame me?'

'You were always such a naughty boy, Scott. Reputations are much harder to leave behind than places and people.'

'What's that supposed to mean?' He splashed red into his glass. 'Michelle. Right.'

His mother just looked at him. And saw right through him. 'Scott, do you want the baby?'

Cullen sat quiet for a few seconds.

Losing my temper like that. Venting my frustration on my mother. Just because I can't tell her what's really...

The wine made the decision for him. 'I don't know.' Felt like his shoulders eased off a few kilos. 'It's such a huge thing. Financially, I don't feel anywhere near ready to do it. I mean, I've got some money in the bank, but we need somewhere proper to live and this demotion...'

'I understand.'

He took a deep breath, but it didn't ease the pressure in his chest. 'Do you think we should have it?'

'Scott, I'm trying not to let my grandmotherly desire answer for me.' She took a sip of wine. 'I don't know if you're mature enough. Remember what happened with you and Sharon last year?'

Cullen cringed. 'We got over that.'

'Have you? That was definitely your fault.'

'Always my fault, isn't it?' Cullen regretted the words as soon as they were out of his mouth. 'Fine. My fault. I was an idiot. But I've apologised to Sharon.'

'And do you love her?'

'Yes.' Cullen didn't even have to think about it. 'Of course I do.'

'Enough to say you'll commit to her and give your child a secure home?'

Cullen looked away. 'I'm not sure I'll ever be able to do that.'

'With Sharon?'

'No, with anyone. I'm an idiot, right?'

His mother laughed. 'What do you want to do, Scott?'

Cullen refilled his glass, right to the brim. *Because I'm a classy guy.* 'I want to get drunk and forget all about it.'

'Scott.'

He sighed. 'Fine, the truth is I don't know. I just don't know what I want.'

'That's always been your problem. Until you joined the police.'

Cullen took a big gulp of the wine. 'Fat lot of good that's done me.'

'Don't overdo it with the wine.' His mother shook a stern finger at him. 'You've put some very bad people away.'

'Aye, but...' Cullen looked into the glass. 'Maybe it's time to take Dad up on his offer.'

'Scott, you can barely bother to be in the same room as him. Don't think I haven't noticed.'

Cullen's phone rang. *Saved by the bell.* He got it out and checked the screen. Guthrie. 'Mind if I take this?'

'Like father like son.' Mum waved him off.

Cullen walked over to the kitchen with the phone to his ear. 'What's up, Goth?'

'Pub?'

34

'You've been drinking, haven't you?' Sharon's voice had an edge.

Cullen knew better than to blame it on the bad reception of his mobile. He walked through his home town feeling like a stranger. Two new charity shops that used to be a shoe shop and a deli. The Earl of Angus was now boarded up, the pub he used to drink with his mates. Probably be a property development soon. Probably be his old boy doing it.

'Just a glass of wine with my mum. Well, a couple of glasses. We were having dinner and—'

'And now you're heading to the pub.'

Cullen stopped in his tracks, looking around as if she were following him.

Of course she isn't. She's in Edinburgh.

'How do you know that?'

'Location sharing.'

'Oh.' Cullen laughed and set off down the road again, catching a blast of frying oil smell from the chip shop. 'You'd make a good detective.'

'And you'd make a good boyfriend if you were here.'

That stung. Cullen stopped and leaned against a wall by the war memorial. 'I miss you, Sharon.'

'Me too. You know, this is the first night we're spending apart since you moved in.'

'Really?'

'I've got a good understudy to take you place, though.'

'Fluffy isn't ginger enough.'

She laughed down the line. It made him miss her even more.

'Well, he'll have to do for tonight. I'll try my best to be back tomorrow.'

'What's on tonight, then? Watching football with your dad?'

'God no.' Cullen set off again, catching coverage of the pre-match buildup through a window on the opposite side. The telly must take up half the living room. 'I'm meeting up with Richard for a pint.'

'McAlpine?'

'No, he's still in Edinburgh.' *No doubt typing away at that novel of his.* 'Richard Guthrie.'

'As in DC Richard Guthrie?'

'Don't tell me you know him?'

'Not in a biblical sense.' Sharon laughed. 'I gave a course at Tulliallan a few years ago. He's from Dundee, isn't he?'

'Sort of. He's Dalhousie too. Went to school together. Him and Rich McAlpine. Small world, eh?'

'Aye, that's almost spooky.'

Cullen took the steps to the town's harbour, the sea salty in the cold night air. A wave crashed off the harbour wall, the spray misting up in the yellow glow. The Ferry glowed at the end of the pier, the only trace of the town's ancient route south to Edinburgh and civilisation, long since lost to the trains. 'How are you?'

'Alright, I suppose. Sorry for being a selfish bitch earlier.'

'You were fine. I was being a selfish prick. Not just last night. But we should've had that talk. I shouldn't have gone to bed.'

'I'll remind you next time.'

Cullen laughed. 'You better not plan on getting pregnant again.'

'Scott...'

'Sorry.' A fresh blast of salty air hit his face, the cold mist soaking his hair. 'Coming up here was definitely the right thing to do. I had a good chat with my mum.'

A long pause. 'And?'

'And that's all. For now. My head's still spinning, but I think I'm slowly pulling it out of my arse.'

'Good progress for one day, I suppose.'

'Well...'

'You better go. Guthrie's probably waiting for me in the pub. Love you, Scott.'

'Love you, too.'

≈

'Two pints of Peroni.' Guthrie propped himself up against the bar, legs dancing. 'Need a slash.' He sauntered off to the toilets.

Amazing he'd kept a job in the police with his timekeeping. Then again, he's out in the wilds with nobody watching him.

The barman popped two pints on the bartop, golden and fizzing away in their posh glasses. Cullen handed him a tenner and was surprised to get change. Quite a lot of it, too. He carried them over to a table by the window overlooking the harbour. The waves seemed larger at such close range.

The football filled the large screen — Liverpool already dishing out a solid hammering to Newcastle. The place was dead, only a few middle-aged men propping up the bar, eyes glued to the telly, nursing a pint for as long as they could.

Guthrie ambled out of the gents like he owned the place, the town sheriff. He picked up his pint and sucked the foam off the top, then gasped. 'Ah, that's the ticket.'

Cullen clinked his glass. 'Cheers.'

Guthrie pointed at the football. 'Can't believe how bad Aberdeen are doing this season.'

'You still go?'

Guthrie nodded. 'For my sins. Still got a season ticket. One of the best things about CID was it's nine to five, give or take, so I get my weekends off for football.'

'I'm supposed to be the same, but it never quite works out like that.'

'You were always ambitious, though, Skinky.'

Cullen shrugged. 'All drive and no direction, that's me.'

Guthrie gave a nod. 'You got a bird?'

'Sharon, but she'd hate to be described as a bird.'

Guthrie nodded again. 'One of them, eh?'

'Jesus, Goth.'

Guthrie grinned. 'Just winding you up, dude. Get over yourself.'

Cullen stared at the football again, just in time to catch a vicious sliding tackle. 'Sharon and I moved in together last year. Turns out you know her. Sharon McNeill.'

'Holy shit.' Guthrie's eyes bulged. 'Punching above your weight there, mate.'

Cullen laughed.

'How's she doing?'

'Alright.' Cullen looked away. 'She's in line for a DI position.'

'You'll be a proper little house husband soon.'

'Something like that.' Cullen took a gulp of beer, but it didn't dislodge the lump in his throat. 'She's going to be a DI sooner or later, so if...' He took another sip of bear. 'If we ever have a family, we'll be fine.'

Guthrie was staring into space. 'You ever think about jacking it in, Skinky?'

'Maybe.' Cullen sighed, then took his pint past the halfway mark. 'My old boy offered me a job tonight.'

'He's doing well, isn't he?'

'Yeah, but it's my dad. Could you work for yours?'

'He died five years ago.'

'Oh, shit. Sorry.'

'It's okay. He was a wanker. Crashed his motorbike. Seeing him on a ventilator for months before Mum pulled the plug, well. He deserved to suffer.' Guthrie looked away with a crooked smile. 'My love life's on a ventilator, too. I can feel my virginity growing back.'

Cullen laughed. 'That's my line.'

'It's not like you've copyrighted it, though, is it?' Guthrie took a long drink. 'I don't mind being single. See enough arguments in the job.'

'You happy as a DC?'

'I'm solving crimes, helping people. If I got promoted, I'd be overseeing half of Angus. I'd be like a supermarket area manager or something. I get paid the same as you and it's cheap as chips to live up here, so yeah, I guess I'm happy.'

Cullen filled his mouth with the rest of his beer.

An explosion of shouts came from the bar. An OAP waved at the screen where the ref pointed to the spot and showed a red card to the Newcastle goalkeeper.

Guthrie winked. 'Someone's lost a bet.'

The front door opened and three men walked in. Cullen recognised them — Alan Thomson, Andy MacLeod and Gregor Smith. All total wankers from their year at school, and all looking three sheets to the wind.

Guthrie turned away again. 'Wankers.'

Cullen laughed. 'Not seen those pricks since uni.'

'They've got worse.'

Despite all the empty tables, Andy MacLeod sat down at the one next to theirs. 'Look who the cat dragged in.'

Cullen took a sip of beer, ignoring him.

'Skinky, I'm talking to you.' MacLeod stabbed a finger at Cullen. 'You're a pig, aren't you?'

Cullen finished his beer and looked at his empty pint glass. 'Oink!'

Thomson and Smith wandered over. 'Oink! Oink!'

Cullen sighed and got out his warrant card. 'We can make this official, if you like?'

MacLeod raised his hands like he was a lady lifting her handbag. 'Where's your boyfriend, Cullen? Rich McAlpine. Someone told me you were living with him. Must be nice.' He was lisping now.

'I see you're still a wanker.'

'That the best you've got?' MacLeod burped. 'How's your sister, by the way?'

'My sister?'

'Tidy, she was. Still got it?'

Cullen picked up his empty glass, gripping near the base, where he could apply the most force. Then he set it down on the table. 'Come on, Goth. Plenty other pubs in this town.'

∼

'STILL THE BEST BAG OF CHIPS IN SCOTLAND.' GUTHRIE MUNCHED noisily, his lips slapping together, hard to follow the words coming out of his mouth.

But he had a point.

Cullen leaned back against the chipper's wall. 'You know they call it a chippie in Edinburgh.'

'Aye?' Guthrie wiped his mouth with the back of his hand. 'What do they call a chippie then?'

'A joiner.'

'Huh.'

Church Street was all lit up in yellow and they were the only people around.

Guthrie finished his chips with a burp. 'See those pricks back at the Ferry? Said you were living with Rich McAlpine?'

'I was.'

'Thought he was getting his arse pounded in London?'

'Come on, mate.'

'Sorry. But he lived there, right?'

'Moved back to Edinburgh last year. We shared a flat for a bit, before I moved in with Sharon.'

'But he's still doing all that gay shit?'

Cullen had to laugh. 'Christ's sake, Goth, he's gay. Get over it. You used to wear makeup.'

'That's different.'

Cullen balled up his bag, feeling woozy from the beer and wine. 'I can see why you never left Dal.'

'Nothing wrong with this place.' Guthrie shook his head. 'Still don't get the gay thing but... Holy shit!'

'What?'

Guthrie pointed inside the chipper at a lone figure feeding pound coins into a fruit machine, just opposite the fryer. 'That's Paul McKay.'

Cullen squinted through the glass door. The guy was skinny and tall, but had a paunch barely hidden by his hoodie.

'Oink!' Thomson and Smith wandered towards them, knuckles almost scraping the pavement. 'Pair of poofs!' Thomson put his hand on the door to push it open.

Cullen got in front of him. 'They're shut.'

'Aye?' Thomson stared over Cullen's shoulder. 'Looks open to me.'

'Well, I'm telling you it's shut.'

Thomson frowned at him. 'You wanting a fight?'

Cullen laughed. 'You and whose army?'

'Don't kid yourself. I can handle you. Oink!'

'Get out of here or I'll arrest you.'

'Aye?' Thomson made a show of looking all around the empty street, ignoring Guthrie as he stared back at Cullen. 'This prick isn't going to help you.'

Smith clapped him on the shoulder. 'Come on, Greg. He's not worth it.'

'Can't handle getting the shit kicked out of him, that's for sure.' Thomson turned around and gave Smith a clumsy high-five as they shambled off. 'See you poofs later.'

Cullen watched them go.

Guthrie just shook his head. 'Sorted them out a few times over the years, when I was in uniform. Couple of times, the pool league got a bit rowdy.'

'They've lost their leader.'

'Aye, MacLeod... Few years back, the prick went on a bit of damage, walking on cars and shit. Had the whole gang out, half of Arbroath, Carnoustie, Montrose. Meat wagons. He'd cleared off, no sign of him. I had to track him down. Found him in Edinburgh. Arrested him and charged him. Sheriff court, but he got off with a fine. Then he dropped off the radar. No idea why he's back now. And here.'

Cullen finished his bottle of Irn Bru and walked over to chuck the empty in the recycling bin.

'Scott Cullen!' Over the street, a woman was pointing at him. The mad woman from the other night. 'You big bully!'

Cullen's shoulders slumped. *Here we go again.*

She marched up to him, her voice rising with every angry step. 'You bullied me!' She reached her arm up to strike.

'Oy!' Guthrie got between them. 'I'm warning you, clear off or it's a night in the cells for you.'

Her eyes flickered between them. She turned and walked off the way she had come, looking back over her shoulder as she went. She got out her keys and took a few goes trying to put them in the door, like a ten-pint drunk. Then she slipped inside the stairwell.

'That's the second time she's done that in one week. I've no idea who she is or what I've done to her.'

'Really?' Guthrie raised his eyebrows at him. 'She was in our year.'

Cullen shook his head. 'Nope, still don't remember her.'

'You sat next to her in French.'

Cullen tried to strip back the years, and the fat from her face. 'She must've put on a lot of weight.'

'Haven't we all?'

'Speak for yourself, mate. But bullying? What was that about?'

'Beats me. You were a bit of an arse at times, but I don't remember you bullying anyone. Too obsessed with yourself for that.'

'Why she's so pissed off with me?'

'Maybe something to do with you investigating her brother's murder?'

Cullen stopped dead. 'What?'

Guthrie pointed a greasy finger at her door. 'That's Audrey Strang.'

'Shite. Of all the people...' Cullen started off after her.

Guthrie grabbed his shoulder, tugging him back. 'What are you playing at, Skinky?'

'I need to speak to her.'

'Not in this state.'

'I'm not pissed.'

'No, but you've had a few pints. Enough for her to smell the booze on your breath as you interview her about her dead brother. Leave it till tomorrow. We'll get in there first thing.'

Cullen looked up into the dark night sky. 'Fine.'

Guthrie balled up his chip wrapper. 'See you in the station first thing?'

'Aye. And first thing means seven.' Cullen clapped Guthrie's arm and headed in the opposite direction, relieved there was no offer of a whisky in Guthrie's flat.

DAY 5

Tuesday

35

MARTA OWENSON WAS A WHIRLWIND OF WILD ENERGY, GYRATING through the messy living room at breakneck speed, her three children whirling around her so fast their faces were a blur. Then they all stopped, froze dead, and stared at Cullen.

On the tiny child bodies were the heads of Alan Thomson, Andy MacLeod and Gregor Smith.

Cullen jolted awake, his heart hammering in his chest. He blinked, but in the darkness all he could see were traces of yellow creeping in under the blinds.

Where the hell am I?

Cullen fumbled around for the bedside table and touched a lamp. He ran his fingers down the cable to find the power button. Bright light stung his eyes. He blinked again, sunspots bursting in his head. Took a few seconds to get his bearings.

He was back in his old room. Barely recognisable, the mid-grey walls now the same cream the rest of the house was done in. His mind was fuzzy. Maybe from the nightmare, maybe from a hangover.

How much did I drink?

He spotted a pint of water beside the bed and smiled. Drunk Cullen looking out for hungover Cullen.

Couldn't have had that much, then.

He toasted drunk Cullen and downed the water, soaking his dry throat. He checked his watch — just after eight.

Shite.

No, wait. I'm out in the sticks. Got ages until I need to be in the station.

He slumped back and rubbed his head.

Another few hours' sleep and I'll be as good as new, ready to show—

Then his phone chirped. A text from Chantal:

You in yet?

He struggled out of bed and started looking for his trousers.

~

DOWNSTAIRS, NO SIGN OF HIS PARENTS. ALREADY AT WORK, NO doubt. A Post-It note was stuck to the kitchen table. 'Call your sister! Love, Mum.' Michelle's mobile number was underneath.

He crumpled up the note and dropped it back on the table, then went to stick the kettle on. Last night's chips were still heavy in his stomach.

Just a cup of tea, then.

Make it a pot.

He filled the kettle and the dogs skulked through, their heads almost touching the floor as they moved, looking for affection. Or dropped toast.

Cullen knelt down and patted them, getting his face licked in return. When the dogs had enough, he filled the teapot and sat at the kitchen table. The Angus edition of the *Dundee Courier* sat there, already twice read by the looks of it.

He skimmed the sport section, half focused on the Dundee teams and half on Aberdeen. The bloody Post-It kept catching his eye.

Why did Mum say I have to call my sister, rather than the other way around?

Michelle had been an arse ever since she went to uni in Glasgow. Why should I bother? She's a year older, she's supposed to be the mature one.

He shook his head and got out his phone to check if it was the same number he had for her. The one she'd bounced calls a few times.

Nope, new one. That explains the lack of response.

But if she's not even bothered to give me her new number, I'm not bothered to call it.

Instead, he called Sharon.

'Hi, Scott. Good night?'

'Sort of.'

'I'm not even going to ask.'

Cullen laughed. 'It wasn't too heavy. Just a few pints while we put the world to rights. How you doing?'

'Better. Going to show Turnbull what's what.'

'Don't push yourself too hard, okay?'

'I'm pregnant, not disabled.'

'I'm just saying. I don't want the decision taken out of our hands.'

Silence. 'No.' So quiet, Cullen thought it was a dog burping. She cleared her throat. 'Think you'll be back tonight?'

Cullen grinned. 'You did miss me.'

'Of course.' No grin in Sharon's voice.

'I'll see how things are here. Got a lead or two, maybe, but nothing concrete. Hopefully be back tonight.'

'I'm looking forward to it.'

Cullen hesitated. 'I meant what I said last night. We do need to talk.'

'I know we do.'

'Can we do it somewhere other than the flat? I don't want you getting all territorial.'

A sharp intake of breath. 'I'm not *territorial.*'

'Yeah, okay, but let's go for dinner anyway. Neutral venue and all that.'

She sighed. 'Fine. I'll call you later. Okay?'

Cullen stared at his phone, still no idea what to do about the baby.

~

GUTHRIE WAS WAITING FOR HIM OUTSIDE, TWATTING ABOUT ON HIS mobile. He looked up and got in the passenger seat, along with a cold blast of wind. 'What time do you call this?'

Cullen checked the dashboard. 'Half eight. Why what do you call it?'

'Hardly first thing in the morning, is it?' Guthrie burst out laughing. 'Anyway, I've made good use of the,' he tapped his watch, 'hour and a half I've been waiting. Went to look for Paul McKay. Turns out he's doing the odd shift in a cafe down by the harbour. Tell you, he wasn't best pleased to have a cop call on him there, which worked to my advantage. Boy answered my questions in no time.' He sifted through his notebook. 'I asked him if he got any emails from Strang, like we did with...' He frowned. 'What was that boy's name? The guy in Dundee.'

'Sure you're not hungover, mate?'

Guthrie clicked his fingers. 'Mark Agnew, that's it. Christ, I have to put up with that gimp in the pub every Friday.'

'So?'

'So what?'

'So, had he received any emails?'

Guthrie unfolded a sheet of paper like it would have the genuine Turin shroud on it. 'He got one. Sent it to me. Similar to the one Mark Andrews got, but not quite the same. Some differences, shall we say.'

'He mention Black Matt?'

'Oh aye.' Guthrie tapped the page. 'Strang said he was shagging his sister.'

～

GUTHRIE KNOCKED ON AUDREY PATTERSON'S DOOR.

No answer.

He leaned against the tenement wall. 'We should have spoken to her last night when we had the chance.' He shook his head, though that was a mistake. Tea swilled around in his guts, still heavy with the chips. 'It's embarrassing how little we know about her brother.'

Guthrie stepped back and looked up at the weathered wall. 'Do you not remember what he was like at school?'

'No, why?'

'He was a pretentious little prick.' Guthrie chapped on the door again. 'Even though he was three years younger than us, he used to march around like he was... I don't know. Too cool for school?'

Cullen racked his brains but couldn't come up with a single image of the guy. 'How come I've forgotten him?'

'You've just got a shit memory. It was the same with his sister and you sat next to her in French.'

'What?' Cullen rubbed his temples, his head throbbing. The rubbing didn't help, so he took a deep breath and stepped up close to the door. 'OPEN UP!'

'NO!'

Finally.

Cullen filled his lungs again. 'MS PATTERSON, WE NEED TO SPEAK WITH YOU ABOUT YOUR BROTHER.'

'PISS OFF! I KNOW WHY YOU'RE REALLY HERE!'

Cullen frowned at Guthrie.

'YOU'RE GOING TO RAPE ME! LIKE MY HUSBAND DID!'

Cullen took a step back. 'Goth, what the hell?'

'Long story.' Guthrie rubbed his neck. 'Remember Dean Patterson? Big guy, in the year above us?'

Cullen pictured a Neanderthal knuckle-dragger in his sister's class, the kind who was always in the bike sheds but didn't ride to school. 'She married him?'

'We were out here all the bloody time, mate. Domestic after domestic.' Guthrie sighed, deep and long. 'Then one night he raped her, said it was his marital right and all that shite. We put him away for it. Not much later, her brother went missing. She's not been the same since.'

Cullen blew out his cheeks, then looked back at the closed door, slowly exhaling until his lungs felt as empty as the rest of him. 'Christ.'

Guthrie leaned down and pushed the letterbox flap in to call through the gap. 'Come on, Audrey! This is about your brother. Don't make us get your parents involved again.'

The door opened to a crack. Audrey Patterson gave them each a withering look then disappeared, the door wiggling open. She was walking down the hallway, then entered a room on the left.

Guthrie led Cullen in, following her into the lounge.

Audrey sat on a green futon and stared at them. There was no other furniture, so they remained standing, awkwardly looking around the room. As sparse as a heroin addict's flat, but it seemed like actively chosen minimalism, like Audrey was screaming to the world that she was in control of her life. She looked up at Cullen. 'Are you here to say sorry, then?'

Cullen took a long look at her. Now that she wasn't charging at him with flying fists, he could start to recognise her. Used to have a ponytail and a granny cardigan, her face used to be softer, her eyes less intense. 'What exactly am I apologising for?'

'The way you treated me at school!'

Cullen took a slow breath. 'How did I treat you?'

'You used to take the piss out of me. You and your friends. Every day for two years. I had no self-esteem by the time I left.' A tear slid down her cheek. 'Why else would I marry Dean? I still shake when I hear your name, Scott Cullen. I couldn't believe I saw you the other night.'

Cullen looked her straight in the eye. 'Audrey, I'm sorry. Back then, I didn't mean any harm.'

'You said I smelled!'

Shame burned its way up Cullen's neck. 'That was wrong, but I'm sure I didn't mean what I said to you. I was a child. And I was a total dick.'

'Well, you still said it and it still hurt. You used to chip away at me. Chipped away at me all the time. I felt so small.'

'I'm truly sorry, Audrey. I shouldn't have done that.' Cullen still couldn't remember taking the piss out of her, he hardly even remembered her, but he vaguely recalled the other names and he didn't trust his younger self to have been above her accusations. 'Look, I'm a police officer now. I make sure people don't suffer the kind of emotional and physical abuse you've had to endure, and I'm genuinely sorry to have cause some of your hurt.'

Audrey narrowed her eyes at him.

The room went very quiet.

Audrey merely stared at him, but after a long, tense silence, she nodded. 'Thank you for saying that. This doesn't make us friends. Mum told me you found James.'

'I'm investigating your brother's murder.'

Audrey's eyes lit up.

'Did James ever mention Black Matt to you?'

'What?' And just like that the fire in her eyes went out. 'No.'

'You're sure?'

She nodded, but her mind was somewhere else. 'Jimi only used the name Black Matt once, and that was to insult Andy MacLeod.'

Black Matt.

Andy MacLeod.

It can't be him, can it?

'Mind how he was called Slip Mat? Idiot thought he was a superstar DJ. And he always wore black. Jeans, T-shirt, leather jacket, DMs.'

Cullen pulled the print-out from his pocket and read out the relevant lines.

Matte Black walls. Black Matt steals time.

Guthrie sat next to her on the futon. 'Your brother sent someone an email saying you had sex with him.'

Audrey dropped her gaze to her lap. 'That was just once. I don't know what I was thinking. Jimi used to get bullied a lot by some of the boys in our year. Alan Thomson, Gregor Smith, that whole lot. They used to beat him up and tease him for being gay.'

'Was he?'

Audrey laughed through the tears. 'No. Jimi was...' She took a deep, sobbing breath. 'Andy MacLeod was the worst. Even worse than you, Scott. What the hell was I thinking?'

'What happened?'

'What do you think? He stuck his tiny little cock up me.'

Cullen blushed.

'I felt awful. I was still married to Dean and... I told Jimi. Asked him what I should do.' She sighed, her eyes losing focus as she seemed to picture it happening all over again. 'He went apeshit. Started screaming at me, calling me a traitor. He kept on shouting about hunting Andy down and making him pay...'

Which, given we saw Andy last night, obviously hadn't happen.

At least, not that way round.

'That was the last time I saw my brother. Andy moved to Edinburgh around then. Haven't seen him since.'

36

TORRENTS OF WATER SLUICED OFF THE WINDSCREEN, THE BROODING sky over Dalhousie coming into view with each brush of the wipers.

Cullen glanced at Guthrie, eyes trained on the road, hands full trying to keep the car from drowning in the nearest ditch.

Did we really bully that girl to the point of losing all self-worth?

Did we really kick her down that slippery slope, our casual piss-takes leading to an inferiority complex and an abusive marriage?

'Reckon she's reliable?'

'Eh?' Guthrie frowned. 'Oh, right. Could be on to something, I suppose.'

'What I'm worried about...' Cullen hesitated for a moment. 'So, Andy MacLeod.'

'I know, man...' Guthrie nodded. The only noise was the rain spattering the roof.

Cullen shook his head with a heavy sigh. 'I still can't remember her from school.'

Guthrie laughed. 'You're losing your mind, Skinky. Alzheimer's?'

'My gran had that.'

Guthrie did a double take. 'Maybe you should get it checked out?'

'That's not what I meant, you sick bastard.' Cullen didn't want to think about it. 'I'm just tired. Not sleeping. And I've been under pressure.'

'Did you mean it when you said sorry to her?'

'Christ, you really know how to lift someone's spirit.' Cullen rubbed his neck. 'You said I was a wanker at school. I was.'

'You totally were.'

'That place was dog eat dog, though.'

'True. I think it's got a lot better since they moved to the new place by the bypass.'

'Couldn't get any worse.'

Guthrie bit his lip when he glanced at Cullen. 'Here we are.'

The MacLeods lived at the other end of the street from Cullen's parents, the houses sharing the same two-up-two-down design, though rear extensions, conservatories and loft conversions had forced some divergence over the years.

Cullen got out of the car as a man in his mid-sixties ambled past them on the pavement, carrying his *Courier* and a bag of morning rolls. He watched him go, then scanned the neighbourhood. 'It's too quiet here these days. Remember playing football when we were kids?'

'Oh, aye.' Guthrie gave him a mischievous grin. 'Mind playing with MacLeod?'

'Well...' Cullen marched past the collection of ceramic frogs on the tarmacked front yard and knocked on the door, warrant card ready.

The door opened and Andy MacLeod peered out at them, wearing a dressing gown and looking like death warmed up. 'Sorry, my parents are at work.' He started shutting the door.

Cullen blocked it with his foot. 'Mr MacLeod, we need to ask you a few questions in relation to the disappearance and murder of James Strang.'

'Piss off.'

'I'm sorry, what was that?' Cullen pocketed his warrant card but kept his foot in the door. 'You wouldn't be obstructing a murder inquiry, would you now?'

MacLeod's bloodshot eyes flicked back and forth between his visitors. 'You pair have a cheek after the state I saw you in last night.'

'That's—'

MacLeod kicked Cullen's foot back out and slammed the door.

Cullen clenched his teeth through the pain numbing his toes.

The key turned in the lock.

'Shite.' He looked at Guthrie. 'Wait here.' He limped round the side of the house, catching his suit jacket on brambles. He hauled it clear with a tear and pushed through the gate. The back door looked like it was slightly ajar.

Cullen sped up, limping towards it as fast as his aching toes would let him.

Nearly there.

A shadow moved behind the door and it slammed in Cullen's face.

MacLeod grinned at him through the distorted glass, then a dark outline retreated into the house. Black Matt indeed.

Cullen hobbled back to the front of the house.

Guthrie watched him, concern etched deep into his forehead.

'He's locked both doors.' Cullen knelt down and shouted through the letterbox. 'Mr MacLeod, I can call your parents if you prefer. I'm sure our fathers play golf together.'

An angry shout: 'I've not done anything!'

'Then let's have a chat.'

Silence, just the drone of distant traffic.

'Come on, Andy. Just a wee chat.' Cullen glanced over at Guthrie. 'I can call backup to knock down this door and take you to the station with a charge of obstruction.'

No answer.

Guthrie cleared his throat with a bored cough, like this was a minor irritation he dealt with on a daily basis. 'Mr MacLeod, if we charge you with obstruction, you'll get a fairly sizeable fine.'

The door snapped open.

~

MacLeod's solicitor was already waiting for them outside the interview room, holding his hand out for Cullen and Guthrie. 'Cameron Leonard, pleased to meet you.' The guy looked like a friendly PE teacher, the polar opposite of the smarmy lawyers Cullen was used to dealing with in Edinburgh. 'So what's this about?'

Guthrie entered the room without shaking and started running through the official interview preamble.

Cullen shook his hand. 'It's just a few questions.'

'Right. The laddie's father sent me. Worried about him, ken?'

Cullen looked into the room at Andy MacLeod. *Hardly a laddie anymore.* And if anything he looked even worse. 'Come on, then.' He sat next to Guthrie and nudged his knee under the table. 'Ready when you are, Constable.'

Guthrie gave MacLeod a tight smile. 'Do you remember James Strang?'

MacLeod glanced at Leonard, who returned the briefest of nods, then he leaned back in his chair. 'This is why I'm in a bloody police station?'

'Sooner you answer the question, sooner you get back to that hangover.'

MacLeod gave a brief chuckle. 'I knew Jimi, aye.'

'You hear that he was found dead in Edinburgh?'

'Aye, I knew that, too. It's been in all the papers.'

'You lived there, right?'

MacLeod shrugged like he couldn't care less.

'And you bullied Mr Strang at school?'

MacLeod jabbed a finger at Guthrie. 'No, I never.'

'Sure about that?'

MacLeod leaned forward.

His lawyer cleared his throat. 'Have you got any official state-ment from the school or other appropriate education authorities to that effect?'

'We have witness statements.'

'Bullshit.' MacLeod crossed his arms. 'You've got nothing.'

'You know his sister though, aye?'

'Bumped uglies with her once, but what's it to you?'

'When was this?'

'Cullen, Cullen, Cullen.' MacLeod curled his lips in disgust. 'Audrey told me you bullied her at school. Shouldn't you be under investigation?'

'Just answer the question.'

'You're wasting everyone's time.'

Cullen looked at him with zero humour in his eyes. 'Why are

you back in your home town after James was found dead? You've not gone to ground, have you?'

'What?' MacLeod shook his head. 'The reason I'm here is I've got a few things going on in my private life. My girlfriend left me and I'm between jobs, so I'm staying with my folks while things sort themselves out in Edinburgh.'

Cullen nodded at him like he didn't believe a word, long and slow, eyes wide.

'Come on. If I was lying low, why the hell would I go out on the lash on a Monday night?'

Cullen just stared at him. 'You had sex with James Strang's sister not long before he went missing, didn't you? And James wasn't very pleased with what she did, was he?'

'So what if I shagged her?' MacLeod sighed with boredom. 'Stop trying to frame me for his murder. I know my rights, Skinky.'

'Don't call me that.'

MacLeod smirked. 'Touched a nerve?'

Cullen forced himself to smile. 'Does Black Matt mean anything to you?'

MacLeod frowned. 'Should it?'

'Well, Mr Strang sent a couple of emails which included the term Black Matt. Also mentioned it to his psychoanalyst. I seem to recall you were called Slip Mat at school. Right?'

MacLeod held up his hands. 'I'm not black, am I?'

'So, just for the record, the phrase Black Matt means nothing to you?'

MacLeod leaned forward again. 'Speaking of sisters, this wouldn't have anything to do with yours, would it now?'

Cullen scowled at him. 'My sister?'

MacLeod winked at Cullen, then looked at Guthrie. 'I slipped his sister a length back in the day.' He breathed on his fingernails then brushed them on his shirt. 'Don't think Skinky ever got over that. Probably fancied a go himself.'

Cullen stood up, his chair scraping over the floor with a loud screech. He stood there, fists clenched. Then he flashed MacLeod a professional smile and handed him his business card. Still on Lothian & Borders stationery, still with DS Scott Cullen. 'Thank you for your time, Mr MacLeod. If you think of anything else of such relevance to our inquiry then please don't hesitate to call.'

'Of course I won't.' MacLeod got to his feet and waited while his lawyer packed up his things. 'How is the luscious Michelle?'

'She's fine.'

A uniform stepped in with a grunt.

'Show them out, Stevie, aye?' Guthrie perched on the desk and watched the door close. 'Tell me this has nothing to do with him pumping your sister.'

'Pumping?' Cullen scowled at him. 'Come on, mate, you're better—'

'I'm not better than that. But just tell me it's got nothing to—'

'I'd totally forgotten about it, Goth.'

'Really?' Guthrie's frown deepened. 'You've been forgetting a lot recently.'

~

'OF COURSE HE'S A SUSPECT, CHANTAL.' CULLEN GRIPPED HIS PHONE like that might strengthen his case. 'MacLeod's got means and opportunity.'

'And you've got no evidence.' Chantal sounded far from convinced. 'What's his motive?'

'He bullied Strang at school. And he was living in Edinburgh at the time of the murder. And he slept with Strang's sister, which upset Strang.'

Chantal's sigh betrayed his lack of evidence. 'Killing him still seems extreme.'

'The discovery of the body was all over the papers. So the murderer will be keeping a low profile, right? MacLeod's lying low in Dalhousie, waiting for the coast to clear.'

Chantal sighed. 'Come on, Scott. This is pish. If you lie low, you go to Brazil, not Brechin.'

Cullen gripped his phone even harder.

'What do you want to do, Scott?'

'I...'

'Let him go.' She sighed again. 'Look, I've got a meeting. I need to go. And I need you back here.'

Click.

37

JUST AFTER ONE O'CLOCK, AND THE OFFICE WAS DESERTED. CULLEN'S stomach rumbled, the booze and chips calories long spent. He slumped at an empty desk and opened his takeaway box, the vinegar punching him in the nose. Macaroni cheese and chips. His mouth was watering.

'Hold on.' Chantal pulled up a chair and dumped a plastic tub of salad on the table. 'I need to find the defibrillator.' She tore the lid of and dug a plastic fork in deep. She took one look at his face. 'You've got hangover written all over you.'

Cullen glanced at her but kept his mouth busy chewing. 'I'm just tired.'

'Did you let MacLeod go?'

'He's back out on the street ready to murder.'

Chantal stabbed her fork into a salad leaf. 'Good boy.' She ate her greens. 'Spent all morning interviewing Strang's old work-mates. Last one said Strang was sleeping with the girlfriend of someone in the band.'

Cullen frowned. *Stealing what wasn't mine, taking what didn't belong to me, coveting my neighbour's wife.*

Chantal chewed a cherry tomato. 'The guy I interviewed said Strang was a grade-A shagger. Si's taking a proper statement now.'

'Any idea who this girlfriend is?'

'It's not Beth Williamson. She worked at the shop. They would've said he was getting it on with her, wouldn't they?'

Cullen thought it through. 'It's definitely a girlfriend of someone in the band?'

'Definitely. He told this guy, like it was a moral dilemma. Didn't name any names. Leaving David Johnson or Alex Melrose. Guy's got a type, anyway.'

'What?'

'Well, they're both smack heads, aren't they?'

Cullen groaned. 'So a drug addict has lied to me. Why am I not surprised?'

'Aye, but which one?'

~

CULLEN KNOCKED HARD ON MARTA OWENSON'S DOOR.

No response.

He looked at Chantal, then back at the door. *Give it a few seconds. She's probably busy wiping some kid's arse. Or shooting up in the toilet.* He was about to knock again, when the door finally pulled back on the chain.

Marta's sharp cheek bones poked around the edge. 'What?'

Cullen forced a tight smile. 'Got a moment?'

Marta let the door drift open and gave them a jerky wave to follow her as she staggered to the living room.

Cullen followed her, expecting to be accosted by her gaggle of children, dancing around like in his dream. The place was as quiet as it was empty. 'No kids today?'

'At Mum's.' She retreated to her armchair, but her mind was elsewhere. 'Glasgow police were here earlier.'

Bain...

That prick should've cleared it with Methven. Especially after all that shite at the weekend.

Cullen frowned at Chantal, sharing his rage. 'What did they want?'

'Just asking stuff about Alex. Breaking the news.' She shrugged. 'Can't remember what else.'

Chantal took up position at the far window, the cold light silhouetting her. 'How well did you get on with James Strang?'

'Jimi?' Marta raised a hand to shield her eyes. 'He was okay. Nice enough. Only used to see him when the band played.'

'You never went to the pub or to the same parties, nothing like that?'

'I wasn't much for going out.' She looked down at her bone-skinny legs and started covering them with her ragged wool blanket. 'Would much rather stay in.'

Cullen laughed. 'Taking drugs, right?'

'I'm not answering that.'

Chantal shot a glare at Cullen, her trimmed eyebrows raised. 'Did Alex take heroin with you?'

'Those Glasgow cops tried to bully me into telling them that as well. Gave them nothing, same as I'm giving you.'

Chantal knelt down in front of Marta and offered her a warm smile. 'We heard that James slept with a girlfriend of someone in the band. You were Alex's girlfriend at the time, weren't you?'

Marta nodded, her hard scowl softening a little.

'So. Did you sleep with him?'

'Never.' Marta stared into space, scratching her wrist. 'Look, Jimi tried it on with me once. Must've thought I'd be an easy junkie or something. I knocked that prick back.'

'When was this?'

'Few weeks before he went missing, I think.' Marta glanced at Chantal, a smile flickering on her face. 'I'm not too good with keeping track of time. Alex was in Glasgow meeting up with one of his pals, so Jimi knew I'd be alone in the flat, just me and the kids. His hands were everywhere as soon as he was through the door. I had to tell him to fu— to get away from me.'

Chantal nodded. 'How did Jimi respond?'

'He...' Marta winced. 'He got right in my face, started shouting at me, giving me abuse about how I'd led him on and...'

Cullen hesitated, a lump forming in his throat. 'I take it you hadn't led him on?'

A tear streaked down Marta's cheek. 'No. My bairns were here. It wasn't right.'

～

CULLEN STOPPED OUTSIDE THE DOOR OF DAVID JOHNSON'S OFFICE AT Edinburgh University and took a deep breath.

Chantal stood next to him, looking him up and down, frowning as she knocked on the door.

'Come in.'

The office was a pigsty, a tiny, stuffy pigsty. A box of Lego Technic lay open on a side desk. Johnson was halfway through building some sort of complex vehicle. Still had that intense body language and film-star confidence, even while he was playing Lego.

Every wall choked with shelves full of books, the main desk covered in papers, the blackboard next to it filled with scribbles.

Johnson flashed them a smug grin. 'What, are you surprised I'm doing a PhD?'

'A little, if I'm honest.' Chantal joined him by the desk, taking a surprising interest in the Lego.

'It's like a three-year prison term.' Johnson gave her a grave look, then beamed at her again. 'Joking.' Then he frowned. 'You're not going to take me back to that safehouse, are you?'

'You're safe for now.' Chantal coughed. 'Mr Johnson, did you have a girlfriend when you were in a band with Mr Strang?'

Johnson looked away with a nod. 'Ailsa.'

'Did she have a relationship with Strang?'

Johnson's reply flickered and died on his tight lips.

Chantal did her flirty head tilt. 'So, something happened?'

'No comment.'

Chantal batted her eyelids at him. 'Look, this is relevant to the case. If there was—'

'We split up because of it.' Johnson pressed his lips together, but the smile just wasn't working for him anymore. He picked up a Lego brick and stared hard at it. 'Her name was Ailsa McHardy. She lives in Falkirk now. I was working late, had a shitload of work to get through, then Jimi met her for a drink and...'

Chantal threw her hands in the air. 'You didn't think to mention this when we had you in protective custody?'

'I'd forgotten, to be honest.' He gestured around the cluttered room. 'This PhD is turning my brain to Swiss cheese, I swear.'

38

'INTO THE LION'S DEN.' CHANTAL GAVE CULLEN A FLASH OF eyebrows, took a deep breath and walked into the incident room.

Straight into Methven. 'Sodding hell, Sergeant, what's the rush?'

'Uh, well, we're just...' Chantal stepped back and straightened her jacket. She cleared her throat. 'Got a few leads, sir.'

'I can't read texts. Sodding hell, Sergeant, I explicitly...' Methven huffed out a sigh, then shook his head. 'Who is Andy MacLeod?' His eyes shot to Cullen. 'Ah, he's your suspect, Constable. Correct?'

'That's right.' Cullen clenched his teeth. 'It's still early days but there's—'

'What do you think, Sergeant?' Methven switched his glare to Chantal. 'Is he a credible suspect?'

She gave him an even smile. 'After the record deal fell through, anything's possible. By all accounts, Strang was increasingly volatile.'

Methven looked bored. 'Okay, so what happened? How did he die?'

Chantal leaned against the wall and folded her arms across her chest, her forehead creasing. 'Say Jimi was meeting someone in his practice room. Some sort of struggle. This somebody attacks him with a screwdriver, kills him and drags him down the corridor to bleed out and die.' He shrugged. 'It's filled in a bit of time in what happened to him.'

Methven curled his lips. 'I think you're—'

'Colin.' Cargill stood in the corridor, hands on hips. 'Room three.' She tilted her head behind her and set off away from them.

Methven clapped his hands. 'Right. Good work. Feels like we're finally getting somewhere with this case.' He looked at Cullen. 'We, uh, need a word.' He set off in Cargill's wake.

Cullen's stomach dropped as he followed, like he was walking to the headmaster's office.

Methven stood in the doorway, ushering Cullen in, then shutting the door. He took the seat next to Cargill. 'How are you doing?'

'What?' Cullen sat at the opposite end of the table, hands on his lap, fingers twitching. The place stank of whiteboard pen. That or someone had been taking nail polish off in there. 'I'm fine, sir. Might have a cold on the way but—'

'I meant about being a DC again.' Methven's eyes narrowed. 'We, uh, didn't get the chance to speak to you yesterday. What with all the chaos and everything. When I'd restored a bit of order, you'd gone home to your parents, I believe?'

Cullen gripped his thighs tight. 'I was working, sir. DS Jain instructed me to do some further investigation in Dalhousie, which is where James Strang was from. My home town too, so I stayed at my parents'.'

'I see.' Methven arched his giant eyebrows. 'But that doesn't answer my question. How are you feeling about your career situation?'

Cullen paused.

How do I feel?

Like shite. Like a load of dog shite on Methven's shoes.

'To tell you the truth, sir, I've… I've found it hard. I've decided it's just something I need to go through, right?'

Methven smiled. 'That's a very mature attitude.'

'Well, I need to take the rough with the smooth if I want to achieve my goals. I've been a bit too quick to anger before.' Cullen swallowed hard, with something catching. He took a deep breath. 'If I'm being entirely honest I have to say I'm disappointed I wasn't briefed.' He shifted his gaze between Methven and Cargill. 'I understand there's a lot going on just now and you might not have had the time, but it's disappointing.'

Cargill nodded. 'I appreciate your honesty and can only apologise for the oversight.' She cleared her throat. 'It shouldn't have happened.'

Cullen flashed her a smile. *Don't want her to think this is cool.*

'Colin, I need to catch up with Jim.' Cargill got up and left them to it.

Methven stared at the closing door, then shifted his glare to Cullen. 'I've been looking through the case notes. These emails... Can you prove that Strang sent them?'

'Why? Are you coming around to my theory?'

'Not quite. I'm still concerned about the serial killer angle.' Methven laughed, barely masking his fear. 'If you're right about the personal motive, then it's less likely to be a serial killer. Right?'

'I never really subscribed to—'

'And there will be texts or calls or emails between Strang and this Ailsa woman he was sleeping with.'

'Unless he deleted them.'

'Well, can you speak to Charlie Kidd and see what he's got from Strang's laptop?'

～

EARLY AFTERNOON AND EVERY CURTAIN WAS DRAWN, LIKE THE Forensic Investigation Unit was staffed by vampires. Looked that way as Cullen powered through the open-plan office, passing rows of male civilians, skin pallid from lack of natural sunlight.

Charlie Kidd's desk was about halfway down, facing the stairwell, better to watch for the impatient cops trying to sneak up on him with urgent requests. He looked up and clocked Cullen's approach. His pale face darkened. 'Oh, for crying out loud.'

Cullen sat next to him. 'That's no way to greet an old friend, is it?'

Kidd tossed his ponytail over his left shoulder. 'Don't see any friends here.'

Cullen laughed. 'How are you getting on with James Strang's laptop?'

'I was about halfway through when...' Kidd gritted his teeth and sighed. 'These consultants are in to merge the IT systems across the force. And it's an absolute disaster. I've been pulled in to help, despite the fact I'm supposed to be an investigative resource.'

'Want me to have a word?'

Kidd rolled his eyes. 'Should be fine, Dad.'

'But you have got the laptop, right?'

'Aye, and his old mobile, too.'

'Look, I need you to have a quick search for any messages between Strang and an Ailsa McHardy.'

'Right.' Kidd turned to his computer and started hammering the keys.

Cullen settled in for a long wait, but it only took a few seconds.

'Here you go.' Kidd swivelled the monitor round. 'Tonnes of texts and calls. Flirty. Holy shit, is that a dick pic?'

Cullen averted his gaze. 'Looks like those two were at it, then.'

'Aye. And discreetly. No emails, just these texts.'

'You've been through his emails?'

'Like you asked. Got hauled off onto Project Omnishambles before I could finish.' Kidd opened up another window on his machine. 'Found that email from Strang to Mark Agnew you were after. The boy sent a couple of others that day, all with similar wording.' He handed Cullen a few sheets of printouts.

Cullen flicked through them, the same poem repeated in each email, almost word for word until they diverged into a particular flavour of crazy. One to Paul McKay, one to Mark Agnew, one to Alex Melrose, all broadly similar but riddled with ever more typos. He turned to the final page.

M=M=MQ=ATTT=E BLS=ACK WQ=ALLL=S
Black Mattt=t= = = == =str=eak=ls tu=to=ime

CULLEN POINTED AT THE TEXT. 'WHAT THE HELL IS THAT SUPPOSED to be?'

'I know what it's supposed to be — Matte Black walls, Black Matt steals time.' Kidd stared off into space. 'I've seen that before.' He cleared his throat. 'Back at uni, me and my mates used to go to the computer lab after a night out. Like three in the morning.

Bloody idiots, man. Called the place the Deviant Suite. One time my pal Ross got there early, and sent us all a load of weird emails only his drunk self could comprehend.' He tapped the page. 'They were filled with that equals symbol.'

Cullen narrowed his eyes at him. 'Why?'

'Took us a while to figure out.' Kidd smirked. 'That key is next to the backspace on a keyboard. Ross's alcoholically impaired motor skills constantly hit the wrong keys.'

'So, Strang must've been shitfaced while he sent those emails.' Cullen flicked through the pages again. 'They started out fairly coherent but ended up with this gibberish. Agnew was third, so he got one of the more sober emails.' He stared at the text on the last message. Take out the = symbols and Kidd was right:

Matte Black walls, Black Matt steals time.

'Can you search for Andy MacLeod, please? Emails, texts, calls, anything.'

Kidd went back to work with a groan. 'Oh, there we go. Quite a few here.'

'Seriously?'

'And it seems like they met up a few times.'

'When?'

'Ooh, isn't that the night Strang went missing?'

39

CULLEN STOMPED THROUGH THE CAR PARK, HIS MIND ALREADY IN Dalhousie.

Chantal stepped into his way. 'You ready?'

'Jesus, Chantal, nearly gave me a heart attack there.'

Chantal grinned at him. 'Show me.'

Cullen handed her the email printouts. 'Here you go. Kidd's sticking it in evidence. I've called Guthrie and he's gone to take him in.'

His phone rang. Guthrie's name on the screen.

'Goth, you got him?'

'Round at his folks' house now, Skinky. Mum's in, but she said MacLeod drove through to Edinburgh at lunchtime.'

'Shite. Okay, cheers.' Cullen stabbed at the screen and ended the call. Chantal gave him a quizzical look, but he just shook his head, already dialling Control. 'Need an address for one Andy MacLeod. M-A-C-L-E-O-D.'

∾

CULLEN PARKED THE POOL ASTRA PARKED JUST BEHIND TYNECASTLE football stadium, home of Hearts, and looked out of the window at the sandstone tenement across the road, up to the third floor. 'Left or right?'

Buxton frowned. 'Three eff one. That usually means left, doesn't it?'

'Come on, then.' Cullen got out and led them across the road. The red stair door of MacLeod's building hung open. The intercom lay on the patch of weeds outside the ground floor flat.

Cullen jogged up the stairs, Buxton close on his heels. 'Be careful, he's ran away from me before.' He knocked on the door, wheezing like his gran on her deathbed. 'Police! Open up!'

The door opened and MacLeod stood in his dressing gown, looking tired, blinking hard. 'What the hell are you doing here?'

'Need to ask you a few more questions.'

'You've had your go at me, Skinky.' MacLeod glared at him. 'Try bullying some other old school mates for a change.' His glower shifted to a grin. 'Like Audrey Strang.'

'Get dressed. We're doing this down the station.'

∼

THE INTERVIEW ROOM FELT EVEN SMALLER THAN USUAL. CHANTAL was leaning over the table, doing her best to push MacLeod up against the wall just by staring at him, but all he did was look down at his folded arms. 'Mr MacLeod, will you confirm for the record you were acquainted with a certain James Strang?'

'No comment.'

Cullen lost his patience. 'Mr MacLeod, we have you on record in an interview this morning discussing Mr Strang.'

MacLeod looked at his lawyer, who simply nodded. 'Fine, I knew the boy.'

Chantal took over the questioning again. 'How well did you know Mr Strang?'

'Just knew the kid to speak to. If I saw him in the pub, I'd have a wee chat with him. We weren't particularly close. Come to think of it, I only spoke to him twice since I moved to Edinburgh. Once in HMV, once in a pub. That was it. And that one time in the pub, all he did was give me a flyer for a gig, then tried to sell me a CD. As it happened, a mate's band was playing that night, so I ended up being there anyway.'

'That's it?'

'You trying to tell me you've got something else?'

'These tell a different story.' Cullen fanned out the emails on the table. 'Seems like you met up a number of other times.'

MacLeod glanced back at his lawyer, who barely seemed interested. 'Alright, so I hung out with Strang after that gig. Got pissed with him. Met up a couple of other times but never really talked to him, just got sloshed. You know how it is.'

'Where were you on the night of third of Septem—'

'Seriously?' With a sigh, MacLeod pulled out his phone and ran his fingers down the screen like he was scrolling through old messages. 'Ah, there we go. I arranged to meet Jimi at the pub, but he never showed up, so I went to their practise room. He was talking with someone.' He frowned, setting his phone down on the table. 'That Mike Robertson guy?'

Cullen frowned. 'The singer in Expect Delays?'

'Aye, him. He's on the cover of *The List* this fortnight, right?'

Cullen's mouth went dry. 'Were they mates?'

'Can't say for sure, but Jimi kept going on about Expect Delays. He was obsessed with them. Said he was mates with Mike, but I didn't believe him until I saw them together.'

Cullen nodded slowly. 'That was the night Strang disappeared.'

MacLeod shrugged. 'If that's the date, then aye.'

'Did you see or hear from Mr Strang after that?'

'Nah, Jimi said he'd catch up in the pub, so I went down and had another pint. He never turned up.'

Chantal looked at him like she didn't believe a word he'd said. 'That was it? You didn't try getting in touch again?'

'Of course I did. Texted him a few times, sent a couple of emails.' MacLeod nodded at the pages. 'Boy never got back to me.'

'And you didn't think this was weird?'

'People drift apart, eh?'

A sudden memory got in the way of Cullen tearing into him.

When I first went through to Glasgow, Robertson was being interviewed.

Sounds like he was the last person to be seen with Strang and the last person due to see Melrose before he died.

Shite.

40

Methven looked at Cullen like he had lost his mind. 'How do you figure that, Constable?'

Cullen looked around the incident room, curious faces all looking at their exchange. With a slow, deep breath, he calmed his heart rate. 'It's Mike Robertson. He didn't plan a series of murders like you thought, just a targeted attack on two victims, quick and methodical.'

Methven was still staring at him, but his frown had shifted from bewildered to angry. 'Constable, do you know what you sound like? It's him, not it's her, no it's this other guy. I've about had it with your—'

'Sir, I want to go through to Glasgow and—'

'No, Constable. No sodding way. Given your erratic behaviour over the last few days, I want you to obtain supporting evidence before you bother more innocent people. Now, it's late and you look atrocious. Get yourself home. I want you fresh as a daisy in the morning.'

'Come on, sir, I—'

'No, I shall take this forward with DI Bain. Get home.'

～

Cullen slumped on the sofa and tucked into the last of the ice cream.

Sharon wasn't home yet, clearly ignoring his request not to work too hard today. No texts, no emails, no calls.

Getting on fine without me.

At least the cat snuggled up to him, chin on his thigh, for once deigning to let Cullen stroke him. He smiled down at the wee guy until a big yawn pulled his head back up.

Cullen eased the cat off his lap, got up and strode into the kitchen, where he stuffed the ice cream back in the freezer compartment.

His nose found a sharp tang. He followed the stench into the bathroom. A yellow puddle lay in the bath. Fluffy appeared in the doorway and bleated at him. Piddle in the bath, indisputable evidence of two overly busy people not finding time to change the poor cat's litter.

'Is that why you were being so friendly to me? You want me to clean your toilet?'

∿

Cullen half-filled a bin bag with stinking cat litter. Poor bugger. He poured a bag of fresh litter in but didn't even have time to put the lid back on before Fluffy hopped in and got straight down to business.

'Go for it, boy.' Cullen laughed to himself, then left the cat to it and took the bin bag downstairs.

'My God, are you being useful for once?' Sharon stood in the doorway, eyebrows raised.

'Just doing my bit. Don't want to get kicked out.' Cullen's grin didn't hit the mark. 'Besides, I remember Angela saying pregnant woman aren't supposed to change cat litter.'

Sharon came over, puckering up.

'Stand back.' Cullen raised both hands. 'I'm as disgusting as Fluffy's bath toilet.'

Sharon laughed. 'Alright, go get cleaned up then. We have a dinner date, remember?'

∿

CULLEN'S BURRITO WAS STUFFED WITH STEAK, BEANS AND RICE, AND it was hot, probably something to do with all the sauce he'd poured over it. He kept having to rinse his mouth with lager to keep the heat down.

Sharon grinned at him. 'You should be drinking milk.'

'Milk?'

'To kill the chilli. I think it's the lactose. Or something.'

Cullen frowned. 'I can't order a pint of milk.'

'Let your pride get in the way of a burning mouth, why don't you?'

'Thanks for the advice.' Cullen finished his burrito and set his cutlery down, savouring the fire burning his mouth. The endorphins were kicking in and he started to feel okay again.

Sharon daintily ate her huge bowl of chilli con carne, with an arched eyebrow. 'So?'

Cullen held her gaze for a few seconds. He felt a surge of love, his stomach doing cartwheels. He'd never admit it to anyone, but the way he felt about her made every challenge and setback in his life seem banal by comparison. He just didn't know how to act like an adult when it most mattered. 'It's a good burrito. Nine out of ten.'

She dropped her fork and it clattered off the bowl. 'About the baby, Scott.'

'Right.' He stopped grinning and looked her straight in the eye. 'Look, I know one thing, okay? I never want to be apart from you. All that shit we went through in October, which I've apologised for so many times, I never want that to happen again. Whether we have kids or not, I want to be with you. But fatherhood...' He took a deep breath. 'I just don't know. I mean, we can't even look after the cat properly. Forgot all about his litter, so how am I going to look after a child?'

Sharon nodded slowly. 'So, what are we going to do?'

'You tell me.'

She gave him a long look, then picked up her fork, placed it carefully on her bowl and pushed it aside, half the food untouched. 'Scott, this is a decision we need to make together.'

'Then let's do whatever feels right.'

'Jesus, Scott, I've got something growing inside me that I don't know if I even want. You don't just decide something this important because of how you feel after a burrito. Every hour we don't make a decision is an hour closer to not being able to get out of this situation.' She paused, taking a few deep breaths. 'On top of that, I've got all this shit about my promotion. I really don't need this now.'

He reached across and took her hand. 'I'm sorry. I'm not handling this at all well. But whatever happens, you need to stop pushing yourself so hard. If we decide to keep the baby, I don't want it to be unwell because you're stressing yourself out so much. And even if we don't have it, this stress isn't good for you, either.'

Sharon pulled her hand back. 'Do you want to carry it?'

'I'm just saying.'

They looked at each other in silence, so much more between them than a small table and a few dirty dishes.

Then Sharon started crying.

Cullen grabbed her hands again. 'Sorry, I'm being an arsehole.'

'It's not that, it's just... Well, it is. It's just... This is all pretty overwhelming. Whether we keep the baby or... Look, we don't have to decide it right this minute, but we need to make a decision by the end of the week. I don't want this hanging over us.'

He reached out for her hand and stroked it silently. 'We shouldn't rush it.'

She took a deep breath and blinked away her tears. 'Let's go out for dinner on Saturday — my choice — and then make the decision. And if we choose not to have the baby, you're coming with me to the clinic and you're holding my hand. Okay?'

Cullen smiled at her. 'Wouldn't have it any other way.'

DAY 6

Wednesday

41

First thing, the incident room was as busy as Cullen's mind had been all night. Instead of thoughts and concerns and anxieties about fatherhood whirring around his head, officers were catching up on yesterday's paperwork, phones ringing, a pot of coffee burning on the machine.

'Ah, Constable.' Methven was sipping from a mug. 'You're gracing us with your presence at last.'

'You told me to go home. I'd still be working if—'

'I'm joking.' Methven barked out a laugh. 'You look fresh, I have to say.'

'Thanks, sir. Did you get anywhere last night?'

Methven slurped his coffee then passed the empty mug to a uniform. 'If getting DI Bain to catalogue Mr Robertson on HOLMES, then yes.'

'That's it?' Cullen clamped his jaw. 'Sir, he's—'

'—not your concern.' Methven clapped his arm. 'Now, I suggest you get on with your job, and leave the Glasgow work to Bain and his team, yes? After all, we're dealing with two separate cases.' And with that, he charged off.

Cullen stood there, fists clenched.

Am I the only one who wants to solve this bloody case?

'Scott?' Buxton was sitting at his desk. He looked up, brandishing a sheet of paper. 'Mate, have a look at this.'

'Morning to you, too, Si.' Cullen slumped in the chair next to him and took a look at the sheet. A log of phone calls by the looks of it. 'What's this?'

Buxton shook his head, his floppy fringe swinging all over the place. 'I found a connection between those two cases. Alex Melrose made a number of phone calls to Audrey Strang.'

~

CULLEN MARCHED UP TO THE FRONT DOOR OF AUDREY'S BUILDING IN Dalhousie. The wind buffeted down the narrow street, sending mini spirals of dust in the air. Fresh sea air, stale cigarette smoke. Cullen stood aside and pointed at the intercom. 'Want to do the honours, Si?'

Buxton pressed the bell, leaning in close to the speaker.

'Hello?'

'Ms Audrey Strang? Hi, this is DC Simon Buxton. I'm here to—'

The door clicked open.

Buxton shrugged at Cullen, then stepped into the hallway and led the way up to the first-floor flat.

Audrey stood outside her door, smiling until she saw Cullen. 'What do you want?'

'It's about Alex Melrose.'

'What?' Audrey's eyes flickered like a faulty light. 'Right, I see. Well... come on in, then.' She led into the living room, taking her place on the futon.

Cullen and Buxton taking up position at opposite sides of the otherwise empty room.

Buxton went first. 'I take it you're friends with Alex Melrose?'

She shifted uncomfortably on the futon. Kept her silence.

'Your number's on this list of calls. Quite a few times, Audrey.'

'So?'

Buxton snorted. 'What did you two talk about?'

'Alex and I both missed Jimi. That's all.'

'Is that all you were talking about?'

'Amongst other things. Alex was a funny guy.'

'I'm sure he was.' Buxton raised his eyebrows at her, suggesting there must have been a lot more going on between the two than a few shared jokes. 'What did you talk about?'

Audrey was kneading her hands in her lap until she caught herself. She folded her arms and stared at the floor. 'Stuff. Things.'

Cullen was fed up with her already. More than fed up. 'You know he was into drugs, right?'

'Drugs?' Her face seemed to spasm. 'Drugs are bad.'

Buxton laughed out loud. 'You don't say. Did you know that Alex was a drug dealer?'

'I didn't.' Audrey kept her eyes downcast. She sighed. 'We talked about how things could have been. Jimi, Alex, their band. Their record deal. If they'd got it, maybe Jimi would still be with us.'

'Excuse me?' Cullen waited until she looked up at him. 'Are you saying you knew he was dead?'

Audrey's eyes bulged. 'No! No, of course we didn't.'

'Then what did you mean about him still being with us?'

'I...' She started kneading her hands again. 'When he disappeared, I thought he'd run away to start a new life.'

Buxton looked at her like he didn't believe a word. 'What did Alex think?'

'Alex said the record deal would have made my brother stay. They'd agreed a lot of money.' She frowned. 'But the record company took the contract off the table just before they signed it.'

'Why?'

'Alex said Michael used his influence to spoil the deal.'

Cullen raised his hands to slow things down. 'Hold on a sec. Who's Michael?'

'Michael Robertson. From that other band. Can't mind their name but—'

'Expect Delays?'

'Aye. Him. Jimi hated that lot. Said they stole one of his songs.'

'What?'

She started singing, too high and out of tune. 'Where have you gone—'

'I get it.' Cullen put his hands up again. 'Expect Delays stole an Invisibles song? Why? They're doing well in their own right, aren't they?'

'Not back then. Alex says Expect Delays were going down the

toilet. They were about to get dropped, so they ripped off Jimi's song. It was nothing like the rest of their stuff, but it became their bestselling single. Got played on the radio and everything. It was even on an advert on the TV.'

'Okay...' Cullen started pacing the room, his shoes clicking off the wooden floor. 'Sure Jimi wasn't just jealous?'

'How dare you!'

'I'm not saying I don't believe you, I just like evidence.'

She looked at the window, at the grey tenement opposite. 'Alex told me. Sent me some emails to make them safe.'

Please let this be more than some silly fantasy.

Audrey reached behind the futon and picked a closed laptop off the floor. She stared at the screen for a few moments while she swept her fingers over the touchpad.

Cullen had to clench his teeth to stop himself from telling her to hurry the hell up.

'Alex sent me this.' Audrey twisted the computer round to show them.

Jimi's poem.

Cullen clenched his teeth even harder.

Shite.

Here I was expecting a breakthrough and I get...

Don't let your disappointment show. The poor girl has lost her brother and she clearly means well.

He forced his tight lips to spread into a smile. 'What makes you think this is anything to do with the murder?'

Audrey just looked at him. 'It's obvious, isn't it?' When he didn't agree, she read from the poem, slowly over-enunciating every word as if addressing a child. 'In the end, I was reduced to it. Stealing what wasn't mine, taking what didn't belong to me, coveting my neighbour's wife. Betrayal is the hardest part. Dishonesty, theft, hiding.' She paused, looking up at Cullen. 'That first part is from Michael's perspective. He was reduced to stealing what wasn't his, coveting Jimi's musical talent. Alex said Michael loved that song, used to rave about it all the time. And then he stole it. That line about "Dishonesty, theft, hiding" — that's where Jimi switched perspective to say Michael went behind his back, stole his song and then refused to see him.'

'You got all that from...' Cullen tilted his head, struggling to follow her reading of her brother's gibberish. 'Never mind. Let's say you're right, then how did Michael hide it from him?'

'Michael cut him out of his life entirely. Started telling stories about Jimi.' Audrey sighed. 'But Alex had evidence that Michael killed Jimi. He was going to confront him about it.'

Cullen rubbed his face. 'Jesus Christ.'

She took the laptop and went to another email, opened a file and handed it back.

Cullen looked through pages of musical analysis of the two songs, chord progressions and melodies analysed side by side. At most, any two sections differed by a note or a beat. Whether that was fact or simply the biased opinion of Alex Melrose remained to be seen.

'Alex said Expect Delays hit a bit of a dry spell. Almost dropped. But they released that *Where Has He Gone?* song and it went straight to number one. Totally changed things for them. Mind how some lassie off X-Factor covered it? There was that campaign to get their version to number one? Didn't work, but Alex heard they had over eight hundred thousand downloads in a month. And bang, they got a new deal. Re-released their last album with it on it and bang, a number one album. Now they never need to work again. Just because of that one song. Jimi's song.'

Bang, indeed. There's the motive.

Cullen read the rest of the email, his hands shaking with nervous energy.

Melrose had also included a detailed record of Michael's movements the day Jimi was killed. Looked like it had been put together by Melrose himself, acting as PI, seeming to have talked to any number of Michael's friends and acquaintances.

Cullen got his notebook out and cross-referenced the info with his own case notes on Michael Robertson. At the time in question, the closest Michael had to an alibi was 'seeing a mate'. Nobody probed the flimsy alibi because Michael wasn't a suspect at the time.

Cullen's fingers tightened around the computer.

I could've torn the alibi apart, if only we'd known.

He relaxed his fingers and forwarded the emails to his own

account. 'I need to take this machine into evidence, Audrey. Hope you don't mind.'

'What?'

'It's part of a murder investigation. Why didn't you go to the police with it?'

'After how you lot belittled me when Dean...' Audrey looked away. 'I'll never look for a cop's help again.'

Cullen was torn between sympathy and impatience, so he focused on the lead. 'You said Alex went to speak with Michael. How did that go?'

Audrey shrugged. 'Don't know. He was going to see him last Wednesday, but I've not heard from him since.'

42

'Run that by me again?' Methven's voice hissed out of the car's speakers. 'A dossier?'

Cullen's eyes were locked on the car in front. 'That's what I said."

'That's a hell of a serious allegation, Cullen.' Methven took a loud breath. 'You think Robertson went to meet Melrose on Wednesday night? Sodding hell. Are you saying the cases are linked after all? Robertson first killed Strang and then Melrose?'

'That's what it looks like, sir.'

The line was silent for a few seconds.

'I'm going to Glasgow now, sir.' Cullen sheared out behind a bus and put his foot down. 'I'm meeting DS Jain there, then—'

'You've told her?'

'Couldn't get hold of you, sir.'

'I've warned you about your behaviour, Constable.'

'Aye, but I've told you now. That's progress, isn't it?'

'You're a cheeky sod. Alright, go ahead, but if you pull one of your cowboy stunts, I'm having no part in it.'

'Noted. I'll get DI Bain's team to bring Robertson in, then we'll question him together.'

∽

CULLEN DROVE THROUGH THE OUTSKIRTS OF GLASGOW, CARRIED along on a tidal wave of traffic. The high-rise buildings either side of them looked like massive jetties in a sea of council houses. He pulled into Govan station and blagged the last free parking space.

Chantal was waiting by a pool Volvo. 'You okay to take this back, Si?'

Buxton shivered in the bitter wind. 'Sarge.'

'Cheers.' Chantal led across the car park.

Cullen nodded at Buxton, then followed Chantal over to the front door.

She entered and flashed her warrant card at the security guard. 'Here to speak to DS Damian McCrea.'

The guard picked up his phone and made the call. 'On his way.' Then he went back to playing with his phone.

Chantal and Cullen stood in tense silence.

McCrea appeared through the security barrier, wearing a tight black waistcoat over a bright white shirt. 'Morning, folks.' He signed them in with a cheeky wink at Cullen. 'Good to see the beast from the east back so soon.' He held out a hand. 'India, right?'

Chantal gave him a flirty smile. 'Aye, good guess. That's where my grandparents are from. How about you?' She held up a hand, then pointed at his outfit. 'Let me guess. On a snooker table?'

McCrea laughed. 'Oh, I like the cut of your jib.'

'We're here to interview Mike Robertson.'

'Meaning you need DI Bain to approve the obbo, aye?'

～

BAIN LOOKED UP AND GRINNED. 'SUNDANCE, NOW THERE'S A SIGHT for sore eyes. I need my car washed.'

'Very funny.'

Bain laughed like it really was, then looked Chantal up and down, licking his lips like the pervert he was. 'Who's your wee girlfriend?'

Chantal sighed. 'DS Chantal Jain. I worked for you for two years. Sir.'

'Aye?' Bain raised his eyebrows, looking around the room to see who amongst his team had heard. Only McCrea. He glared at

Cullen. 'Methven called, saying you want to speak with Michael Robertson?'

'Lives through here, so I'm following protocol. Unlike you.'

'What's that supposed to—' Bain dropped the daft smile. 'Forget it. We spoke to the boy and moved on.'

'But you didn't ask him about James Strang, did you?'

'Why would I? The Melrose murder is locked down. It was a drug killing, as you well—'

'Sir?' Chantal stepped forward. 'We're not trying to undermine your drug inquiry. We simply need to speak to him. We've got approval from Superintendent Jim Turnbull, and as you know, Turnbull won't tolerate any obstruction.'

'Aye but he's not the boss now.' Bain squinted at her for a few seconds, then turned to Cullen. 'Is this one of your maverick missions, Sundance?'

Cullen rolled his eyes. 'Look, after everything we've been through together, you should know to listen to me.'

Bain scoffed. 'Right, take your best shot at him. Like I care if you ruin your career. But don't you dare make me look bad in the process. I'm warning you, no messing about here.'

∼

ROBERTSON LIVED IN A VICTORIAN PILE IN THE SOUTHSIDE, LARGE enough for two big families, or a single rock star.

Cullen parked along the road, opposite Bain's purple Mondeo, then flashed his lights. Bain returned the signal.

'Always the same with him.' Cullen got out and led Chantal over. He took one look up and down the street and frowned. 'Where is everybody?'

Bain smirked at him. 'It's just me, McCrae, and you two chickens.'

'This is ridiculous. We're dealing with a murder suspect who poses a considerable flight risk.'

Bain just snorted and turned to look at the house. 'No reason to get your panties wet, Sundance. We think he's inside.'

'You *think*?'

'We've just got here, Sundance. But Control had a noise complaint last night. Big racket about three in the morning. Loud music. Party. Sent a few knuckle-draggers round and they shut up.'

Cullen ground his teeth. 'He's probably not alone, then.'

'Mibbes aye, mibbes naw.' Bain stared at the house for another moment. 'Relax, Sundance. This boy is all skin and bone, no danger he's getting away from us.' He grinned. 'But remember, if this goes tits up, it's your fault.'

Cullen shook his head. 'With no backup, any mishap is your fault.'

'Wrong time for politics, Sundance.' Bain pointed at the house. 'You pair go ahead. McCrea will shadow you, so you don't wet your big boy pants, and I'll stay behind in the car just in case Robertson does try to escape.'

Chantal led over to the garden gate. 'You two go to the front door, I'll go round back.'

McCrea nodded, then held open the creaking gate as Cullen hurried across the pebbled front garden.

Cullen knocked.

No answer.

McCrea looked at him. 'What do you want to do?'

'Well, unless he answers the door, we're snookered.'

McCrea glanced down at his waistcoat. 'Ha bloody ha. Now come on, we're going in. The gaffer'll cover us.'

'You're breaking the door down?'

McCrea winked. 'A trick I learned from an old DI.'

'Not the current one?'

'Christ.' McCrea sighed. 'I though you were meant to be the maverick. Let's just get in there and square up the notebooks after, alright? We found the door knocked in.' He braced himself. 'On three. 'One, two, three.' He shoved his heavy shoulder into the door, smashing it into the hallway wall.

Looked like it had been left on the snib. Probably by some party guest last night.

Cullen followed McCrea inside and had a quick look around. Place seemed empty. No overnight guests lay around, no chill-out tunes blasting out.

McCrea pointed at the champagne bottles in the kitchen sink. 'Somebody had a decent time last night. Still be sleeping off his hangover upstairs.'

Cullen headed to the staircase.

Robertson stood at the top, dressed like he'd slept in his party clothes, or not slept at all. A woman stood behind him, tugging at a white T-shirt to cover her bare thighs.

'What the hell is going on here?' Robertson skipped down towards them with a furious scowl.

'Police, sir.' Cullen got out his warrant card. 'Mr Robertson. We'd like to speak to you in relation to the murders of Alex Melrose and James Strang.'

Robertson stopped at the bottom. 'I've talked about this to one of your colleagues. Nothing more to say.'

'Just come to the station with us, sir.'

'You've broken into my house!' Robertson squared up to Cullen. 'Have you got a warrant for this?'

'We do, actually.' McCrea produced a folded sheet of paper from the inside pocket of his waistcoat. 'Not that we would've needed one. The door was open and we were quite concerned a crime may be in progress. Got a noise complaint, you know? But you seem to be in good spirits.'

Robertson shot him an angry glare. 'Like hell the door was open. Do you honestly think you can get away with this?'

McCrea held up his hands. 'Sir, if you'll just come with us—'

'No, I bloody won't. I want the pair of you out of here and then I want to speak to your boss.'

'He's outside but, believe me, he's the last person you want to speak to.'

Robertson sighed. 'Jesus. Just ask your questions and get out.'

'Thanks.' Cullen smiled at him. 'Now, do you know one James Strang, also known as Jimi Danger?'

'Sure, I knew Jimi. Disappeared a few years back.'

'We found his body last week. In Edinburgh.'

'Oh, aye?' Robertson sounded as bored as he looked.

'It was close to somewhere you knew, a medieval catacomb under the Old Town.' Cullen paused. 'When was the last time you saw him?'

Robertson went from bored to irritated in a heartbeat. 'I don't know, do I? That's ancient history, man.'

'Can you try and think?'

'Jesus Christ, it was probably when he played that gig where he cut himself up. I remember that. Wasn't a pretty sight.'

Cullen kept his smile going, if only to push the guy's buttons. Might get more than a shrug from him that way. 'I gather you used to drink with Mr Strang?'

Robertson rolled his eyes. 'Bugger me, what is this? A walk down memory lane? Yes, I drank with him. For a bit. We used to go out clubbing together. Jimi was a good guy, could always attract the ladies, that's for sure.'

'How was your friendship?'

'Fine, I think.'

'He wasn't annoyed with you about anything? No fights?'

'No.'

Cullen nodded slowly. 'What about Alex Melrose?'

'What about him?'

'I gather you were going to meet him last Wednesday evening.'

'Woah, woah, woah.' Robertson made the time-out gesture. 'You come in here and talk shit about—'

'Sir, we also need to know your movements for—'

Robertson lurched forward, shoving Cullen into McCrea. They keeled over like bowling pins. Cullen tumbled over, landing flat on his back.

Robertson bolted for the open door.

'Mikey, where are you going?' The girl was as stunned as Cullen.

Robertson slammed the front door behind him.

'Get up!' McCrea squirmed underneath him. 'Get off us!'

Cullen scrambled to his feet, then helped McCrea up and ran to the door. His fingers slipped off the handle. He wiped his hands on his trousers, then yanked on the handle again. This time it opened.

Robertson was at the bottom of the garden path, his dressing gown flapping behind him. Cullen set off, crunching over the gravel.

Bain headed Robertson off on the street, going straight at him with a huge punch. Robertson saw it coming, stepped into the swing, let it glance off his shoulder and kneed Bain in the groin. The DI sank to the ground like a deflated balloon.

No sign of Chantal.

Shite.

Robertson stepped over Bain and made straight for his purple Mondeo.

Cullen closed in, feet slapping off the pavement, but Robertson was in the car, the engine screaming in protest. The car fishtailed away from the kerb, tyres screeching in a fug of burnt rubber.

Cullen stumbled out into the road just as the car gained traction and sped off. 'Shite.' He stared after the car as it skidded around the bend out of the estate, then raced back to Bain, McCrea already kneeling over him.

Bain spat blood. 'Get after him, you clowns!'

Cullen was panting hard. 'What about you?'

'I'll be fine. Send a squad car for me. Go! Now!'

Cullen's car pulled up behind him. Chantal reached over and threw open the passenger door. 'Get in!'

Cullen jumped in the front, McCrea in the back.

Chantal pulled off, ignoring the oncoming traffic. A car swerved to avoid them, its horn blaring past them.

McCrea's voice was a horse shout. 'Faster! We'll lose him.'

Chantal was hitting sixty in a residential area, Cullen's Golf bouncing over the speed bumps, the suspension crunching.

Cullen pointed at the purple blur turning right a hundred yards ahead. 'There.'

Chantal floored it, one eye on the road, the other on the rear-view mirror. 'McCrea, call it in!'

McCrea reached into his coat pocket for his Airwave and spoke, his voice drowned out by the roaring engine.

Chantal steadied the car as it came out of the bend on to a dual carriageway.

The Mondeo was about ten cars ahead, moving in and out of sight as it overtook further vehicles.

Chantal shadowed every manoeuvre.

Cullen grabbed the handle over the window, then craned his neck round to McCrea. 'If you'd tried to apprehend Robertson instead of seeing to Bain, we'd've caught him before he got in the bloody car.'

'Piss off! This is your disaster, Cullen.'

'No way. There was no back-up. This is on you and Bain.'

'What were we supposed to do? You'd already pissed off the

Chief Super with your antics. The gaffer had no choice but to keep this quiet so don't tell me—'

'Shut up!' Chantal hammered the horn with the heel of her hand, making a white van swerve out of the way. The speedo went past eighty as she weaved through the traffic, managing to narrow the gap to five cars. 'Any idea where he's heading?'

McCrea leaned between them. 'The M74 is just up ahead. From there, it's all quiet back roads into Bandit Country.'

'Bandit Country?'

'North Lanarkshire. Otherwise, it'll be the M8 for him. If he's got any sense, he'll get off the motorway and ditch Bain's motor.'

Chantal flashed at the car in front and got it to pull in. She hit the floor and just about caught up with Bain's Mondeo, close enough to see Robertson spotting them in the rear-view.

She hammered the horn again.

The Mondeo surged forward. Cullen's Golf only had a one point eight engine, no GTI or anything. The sports Mondeo would be at least three litres and stuffed with turbochargers and fuel injections.

Their luck changed — the traffic ahead slowed. They caught up with Robertson, going bumper to bumper.

Robertson jerked into the exit lane, careening on to a residential street beyond.

Chantal hit the brakes, shifted down and went right after him, engine howling as the cars behind screeched to a halt.

A large SUV was too slow to react, clipped the rear of Cullen's car, sending them spinning into a low wall. The car almost tipped over as the metal ground into stone. It fell back down with a deep thud.

Cullen's head whipped back into the headrest.

The purple Mondeo disappeared from sight.

Chantal tried the ignition, but the grinding noise quietly suggested his car was a write-off.

McCrea groaned in the back seat, then somehow found the nerve to chuckle. 'I'm so glad this is your disaster.'

Cullen only had his sore neck to thank for not punching McCrea there and then.

43

CULLEN UNCLENCHED HIS FISTS, THEN STARED AT THE HALF-MOON-shaped marks his fingernails had left in his throbbing palms. His sigh turned into a wince as he started rolling his shoulders. But he kept at it, trying to loosen the tension in his neck.

Car after car sped past them, heads craning around to gawk at the Golf lodged into the wall. A thick white cloud of steam billowed out of the crumpled bonnet.

Chantal sucked a big breath into her lungs. 'Sorry about your car, Scott.'

'Never you mind that heap of junk.' McCrea snorted. 'The ANPR lost Bain's Mondeo coming off the M74 in North Lanarkshire. Robertson will have already dumped it.'

Cullen sat in silence, the kerbstone digging into his buttocks. *We're bollocksed.*

McCrea's Airwave crackled. 'Oh, this'll be good.' He listened for a second, then sighed. 'Terrific. Bain's car's turned up in Hamilton. Empty.'

~

THE PURPLE MONDEO SAT IN A SMALL LANE, WITH A LOCAL uniformed officer stood by the vehicle, trying to act as professionally as he could with a manic DI shouting the odds in his face. A parking ticket was stuck under the windscreen wiper, flapping in the breeze.

'How did it get ticketed before it got called in?' Bain ripped the ticket off the windscreen, a white plaster stuck across his nose. 'What's the point in having a call put out for it?' He stuck the ticket in his notebook. 'Someone's boss is getting paid a visit.'

Cullen approached with caution. 'Shouldn't you be in a hospital bed after what Robertson did to you?'

'Eh? Of course not.' Bain scowled at Cullen. 'I've no time for that shite.'

Cullen's phone buzzed in his pocket. He checked the screen as he walked away a few steps. Missed call from Sharon. Heart thudding, he called her back. Straight to voicemail.

'Hey, it's me. You okay? Give me a call back.'

Not that she ever listened to voicemails.

Cullen pocketed the mobile and hurried back.

'Come on, sir, we need to get going.' Chantal grabbed Bain's sleeve and led him away. 'Let's have a look at the CCTV footage, okay? See where Robertson went after?'

'The boy could be anywhere.' Bain squinted up at the camera fifty yards further along the lane. 'That thing better be working.' Then he turned to Cullen.

'Don't look at me.'

'But you're so good at looking at CCTV footage, Sundance.'

'This isn't my jurisdiction.'

'Nor mine.' Bain sneered at him. 'I'm Glasgow South, not this backwater. And I'm giving you a direct order, Constable. Look into the CCTV.'

Cullen took a deep breath. 'I really don't—'

Bain's phone started ringing. He answered it with a smug grin, his eyes locked on to Cullen. 'What?' His grin faded. 'Shite.' He put his phone away. 'DCS Soutar wants us at the station to go over this clusterfuck.'

~

CULLEN GRIPPED HIS MOBILE TIGHT AND LEANED BACK AGAINST THE wall, feeling like part of his brain had died. 'I think I've caught your cold.'

'You have been pushing yourself a bit hard.' Sharon sounded distracted. 'Where are you?'

'Govan. Long story, but we lost our suspect and Chantal killed my car.'

'She what?'

'Aye, it's getting towed to some garage in Glasgow. Thing's absolutely mangled.'

McCrea, Bain and Graham marched down the corridor

Shite.

Cullen ducked into the stairwell. 'I'm waiting on Turnbull and Cargill to meet us here. We're going in front of Soutar.'

Sharon tutted. 'Jesus, Scott. Remind me why I go out with you again?'

Cullen hesitated. 'Because I sound sexy when I whinge?'

Silence on the line.

Turnbull came barrelling down the corridor, wearing full uniform, nostrils flaring. Cargill and Chantal were jogging to keep up.

Chantal saw him peeking through the stairwell door and waved at him.

Cullen lowered his voice to a whisper. 'Better go. We're heading in. I'll call you later.'

'Scott, I need to—'

'I've got to go. What is it?'

She sighed. 'It'll wait.'

'Alright. Bye. I love you.'

Cullen hung up and started off down the corridor. His phone went off in his hand.

Buxton.

Chantal was holding the meeting room door open for him. *Shite.* He held up a finger, then he took the call. 'Make it quick, Si, I'm in a rush.'

'I've got your CCTV footage. You coming through?'

'Doubt it.'

'You want me to look through it, right?'

'If you wouldn't mind...' Cullen nudged the door open and tried to sneak in.

'Ah, DS Cullen.' DCS Carolyn Soutar sat at the end of the table, frowning at him. She had a commanding presence. Unfortunately, she also had a voice like Margaret Thatcher. 'Sit.' She motioned to the free seat between Turnbull and Cargill.

Opposite Bain, McCrea and their dour-faced superior, DSI Keith Graham.

Cullen sat as instructed, then cleared his throat. 'It's DC Cullen, ma'am.'

'Is it?' Soutar turned her frown on Turnbull. 'I see. Well...' She looked around the room. 'Thank you all for gathering here. I didn't think we'd have to deal with this kind of issue so early.' Her eyes settled on Cullen. 'It would appear we've managed to get ourselves into a bit of a situation here. I don't know or care how, but let there be no mistake, from this point on, both investigations are officially under Glasgow South direction.'

'Carolyn...' Turnbull drew a starched white handkerchief from the hip pocket of his uniform, daubed the spittle off his lips and gave her a tight smile. 'I don't think it'd be prudent to merge these cases. At least not under Keith's remit.'

Graham shook his head. 'I disagree.'

'Please, gentlemen.' Soutar shot them both a stern look. 'Go on then, Jim. Why?'

'Look, we're happy to acknowledge there are certain connections, but are we positive the cases are genuinely one and the same?'

'Absolutely not.' Bain snorted. 'Our boy was killed for drugs. No idea why theirs was. Some rock-star bullshit.'

Cullen raised his hand and waited for Soutar to nod at him. 'Michael Robertson met both victims the nights they died, and he's alleged to have had acrimonious relationships with both. In my book, that makes him a suspect for both murders.'

Turnbull nodded. 'I suggest we pursue a bilateral strategy, Carolyn. You should be aware of DI Bain's reputation for man-management.'

'Now wait a minute.' Bain scowled at him. 'What are you saying?'

'You worked for me, Brian. I'll leave it at that.'

Bain mimicked his voice. 'I'll leave it at that.'

Turnbull ignored him. 'Carolyn, you're aware of the issues surrounding DI Bain's suspension last year.'

Bain stabbed his finger at Turnbull. 'Watch what you're saying.'

'Really?' Turnbull smirked at him. 'You don't want me to go into the reason why you're no longer in Edinburgh?'

Bain looked away. 'I was cleared of any wrongdoing.'

'You assaulted a senior officer.'

'Okay.' Soutar cleared her throat with a sharp cough. She was blushing. 'Jim, time is of the essence here, so I want us to focus on the matter at hand. I've just had a phone call from the Chief Constable's office. Some London lawyers have been making inquiries about this attempt to bring in Michael Robertson. Apparently, it's jeopardised a concert at Hampden Park tonight.'

'Seriously?' Cargill sighed. 'We had a lead and we followed it through. DC Cullen obtained intel pointing to his possible involvement. We confronted him and he fled, stealing DI Bain's car. Our priority has to be finding him, not talking politics.'

Soutar narrowed her eyes. 'What are you trying to say here?'

'I don't think the investigation should be placed under DI Bain. He's not fit for purpose.'

Bain glared at her. 'You better be careful what you're saying, princess. I know our case is a drug-related crime. The evidence I've seen from Sun... from DC Cullen has been sketchy at best. I'm not even sure you've got a case at all.'

'We know that Robertson talked to both Strang and Melrose on the nights they died. End of story.' Cullen blew out his cheeks. 'As far as DI Bain's theory that it was a drug killing? It's a fine theory, but it's wrong. Robertson stole a song from Strang's band and built a career on it. They fell out over that. We know The Invisibles were offered a record deal. Robertson somehow managed to exert pressure and it was withdrawn. The next we know, Strang confronted Robertson in Edinburgh. Robertson must have killed Strang and hid the body away in the abandoned streets under the Old Town which he would have been familiar with because—'

'Okay.' Soutar tapped her pen against her pad for a few seconds. 'Very well, I'm supervising this personally.' She looked from Turnbull to Graham. 'Gentlemen, we're treating this as linked. I'm SIO. You both answer to me. I expect this to work seamlessly and I will hold both of you accountable if this is not a success.' She waited until they both nodded, then clapped her hands. 'Now, I need a private word with you. Brian and Alison, you too.'

Cullen got up first.

'Constable...' Soutar pointed at him with her pen. 'Can I ask you to lead the search for him? Get together all the possible leads. Fifteen minutes and we'll be through to check on progress. Okay?'

44

CULLEN WALKED OVER TO THE WHITEBOARD, FILLED WITH possibilities of who to look for in the hunt for Mike Robertson.

Friends.

Family.

Work Colleagues.

Chantal joined him, uncapping a pen like she had something new to add to it. 'What are you thinking?'

'Very little.' Cullen rubbed at the day-old stubble on his chin. 'Friends and work colleagues would be his band plus a few others, right? Band manager, people at the record label, hangers-on, mates, guitar tech, sound guy and so on.'

Chantal nodded. 'That's a long list.'

'And we need to go through it. Robertson's gone somewhere. Maybe someone on this whiteboard knows where.'

McCrea got up from the table and joined them at the board. He tapped on the friends list, smudging the ink slightly. 'You can tick her off that bird at his house.'

Chantal scowled at him. 'That bird?'

'Christ's sake.' McCrea snatched the pen off her and scored out the name Leanne. 'She was questioned and released. Just a groupie he'd picked up at the backstage party. Never met him before.'

'Great.'

McCrea looked at the board and his shoulders slumped. 'We know so little about him.' He scanned the rest of the lists. 'This is a shambles.'

'Aye.' Cullen glared at him. 'But at least it's my shambles, right?'

'We'll see.'

The door opened and Methven strode in, his thick eyebrows knotted into a tight frown. 'What's the plan of attack here?'

'We're thinking, sir.'

'Thinking?' Methven jangled the change in his pocket. 'We need to round-table this.'

McCrea laughed. 'What the hell does that even mean?'

'It means we need to get round a table and plan this out, Sergeant. Properly.'

Chantal nodded. 'We need to think about press releases, probably Crimewatch.'

'Very good.' Methven gave her the thumbs-up. 'That'll be good publicity for Police Scotland.'

Cullen walked back to his chair and collapsed into it. 'It's not going to find him any faster, though, is it?'

'Sundance is right.' Bain was standing in the doorway. 'We need to find this boy and quickly. From the way Robertson bolted when Cullen ploughed in, we can assume he's guilty of one crime or another. We just need to get him in a room and pile into him.'

'You've changed your tune.' Cullen's phone rang. He got it out of his pocket and checked the display — Buxton, again.

Bain scowled at him. 'Turn that bloody thing off.'

'Sorry.' Cullen flicked the ringer off and walked back over to the board. 'Let's focus. His friends and workmates will heavily overlap. The guys in the band were probably his best mates, though most likely they'll hate each other by now. Either way, they should be able to give us a lead.' He started drawing on the whiteboard. 'Neeraj Patel on guitar, Jenny Stone on bass, Brian Hogg on drums.'

'Sundance, you and McCrea can do the rhythm section.' Bain sneered at him. 'That's the bass player and drummer.'

Cullen clenched his teeth. 'I know what it is.'

'Bravo.' Bain grinned at Methven. 'You all right to sit and fiddle with your phones while young Scotty takes his swimming lessons?'

'Will you just sodding grow up?' Methven gave a tired sigh. 'This is your fault.'

'Aye?' Bain folded his arms. 'You've got an extra stripe and you think you're Billy big balls now, do you?'

Methven ignored the insult and looked at the rest of the team.

Bain sighed, probably disappointed not to get a rise out of him. 'Sundance, how's the CCTV from Hamilton?'

'Got it, Simon Buxton's going through it.'

'In the name of the wee man.' Bain shook his head in disbelief. 'Robertson could be anywhere and you've got that chump on it?'

Methven cleared his throat. 'Cullen, the band will be at Hampden, sound-checking for the gig tonight. Can you please speak to them?'

45

CULLEN WALKED ONTO THE PITCH, HAMPDEN STADIUM SPREADING around them. Always looked small on the telly, especially compared with others, but being inside it... It was massive. A snare drum echoed around the empty stands over and over again, changing ever so slightly with each beat. The stage was in the goalmouth at the far end, alive with roadies carting amps and cable rolls back and forth, like ants swarming around under the massive black screen. A walkway extended into the crowd towards them.

'Amazing.' McCrea looked around, wide-eyed. 'Always told my old man that I'd get on the pitch here, just expected it to be scoring against the English.'

The drum sound changed as Cullen walked towards the stage, getting deeper with each step, now a low *booov*. Someone turned up the volume, the beat approaching ear-shattering levels.

Cullen waved down a security guard and showed his warrant card. 'Looking for Expect Delays.'

The guard pointed at the stage. 'The drummer's doing his soundcheck now.'

'Has the singer shown up?'

'No idea.'

'No other band members?'

'Nah, just the manager.' The guard looked around. 'At least he was here earlier. Oh, hang on, there he is.' He pointed at a tall man coming out of the VIP toilets, rubbing his nose. 'That's him.'

Cullen nodded, then headed over, McCrea cursing under his breath as he struggled to keep up.

The drums cut out. In the throbbing silence, the guy behind the drum kit leapt to his feet and tossed his sticks to a waiting roadie. A small Expect Delays banner hung above him, dwarfed by the huge U2 light show.

Cullen headed the manager off just before he reached the stage. 'Excuse me, you the manager of Expect Delays?'

'Aye.' He swept his salt and pepper fringe out of his ridiculously handsome face and gave Cullen a piercing look. The guy had the bluest eyes cocaine had ever seen.

'You got a name?'

'Lennethy.'

'That a first or second name?'

'Who are you?'

Cullen flashed his warrant card just as McCrea caught up. 'Police. Looking for Mike Robertson.'

'Finally.' He sniffed as he nodded a rock-star welcome at McCrea. 'Been meaning to call you boys and put out an APB on the wanker.'

'You heard from him today?'

'Naw. We were in Birmingham last night. Amazing show, got on the bus after it, had a wee party on the road, then dropped them off at their homes. Night in their own beds, eh? Bloody Mikey pulled some lassie when we stopped at the services. Some shagger that guy, eh?' He gave a mad cackle.

Cullen humoured him with a quick smile. 'You know if anyone else has heard from him?'

'How the—' He sniffed again. 'Wee Brian's up there just now.' He pointed up at the stage, where wee Brian was just starting to sound-check the rack toms. 'Christ, can't hear myself think!'

Cullen raised his voice. 'Where are the other two?'

'Ever heard the phrase herding cats? That's my day job, pal. Every single day. This lot, I swear. Let them out of your sight for one minute and—' Lennethy sniffed, again. 'Just a sec, I need to go to the bogs.'

Cullen stopped him. 'You've just been.'

'Have I?'

'Are you serious?' Cullen frowned at him. 'Where is Robertson?'

'Far as I know—' Lennethy flinched, then got out his mobile. He glanced at the screen and a smile spread over his face. 'Mind if I takes this?' Didn't wait for an answer. Must've felt the buzz, the drumming was way too loud. 'Hey, Splodge, can I call you back, man? Four should do it, aye. Usual.' He hung up and made another call, then hung up again. 'Only got Mikey's voicemail. What's he done?'

Cullen dismissed the question with a wave. 'Did you know James Strang?'

'Nope.' Lennethy was looking over at the backstage area, and the toilets.

'Jimi Danger?'

'Him.' Lennethy stared hard at Cullen. 'What's he got to do with Mikey?'

'Found his body in Edinburgh last week. We need to—'

'Wait, wait, wait. You think Mikey murdered him?' Lennethy raised his eyebrows, his blue eyes as big as the sky. 'Are you mental?'

'We understand Mr Strang had a grievance with Mr Robertson.'

'Stupid prick.' Another sniff. 'Listen to me. Mikey didn't steal *Where Has He Gone?* from anyone, least of all that twat. What a load of shite. You ever hear the phrase Where there's a hit, there's a writ?'

McCrea shook his head. 'We have a musicologist proving that song and *Goneaway* by The Invisibles are the same piece of music.'

'Glad to see my tax bill being spent wisely...' Lennethy sighed, then leaned in close as if confiding a terrible secret. 'Jimi Strang was a radge wee walloper. A jealous has-been. I saw his last gig. The boy had totally lost it, man. You know that Morrissey song, *We Hate It When Our Friends Become Successful?* That's Jimi to a T.'

Cullen nodded. 'Okay, let's say Mr Strang just imagined it. He'd still have had cause to resent Mr Robertson, wouldn't he?'

'Why would Mikey kill him, though? Doesn't make sense.'

'To keep Mr Strang quiet? How big would the lawsuit have been, do you think?'

Lennethy didn't say anything, just rubbed his nose.

Cullen narrowed his eyes at the shifty hustler. 'Did you know Mr Strang was also under the impression that Mr Robertson personally ruined a record deal they'd been offered?'

Lennethy's eyebrows shot up all the way up to his fringe. 'Bollocks. Listen, I knew a couple of labels were sniffing around his piece of shit band, but that's not the same thing as a contract being on the table, you know? Jimi could be a bit delusional at times.' He rubbed his eyes. 'Don't get me wrong, I liked the boy when I first met him, but he just didn't operate by the same rules as the rest of us.'

'I'm more concerned with actual rules.' McCrea folded his arms. 'We call them laws, and Mr Robertson broke several this afternoon when we went to speak with him—'

'What!' Lennethy's arms went wide. For once, his emotion seemed genuine, not some contrived act. 'He's supporting U2 tonight! Look around you, man. There's going to be fifty thousand people here. Probably at least half of them to see my lot and most of those will buy a CD. You know how hard it is to sell CDs nowadays?'

'No, I don't. I need to find Mr Robertson as a matter of urgency. Can you think of any family he might've turned to?'

Lennethy rubbed his nose. 'Would need a long, hard think about it, man.'

Cullen stared at the manager. *Prick's playing for time.* 'No brothers or sisters that came to gigs?'

'He's an only child, man. You boys have clearly not done your homework. His folks live in Edinburgh. Sorry, lived. They carked it a few years back. Gives the boy his haunted look.' Lennethy glanced up at the stage. 'Where the hell is Jenny?'

Cullen frowned at him. 'Isn't she here?'

'Like I say, man, herding cats. She's meant to be up next, once Bongo up there's finished his test. Her bass rig's set up but she's not. Christ, man.' He sniffed. 'Tell you, I'm bursting for a slash.'

Cullen pointed at the stage. 'You can probably tell Mr Bongo here to stop. The gig isn't happening tonight.'

⌇

Cullen walked up to an expensive Victorian terrace in Glasgow's West End. Huge bay windows either side of a columned portico. He hit the buzzer and waited. 'Nice pad.'

'Aye.' McCrea was peering inside. 'Tell you, I can play bass better than—'

The buzzer sounded. 'What?'

Cullen cleared his throat and leaned close to the intercom, a silvery box mounted in the middle of the pale-green door. 'Ms Stone? It's the police. Please open up.'

A pause, just hissing static. 'Fine, I'll come down. Got a cab coming to pick me up anyway. We can talk while I wait.'

McCrea grinned. 'The things I would do to her, I tell you. Not hard to see why she's in the band, mate, and it's not her prowess on the bass. Like I say, I'm miles—'

The door thunked open and Jenny Stone stepped out, looking as bored as she was beautiful. Classic rock chick — dyed blonde hair with dark roots, tight denim skirt, red leather jacket, her fitted white blouse pulled down to show a black bra and lots of cleavage. 'Oh, there's my cab. Can we do this later?'

McCrea was practically drooling.

Cullen stepped in her way. 'Your gig's cancelled.'

'What?'

'We're looking for Mike Robertson. You know where he is?'

Jenny was staring at her phone. She put it to her ear. 'Lennethy, what the—' She turned away, frowning. 'Right.' Then back at Cullen, as she pocketed the phone in her jacket. 'I've not seen him since last night.'

'Mind if we come inside?' Like a creepy uncle at a sweet sixteen party, McCrea put an arm around her waist and led her into the house.

Inside, Cullen felt like he'd walked into a Turkish coffee house.

Jenny wriggled out of McCrea's embrace and hurried into a bohemian lounge full of low-slung sofas and bean bags under a canopy of colourful printed sarongs draped all over the ceiling. 'So what's this about?'

'Alex Melrose and James Strang. We think—'

'Wait, what?' Jenny sunk on to one of the sofas and her eyes bulged. 'Jimi's *dead*?' She stared at Cullen as if he'd slapped him in the face, then burst into tears.

'You were close?'

She looked up, startled, as if surprised to find she wasn't alone. 'Kinda. He used to follow me around like a little puppy.'

Cullen put a couple of pieces together in his head. The name, the reaction — the Jane that Strang's mother had mentioned was, in fact, Jenny.

McCrea leered at her. 'I bet you get that a lot, eh?'

Jenny ignored him, so Cullen continued the questioning.

'Did you ever reciprocate his feelings?'

'Hardly. He wasn't my type.'

McCrea licked his lips. 'What is your type?'

Jenny scowled at him. 'Is that relevant? Listen, Jimi was a good friend, so this is sad news to me and I'd appreciate if you could let me grieve in peace.'

'Of course.' Cullen held up his hands in apology for McCrea. 'Just one quick question before we go. Do you have any idea where Mr Robertson might be?'

Jenny folded her arms. 'You'll have spoken to Beth, right?'

'Beth Williamson?'

'Of course Beth Williamson. She used to go out with Mike.'

46

Cullen jogged into Leith Walk incident room, looking for Buxton. 'Ah, there you are.' He rested a hand on the desk, trying to catch his breath. 'Why aren't you answering the phone?'

Buxton waved a hand at the screen. 'Because I'm searching through the CCTV like you bloody asked.'

'Got anything?'

Buxton didn't even reply, just stared hard at the screen.

'Si?'

'What?'

'Have you found Robertson after he dumped Bain's motor?'

'I think I'm going blind from watching CCTV footage in Hamilton.' Buxton hit a few keys on his laptop and showed him a freeze frame. 'Taken me ages, but Robertson got the bus to Edinburgh.'

The image on the screen was fairly pixelated, and Robertson was keeping his head down in the queue, but it was definitely him.

'He hopped on a coach at eleven fifty this morning, destination Edinburgh.'

'Okay, so is he here?'

'That's the thing. We don't know if he made it all the way. The CCTV camera on the coach was out.'

'You can't get footage from any of the stops?'

Buxton sighed. 'I've been through what I can get. There are a couple of guys who could pass for Robertson getting off, one at the stop just by the zoo and the other at the bus station, but that's it. That geezer's going to email the high-res screen grabs across but I've not got anything yet.'

Cullen nodded. 'What are you doing now?'

'Going through the onboard CCTV from the bus company to confirm it.'

'Thought the camera was broken?'

'The external one still worked.' Buxton fast-forwarded through the footage.

Cullen yawned, tears blurring his vision even more.

'Scott!' A gruff voice called from the other side of the room. Craig Hunter was staring at him, in uniform, his disco muscles poking out of his black Police Scotland T-shirt. 'Chantal asked me to get you to join her downstairs.'

'Eh?'

'I brought Beth Williamson in.'

'You found her?'

'When we were in the safehouse, she... She was flirting with me. Gave me her mobile number.'

'A fetish for pregnant women, eh?'

Hunter blushed. 'Piss off.' He turned on his heel and walked back out. 'Come on, she's downstairs.'

≈

CULLEN OPENED THE INTERVIEW ROOM DOOR.

'Ms Williamson isn't a suspect. She's merely being asked to assist with our investigations.'

Cullen walked into the dark room and sat next to Chantal, his brain fizzing with energy.

'DC Cullen has entered the room.' Chantal gave him a luke-warm smile, then looked over the table. 'You don't need to be here, Mr McLintock.'

Ah shite.

Campbell McLintock flicked an imaginary dust mote off his navy pinstripe suit, then glanced down at his lime green shirt and straightened his purple tie with the same smug grin that had graced countless newspaper front pages in his storied career. 'I'll be the judge of that, Sergeant. Given the recent changes in our country's criminal justice system, I think it is in both of our interests that I'm present, don't you?'

'Nothing to do with the fact you're charging Ms Williamson by the hour?'

'I beg your pardon?'

Chantal mirrored McLintock's smug grin, then looked at Beth. 'Ms Williamson, can you please detail your relationship with Michael Robertson?'

'We knew each other from music.' Beth looked like she hadn't slept since Cullen had last spoken with her, her deep bags acting like eyeliner. 'We both played gigs in Bannerman's and we had practice rooms in Niddry Street, where you found...' She took a sip of water. 'We did a few gigs together in Glasgow.'

'That's it?' Cullen frowned at her. 'That's the extent of your relationship?'

'I'm sorry?'

'You and Mr Robertson were no more than friends?'

Beth glanced at her lawyer. 'That's what I just said.'

'I've heard that you were—'

'Constable!' McLintock went wide-eyed. 'My client has already defined the nature or her relationship with Mr Robertson. Please drop the matter.'

Cullen kept his eyes on her. 'That's your final answer, is it?'

She nodded but evaded his stare.

'A good friend of yours told us otherwise.' Cullen opened his notebook. 'Jenny Stone.'

Beth's forehead creased. 'Jenny?'

'She's the bass player in Expect Delays. You knew her too, right?'

Beth gritted her teeth. 'I know her.' She slid her wedding ring up and down her finger. 'Sod it. Mike and I went out with each other for sixteen months. So what?' A tear escaped from her closed eyes. 'We broke up when he made it.' She rubbed her eyes. 'It was for the best, I suppose. I'm not the most trusting and him being away on tour or in a studio for months on end wouldn't have been good for me.' She looked down at her belly and her lips tightened into a grim smile. 'Besides, I probably wouldn't have this one on the way if he hadn't broken up with me.'

Cullen shrugged. 'It might have been useful for your career, though, right?'

'I'm sorry?'

'Remember when I asked you if you knew why your band's offer of a record contract fell through? And remember how you said you didn't know? Well, Mike Robertson was responsible for that.'

Beth's face went white. 'Where did you hear that?'

'Is it true?'

'I don't know.' Beth started wringing her hands. 'Jimi thought it was true. Why would Mike have done that? I don't get it.'

Chantal referred to her notebook. 'Mr Strang was under the impression that Mr Robertson had stolen *Where Has He Gone?* from your band.'

'Shite.'

'It's true, then?'

McLintock cleared his throat with a sharp cough. 'Sergeant, my client wishes to make no further statement on the matter.'

Chantal gave him her best impression of his smug grin. 'This isn't going to look good for your client. As it stands, Ms Williamson lied to us on the record. We have enough here to prosecute her. She'll get a fine, probably. But it'll be hefty.'

McLintock looked away.

Chantal turned back to Beth. 'So, Mr Strang told you his theory?'

Beth shrugged. 'Jimi certainly thought it was the same song.' She looked down at her interlocked fingers. 'You've got to admit there's a big similarity between them.'

'Did Mr Strang do anything about it?'

'No idea.'

Chantal nodded. 'We tried to speak to Mr Robertson earlier today, but he assaulted three officers, stole a car and ran off.'

Beth just laughed.

'Have you had any contact with him?'

Beth scowled at her. 'Mike is the last person I'd want to see, believe me.'

'That's a definite no?'

Beth looked away again. 'We just had sex with each other for sixteen months. He isn't the love of my life or anything. And he ended it, not me. I wasn't pleased, so if I saw him now, I'd kick him in the balls and tell him where to go.'

Chantal pursed her lips. 'Can you think of—?'

Beth flinched slightly and touched a worried hand to her large stomach. 'I need to lie down.'

McLintock jumped to his feet and helped Beth off her chair with a furious glare at Chantal. 'I think my client has assisted you quite enough now with your inquiries, Sergeant.'

∽

METHVEN WAS IN THE INCIDENT ROOM, FINGERS BATTERING A laptop's keyboard. He looked up, then shut the screen and sat back, arms folded. 'Well?'

Cullen smiled. 'She pretty much confirmed our theory.'

'Pretty much isn't good enough.' Methven raised his bushy eyebrows. 'I'd expect pretty much from our colleagues in Glasgow South. Not from you.'

'Alright, let me rephrase.' Cullen perched on the desk. 'I think she knows something. Do we have the manpower to put a tail on her?'

'Graham and Jim have half of Scotland at their disposal.'

Chantal nodded. 'Can we make it some of our better officers, though? I'd like DC Murray and PC Hunter.'

'Stuart Murray is coming on shift just now, I think.' Methven opened the laptop again and checked the roster. 'Aye, he is. You can have him. As for Craig Hunter, he's back in uniform, so he's out of our grasp.'

'Can you try?'

'Fine.' Methven nodded, then looked over at Cullen. 'Now, Constable, can you get back to that CCTV?'

Cullen got a call and checked the screen. Sharon. *What the hell?* 'Sorry, sir, I need to take this quickly.' He didn't wait for a reply, just answered the call.

She wasn't speaking, just crying.

'Sharon? Are you okay?'

'No.' And she was gone.

Cullen tried calling her but she bounced the call. He looked back at Methven. 'Shite, I need to go.'

'Now? When we've got a manhunt on.'

'I'll be back as soon as I can.'

47

CULLEN JOGGED UP THE ROYAL MILE, SWEAT TRICKLING DOWN HIS back, feet hammering the cobbles. He tried Sharon again. Straight to voicemail. Again. He pushed the pace even harder up the hill, panting as he dodged between two Chinese tourists photographing everything, weaving into their shots of pub fronts and gaudy shop windows stuffed with tartan trinkets.

He dived into World's End Close and fumbled his keys in the door. Then he bombed up the stairwell, pounding away.

Footsteps came from above.

Cullen stopped and pressed himself against the wall.

Shite. Has someone got her?

'There you are.' Michelle Cullen stared down at him, looking as harassed as ever. She'd put on quite a bit of weight recently, her dark clothes all a number too small. Her hair was dyed a matt black, entirely the wrong colour for her pale skin. And yet she still looked like a shorter version of him with long hair.

Tough luck, sis.

Cullen huffed out a sigh, but he was so far away from catching his breath. 'Not the time, Michelle.'

She scowled at him. 'Thanks for calling me.'

'What? I didn't.'

'I know.' She stuck her hands on her hips. 'Mum gave you my number, but you didn't call. Even with all that's going on?'

Cullen tried to barge past, but she wouldn't let him. 'What's going on?'

She thumbed up the stairs. 'Sharon being pregnant?'

'You spoke to her?'

'No. I rang the bell, but there was no answer. She's either out or ignoring me.' Michelle gave him a hard stare. 'Like you. You didn't think to call me, Scott?'

'I tried a while ago, but you never got back to me. I figured you wanted time away.'

'You had the wrong number.'

'You didn't think to tell me you got a new one?' Cullen sighed. 'Look, I need to speak to Sharon. Do you want to come in?'

'I've got to get back home to my jailer. Sorry, daughter.' No hint of a smile, deadpan as ever. 'I was in Edinburgh for meetings, so I thought I'd just call in. Should've rung, eh?'

'You should've. How's Emily?'

'Fine. Full-on, though. It's hard having a small child, Scott. And I'm not talking about Jeremy.'

Cullen laughed. 'How's he doing?'

'He thinks a screenplay is going to be his saviour now.'

'Gave up on the books, then?'

'They gave up on him, more like. He's still not working, though, so I'm the only breadwinner.' She took a deep breath, then gave him a tired smile. 'He does a good job around the house, to be fair. We're having so much work done and he's great at managing builders and plumbers and electricians.'

'Finally found a use for him, then?'

'I hate dealing with workmen.'

'Sounds like Dad.'

'Scott, that's not even funny.' She was still laughing, though. 'He's really good with Emily. Much more patient than me.' She stared into the middle distance. 'I mean, I'm working long hours and I don't usually get home till after seven, so I barely see her.'

'Must be tough.'

Michelle shrugged. 'So. Sharon's pregnant?' She grinned. 'I didn't think you had it in you.'

'Very funny.' Cullen looked away. 'I'm shitting myself.'

'You'll make a good dad. You're a total idiot but I think you've got a good sense of what's right.'

Cullen squinted up at her. 'An idiot?'

'I mean it. Not the idiot bit. I mean about you being a good dad.'

'Aye, maybe when I'm ready.'

'Scott, you're thirty-one next month.' Michelle gave him her best no-nonsense-stare. 'When are you going to be ready?'

'Maybe when I earn more than sod all and enjoy a bit of job security, for a change.'

'What about Sharon? Is she ready?'

'I don't think either of us are. We had all that shite last year as well.'

'Mum told me.' Michelle bit her lip like she shouldn't have let that slip. 'She was pretty upset about it.'

Cullen shook his head. 'Look, Sharon's pushing for a DI position. She's under a lot of stress. I don't think it's good for her in that condition.'

'Look after her, eh? I liked her the one time you let us meet. She's a keeper.'

'Let us meet?'

'You know what I mean. You can be a bit of a stranger at the best of times.'

'It's called being busy.'

'Tell me about it.' Michelle ran a hand through her dark hair. 'It's good seeing you. You really annoyed me, you know?'

'I'm sorry. Really, I am. But you need to stop being so precious.'

'It wasn't funny, Scott. Jeremy and I had a huge argument about the card you sent when Emily was born.'

'Why?'

Michelle glared at him. 'Congratulations, see you in eighteen years?'

'And? I'm your brother. I was just taking the piss. You'd do the same to me.'

She gave him a hard look.

Cullen hated that look. For as long as he could remember, it had always made him feel guilty as hell. 'Look, I'm sorry, okay? I didn't mean to upset you. I take it all back.'

Michelle's face softened into a smile. 'Apology accepted, I suppose.'

'Thanks.' He grinned up at her. 'You know that feeling you

always give me of being a small child? That reminds me. I was dealing with someone you knew back in the day. Andy MacLeod.'

Michelle rolled her eyes. 'That wanker.'

'You went out with him, though, didn't you?'

'For my sins.'

'Or for mine. I hated that guy. I think he went out with you to piss me off.'

'Nothing to do with my legendary blowjobs?'

'Jesus Christ.' Cullen laughed. 'I forgot you're as depraved as me.'

'Blame Dad. Anyway, what's Andy done to you?'

Cullen pressed his lips together. 'I probably shouldn't be telling you this, but he was a suspect in a murder case.'

'Andy?'

'Aye, but we cleared him.'

'Good, I'm relieved to know it. Would have totally ruined my day to find out I'd let a murderer put his hands on me. Sorry, in me.' She winked at him, then checked her watch. 'I need to run. This has been good, though. We should do it again soon. Maybe not in a stairwell, but don't be a stranger, eh?'

'Yeah, I'm glad I bumped into you.'

'Bye.' She squeezed past him down the stairs, pressed a quick peck on his cheek and was gone.

Cullen stood there, wondering what the hell just happened. *No contact for yonks and now she's as familiar as when we were kids...*

KIDS!

Shite, I forgot about the baby.

Does that mean I'm used to the idea?

Maybe.

But how about Sharon?

And why didn't she open the door when Michelle rang?

He ran up the final steps, unlocked the flat door and rushed inside. The cat came up to meet him with a high-pitched bleat.

Cullen went into the living room. Sharon was sitting on a stool at the breakfast bar, her head slumped on the counter.

Cullen raced over to feel for a pulse.

His hand got batted away. 'Get off us!'

'Are you okay?'

Sharon half opened her eyes. 'Where have you been, you

prick?' She was slurring her words.

'At work, but what's—'

'I called.' She made it sound like an accusation. 'No answer.'

'I've been... Hang on.' Cullen sniffed her breath. 'Have you been *drinking*?'

'Maybe.'

Cullen glanced around the kitchen. Two empty bottles of white wine in the sink. 'You're pissed.'

'Why didn't you answer your phone?'

'I did, but you didn't say a word, just cried in my ear, remember? I've tried a few times since.'

'My phone.' Sharon jerked her head around to look for it, her eyes rolling back in her head as she got dizzy and slid off the stool.

'Jesus Christ!' Cullen caught her under her slack arms. 'You're pregnant. You can't do this.'

Sharon started crying. 'You don't want the baby.'

'I... I do.'

Sharon stared up at him as he helped her back on the stool. 'What?'

'You need a coffee.' Cullen went over to the sink and started filling the kettle. 'What are you playing at?'

Sharon rubbed her eyes. 'Lamb got the job.'

'Oh. That's what you were calling about?'

Sharon avoided his eyes, and instantly started swaying on the stool again. This time she caught herself. 'I needed to speak to you. But you were too busy. Always too busy.'

Cullen walked over and gently stroked her arm. 'We've got a manhunt and—'

'I'm more important.' She said it like a fact. Which it was.

And Cullen knew it.

He waited until she looked at him. 'You are more important.' He ran his hand through her hair, then gave her a pained smile. 'Jesus, I can't believe this.'

'I'm sorry.' Sharon buried her head in her arms, heaving with sobs. 'Nobody wants me. Turnbull turned me down. You weren't there. I needed you, Scott.'

'I'm sorry.' Cullen stroked her hair again, sympathetic, resentful and useless all at once. As if he was the one suffering the hormone chaos.

'I needed a drink.' Sharon sniffed. 'That's the second time Turnbull's turned me down for a promotion.'

The kettle clicked off. Cullen spooned coffee grounds into the cafetière and filled it with hot water. The dark liquid swirled as he stirred it, thick brown bubbles rising, caking the surface in a foamy sludge, swelling bigger and bigger, like the problems in his life. He stuck the plunger in and poured Sharon a mug. 'Drink this.'

She took it with a frown, her eyes all smudged with mascara. 'I'll be up all night.'

'But you'll be more sober.'

She stared into the mug, steam wafting into her face. 'I thought I'd get promoted when Crystal got his.'

Cullen sighed. 'You'll get there eventually. You're too good at your job not to. Turnbull's worked with Lamb for years, that's all.'

'Lamb's an arsehole,' Sharon told her coffee. 'He's driven like a psychopath. Won't stop at anything to get the job done. Wouldn't be surprised if he crossed the line one day.'

'Oh, come on now, he's hardly—'

'Turnbull asked if I wanted to go on the rape task force in Bathgate.'

'Bathgate?'

'I've been looking at houses there.'

'Sharon, stop.' He gently took her face in his hands and made her look at him. 'You need to slow down and sober up.'

'I need the toilet.' Sharon slapped his hands away and trundled off.

Cullen watched her go, then held his own head in his hands. *What a bloody mess.*

His phone rang.

Chantal.

With a deep sigh, he took the call. 'Aye, what is it?'

'Scott, you'll love this.'

'Try me.'

'Hunter just followed Beth Williamson to the practice rooms on Niddry Street with a backpack full of food and clothes, and a sleeping bag.'

Cullen shot to his feet.

Robertson.

48

CULLEN JOGGED ALONG THE ROYAL MILE, CLUTCHING HIS PHONE TO his ear. 'Michelle, if you can just stay with her. She's pissed and I don't know what else to do.'

'Right.' She sighed. 'I'll head back up there. You owe me.' Click.

Cullen pocketed his phone and set off down Niddry Street. Unmarked cars were parked across the top entrance and down at the Cowgate below. Robertson was trapped. Down the hill, a police car pulled up opposite the practice rooms, joined by another from below, boxing in a black Land Rover. Beth Williamson's yummy mummy Chelsea tractor.

Chantal jumped out of the squad car and pointed up the slope and calling some inaudible command to Buxton.

Cullen raced down the road to join them.

Bain climbed out of the car above the Land Rover and shouted across the roof with a bright red face. 'We need to get in there, Col!'

Methven got out the other side, teeth bared. 'For the last time, Brian. This isn't your investigation. Follow. My. Lead.'

'Wanker.' Bain strode towards the front door. 'He's got a hostage now.'

Methven had to jog to keep up with him. 'You think?'

'You don't? Are you stupid or something?'

Cullen darted between them and put his back to the door, hands up. 'Calm down, the pair of you. You're acting like children.'

'Shut your pus!' McCrea was lumbering down the road, slow to get out of Bain's car and even slower to catch up with him. 'It's always cheek with you, Cullen. Show the gaffer a bit of respect, man.'

Cullen raised his eyebrows. 'Last time he led an arrest op, the suspect nicked his car and got away.'

'Robertson wasn't our fault.' McCrea said it like he didn't quite believe it himself.

The door burst open behind Cullen.

Beth Williamson charged past him, in floods of tears, a tissue clasped to her face. She slumped against her Land Rover, her body racked with sobs, no longer carrying the bags she arrived with.

Methven held his hand up, signalling: *Retreat!*

Cullen grabbed Beth by the arms and pulled her away from the car. 'Keep quiet.' He led her back up the hill.

Beth's eyes bulged. 'What's happening?'

'Mike Robertson is down there, isn't he?'

She looked like she was going to deny it, then her lips puckered and fresh tears streamed down her face. She nodded.

'Is he armed?'

'I don't know. He met me on the stairs just by where our old practice room was.'

Methven walked up to them, shadowed by Hunter. 'Right, Constable, get her processed.'

Hunter led Beth up the street to the meat wagon, one arm firmly clamped around her shoulders, the other waving ahead to disperse a crowd of gawkers.

Methven turned to Chantal. 'What are we thinking?'

'We could bide our time.' She pointed at the reinforcements. 'Man all the exits and wait. He'll run out of food quickly.'

Bain snorted. 'There's a huge bag of messages just gone in there. It'll be a week before he runs out of Doritos.'

Methven glared at him. 'What do you propose instead?'

Bain shrugged. 'I want to know how public enemy number one can march through Edinburgh and not be spotted.'

'Park the politics. What strategy do you suggest?'

'Pile in there. If we can't arrest a single, unarmed man, we should quit the job now.'

Methven stared at the door for a few seconds. 'Cullen?'

Cullen was surprised to be asked. 'Much as I hate to admit it, I'm with Bain. Let's just go in there and arrest him.'

'What if he's armed?'

'We take it slow, assess the situation. Then if he is, send in an ARU. Armed officers are trained. But I doubt he's got a gun. A knife, maybe.' Cullen snapped out his baton. 'We've got these.'

'I'm not sure.'

Cullen glanced at Bain. 'Sir, if Robertson gets into the tunnels while we stand around and debate, he might find another exit.'

Bain frowned. 'Where do they lead?'

Methven shrugged. 'We don't know. It's a warren. The council were going to send in a team of archaeologists but they're waiting on our case concluding. All we know from old city maps is that the you can get into the tunnel here.'

'Col, these catacombs used to be the city's road network before it all got built on.' Bain snorted. 'Where did you find Strang's body?'

'Just under South Bridge, I think.'

'Right. So, it's miles away.'

Methven nodded. 'We've no choice, then. We have to go in. Cullen, McCrea, Bain and myself first. DS Jain, can you manage the entrance here.'

'Great.'

'It's an important task!' Methven's eyes flickered, looking the most nervous Cullen had ever seen. 'Okay.' He nodded at Bain and McCrea. 'Are you ready?'

'I was born ready.'

Cullen looked at him. 'So what happened?'

'Shut it, Sundance.'

'Quiet!' Methven led them inside, clicking his torch on within the first few tentative steps down into the damp, whitewashed space.

The practice room door hung wide open, the room empty but for assorted musical equipment. The police tape was still hanging over the mouth of the stairwell, billowing in the draught as the front door fell shut with an echoing bang.

Cullen flinched.

Bain took a while to get his cynical sneer back in place, glowing in the darkness like a Hallowe'en lantern.

Cullen led off in single file, training his torch on the stairs. He ducked under the cordon and skipped down the stairs, his shoes like sandpaper on the worn stone steps. At the bottom, the ancient wooden door was closed and cordoned off with more police tape. He pushed the metal handle down, then gave the door a hard shove. A loud screech cried out into the dark, making the hair on the back of his neck stand on end.

Bain sneered at him, but there was a twitch in one corner of his curled lips. 'You first, Sundance.'

'Alright, off we go.' Cullen led the way, the torch light bouncing off the walls in jerky movements. He tried to steady his hand as he strained his ears, listening out for any strange sounds, but all he could hear were the quiet footsteps behind him.

The torch hit a wall, a bricked-up doorway. The old crossroads, more bricks blocking their way on the left, leaving only way to go, on to where they had found Strang's corpse.

Cullen was breathing hard now, his eyes flicking around the damp walls, chasing the nervy spotlight of his torch, trying not to blink. Trying to keep his mind from straying to the image of that screwdriver impaled in rotten flesh. His heart hammered in his chest. He stopped and swung his torch around the walls.

Bain walked into him with a grunt. 'Christ's sake, what's wrong?'

'This where Strang's body was found.'

They gathered round to take in the scene, torches focused on the area. The writing on the wall was still there.

I WILL KILL AGAIN.

Bain was the first to break the eerie silence. 'So, where is Robertson?'

Cullen shone his torch further down the tunnel, the light hitting nothing but cob webs and more tunnel. He walked on, slowly.

Robertson has to be somewhere ahead, we just don't know where.

Or if he's armed.

Not like he hesitates to use violence...

Cullen stopped at another crossroads, this one not bricked up.

One tunnel led straight on into darkness, one off to the left, another to the right. He shone his torch down all three of them, then turned to face Methven, his face unreadable in the flickering shadows. 'What now, sir?'

Methven frowned, his face distorting. 'This is what we don't sodding need.' He shone the torch back the way. 'There are only four of us but three routes Robertson might've taken.'

Silence.

Bain cleared his throat with a dry cough. 'So, what are you suggesting, dungeon master?'

'We need to be systematic.' Methven pointed at McCrea. 'Sergeant, you and I will investigate this passage.' He pointed to the right. 'You two—'

'What?' Bain's voice was at least an octave higher than before. He cleared his throat again. 'You want Cullen and me to take the left tunnel and leave the way ahead open? Are you serious?'

Methven shook his head. 'You two stay here until we return. If it's another long tunnel then we have no option but to call for reinforcements.' He turned to McCrea. 'Ready?'

'Born ready.'

'Bain said that.'

'Piss off, Cullen.' McCrea shuffled off after Methven, the torch light fading to darkness as soon as they took the first bend in the old road.

Bain got his Airwave out and shook it, then did the same with his mobile. 'I've got absolutely no reception down here.'

Cullen shrugged. 'Reckon we should send for back up?'

'Probably just shite it.' Bain shone his torch the opposite way to where Methven and McCrea had gone. 'Right, bugger this, I'm off. You coming?'

'You heard Methven's orders. We need to stay.'

'And do what? Let a murderer get away?' Bain sounded as nervous as Cullen, but he wasn't letting it stop him. 'Robertson clearly knows these catacombs if he dropped the body off down here. He could be heading to some secret door on to the Cowgate for all we know.'

Cullen shook his head. 'I'm staying.'

'Christ's sake. Teacher's pet to the end.' Bain took a ragged breath, then walked off into the gloom.

Soon, Cullen couldn't see or hear the slightest trace of him. Alone in the dark.

We could be down here, searching for Robertson for weeks.

Chances are, this isn't the only set of crossroads in this maze, and with each of them, the possibilities expand.

But Robertson will eventually have to surface for more supplies, but if he rations what Beth just gave him and—

What the hell was that?

Sounded like a choked scream, echoing out of the tunnel Methven and McCrea had disappeared in. He shone the torch into the dark. Nothing. Then another scream ricocheted off the stone walls.

He cupped his hands around his mouth and took a deep breath. 'Bain!'

No response.

What the hell do I do?

Sod it.

Cullen ran down the tunnel, his torch beam bouncing off the dusty old path and damp walls, his feet slapping off the stone floors, his mind alive with fear.

He passed through an open doorway, skidding to a stop a few steps into a large vaulted chamber. Methven and McCrea lay in a heap in the middle of the room.

Then he heard a click behind him.

He spun around and stared straight into a blinding torch. He blinked, yanking his head to the left to be out of the light, but a fist caught him square on the cheekbone. His head snapped the other way and he thumped on the floor, the rough stone juddering into his coccyx.

Robertson stood over him, holding his torch under his own chin to light up his face like in a horror movie. 'Well, this is slightly ghoulish, don't you think?'

Cullen shuffled back, then scrambled to his feet.

Robertson just stood his ground.

'Mike Robertson...' Cullen's head was nearly exploding with the pain. 'I am arresting you for the murders of Alex Melrose and James Strang. You are not obliged to say anything but anything you do say will be noted and may be used in evidence. Do you understand?'

Robertson grinned. 'No, I don't.' He pulled out a large knife. 'But you understand what this means, don't you?'

Cullen looked at Methven. 'How do you want us to play this, sir?'

No answer.

Robertson slashed the knife through the air.

Cullen retreated deeper into the cavernous dark behind him. He kept his eyes on the knife. 'Give up, Robertson. You're surrounded.'

'Am I really?' The torchlight flashed across his face as he swiped the knife again. 'Just keep on backing yourself into the corner.'

Cullen felt cold stone against his shoulders.

'Drop your torch.' Robertson pointed his knife at Cullen's chest as he kept advancing. Slowly. Only three steps away now. 'Drop it or I will kill again.'

Cullen took a deep breath, then tossed his torch straight at Robertson. He jumped after it, swinging his baton as Robertson dodged the torch.

Robertson was too quick. Somehow, he saw the baton and caught Cullen's wrist, twisting it with a jerk that set Cullen's whole arm alight with pain. Like an electric shock. It carried on flashing up and down a fuzzy nerve in his forearm.

The baton clattered off the stone.

And Robertson was still holding his knife. 'Get up.'

Cullen stumbled to his feet, hands raised.

'No more funny business. Now...' Robertson pointed his torch at Methven and McCrea, still lying in an inert pile. 'Get over there.'

Cullen walked slowly, trying to cross the darkness without taking another fall. His discarded torch lit up a narrow shaft in the ancient stone floor.

Robertson waved his own torch around, impatience making his hand judder. 'Just keep on walking that way.'

Cullen looked down at Methven and McCrea. Neither moved. 'You'll go away for a very long time, Robertson.'

'You'll have to catch me first. This tunnel has several exits. Won't have to go out the way I came in.'

'So what? Once you're outside, you won't escape us for long.'

'Shut up.' Robertson grabbed Cullen by the wrist and spun

him around, pressing the blade against his throat, cold steel kissing his skin, pricking it just below the Adam's apple.

'You're surrounded, Robertson. You won't get away.'

Robertson kept the pressure on the knife. 'I've got a hostage, now.'

'How's that going to help when we're out in the open? You won't get anywhere.' Cullen was trying to make his voice sound as hard and sharp as the blade. Trying and failing. 'Come on, man, you're a celebrity. You'll get caught eventually. Be smart and turn yourself in now. It's the only thing that will work in your favour. Reduce your sentencing. Might even—'

'Shut up.' Robertson sounded like he was about to lose it. 'I'll take my chances.' He drew the knife back.

Cullen shut his eyes, waiting for the blade to slice his throat.

An arm wrapped around his neck from behind. The tip of the knife prodded his lower back.

Robertson had his mouth right beside his face, hissing hot breath into Cullen's ear. 'We're going to try the front door. See if your pals haven't all gone to cover the other exits. We'll go slowly. Back the way you came. Okay?'

Fear hit Cullen's stomach like a punch. *We'll walk right into Chantal and what's that knife going to do when he gets a fright or—*

'Okay?'

'Fine.' Cullen started walking.

Another pair of footsteps joined them, quicker and heavier.

Something thumped Cullen from behind and send him sprawling forward.

'Get off me!' Robertson, by the sounds of it.

'You absolute bastard!' Bain, screaming.

The knife tinkled to the ground.

It was still too dark to see anything.

A new torch lit up the room, roving through the dark like a searchlight beam. It landed on Robertson and stopped, then tracked him as he got to his feet, unarmed, his knife nowhere to be seen.

Cullen charged at the guy, sending him flying back to the ground. He buried Robertson underneath his body, pinning him down while he forced his arms behind his back. He reached into his pocket and retrieved his handcuffs to secure the squirming bastard, breathing hard.

A squad of uniforms entered the room and took control of the situation. Two officers grabbed Robertson's arms while a third held him still in a headlock.

Bain stood off to the side, dimly lit in the criss-crossing beams of several torches, clutching his hands to his stomach. His eyes were wide with shock, his fingers covered in blood. Then he slumped to the ground.

Cullen lurched forward and emptied his lungs with an echoing shout: 'GET AN AMBULANCE!'

'Bastard stabbed me.' Bain's voice was wet with pain.

Cullen put both hands on Bain's stomach, the blood hot on his cold skin. 'Are you okay?'

Bain looked up, his eyes glassy. 'I'm pretty far from okay, Sundance.' He closed his eyes and his body went limp.

49

CULLEN STOOD ON THE ROYAL MILE, UNABLE TO STOP SHAKING. Someone put a blanket around his shoulders but it wasn't helping.

Methven sat in an ambulance, a paramedic bandaging his head. 'You'll be fine, sir. Just a graze.'

McCrea sat next to him, his paramedic doing the old counting fingers trick. 'You're concussed. A torch to the head will do that to you.'

Cullen looked up and down the street. The press had arrived, telephoto lenses defeating even the most assertive officers. He shivered at the thought of seeing his face on the front page.

Chantal rushed over. 'Are you okay, Scott?'

'Nothing damaged. Any news about Bain?'

Chantal bit her lip. 'Nothing yet.'

Cullen just nodded, close to tears.

She hesitated, then pointed out the obvious. 'Bain saved your life.'

'I know.' He looked away, the tears flowing freely now.

Another lost officer on my conscience.

Chantal tried to smile but by the looks of it she failed to convince even herself.

Cullen couldn't process what had just happened.

Bain, for so long his annoying mentor, or tormentor, was on the way to A&E because he had got in the way of a knife meant for

Cullen. Everything Bain had gone through in the last year and now this. The guy was lucky to still have a job, and even luckier to still be alive. After the way he had behaved for the best part of a decade, the police force would be better off without him, that was for sure, but him dying would be hard to take, not least because Bain would die a hero and redeem himself with his selfless sacrifice, all the shit he'd made Cullen suffer over the years forgiven and forgotten.

Jesus, I'm turning into a bitter old man.

And if he survives? Bloody hell, that would be even worse. I'd never hear the end of it.

You owe me, Sundance. Big time.

Cullen tossed the blanket to the floor and got to his feet. 'I really hope I don't have to live with his death on my conscience.'

Chantal rubbed her forehead. 'That's a weird thing to say.'

'You know what I mean, though.'

She thought about it for a moment. 'Aye, I suppose I do.'

Cullen looked up at the grey sky, replaying the scene in the catacombs. Then his phone rang. Didn't recognise the number so he bounced it. But it started ringing again. With a sigh, he answered. 'I'm a bit busy.'

'Scott, it's Michelle. Sharon's collapsed.'

'What do you mean?'

'She fell over.'

'Call 999!'

'I have but they'll be forever.'

The paramedics.

Cullen bolted over to the last remaining ambulance. 'Help!' He ran to the nearest paramedic, already in the process of packing up. 'I need help.'

'What happened? Are you okay?'

'It's not about me. My girlfriend... Something's happened to her. She's unconscious. She's pregnant.'

'Show us.'

The paramedic made to jump in the ambulance but Cullen held him back.

'I live just around the corner. Follow me.'

He rushed back to the flat, barging through the crowds on the

Royal Mile, then darted into the close and bounded up the stairs and through the wide-open door into the flat.

Michelle was kneeling over Sharon's limp body.

Cullen pulled her away.

The paramedic tested for a pulse, his head against her chest. 'Got a heartbeat.'

～

Cullen sat in the waiting area at Edinburgh Royal Infirmary.

'Here.' Michelle handed him a coffee and stroked his back. 'You okay?'

'Pretty far from okay.' Cullen filled his lungs with the acidic aroma of the coffee, then breathed it all out again until there was nothing left in him. 'I don't know anything, except that Sharon's still breathing.'

'That's all that matters right now. She's tough, she'll be back at work in no ti—'

'Scott?' Chantal stood at the information desk, looking wary.

Michelle gave him a nudge. 'Go talk to your friend. I'll check on Sharon. Let you know if there's any news.'

Cullen's feet carried him over to Chantal, his mind paralysed with worry.

Chantal took one look at his face, then took his arm and gently guided him to another waiting area surrounded by plastic plants. The coffee table was covered in information leaflets on how to act in various medical emergencies. And not a single scrap of advice on how not to go crazy while you wait to hear from the doctors.

'How's Sharon?'

Cullen didn't make eye contact. 'We'll see.'

She cleared her throat. 'He confessed, by the way. Robertson. Says Strang attacked him with the screwdriver and it was sort of an accident but he didn't think we'd see it that way, so he hid the body.'

'And that message?'

'To throw us off the scent. He did Melrose the same way.'

Cullen didn't look at her, just kept staring at those leaflets. 'So, I was right?'

'Aye.'

It gave him no satisfaction to be proven right. Not at this cost. 'How's Bain?'

'I don't know yet. Haven't heard any news since.'

Cullen didn't know what to say. 'I hope he pulls through.'

Chantal just nodded, then sighed and joined him in gazing at the emergency leaflets. All they could do was wait.

'Scott?' Michelle was standing on the other side of the table, smiling at Cullen. 'You can go see her now.'

The information didn't register with Cullen.

Michelle cleared her throat. 'Scott! Sharon's awake.'

Cullen staggered to his feet. 'Thanks. Chantal?'

Chantal got up too. 'I'll wait here. You go.'

A smiling nurse led Cullen through to Sharon's room. She lay on the bed, tubes and wires coming out of her bare arms, the skin as pale as the sheets. Her bloodshot eyes looked up at him, brimming with tears. 'I lost her.'

Cullen felt like he'd been shot.

Her.

'I was eight weeks pregnant. I had a daughter. And now she's gone.'

Tears ran down his cheeks. They would never stop.

My daughter.

Sharon looked him in the eye and lost all control over her face. 'Oh God, I'm so sorry.'

Cullen sucked in deep breaths, trying to stop the tears. 'Don't be sorry.' He leaned in, hugging her tight. 'I thought I'd lost *you.*'

They stayed like that, silently hugging each other far too hard for their fragile state.

Then she sniffed and started caressing the back of his head. 'It'll take more than that to get rid of me, Scott Cullen.'

He laughed, tears choking him up as he pulled back his head and stared at her. 'Don't ever leave me.'

'I won't.'

He collapsed on the chair beside the bed, all energy sapped from his body. All he could do was hold her hand. 'I think I wanted a child.'

Sharon looked away. 'When Chantal showed me the test kit that first time, I felt so angry. Kept berating myself. How could I let that happen? Now...' She looked at the ceiling and fresh tears streamed down her cheeks. 'Now I've lost our daughter, and I don't think I've ever felt so lost myself.'

Cullen clenched his teeth to suppress a sob. 'What... What happened?'

'Stress.' She shook her head like she still couldn't believe it. 'The job. The cold. Drinking all that wine. Or some combination of the three. They don't know but my body didn't take to the baby very well. The doctor said it's actually really hard to get and stay pregnant. Three in four pregnancies end in miscarriages. But I shouldn't have been pushing myself so hard.'

'Hey, it's okay.' Cullen squeezed her hand. 'This isn't your fault. We've still got each other, remember?'

She glanced at him, but her eyes wouldn't stay with him. 'I know.'

Cullen heard the words, and the lack of conviction they carried. He squeezed her hand again, but she wouldn't look at him. 'Listen, Sharon, this has really scared the shit out of me. I thought I'd lost you.' He staggered to his feet. 'It's made me think about everything and put it all in context.'

Sharon took one look at him and her eyes widened. 'Scott Cullen, don't you dare get down on one knee.'

NEXT BOOK

The next Police Scotland book is out now!

"LIARS AND THIEVES"

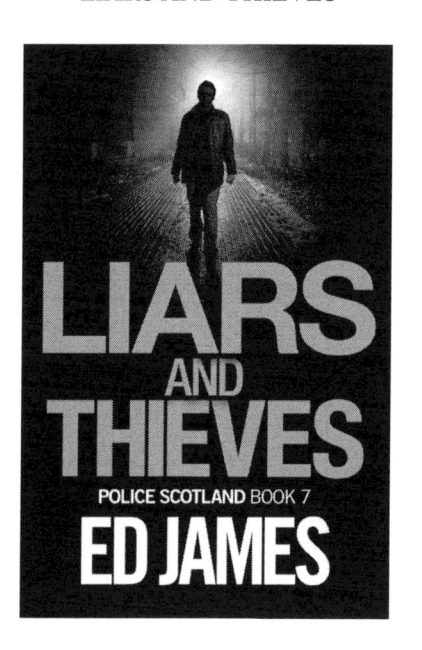

Get it now!

If you would like to be kept up to date with new releases from Ed James and access free novellas, please join the Ed James Readers' Club.

AFTERWORD

Thanks for taking the time to read this book and I hope you enjoyed it.

I originally published this book back in 2014 as BOTTLE-NECK. So why the hell have I edited it and renamed it? Because I'm a bloody idiot, as my four-year-old nephew called me. He's so right.

Well, one of the reasons is I'm restless. But the main one is that I looked at the text and just couldn't stand it. It's the only one of my original books from before I went full-time that I haven't redrafted. This one is tighter and better, at least I think so. I cut a fair few characters and retconned the introduction of one Craig Hunter, who stars in two novels of his own (with Cullen being a bit of an arse in them) as well as in Cullen 8. Couldn't help myself. If you've just met him here for the first time, then the subplot about Cullen and Hunter's antagonism is resolved in that book.

Anyway, that's me done with nipping and tucking the Cullen books. I hope you enjoyed it.

— Ed James
The Borders, March 2019

Without the following, this book wouldn't exist:

Development Editing

Len Wanner

Editing
John Rickards

Proofing
Eleanor Abraham

As ever, infinite thanks to Kitty for putting up with me and all of my nonsense.

Original afterword:
This was a tough one to research. As you'll have discovered, Police Scotland was formed during this time. I've just been on Radio Scotland talking about how difficult it was — I had to do a lot more research than usual, especially given how central it was to the plot. The information here is accurate — at the vantage point of a year after the implementation, I'd say the whole thing seems to have gone well, with some notable convictions under their belts.

The first novel I ever wrote was about music and a band called The Invisibles. It's been immense fun to reuse that world in a Cullen novel and reacquaint myself with the characters. I also butchered EVIL SCOTSMAN (for Matt MacLeod), a book I'd partly written a draft of and gave up after GHOST IN THE MACHINE started clicking into gear. I did this re-engineering not out of writer's block but to stop me picking up flawed books again — the word count in the bag is illusory and I've finally put them to rest. There's only one more left in my cupboard and I've got concrete plans for that.

— Ed James
East Lothian, March 2014

ABOUT THE AUTHOR

Ed James is the author of the bestselling DI Simon Fenchurch novels, Seattle-based FBI thrillers starring Max Carter, and the self-published Detective Scott Cullen series and its Craig Hunter spin-off books.

During his time in IT project management, Ed spent every moment he could writing and has now traded in his weekly commute to London in order to write full-time. He lives in the Scottish Borders with far too many rescued animals.

If you would like to be kept up to date with new releases from Ed James, please join the Ed James Readers Club.

Connect with Ed online:

Amazon Author page

Website

OTHER BOOKS BY ED JAMES

DI ROB MARSHALL

Ed's first new police procedural series in six years, focusing on DI Rob Marshall, a criminal profiler turned detective. London-based, an old case brings him back home to the Scottish Borders and the dark past he fled as a teenager.

1. THE TURNING OF OUR BONES
2. WHERE THE BODIES LIE (May 2023)

Also available is FALSE START, a prequel novella starring DS Rakesh Siyal, is available for **free** to subscribers of Ed's newsletter or on Amazon. Sign up at https://geni.us/EJLCFS

POLICE SCOTLAND

Precinct novels featuring detectives covering Edinburgh and its surrounding counties, and further across Scotland: Scott Cullen, eager to climb the career ladder; Craig Hunter, an ex-squaddie struggling with PTSD; Brian Bain, the centre of his own universe and everyone else's. Previously published as SCOTT CULLEN MYSTERIES, CRAIG HUNTER POLICE THRILLERS and CULLEN & BAIN SERIES.

1. DEAD IN THE WATER
2. GHOST IN THE MACHINE
3. DEVIL IN THE DETAIL
4. FIRE IN THE BLOOD
5. STAB IN THE DARK
6. COPS & ROBBERS
7. LIARS & THIEVES
8. COWBOYS & INDIANS
9. THE MISSING
10. THE HUNTED
11. HEROES & VILLAINS
12. THE BLACK ISLE
13. THE COLD TRUTH

14. THE DEAD END

DS VICKY DODDS

Gritty crime novels set in Dundee and Tayside, featuring a DS juggling being a cop and a single mother.

1. BLOOD & GUTS
2. TOOTH & CLAW
3. FLESH & BLOOD
4. SKIN & BONE
5. GUILT TRIP

DI SIMON FENCHURCH

Set in East London, will Fenchurch ever find what happened to his daughter, missing for the last ten years?

1. THE HOPE THAT KILLS
2. WORTH KILLING FOR
3. WHAT DOESN'T KILL YOU
4. IN FOR THE KILL
5. KILL WITH KINDNESS
6. KILL THE MESSENGER
7. DEAD MAN'S SHOES
8. A HILL TO DIE ON
9. THE LAST THING TO DIE

Other Books

Other crime novels, with Lost Cause set in Scotland and Senseless set in southern England, and the other three set in Seattle, Washington.

- LOST CAUSE
- SENSELESS
- TELL ME LIES
- GONE IN SECONDS
- BEFORE SHE WAKES

LIARS AND THIEVES

PROLOGUE

HE TRIED TO KEEP IN THE SHADOWS AS STEVEN OPENED THE FRONT door. Blinking, he stepped back as the taxi swept past the house before it trundled up the hill, headlights illuminating the wet street. He waited for it to pass and the dim glow of the street lights to return. 'Can you not hurry up?'

A man passed them on the opposite side of the street, coat tucked tight against the rain, looking overweight. Had he seen them? His breath quickened.

'Got it.' Steven fumbled with the front door, finally nudging it open. 'Sorry about that. Too much to drink, obviously. Come on in.'

'Thought you'd never ask.'

Steven looked down at the cream carpet in the long hall. 'Can you at least take off your shoes?'

'No.' He smiled before walking through to the living room, flicking on the mother and child light by the sofa, but remained standing. 'I'm fine as I am.'

Still standing in the hall, Steven reached down to untie his own laces. 'Can I get you a drink?'

'Now that would be good.'

Steven marched across the wide room, switching a side light on. He paused in front of an oak cabinet behind a leather recliner, like he was going to say something, before pulling down the horizontal cabinet door, revealing a sizeable collection of spirits bottles. His hand hovered over them before settling on a whisky, black label embossed with silver. He sniffed it then poured healthy measures into a pair of glasses. 'Here you go. Hope it's still to your taste.'

'Dunpender, right?'

Steven took a sip and nodded, eyes staring into space. 'Right.'

He took the glass and wandered over to stand just to the left of the window, before sniffing the drink. Pure darkness. 'Still think it's the best whisky in Scotland, Steven?'

'I like it. Get through a bottle every month.'

'That's a lot of drinking.'

'Helps with the stress. You know how it is.'

'Don't I just.' He finished the whisky in one, the liquid burning his tongue and throat. Sucking in a mouthful of air, letting it dampen the heat. Bliss. He held the glass up to the light and inspected the lines of the crystal.

Steven finished his dram and put his own glass down, hand shaking. 'What is it you want?'

'A chat. One that can't wait. It's important.'

'Why?'

'It just is.'

'Come on. You dragged me from the pub to hear whatever it is.'

'You'll want another drink.'

'Do I?'

'Aye, I think so.'

'I've had a skinful already.' Steven turned his back and poured out another measure of Dunpender, his head bowed. 'Fine.'

He spotted a crystal quaich, *Dunpender 100* etched into it, next to another tall bottle matching the design but gold replacing silver. 'Nice little trinket you've got there.'

Steven ran a finger over it and nodded. 'Cost me a pretty penny.'

'Disappointed you're not opening that one for me.'

Steven sighed as he looked down at his glass. 'Like I've got anything to celebrate.'

'Quite.' Taking a deep breath, he set the empty glass down on the dark brown window sill. He lashed out, connecting the base of his hand with the back of Steven's neck, forcing him against the cabinet, fingers clutching at the glass doors. Steven fell forwards, grasping for the hinge as he sprawled across the machined wood flooring, the bottle of Dunpender tumbling and smashing, a pool of gold liquid forming around his prone body.

Stepping forward, he followed through with kicks to Steven's stomach, head, balls. He kicked the head again. And again.

He knelt down, breathing heavily, fingers crawling up Steven's throat, clasping the pulse point. His heartbeat was faint.

Still alive. Good.

~

HE DROPPED THE TOOLBOX IN THE MIDDLE OF THE LIVING ROOM, THE trail of oil muddying the bleached wood of the floor, before sifting through the tools inside.

Pliers. Excellent.

Hammers. Two of them. Which one? The ball-peen for definite, its small head giving precision. The claw hammer was all about brute force. Maybe he'd need both.

He rummaged through the second layer of tools, finding a long cord, the sort used on a drying green. That's the ticket.

He got to his feet and untied the kitchen cloths on Steven's wrists, replacing them with the cord, the solid knot at the back of the chair just out of reach.

Breathe. Slowly, deeply. Take your time.

He picked up the glass of water from the coffee table and tipped it over Steven's head. He didn't wake up.

He raised the hammer, bringing it down on Steven's middle finger.

Steven's eyes shot open. He screamed, a primal roar from the pit of his gut, his gaze darting around the room.

The noise curdled his own stomach. He swallowed, his throat constricted. 'So you're awake then?'

'What are you doing?'

'Come on, Steven, you know what I'm doing and why.'

'I can pay you.'

'Can you really?'

'Please, how much do you want?'

'This isn't about money. At least not to me. No, it's about the betrayal of trust.' He reached for the pliers, gripping the fingernail on Steven's left thumb and yanked. The scream turned his stomach anew.

~

ONE, TWO, THREE...

Two minutes — one hundred and twenty — that's all he'd allow himself to enjoy his work.

He stayed in the shadows, watching the yellow flickering in the living room and kitchen windows at the back. The briefest smell of charcoal and petrol.

Glancing around the street, he couldn't see anyone.

One nineteen, one twenty. Time up.

A cough. Somewhere to the left.

He looked around. There — a fat man stood a few doors down, focused on his phone as a small dog ratted around the bushes of the compact front garden, cocking its leg as it sniffed the air. It was the man who'd almost spotted him as Steven made a hash of getting in.

The dog sensed him, its brown eyes locking on, its mouth curling.

He stepped back into the shade. The dog's bark rattled around the small space.

'Benji, will you bloody quit it?'

One, two, three...

After sixty he peered out, the phone's backlight illuminating the man's face, thumbs working at the screen, the dog pulling the lead tight.

He clenched the claw hammer, hoping he wouldn't have to resort to another murder just to get away.

'Come on, Benji.' The man tugged at the dog and led him inside.

He let out a breath, watching it mist in the cold air, before walking off. He headed for home, his work complete.

He allowed himself another glance at the house, the flames now visible and obvious to anyone who cared to look.

~

THE SEVENTH POLICE SCOTLAND BOOK, LIARS AND THIEVES, IS out now. You can get a copy at Amazon.

If you would like to be kept up to date with new releases from Ed James, please join the Ed James Readers Club.

Printed in Great Britain
by Amazon

37619432R00209